NOBODY'S CHILD

When their mother dies and their father, in his grief, burns down their wagon and runs away, Kath and Ella – gypsy sisters – suddenly become orphans. With no one to turn to for help, they face hardship and hunger at every turn. Will their special sisters' bond be strong enough to see them to safety?

NOBODY'S CHILD

NOBODY'S CHILD

by

Elizabeth Gill

Magna Large Print Books
Long Preston, North Yorkshire,
BD23 4ND, England.

British Library Cataloguing in Publication Data.

A catalogue record of this book is
available from the British Library

ISBN   978-0-7505-4421-4

First published in Great Britain in 2016 by Quercus

Cover illustration © Gordon Crabb by arrangement with
Alison Eldred

Published in Large Print 2017 by arrangement with
Headline Publishing Group Ltd.

Magna Large Print is an imprint of Library Magna Books Ltd.

Printed and bound in Great Britain by
T.J. (International) Ltd., Cornwall, PL28 8RW

For my sister, Julia, who gave me the idea
for the story and who loves horses as
much as any gypsy lass ever did.

Author's Note

One of my oldest and dearest friends, Ann Hudson Calvert, lives in Middlesbrough and I have been visiting her there and she has been coming to Durham for over thirty years. Trying to get my head around the differences between Middlesbrough after the First World War and Middlesbrough now is not easy to envisage but she duly ferried me around, recreating the old place for me. It was and is a vast and fascinating place. Thanks, Ann, not just for that but for being such a good friend all this time. We have been there for one another during the worst times of our lives. Now we go to beautiful places to eat and congratulate one another on getting here.

One

1930 Durham Fell tops, Castle Bank Colliery

Christmas was all around. The shops had coloured streamers crisscrossed in their windows and Kath Watson could see chickens, geese and turkeys hanging up in the butcher's. She thought it might be nice to have something good to eat on Christmas Day. The shop had a queue; people here must eat a lot of meat.

She lingered outside the shoe shop. Her family bought their shoes off markets so a shoe shop was a strange place, with its boxes everywhere. She looked through the window and her attention was caught by a pair of black patent leather shoes that she instantly longed for.

She was surprised at herself. Clothes were just something to wear to keep you warm and cover you up; she thought pretty clothes were nothing more than a come-on to coarse mucky lads who only wanted to take you behind a hedge.

Her father had wished her married long since and didn't understand why she was so picky. A lot of the gypsy lads had money – those that dealt in scrap metal or horses – but Kath had seen inside other families' wagons and they reeked of filth and disarray. She did not see herself turning out baby after baby, clearing up and putting up with the likes, so she wouldn't have any of them.

13

Her father called her unnatural and asked her what in hell she thought she would do instead.

Her mother had shuddered and said when he was gone, 'I want a better life than this one for my lasses. I don't want them on the road like we are.'

Kath had never ventured this far up the main street of the little pit town, where many people shopped and went out. The street had as many houses on it as shops and children played in the road. She was always afraid that she would be shouted at and since at the moment they could not move on, she didn't want to face their scorn.

Today, however, she made herself take it on. She thought that people stared but that could have been simply because they didn't know her.

The shops were mostly repeats of the co-operative department store and every so often there was a little run of terraced houses among them. A picture house called The Palace was at the top of the slight hill that led up past the railway gates where the cattle market was on one side and a foundry on the other. After the petrol station and some buses, the street evened out and straggled away until it split in two at the top.

Yards or passages led into the back streets and she passed several pubs with archways which must have been where the horses and carriages were kept in older times. There were also a number of churches. She didn't know much about churches. When she reached the top of the street, she crossed over and began to come down the other side until she became aware that somebody was following her. When she stopped and turned around, a middle-aged woman was behind her.

She stared at Kath. 'You're Rose Gurney's lass, aren't you? You look just like her, the mucky slut.'

Kath stared back and replied, 'My name's Watson.'

The woman chuckled but her eyes were full of scorn. 'Is that right and where did you get that from?'

She walked off before Kath had a chance to say anything more. Kath tried not to think about it, but flustered, she hurried home without the shopping she had meant to buy. She had had such plans for Christmas – she was going to bake a cake and stuff a goose. She was so determined that they would have a good holiday this year.

She had not been back long when there was a heavy knocking on the back door. She opened it and beheld a policeman, large and fierce-looking.

'Is your father at home?'

'No.'

'Your mother?'

'My mother is very ill and in bed.'

As she spoke her father appeared behind her. She thought he had gone out and was relieved he was there to handle the problem.

'What's this?' he asked and she stood back and let him go to the door.

The policeman stared at her father and said, 'You can't stay here. This house is Jonathan Gurney's.'

'He's not here,' Kath's father replied. 'I had to pull the boards from the windows so that we could stay. My wife is ill. When she's better, we'll go.' He slammed shut the door.

Late in the morning she went upstairs to check on her mother. She was worried by what she found. Her mother was asleep and her breathing was harsh and uneven. She didn't open her eyes when Kath entered the room. She didn't look like Rose any more. She had turned old, her yellowing skin stretched across her face as though there wasn't enough of it. She was getting worse.

Kath lingered. She wished her mother would open her eyes, that she would say something. Kath didn't like to make any noise, though she hoped her mother would be aware of her presence. It was better for her to sleep.

She swept the ashes from the fireplace then laid sticks and paper and a little coal inside. She put a match to it and watched it light and lick. The growing flame gave her a measure of satisfaction.

The sheets didn't seem to need changing; everything smelled fresh. She was thankful she didn't need to open the window to clear the air – when she drew back the curtains to let a little light in, snow began to fall. She stood there for a few moments, watching it.

She could remember last Christmas. They had gone south as they often did and met up with friends at Thirsk. It was such a pretty town and unlike many places, there were fields they could stay in. Nobody had tried to move them on or got in the way. The man who owned the land wanted payment, but that was no problem – they had plenty of money and her father was thought by other men to be silver tongued, which helped. Kath's father was a harsh but decent man and kept his family well. He could read and write and talk to the authorities. They stayed several weeks while the weather was bad and left in April when things picked up.

She enjoyed their time there, surrounded by friends and music and dancing. Her pleasure wasn't even diminished by her father's attempts to marry her off. He had insisted that Kath wear beautiful dresses in the camp so that the young lads would court her, which they did. She braved her father's anger when she refused to marry any of them.

She had other things to worry about now. Her mother had been ill for four months and was becoming worse each day. Their father had brought her back here to her hometown only when she broke down and begged. Kath did not think her father told the truth to the policeman about when they would leave – he would never have come back here but to let his wife die where she chose. It was just a question of time.

Christmas morning dawned and was nothing like other Christmases that Kath had known. The house was like a tomb; it had its own atmosphere. She heard voices, sound raging beyond her room.

She got out of bed, pulled open the door and in the dimness of the shadowed hall she could see the figures of two men, one half-turned toward her and the other almost completely away. She heard a sound she didn't know, a man crying. It was her father. The other man was the doctor, whom she recognised from his visit two days before. He was in his shirtsleeves, white shirt stark against the gloom, a jacket over his arm and the black bag he carried in his other hand.

The doctor, ignoring her, went down the stairs. Her father hurled himself into the room and slammed the door. Kath was left in the freezing hall. She wore nothing but a shift and began to shiver, but it was not from cold, it was from dread.

She could hear her father sobbing. Had her mother died? Her father was crying now as he had never cried before. Kath was confused. He had never taken her mother's happiness into consideration. Like most of the travelling men, he pleased himself and did whatever he liked. He was the person who dictated how the rest of them went on. It could be nothing but guilt bringing him to tears. As Kath stood there, Ella, her younger sister, came to the door. Hearing her father crying, she turned back into the room and Kath followed her.

Kath thought that her father would eventually come out and tell them that their mother had died, but he didn't. As the morning wore on, she dressed, went downstairs, saw to the dogs and lit the fire. Ella said she didn't want anything to eat but when Kath made toast over the fire, slick with butter, they downed it with hot, sweet tea.

She could not believe that their father had not invited them to say goodbye to their mother. She felt as though she would never have the strength to move away from the fire again.

When her father staggered down in the early afternoon, she could see that he was drunk. Kath had seen him drunk before but this time felt different. He looked years older. His face was harsh,

18

his hair wild and his eyes unseeing. He blundered to the cupboard where he kept a couple of bottles of whisky, took a bottle and staggered back upstairs.

'I'm scared,' Ella moaned in a tiny voice and she ran from the house and into the wagon that was their usual home.

Ella came back inside when dusk fell and Kath was glad of her company. It was mid-evening when she took Ella upstairs to their bedroom. There was no sound at all from her parents' room. It took a long time for Ella to go to sleep; she turned over and over. She was cried out and exhausted and when she finally slept, Kath listened to her breathing and was thankful for it and for her warmth. Outside a keen frost had set about the town though the snow had stopped falling and the air was clear.

She must have slept at one point because when she awoke in the darkness she knew that something had changed. She didn't know what it was. She thought she heard footsteps on the stairs.

The curtains were pulled across the windows but she could see a light from outside. It was not the moon – it was too bright and too big and too low and the wrong colour. She didn't want to disturb Ella so she slid from the bed and gently pulled aside the curtain. She gasped in horror at what she saw.

Their wagon was on fire. It was made of wood and was well alight. She could see her father standing, a tall black silhouette in front of the flames, watching as it grew. She did not know how long she stood there, knowing that there was

19

nothing she could do. It was too late for so many things.

Ella slept on but after a while Kath slipped from the room. Her parents' door was open and a lamp burned inside. The room smelled of death and the fire had long since gone out. It was cold, and her mother's body was all that was left of her existence. Kath could see that she was dead and that there was a complete absence of anything that had been like her mother. She didn't stay. There was nothing to stay for.

Her great fear had been that her father had burned her mother with the wagon. Since her mother had not traditionally been a traveller, it would not have been right. Indeed, it was only his anger and spite that made him burn everything they owned – only necessities had been brought into the house. Now they had nothing except the money that Kath's mother had given her long ago to keep in case of emergency. Thank God her mother had had the sense. Everything else was over.

The only things that mattered now were outside that room. She would wait until her father had spent his rage and grief on the fire before trying to comfort him. If he was too drunk, she would wait until morning.

How they would leave this town now was her next concern. They could go nowhere without the wagon. Her father seemed to have lost all reason though Kath did not understand why when he had always treated his wife as nothing more than a possession. Most men went on beyond their dead wives.

She watched her father throw what she thought was everything her mother owned on to the fire. When it began to die down, she thought he would come inside – maybe even sleep – but he didn't.

He went out of sight and Kath went downstairs to wait for him. She heard him calling the dogs. They whined and scratched at the door so she let them out. Then she heard the galloping hooves of a horse on the crisp frost. Her father, like a madman, had taken Diamond and was riding away, both dogs hurtling behind him.

Kath had never laid out a body before. She closed the bedroom door with Ella asleep inside and went back downstairs.

There was water still warm in the boiler. She ladled it into a bucket, took clean cloths and went upstairs. Steeling herself, she went into her mother's room and here she made everything right. She took off the clothes her mother had died in, washed her body and put her into a clean nightgown. She removed the soiled sheets and everything that held any evidence of illness or death.

Kath steeped the sheets and clothing in soda and water again and again. She rinsed them and wrung them out and when there was no more clean water, she left them bundled in the basket. Later, when the smoke had died away, she would hang the sheets and her mother's clothes on the line. The wagon was still smoking when the sun came up.

She went upstairs and cleaned out the fireplace and laid the fire as though her mother would awaken. Her father would find his sanity and come home.

Late in the morning, she went to bed. She lay down and closed her eyes and this time she fell asleep.

She awoke when somebody tugged hard at her arm. She was about to protest when she opened her eyes and saw her sister.

'Kath, the wagon burned. Come and see. There's nowt left but a pile of sticks. Everything. All my stuff was still in there. Look, Kath, look!'

Kath, not wanting Ella to know what had really happened, got up and went to the window and showed horror.

'We have to tell Dad,' Ella said.

'I think he went out earlier,' Kath said.

'He did? What about Mam? What about ... what happens now?'

Kath had thought about this. She should go to the undertaker but she didn't know if he would be at work on Boxing Day. She had thought that her father would take care of such things. Now she must try to do it herself, though she didn't want to leave Ella alone with her mother's body or take her to a place where there would be coffins. Ella, now fourteen, had always been the baby of the family and close to her mother. Kath was seventeen and quite old enough, she thought, to cope until her father remembered his responsibilities and came home.

Ella would not go near her parents' bedroom. Kath did her best to avoid it when they went out on to the landing. Ella sidled down the hall and the stairs and into the kitchen. Kath wished she could run away, that she had a horse and could gallop off like her father had done, but she was bound here by her duty to Ella and her mother.

The frost gave and more snow fell. It went on and on. It would have been comforting had her father been in the house, but she was too worried about where he had gone. Ella kept asking when he was coming back and Kath made excuses so she stopped asking. When it grew late, they didn't go to bed. Ella didn't want to go upstairs where her dead mother was and Kath didn't want to go upstairs because her father wasn't there.

They curled up together on the floor, wrapped in blankets in front of the fire. Kath had visions of her mother appearing in ghostlike form. She didn't know where the idea had come from. Was her mother trying to return to them? She knew that wasn't possible, but it was comforting none-theless.

All that night she waited for her father to come home. She didn't sleep. She felt as if she would never sleep again. But he didn't come back, even when the snow stopped and the pale winter light arrived in the silent yard. Kath decided that she must act. She found a key and locked the door of her parents' room and then she told Ella to stay inside by the fire. She promised she was only shopping and would bring some chocolate back.

She had no idea where the undertaker's was and didn't like to ask. People stared at her. She thought they knew who she was by now. She made her way quickly up to the store and went into the grocery department. She was greeted with a smile by Mrs McGregor, who had previously served her potatoes and yeast and flour.

'Why, lass,' she said, 'I thought you'd be with your family today. I didn't think to see you in here.'

Kath looked around her. The shop was full of people so she whispered, 'My mam died. I need to find an undertaker.'

Mrs McGregor looked startled. 'I had no idea. You poor soul.'

'I only need to know where he is. I don't want to interrupt your work,' Kath said hastily.

'Oh, bless,' said Mrs McGregor. 'Just along the road, toward the end. It's on the left-hand side. He's called Donald Lawson.'

'The bloody gypsy. She got what she deserved,' someone muttered behind her. It was not the first time that Kath had wished she did not have such good hearing. She knew that they were talking about her mother.

She set off along the icy street. A nasty wind, low and keen, was swirling through the town and her shoes were letting in the damp. She had had them a long time and they had not been good when her mother bought them. Rose loved them for their red colour.

Her mother had liked pretty things, she was not practical like Kath. Kath thought sorrowfully about her and wondered not for the first time why she had run off with a man like her father. She must have been drawn to his wildness and the romance of gypsies, campfires and the open road. She had paid for it ever since, Kath thought.

Her mother could not have thought that Kath would spend a second winter in these damp shoes. Each step was hard, her feet frozen so that her chilblains itched. Every time her shoes encountered water, they shrank a little more.

She was almost as far as the fell when she found Mr Lawson's establishment. The door was unlocked so Kath ventured in. A tall thin man peered at her over the top of his spectacles.

'Ah,' he said, 'good morning.'

She said good morning in return and then hesitated; she didn't want him to know who she was. Then she realised it was unavoidable. She explained that her mother had died and her father was not at home and asked if he could help her arrange a funeral. She had money, she assured him.

He gestured for her to sit down across the desk and there he eyed her for several moments.

'I'm afraid that you must pay for this now.'

He thought she had nothing. She looked squarely at him.

'If you tell me what I can have and how much it is, then I will tell you what I want,' she said.

He told her about the graveyard, about the coffin, how much it would cost to lay out her mother's body–

'I've done that,' Kath said.

'Do you want some kind of service in a church?'

'No.'

'Will you need a place for people to go who have come to the funeral?'

'Nobody will come,' Kath said.

'No food or drink then?'

'Nothing like that.'

'A tombstone?'

Kath couldn't see the point to it and shook her head.

'I don't want anybody to know. I just want to be able to say a few words over her grave with my sister. How much will that be?'

Mr Lawson worked this out and gave the total to Kath. She thought it was reasonable so she brought out her purse and counted the coins, slowly and deliberately. After this he was a lot more cheerful.

Managing her mother's funeral was the hardest thing that Kath had ever done. Her father did not come back and she was astonished at how fast things were happening.

Gypsy funerals always had a closed coffin on a flat cart pulled by a horse, but since Kath's mother was not a traveller, she had neither of these things. Kath requested a straightforward burial and was thankful when her mother's body was finally carried out of the house by lads that Mr Lawson had sent.

The cemetery was a strangely welcoming place. It looked out from its hill down to Weardale. They buried her mother's body in a particularly good spot. Her mother had liked looking out at the world, and Kath hoped she would be comfortable here. She couldn't pray, she didn't know how to, so at the graveside she stood silently, accompanied by Mr Lawson, the lads, Ella, and a grave digger who stood slightly apart, leaning on his spade.

She had no idea what to say. Ella hid against her and after a few moments, the man began to fill the hole with earth and Mr Lawson and his boys departed. It was not much of a burial for a woman like her mother, who had been so vital, so alive.

She and Ella left without speaking. Neither of them cried. Kath thought that Ella would ask where their father was but she apparently understood that it was pointless.

The house had a different atmosphere without her mother's body in it. Already the place was lighter. Kath felt certain that her father would come back that night, now everything was done. He would come home and face the future. Kath didn't know what it held but he would. He was good with money and would take care of them. He would come back and have a new wagon and a plan and he would know where they were going next.

That night felt very long. Kath lay awake from dusk to dawn and still nothing. She was beginning to panic.

The day passed and the one after that. Ella continued to ask where their father was. Had something happened? Kath had no answer. The longer her father was gone, the more she worried.

It was five days before the constable came to the door. Kath stood back when she saw who it was and quaked before his uniform.

'Right, Miss,' he said. 'Can I come in?'

Two

1930 Weardale in County Durham

It was almost Christmas when Jake's mother died. The doctor had said he thought she would live until the spring but Jake thought he was simply being kind. For his mother to survive the bad winter weather and the hard spring storms seemed unlikely and proved so. When the wind came screaming down the dale in late October he had known that she wouldn't last much longer.

She was stubborn. She wouldn't let him light a fire in her room, nor carry her downstairs to the big stove in the kitchen, which was the only fire they could afford to keep lit all the time. So he sat in her bedroom, windows wide open at her insistence, frozen and terrified, listening to her taking gasping breaths, day after day, night after night.

Jake would lean against the cracked window-pane, curtains drawn back at her request, the howling bloody gale turning his body to frost. He sighed a dozen and more times each night and wished that his mother was not so damned stupid and stubborn, yet he was still proud of her for not giving in.

She might have lasted longer had she gone downstairs, but then again she couldn't eat and she would barely drink. She would not have death defy her, she would defy it and go out when she

28

chose. It was not a view that Jake shared. His father had dropped dead years ago in a low field next to the river. It was his heart, the doctors said. Jake couldn't disagree with that. It had broken his father's heart when two of his sons did not come back from France. Jake was only glad his father was not there to see when his eldest son, Patrick, came back without his mind.

His mother had endured all that time – she fought so hard – but she too had suffered much during the years. In addition to all her work in the house, she had been obliged to help Jake with the milking, the butter-making, the dairying and taking care of the animals.

She helped him with the lambing because there was no way he could do it alone, but in the bad years, the sheep and lambs were lost in snowdrifts and in the good years, the harvests were so fruitful that the work was never finished. They both worked to the bone and still the farm brought in less money each year.

One morning in August his mother was so unwell that she went to lie down. Jake came back at teatime to find the kitchen stove extinguished, no dinner made and his mother asleep in the rocking chair. He went up to check on his brother, as he always did at that time, and found Pat's bed empty.

Jake went back out into the early evening to discover that the warm weather had left. It was raining hard and the day was so dark and cold that it could have been November. He went back into the hall and pulled on his coat, setting off again with Nell, his sheepdog, by his side.

He shouted Pat's name up the yard in a panic. Pat rarely went out.

Jake searched the buildings, calling Pat's name. Nell was sniffing here and there and despite the rain would have found Pat's scent had there been any sign of him. Jake could feel his heart pounding with fear. What if Pat had gone beyond the gates, wandered into the road?

He would probably not be knocked over, Jake reasoned, because the road was quiet. It was only traversed by bicycles, the bus that goes up and down the dale, and the odd car belonging to the better-off folk. But if the night was cold and Pat could not find his way back, he might despair and lie down.

Jake shouted across the road. He considered whether to go up to the fields or down to the river, but he was equally concerned that his mother would awaken to find neither of her sons in the house. He retraced his steps back to the yard and beyond the buildings to the field where the hen house stood. The hens very sensibly had gone inside to get out of the weather.

Nell followed him there and began to whine. Jake opened the hen house door. It was all shadows inside and he could see very little. The hens blinked their tiny jewelled eyes while Nell hovered, crying in a low voice because she knew that she must not go inside or frighten the hens. Jake gradually saw a shape right at the back of the hen house. He got down and said his brother's name very softly.

'She's going to die,' Pat said, in strangled tones.

'No, she's not, she's just asleep. She was tired,

that's all. Come in and I'll light the stove and we'll have some tea.'

In a way, Jake thought, Pat had seen before he did that their mother was worn out, but then Pat had seen so many deaths. Even though his mind denied such things, his body had grown accustomed to it and this was what he could not bear. Jake couldn't bear his mother's death, either. How on earth would he manage without her?

Jake was familiar with Gold Hill Hall. Colonel Banks had always had parties at Christmas and harvest time for his tenants and their families. Then the Colonel had died and Mrs Banks was only seen by the farmers and villagers at the parish church on Sunday, dressed in black, heavily veiled. She would walk up the aisle to her family pew, ignoring everyone as she made her slow progress towards the front.

She always arrived just as the first hymn ended – with Miss Banks falling behind, cheeks flushed – and Jake was forever amused by the consequent annoyance of the new vicar, Robert Black. Mr Black would have to wait in the quietness until Mrs Banks, assisted by her daughter, was seated. Taking off her gloves, she would settle herself with a great flurry of veil and scarves before kneeling down to spend a considerable amount of time communing with her maker.

Because God was listening to Mrs Banks, there was no way He could also hear the new vicar attempting to greet and welcome his parishioners, and so Mr Black waited. Inevitably, as soon as he had deemed it safe and began to speak again, Mrs Banks would finish and need to be helped off her knees and back onto her pew where her daughter waited with her hymn book and beautiful white leather-bound Bible. It was only then that she would sit back and look at the vicar, wondering why on earth he was taking such a long time continuing with the service.

The congregation, having waited all this time in silence – barring the odd cough or already bored child kicking the pew in front – gave a collective letting go of breath as the vicar was allowed to go on.

After the Colonel died, the festivities at the hall – so much looked forward to and appreciated by the tenants – had ceased. Since this was several years ago, Jake had been astonished, one cold dry afternoon just after his mother died, to find Miss Banks at the back door at teatime. He ushered his guest into the cold back kitchen where she got right to the purpose of her visit: she hoped he would accept her offer to serve refreshments up at the hall after his mother's funeral.

Jake's biggest worry until this point was whether he ought to offer tea to Miss Banks. He was aware of the unwashed pots in the small kitchen sink and how messy the house was because he had no time to see to it. He was ashamed that there was a dark empty grate in the front kitchen instead of a roaring fire and that if Miss Banks cared to look about her at the various downstairs rooms, she would notice the thick dust on every surface. The unforgiving sun, which was even now going down at the front, was casting light through the rain-

streaked windows into the room so that the cob-
webs and dirt might be seen more clearly.

Miss Banks, however, did not notice. Jake
thought she looked uncomfortable. He thought he
could understand why. Without his mother's
supervision, a woman could not come to the farm
alone without running the risk of people talking.

Miss Banks was probably above such things,
but when she saw how astonished Jake was at the
offer, her face coloured to the point he might
have warmed his hands by it.

He wanted to say that he had never heard of
such a thing, that it was far too generous, but he
couldn't. Words seemed to have escaped him. He
wasn't used to talking to people outside of the
marts where the sheep and cattle were bought and
sold. He conversed in the general run of business.
He was also painfully aware that Miss Banks was
an educated woman and he was a tenant farmer.

Miss Banks, however, ploughed on.

'My mother thinks that it is the right thing to
do.' She smiled slightly and the blush on her
cheeks faded. Jake thought that was a shame; the
colour suited her usually pale face. 'And if this
goes well, then she might agree to reinstate the
parties for the tenants. I miss them very much
and I'm sure everyone else does.'

Miss Banks, Jake thought, always sounded as
though she had just read a book. He found his
face warming, too, but that was at his sudden
awareness that he owed her several months' rent.
It was yet another problem he had been trying to
put to the back of his mind.

'It's ... it's very good of you.' He hoped he

sounded as educated as she did. Perhaps it was just her presence. He wanted to talk to her about the rent but since there was no way he could pay it, it seemed pointless. The growing misery that always fell on him when he thought about the farm's financial state was broken by Miss Banks saying, 'My mother was very fond of yours.'

Jake's mother had been a maid at the hall when she was a young woman. Jake could remember her saying that Mrs Banks had remonstrated with her when she gave her notice to marry his father; she told her what a fool she was. His parents' marriage had been a good one, but Mrs Banks never took back her harsh words. It seemed strange that she should want to do this now.

Jake thanked her and Miss Banks departed with assurances that his mother's tea would be in good hands. He helped her back onto her horse and opened and closed the gates for her.

He tried not to notice, as he did several times a day, how gloomy it was without his mother presiding over her kitchen. The warmth was gone and not just from the stove. He went through into the big kitchen at the front of the house and noticed how dirty the windows were that looked out over the lawn. The garden was a jungle. His mother had loved it, cared for it. Now it was just something else that he had failed to do.

He plodded up the stairs and opened the bedroom door. Pat was either asleep or hiding from their visitor. He quickly confirmed this second notion by whispering to Jake, 'Has she gone yet?'

Jake sat down on the bed. Before their mother died, Pat would occasionally get up and sit near the stove in the afternoons, but her loss had sent him back to the safety and relative silence of his bed.

'She's offered us the hall for Mam's funeral tea.'

Jake was rather satisfied when his brother sat up in astonishment. Pat's face was pale in the dimness of the light that came from the one candle on the side table.

It was a lovely room, Jake thought, with its small black fireplace and wallpaper of pink roses. Jake had never yet lit the fire there.

'Why?' Pat said.

Pat may have suffered badly during the war but sometimes his utterances were acute.

Jake told him what Miss Banks had said about reinstating the festivals but Pat frowned. Even so, he said, 'That would be nice for people.' Jake wondered again whether he would be able to persuade his brother to wash, shave, dress and follow the coffin the half-mile or so to the village church. He knew it wasn't likely; Pat had not left the farm in twelve years.

'It will likely be a good spread,' Pat allowed. 'Mam would have been pleased,' and he lay back down with a sigh.

'Will you come downstairs if I make you some tea?' Jake offered. 'I can have the stove going in no time at all.'

His brother considered the bribe.

'Yes,' he said, after a few seconds, 'that would be nice.'

Three

Kath duly pulled back the door even further and the policeman took off his helmet and went with her into the kitchen. When he saw Ella he said, 'Is there another place maybe where we could talk?'

She took him into the icy living room and he shivered. She was not surprised. They had never lit this fire and the walls were almost running water.

The constable collected himself. 'I have to tell you, miss, that we have found a body up on the fells–' he hesitated there as though she should react but Kath only went on looking at him '–and it is your father's. He has been identified by the doctor.'

For some stupid reason she thought first of the horse.

'It looks as if the animal stumbled and threw him and then he hit his head on a stone. There'll be an inquest.'

'And Diamond?' she said.

He gazed at her. 'If you want the animal's carcass moved, it will cost you a great deal of money. And then what would you do with it?'

Kath didn't know. Perhaps Diamond was better up on the fell, so that the crows and the land could take him. She didn't bother to ask about the dogs. Why would he care?

'You'll have the funeral to pay for unless you

want a pauper's funeral for him. And you need to leave this house in the next few days. You won't have to go far – there are plenty of farms here looking for hiring maids. But I warn you that local folk don't like gypsies, so if I hear of anything going missing I'll know where to look.'

The policeman left. Ella waited until he had gone and then she came into the hall.

'I heard,' she said and she didn't cry, she just stood there. 'Did Daddy do it on purpose, Kath?'

'Of course he didn't,' Kath said, soothingly. She didn't say that her father had been mad with grief when he left. He hadn't known what he was doing, was all she could think.

'We can't stay here now, Kath. I don't want to go and live in the middle of nowhere with some mucky old farmer.'

'Don't worry, we won't.'

'What about the dogs?'

'I don't know,' Kath said.

When it had been established that her father's death was an accident, she went again to Mr Lawson and gave him the money that he needed. It was also all the money she had left.

Kath was fighting back panic; she didn't know how to go on. Her father was buried beside her mother and she and Ella were on their own. After the funeral they went back to the house, not speaking. There was nothing left to say. Kath didn't know what to do. She had no money, no friends to call.

She thought briefly, absurdly, of Will, the richest gypsy lad she knew. He had offered to marry her last Christmas. How much she wished now that she had accepted the offer. How right her father had been to urge her. She needed help now and the support of a family.

She and Ella slept in the same bed, hugging one another for comfort and warmth.

'It'll be so cold on the road,' Ella said.

'Anything has to be better than staying here,' Kath pointed out. She thought of Thirsk. Their friends would be gathered there as they did most winters. She couldn't allow herself to think that they might be somewhere else this year, and that Thirsk was very far away.

As soon as it was light, Kath took what they could carry, and they wore as many clothes as they could. Kath thought she knew which way was south and so they set off across the top of the hills, past a long row of houses some way beyond the town. The land began to fall away into the valley and up the other side. She started to think that things might improve – there could even be a horse and cart or some other kind of transport that might help to carry them away from here. They picked up the pace and Ella even managed a smile.

They had not gone much further when she heard a noise behind her. Turning, she saw that two policemen approached on bicycles. They angled these in front and behind her, while Ella drew back.

'Leave us alone. We're not doing anything.'

'Except trying to run out. I thought you might

do something like this,' said the first constable.

'What difference does it make to you?'

'Sergeant Birton and I are the law around here and you are mucky gypsies who need to be taught better.' His gaze went to her breasts. Kath looked at the other man and saw nothing better.

'Just leave us alone,' she said.

The two policemen laughed.

'A bit lass like you shouldn't be going no place,' said Sergeant Birton, getting off his bicycle.

Kath waited until he was close and then she moved forward and rammed her knee in his groin. He staggered and let out a groan of pain. The other officer grabbed Ella and pulled her arms behind her back. Sergeant Birton tried to grab Kath again and when he reached between her legs, she elbowed him hard in the face, hearing a satisfying crack. Ella was screaming as the other man took her away. Distracted by her sister's cries, Kath didn't see Birton's hard, fat hand coming until it struck her across the face.

Kath fell to the road, rolled, and leaped back to her feet. She crouched, ready, and looked him in his piggy eyes.

All she could hear was Ella screaming. She wanted to kill him.

He came forward, truncheon in hand. He swung it clumsily and she weaved and dodged it easily. Ducking behind him, she chopped her hand into the back of his neck. He fell to the ground and lay there.

She turned to see where Ella was. The other policeman had dragged her down the street. Kath started to run in their direction when she saw a police car pull up to the pair. She halted in her tracks – they were bundling her sister into it. She dropped to the ground until they were gone, and then seeing the prostrate sergeant stir, she pulled her thick coat around her torn clothes and ran.

When she got back to the village, she saw the car parked outside the orphanage. She watched the building for any sign of Ella but there was none. She knew better than to approach. She had hurt a policeman and she appreciated what would happen if they caught her. They might put her in Durham gaol, they might even hang her. Women had been killed for lesser things, and she was a traveller.

She waited outside the orphanage all night and it took some doing. It was so cold that her teeth refused to chatter, even after the sun came up. She had nothing to eat or drink and the late winter morning progressed so slowly that she could have screamed.

Ella still did not come outside. Kath considered going in, but they would surely hand her over to the police and what would happen then? If they put her away she certainly couldn't help Ella. She must go find help and return. Without knowing where to start, she turned away blindly and started walking.

It took both policemen to get Ella into the orphanage. She was in full panic and didn't understand why they were taking her away from Kath. She had never been away from her sister before. She screamed and scratched and clawed.

Her anxiety levels grew when they hauled her into the car. It was her first time in one and when it started up, she began kicking and punching in terror. The tears fell hot on her cheeks until her eyes were sore. They attempted to restrain her to no avail. She fought all the way and by the time they got her back into the little town, she was exhausted and could cry no more. She fell to whimpering like a small animal, curled up as tiny as she could be. She thought they were going to kill her and she would never see Kath again.

She did not notice the building they took her into. She twisted and turned so much that the policemen could barely hold her. Her face burned with frustration. It must be prison, this place.

Once inside, she was dragged into a small room where a woman sat behind a desk. Released, Ella could barely stand. The floor came up to meet her and she fell into a sweet dark nothing.

She dreamt of the view of stars from the wagon. Home. Joy. It wasn't until she began to come round that she remembered the nightmare was real.

She opened her eyes. All rooms were small and dark to her. This one had a lot of furniture, which made it even smaller and darker. A dim light fell through the only window and she could see the two policemen and the woman. Ella was lying on a most uncomfortable couch of some sort. The room smelled of overcooked vegetables and was musty like old wagons that had long been abandoned. As she looked up the woman said, 'She cannot stay here. She's no bairn.'

'It's just for now. Don't you worry, we'll sort her out when we find the other one. I dare say you could find use for her in the meantime.'

'I want our Kath,' Ella managed.

'Your sister is not here. The police have taken her away. You should be grateful that they have brought you to me. You couldn't have survived out there in this weather. Whatever was she thinking, taking you out like that? We are only trying to help you but she wouldn't be told, would she? She is a very bad example to you, a very bad girl.'

'She's nothing of the sort,' Ella said crossly, sitting up carefully.

'You must not speak to me like that. I am Miss Timpson. I run the orphanage and I demand respect.'

'I want our Kath.'

'I have no doubt that you will see her soon. The other constable has her and if you behave well you will probably see her later. Gentlemen, I have it from here. Please keep me informed.'

The two policemen retreated and left the room.

'Now if you can manage it, you may come into the dining room and have some breakfast with the children.'

Ella was not hungry. She thought she would never be hungry again. Her throat was raw from tears and fright and all she wanted was to have Kath close to her as she always had been.

The woman led her out of the room, down a corridor and into a long narrow room where a dozen children of varying ages sat at either side of a table on long wooden benches. None of them was nearly as old as she, but she was tiny and people always mistook her for younger.

Ella sat down and a dish of food was put in front of her. She had no idea what it was. It was the first time she had ever seen badly-cooked food. Kath had done their cooking for as long as she could remember and she was good at it. Ella hadn't thought about that before now.

The children were scooping up the mixture. Ella gazed into it. She was not used to people she didn't know and didn't want to look at any of them. Gradually she became aware of the boy sitting next to her. She thought that he was extraordinary looking with his hair the colour of carrots and dark brown eyes. She looked quickly back down at her bowl. After a little while he said softly, 'Can I have it?'

She was brave enough to look at him again.

'Can I have your porridge?' he repeated.

It was porridge? The stuff that Kath made with milk and sugar, thick and creamy?

She peeked around her but none of the other children was looking at her so she pushed the dish towards him.

'Thanks,' he said.

Ella had met a lot of lads. The travellers all had big families and she knew many boys of all ages – the little ones she loved – but this one was not like anybody she had seen before. Gypsy lads were mostly dark-haired, very often black-eyed and dark-skinned. Some who came from overseas were as fair as she was and even more so. But mostly they looked like Kath. It made her miss her sister all the more.

When the meal was over, the children were lined

up and marched away into another room. Ella had never seen anything like it. It was full of desks and seats and at the front was a black-board. When they were all seated, a short, stout man with a red face wrote words on the blackboard.

'Now then, who can tell me what this says?'

Nobody moved, nobody spoke. The man surveyed them. Then he walked up and down, finally pausing before Ella.

'Ah,' he said, 'a new girl. Do you know what the words say?'

Ella shook her head.

'You must say "yes, sir" or "no, sir".'

Ella gazed at him. She had died and gone to hell for sure. And then she spoke up as she had always been encouraged to.

'I don't read or write,' she said. 'I'm a traveller.'

The man looked perplexed.

'A gypsy?'

Ella considered his ignorance.

'It's not the same thing at all,' she allowed.

'Perhaps you would like to enlighten us as to the difference.'

'Well, gypsies were originally from Asia,' Ella said, 'tinkers are from Ireland and travellers are from all over the place. My dad's family have been travellers for hundreds of years. My mam came from here.'

'Would you like to tell us your name?'

'I want to go back to my sister,' she said.

Four

Caroline Banks, who had owned Gold Hill Hall since her father had died several years ago, was standing in front of the study windows considering what to do next. When her father made his will, he left her everything, knowing that his wife did not care and wouldn't be able to cope. He trusted Caroline – or 'Caro' as he affectionately called her – to look after her mother and the estate and the farms and everything that went with it.

The Colonel had been a good man, a kind father and an astute businessman. He loved the countryside and he cared about the people who worked for him. He often noted that some of his tenants had likely been on the same piece of land for a thousand years, hundreds of years more than any of his ancestors. He respected their heritage.

He kept the farms in very good repair – if the harvest failed or the winter was bad and the sheep and lambs died, he made sure that the men and their families had more than enough to feed and clothe them. Caro started visiting the farmers' wives when she was a child, and although she would say little, she knew the problems they had. She would discuss them with her father, who would help to sort them out with discretion so nobody was embarrassed or humiliated.

He didn't expect any of his tenants to go to

45

church. He believed when people had free time, it was up to them what they did with it. His wife was a big churchgoer but he only went to weddings, christenings, funerals, Christmas and Easter. He had loved shooting in the autumn and fishing in the spring and summer. He encouraged the tenants to shoot over their own land and fish in the tributaries that adjoined their farms.

Caro went to church every Sunday with her mother. She knew her father was grateful to her for this. She adored him. He had been her whole life, and when he died, all happiness ceased and her work began. She had no one to turn to now, nobody to help.

Caro always recalled him with affection and pain. She knew he had wanted a son – he must have done, though he never said – and she had the feeling that her mother could have provided one but had chosen not to try after her first child was born.

Her mother had been an aristocrat and married beneath her with Caro's father. She never let him forget it, either. Caro suspected relations in the bedroom had stopped with her birth or because of arguments and dissent. Certainly her parents were never happy. Every year on her birthday her mother would tell her how hard her birth had been until Caro longed to stop her mouth with cake.

Not that her mother ate cake. She ate nothing and drank nothing but weak tea pale with milk. Her mother was skinny and was always looking her daughter up and down because Caro was podgy. There was no other word for it. She was like a little square, very short and rather round. She was just over five feet tall and had always hated it, though she knew that it didn't make any difference what size people were. In fact, she thought, smaller people tended to be more successful. Perhaps they had bigger brains. What a lovely thought. She looked like her father, who had also been short and portly. She liked being like him; it was better than being mean and tall and skinny like her mother.

Her father had had a fancy woman for years. Caro wasn't sure whether her mother knew or cared. He said nothing and was discreet – he never took his car and was not often seen – but the dale was a series of villages and there was nothing for people to do but work and gossip. Miss Turner was one of the local schoolteachers, most respectable.

When Miss Turner went on her holidays to Whitley Bay in the summer and to Newcastle to visit her family at Christmas and Easter, the Colonel would make business trips to join her. He was happy, his wife was delighted to be left alone, and Caro enjoyed the consequent peace and quiet.

Miss Turner did very well for a schoolteacher. She had pretty clothes and good jewellery and she lived in one of the Colonel's houses in the village, a lovely place with double bay windows at the front and a big garden at the back. He left it to her when he died, along with a substantial amount of money that only Caro and Adam Wilks, the solicitor, knew about.

Caro begrudged Miss Turner nothing. She had made her father content; she had been good for him. He made sure when he died that she would be financially independent. He wanted her to have the freedom to move away if people talked, or give up work if she chose. But nobody said anything and Miss Turner stayed where she was. Sometimes the people here were outwardly respectable and inwardly forgiving. It helped that Miss Turner was a very good teacher and people wanted their children to be well-educated and capable, and have the ability to succeed both inside and outside of the dale upon graduation.

Mrs Banks would never admit to any kind of good humour. She had, Caro thought, spent her whole life complaining. Her family had a very old name but they were potless. She had landed on her feet, the community said, when she married a lovely man like the Colonel. His match had disappointed a lot of local women who would have appreciated marrying him, but Caro's mother could not forgive her family for having no money nor the Colonel for having enough to buy her for his wife.

After he died, Caro's mother wanted no part of his tenant parties. Few people came to the hall. Initially Caro had endured her mother's wishes because it caused shrill complaints from her when she didn't. But as she gained in confidence running the estate, she learned not to care about or listen to what her mother thought, though it wasn't always easy.

Her mother had never liked her; she wanted her to be dainty and catch a rich husband as her mother's generation had been obliged to do. Caro understood that her mother wanted better for her, but was not the kind of better that Caro would have enjoyed. She did not want some man to tell her what to do. Her father never did, but she saw around her a lot of women who would not have been allowed to do what she was required to every day.

The work may not be considered womanly, but she liked the challenge. She liked going to the marts and talking to her solicitor and her accountant, she liked driving up and down the dale. And in a shameful kind of way, she liked that people knew who she was.

She was happy with herself, but she did not think that any man – or at least, any that she would consider for marriage – would like her. She was plain and fat and Miss Banks.

Caro was twenty-one when her father died. She thought he had hung on until she was old enough to be given the responsibilities he had no intention of leaving to his wife. For years after, she put up with her mother telling her what to do.

Business was hard. There had been several awful years during the war when a lot of men went away. Families like the Sutherlands had an even harder time after the war when their sons did not come home and they struggled to keep their farms. Now she was tired of her mother's wishes and her mother's commands and her mother's needs.

She had lied to Jacob Sutherland – it had not been her mother's desire to help when his mother died; she had suggested it to her mother and her mother had finally agreed. Emboldened by this success, Caro decided that she might alter a great many things. She was tired of fighting so hard for everything.

She decided to start with the tenants' festivities. Soon after her mother acquiesced to the funeral reception, Caro went into her sitting room in the middle of the morning when she knew her mother would be taking tea. She got straight to it.

'Mother, the tenants work hard and I would like to reinstate their parties.'

Her mother sniffed.

'Out of respect for your father, I think we had better keep things as they are,' she said.

'He's been dead for many years and the people are having a bad time. The parties at Christmas and harvest time will boost morale.'

'I couldn't allow it.'

Caro looked at her. Why did her mother not understand that she was being consulted purely from a respect that she did not deserve? She had no power here.

'I think we should,' Caro said.

'Whatever for?'

'Because we look ungrateful.'

'Ungrateful?' Her mother looked sharply at her. Had her mother ever looked at her any other way? 'These people should think themselves lucky that they have these farms. If it wasn't for us they would be homeless.'

'Mother, people like the Wears and the Sutherlands have lived on these farms for hundreds of years. It's a question of cooperation.'

Her mother looked tired. Her face drooped. She wore too much white face powder which only served to offset the thick black eyeliner and

50

mascara on her well-divided lashes. Her mouth was a thin slick of tangerine and her cheeks were round and pink like a doll. It was gruesome, a mask, Caro thought.

'Dear God,' her mother said, 'you sound like a man. No wonder no one will marry you.'

That stung because there was truth in it. Caro knew that most of the men in the dale didn't consider her a proper woman, if they thought of her at all. And yet she still wasn't one of them.

She belonged nowhere, she had no friends. The women shunned her because she ran her father's business. Women her age had been married for years and had two or three children. She had nothing in common with them. She was Miss Banks.

When she went to bed at night – in a room much too large for comfort – she looked at herself in the mirror. She saw the lines on her face, how she was too fat and too pale, with eyes that were too dull. She remembered when her father had sent her to London when she was seventeen for her coming-out season.

She had been so excited. She was not a beautiful girl but she was pretty and her figure had been attractive then – hourglass, that was what men called it.

Her father was generous with his money so that she could have anything she wanted. Her mother's family had connections and she lived in London for the summer season. She wore lovely dresses, her hair was looked to each day, and she strolled on slippers that suited her tiny feet – they were the one claim she had to beauty. She had admired the slender elegance of her own ankles and wrists. Her skin was milky and her eyes were bright. She saw men admiring her breasts, her small waist and swelling hips.

The trouble with an aristocratic mother and a rich father was that the men who danced with her were those who needed money. The cream of the aristocracy would not have aligned themselves with a mere colonel's daughter, no matter how well-connected her mother was.

Caro was undeceived and too sensible even then to marry a mere handsome face; she was not taken in for a second. She sometimes wished that she had been swept up and could look back on that time with affection, but she was far too rational to join her life to some idiot who only wanted her money. She knew it would lead to lifelong misery. So even though she received half a dozen offers of marriage, she would have none of them.

Her mother was horrified and said she would die an old maid. Her father had told her she made the right decision; he would never want her to marry a man who did not love her.

When she came home, men still vied for her hand because she was her father's heir but they were middle class, cunning solicitors or rough farmers who were so uneducated that she could not converse with them nor overcome her distaste. She had given up thinking she would ever have a man to call her own. She would rather die alone in her bed, unloved and unwanted, than to give herself to one who didn't care for her.

The trouble was that, despite everything, she had ultimately fallen in love, and so unsuitably that when she stood in front of her mirror at night she laughed disparagingly and called herself foolish. Her face warmed just thinking about it.

She had not known then that it was love – she was sure it was just a silly fancy – but when she stood in Jake Sutherland's kitchen, all her feelings for him were reinforced. She couldn't understand it.

The man had no education, he had never been anywhere, and he had been a child during the war, slightly younger than she was. He spoke like a rough farmer, of course, but she had seen him fighting to keep the farm going even after his brother had come home broken, and she respected that.

Now his mother had died and she could not stop herself from offering him the hall for his mother's funeral tea. There was no reason why she shouldn't – the whole village knew that Jake's mother had been in service there so it was common enough – but Caro knew that it mattered too much to her and she needed to dismiss him from her mind.

Could she ever marry Jake? He was so far beneath her station – and aside from that, he would never choose to – but she could not shake the idea. He couldn't marry either because he was penniless. No woman would have him in such circumstances. The local farmers' daughters knew that he had no money and that his brother had lost his mind, so there was nothing to be gained from marriage to such a man, only burdens. Their fathers might speak to Jake at the mart but none of them visited.

Jake seemed to understand his place in the world. He did not leave his brother, not even to go to a dance or to have a drink in the local pub. He didn't fuss with nice clothes – he probably didn't have any. Even when the evenings were long in the summer, he went nowhere. His brother was his whole life.

He did not look at any women except to say a polite hello, and then he always left first.

Jake's life was impossible, Caro thought, and yet he led it. She took comfort in that. She felt as though they had at least that much in common. She wished she could ease his life and that he could ease hers, but it would never happen. He went to bed half a mile away. Sometimes she thought she could see the odd dim lamp in the house when Jake closed everything up for the night.

She wished she could visit him and talk about the animals and the farm but she knew it would look bad, so all she did in the dark nights was watch for the tiny glow as the farmhouse windows were briefly lit before the whole place descended into darkness.

In the summer she lay awake, sweating with the windows open. The cries of the birds beyond the river made her wish she could fly away. Did he ever lie awake and wish that he would have some-one of his own? Men usually thought they were entitled. All he did was work and keep the farm and his brother. What he did during the long summer nights she could not – tried not to – imagine.

Winter was bad enough but summer was particularly cruel to those who lay alone. There was no comfort in the sunshine when families picnicked by the river, young couples held hands walking, and on Sundays children hopped and skipped their way to church.

She ached for a child to call her own, but she carried on doing what she must do, keeping the dale going. Sometimes she didn't know why she bothered when she had no heir to take up the work when she was gone, but her sense of responsibility drove her forward.

She did, however, have this one victory over her mother. She reestablished the summer and Christmas parties and she called at every farm in the dale that had been her father's and was now hers and told them so. She saw the joy in their faces when she gave them the news, and that was enough.

She would give a lavish party each summer like her father did, tables set up outside, heavy with food. At Christmas she would make sure that the children had gifts, wonderful treats that they would never have otherwise. She would fill hampers with hams and smoked chicken and orange chocolate and ginger snaps. There would be bottles of sherry and whisky and brandy.

There would be dancing. Sweets for the children and ribbons and books for the older girls, fishing rods and kites for the boys, and marzipan dainties for their mothers. She would grant the men more opportunity to fish and shoot over her land. She wanted to make sure they had everything they needed so that they could lead lives of more than enough, and merriment. This much she could do and was glad to do it.

Five

Kath walked down the banks from the little pit town. It was the only way out of the village other than the route she had already attempted, and she didn't think they would look for her going this way. She kept to the side of the road and spent a good amount of time watching behind her. She wouldn't be caught unawares again.

When she reached the bottom, after about three miles, there was a pretty little town ahead. She walked through the middle of it and out the other side. It didn't take long, but as she made her way up the road, not knowing where the next town was or how far, the snow came down so thickly that she could barely see. Darkness began to fall, though it was but early afternoon.

She grew weary. She wanted to lie down in the snow and sleep, but she knew that she must go on as far as she could. She had no money, she had to help Ella, and she could not go back.

The narrow road wound and wound and there was no car and no cart and nobody to help. The snow came down even more thickly and darkness gathered. She couldn't see at all. Her steps began to flag and her feet to numb. She couldn't feel her fingers and the snow was clinging to her clothes and her feet were getting heavier with each step. Soon the snow was so deep that she could not lift her feet out of it. She kept going, pushing through.

When the snow stopped, the sky cleared and a great big moon and thousands of stars came out. She remembered what her mother had said, that each star was a traveller. She felt the crispness of the ice above the snow. It held her feet up but her shoes were disintegrating and she couldn't feel her feet any more.

There were no lights other than the moon and stars, so high in the heavens, where Kath felt sure her parents were among friends. She saw her mother laughing and dancing, the bright lights of a party. Kath could hear the fiddler playing while her mother spun in a rich, red velvet gown, her hair loose and shining as it had been before she became ill, gold and pearl earrings swinging, coral bracelets upon her slender brown wrists which twirled as she moved. Their father was laughing and Ella was smiling. The music wove its magic around her.

Kath came to and there was a sweet doggy smell and a warm tongue licking her face. At first she thought she was back in the wagon and her mother had sent one of the dogs in because she was sleeping late. She could hear gentle waves spreading across wet sand, and then she opened her eyes, moving slightly. The dog sat back.

It was a sheepdog, black and white, with one ear that was imperfect and flopped forward. The dog gazed down at her from big liquid brown eyes, its head tilted to one side as if it expected her to get up. Kath couldn't. She couldn't feel anything other than pain in her feet and hands. She closed her eyes to shut out the hurt and then she heard a voice.

'Come away, Nell, and let me see. What have we got here?'

He bent down, swore and then picked her up. Kath kept her eyes closed. She didn't want anything to do with this. She just wanted it all blocked out and never to have to think about anything again. He set her back down and she almost cried out with pain. The next minute he had wound something thick about her feet and legs, enveloping her in a big garment, and lifting her again, he began to carry her through the snow.

She wanted to return to sleep, back to when her parents were alive and they were all at a party and everything was as it should be, but the dream was fading against the movement and the reality. If she could have cried, she would have, but it was too much effort. She felt every step as he walked. She was huddled in his coat; it was itchy against her cheek and her face grew hot. Her body ached everywhere.

It seemed to her a long time before she heard his voice again and when she opened her eyes a man was gazing down at her and another was almost out the door.

'I'm going for the doctor, Pat. Watch her until I get back.'

'She's wet through,' Pat said.

'What?'

'We need to get her clothes off her or she'll die of the cold.'

Kath wanted to tell them that she could do it herself but she couldn't move; her body was not obeying her. Rather clumsily and hastily, they took off her shoes and dress and wrapped her in warm rough clothing, thick woolly socks, and two huge blankets.

She began to shiver, lying there with her eyes closed, not wanting to acknowledge that she was still alive. Heaven had been so close and now she was shut out and would have to face further horrors.

She couldn't conjure up the party she had thought she was attending. She opened her eyes again and started to take in her surroundings.

A man in his mid-thirties was sitting in an armchair to one side. He smiled at her but didn't say anything at first, and then in a kind and gentle voice he said, 'Don't fret, lass, it's all right. Nobody's going to hurt you.'

It was the most reassuring thing Kath had heard in a long time. She was lying on a sofa, and there was an enormous fire in the grate. Perhaps it was the only room they had – the ceiling was so high and the room seemed endlessly wide, though she couldn't see much of it. She thought that the fire was the most wonderful sight she had ever seen, entire logs with flames licking the roundness of them so that they glowed against one another. As the man moved his gaze to the fire Kath felt nothing but relief and closed her eyes again.

She fell sleep, she didn't know how long for, waking only when she heard a new voice in the room. It was the doctor. She opened her eyes and found she was being offered a large white cup of tea.

It smelled like heaven on earth. She sat up, with help, and drank from the proffered cup, enjoying the sweet milkiness as she leaned back against the softness of a cushion. It was only when the cup was empty that she looked up to see three pairs of eyes looking intently at her. One of the men wore a suit – that must be the doctor – while the other two appeared to be farmers, one in his mid-twenties and the other the man who had stayed with her.

The doctor smiled reassuringly and then he seemed keen on seeing the state of her toes and fingers. He asked her some questions and nodded.

'You're a very lucky girl,' he told her. 'You're going to be all right.'

He took his leave with an encouraging pat to her shoulder and the young man saw him out. He was the one who had found her, she knew. She thought he had a voice like warm treacle and wondered at his accent; she had not heard one like it before.

The older one urged her to drink more tea. She thought there was something curious about him; his round face was wiped almost clean of expression, like a small child, but there was concern for her in it. She managed another cup and was soon asleep again.

When she came round the second time she was alone, lying comfortably on the sofa, trying not to think about what had happened, especially about Ella. She must get back, yet how could she? They would not let her take her and they would doubtless haul her off to prison because of what she had done. She must lay low if she hoped to keep Ella safe and have the hope of a future reunion.

She was desperate to pass water and when the man who had rescued her came back in she said, 'I – I need a – a chamberpot.'

'Oh, right,' he said, as though this happened every day, and he carried her and a candlestick through the room and up the stairs and into a bedroom. He asked her whether she could manage and when she said she could, he said he would come back and knock in a few minutes to see if she was ready to go back downstairs.

She wanted to say to him that she could get back downstairs by herself but this short interval proved to her that she could not. She managed her business and to pour water from the jug into the bowl and wash her hands, but the feat left her exhausted.

It was a fine room, she thought, with a woman's touch. The bed was big and the covers were white with a quilt on top stitched with intricate patterns of pink and red. The floor was wooden but had lovely rugs, the likes of which she had never seen before, thick and dark red, possibly made by the same woman who made the quilt. The washstand was tiled in blue and white.

Her saviour had left her a huge nightgown, socks and a housecoat made from pink wool which she guessed his mother or grandmother must have worn. She put these on and discarded the blankets.

'Are you all right in there, Miss?' came the voice from the other side of the door.

She answered and he came in.

61

'What a lovely room,' she said.

'It was our mother's.'

'She was a woman of taste.'

'Aye, she was,' he said, smiling just a little and almost to himself, 'and temper, too.'

'My mother was like that.'

He smiled at her and his eyes were dark and gentle.

'I would let you stay up here but you need warmth, so just for tonight we thought you would be better staying in the kitchen. Tomorrow we will fix this up for you.'

'You're very kind. I didn't thank you, sir. What's your name?'

'I'm Jacob Sutherland and my brother is Patrick, so that's Jake and Pat.'

'I'm Kathleen. My family called me Kath. I'm so sorry to bother you.'

'You're no bother, Miss Kath. I just thank God Nell found you.'

'Where is she?'

'She sleeps outside, in a little hutch turned from the wind that blows down the yard. She won't go in the barn for warmth and I would have her in here but she won't come. She guards the door.'

'I would like to see her and thank her as well.'

'You can do that in the morning,' he said, and smiling, he scooped her up as though she was nothing heavier than a basket, taking the blanket with her. He carried her back down the stairs, telling her without embarrassment that she need not fear, they would leave the fire lit and the chamber pot nearby, as well as a bowl with water and a cloth to wash with. She must not worry because everything would be all right.

She was impressed with how easily he told the lie, as though he had said it many times before. She didn't think he was much older than she was, but he acted like a parent. She was grateful for it. She had rarely needed a parent more than she did now.

She went back to sleep. It was long and peaceful and she slept so well that she was reluctant to leave her dreams. When she finally awoke, she realised that the rest of the household must have been up for hours. They were outside by the sound of it, so she climbed slowly upstairs into the bedroom she had been in before and washed without being interrupted. She wanted to dress but she couldn't see her clothes or her shoes. She went back downstairs in her nightgown and hesitated by the fire. Perhaps hearing her, the younger man, Jake, came back in.

He greeted her with warmth and smiles, said she looked much better and offered her food. He went into the back room so she followed him there. It was much smaller, a proper kitchen with a big stove which threw out tremendous heat.

Never before had she considered the heavenly smell of frying bacon and she had not seen a man look so competent in a kitchen. He fried eggs that sputtered delightfully in the pan and Kath could have wept with hunger. They sat down at the table and he put a huge plateful in front of her. She tried not to eat too quickly. The eggs had yolks so golden that they were almost orange and the bread was brown and there was a lot of it, cut into great chunks and fried in bacon fat. The bacon was the best she had ever tasted and she said so.

His brother came into the room. He was very thin; she had not noticed before. He had about him a vague air that she had seen on people who were daft, like he wasn't sure which world he was in. He didn't eat much, but they all had several cups of tea from a huge brown teapot which Jake kept replenishing with water from the big silver kettle. Kath took her courage and asked about her clothes.

They looked one to another until finally Jake said, 'We had to throw them out. They had rotted with the wet.'

'Shoes?'

Jake looked at her.

'Gone to nothing.'

She knew what he meant.

'We have our mother's clothes but we weren't sure whether to say. We don't know what your circumstances are—' Here he hesitated and she thought it best to be as truthful as she could. She told them about her parents' deaths and that they had been travellers. She told them that her four-teen-year-old sister had been taken to the orphan-age and kept there. And then, rather ashamed, she told them how she escaped from the police by hurting one of them, and how she was afraid to go back because she would be put in prison. They smiled over the bit about her besting the sergeant but looked grave when she told them that she wanted to rescue her sister from the orphanage.

'I'm afraid they won't keep her there because

she's too old and they'll send her to people who will be horrible to her. She doesn't look fourteen, she's so little and skinny. She's never been alone before.'

They gazed at one another for a few moments then Jake said, 'We'll think of something. If she looks young, they'll probably look after her for the time being. When the weather gets better, I'll borrow a car and go and see if I can discover anything.'

Kath's heart began to lift.

'You would?'

'Aye, of course,' he said.

Kath was so relieved she could have cried.

'Now about those clothes–'

'Ma was a bit bigger and would have made two of you, and we don't think these are owt much, but maybe something will suit,' Jake said, opening the wardrobe back upstairs in the room that she had liked so much.

He went tactfully from the room and she pulled down the first of them. It was washed out but clean, grey and smelling of lavender. When she put the first of them on, it was huge on her but not too long. She found a kind of sash in the drawer so she put that three times around her waist and knotted it. When she looked in the long, spotted looking glass she thought she didn't look too bad for a woman who had almost died in the snow.

Pulling the dress back off, she tackled underclothing. There was some in the drawer, worn thin again, and she looked at the vests and laughed.

Her figure didn't need any help there. All she needed was a pair of knickers for respectability. She knotted the elastic undergarment at the top and donned the vest for warmth before pulling the dress back over her head. The shoes didn't make her feet hurt, so in almost every way they were better than the ones she had had. She was not going anywhere for the moment so the fact that they didn't quite fit, being rather wide, didn't really matter. She could wear extra socks and there were plenty of those in the drawer. She finished off her ensemble with a huge cardigan that she pulled down low over the dress, and tied the sash on top and around it.

When she went downstairs in such finery the two men started. They clearly remembered their mother in these clothes. She fell asleep again on the sofa but this time it was not for long and when she woke she felt better, although the chilblains on her hands and feet were vile in their redness and itching. She found bicarbonate of soda in the kitchen cupboard and that helped. She was relieved at not having to walk anywhere in the snow and ice and wet.

There was a little room near the back door which seemed to be used as a kind of office with a desk, a chair and lots of papers in it, and in the hall were coats, wellingtons, boots, hats and scarves. Across the passage was where they had eaten breakfast.

The back kitchen was not big and rather narrow, but it had two windows which looked out onto the yard beyond and the light was good. The stove where Jake had made breakfast was projecting a strong and steady heat. Kath hadn't noticed it before – she had been too hungry – but now she studied it. It was big and cream-coloured and had ovens to one side. There were covers for the top and when she lifted one of the lids and put on the kettle, it boiled in minutes. The stove ran on wood, which Kath thought a very practical idea, and the smell was so familiar to her as a traveller – woodsmoke and fires – that she felt an immediate affection towards it.

There was also a big white sink, cupboards on the back wall, and a pantry across the passage, dark without a window, with marble tops. The stone-flagged floor held big glass jars with various liquids in them – lovely honey colours of raspberry and clear.

She discovered box after box of apples in sand, turnips and potatoes in sacks, parsnips, and Brussels sprouts on long stems. Strings of onions hung from the ceiling. There was a huge tin of sugar and milk further back. Beyond that was a white-coloured substance in big clumps; when she tasted it she discovered it was cheese, sour and crumbly. There was also a big jug of thick cream.

There were great pieces of bacon and ham and preserves which made her think that their mother had not been dead long. Jam, plum and gooseberry and rhubarb, raspberries, strawberries. Also chutneys labelled apple, redcurrant, crab apple. There was a sack of flour. They obviously ate well and looked after themselves.

She heard footsteps behind her and when she turned around she saw Jake smiling.

'You're feeling better,' he said.

'What store cupboards you have!'

He looked sad. 'Our mother died but she laid in stores to see us through the winter.'

'She was a very good housekeeper.'

He beamed.

'Aye, she was a grand woman.'

Kath hesitated. 'I know how to make bread. I don't know your stove but I could try. I will need yeast.'

He looked pleased.

'I'm going into Stanhope tomorrow for various things so if you think of anything else, I'll make a list.' Then he hesitated. 'Can you cook?'

'Sort of, yes,' she said.

'We could certainly use your help there, though you should probably rest for a few more days.'

She smiled up at him. 'Do you have butter?'

Six

Ella waited out the afternoon but by the time it got dark she didn't understand why they didn't take her to Kath or why Kath didn't come to her. Nobody said anything and although there were people about, she did not see Miss Timpson again.

There was dinner – once more she did not recognize the food and did not eat it – and before he even asked, she gave it to the boy who sat next to her.

The children went back to the same room and the same man taught them even more difficult things she did not understand. There was a lot about kings and queens, whoever they were, and then a Bible story.

She knew about God, who preferred travellers to anybody else, but the next subject, about the locations of places, perplexed Ella. She only knew about regions that were on their ·route. However, when they had what he called 'mental arithmetic' time, she was calling out the right answers much quicker than anybody else, which pleased her. The afternoon went on until she felt she had been there at least a month. When the lessons were finished and afternoon grew into evening, she became more and more anxious. Where was Kath and when would she see her?

There was eventually tea – and even she recognized bread and butter – but she wouldn't have any of it, convinced that she would be called at any moment and Kath would be there.

They were allowed to play after the evening meal. Ella had not seen children allowed to play before and could not do such a thing simply because somebody had decided that it was time. It was all very odd.

The girls played skipping games and the boys kicked a ball. She stood by the wall and wished with everything she had that she might get out of there.

Bedtime came, so early that she was amazed, and she was taken into a big room with a lot of small beds and instructed to take one of them. She was appalled. She had never slept without her sister in her life and now she was expected to sleep with a dozen other girls.

The bed had a pillow and blanket, but the room was so big it was like a cavern she had once been taken to in Yorkshire by her father and been so afraid of that she screamed to be out. She had already learned that if she screamed here nobody would care. She lay down when the lights were out. There was not a sound other than some muffled whispers and giggles and gradually – she could tell by their heavy breathing – the others slept.

She couldn't stay. She must go to Kath. She waited until it felt very late and then she got up and slid to the door. She could move silently, her father had taught her when she was small; he had told her to be nothing more than a shadow.

She made her way into the passage in the middle of the building and then slid toward the front door. The key was in the lock – nobody had imagined that she might try to leave, she thought, how odd. She turned the key noiselessly and opened the door. The world was covered in snow and ice but she was so convinced that her sister was nearby that she had no compunction about leaving the safety and comparative warmth of the orphanage. It was only when she got outside and the ice nipped at her face and toes and fingers that she realised she didn't know where Kath was.

She couldn't think beyond the house and it was only down the bank, so she made her way there, slipping as she went because the soles of her shoes were so thin. It did not take her long to reach the property.

It was in darkness. She had half-believed her

mother and father and Kath would be there, but of course they were not. In the yard was the ruin of their caravan. She stood still for a little while as though some spell would take her back to when the wagon had been their home, everything had been all right and she had been able to behave like a child.

She didn't cry, she couldn't see the point in it, but she went into the stables. She no longer expected Diamond to be there but somehow the sweet smell of horses and hay lingered. She thought fondly of the dogs. She lay down where Diamond had been even though she knew that she mustn't stay long; she had to be gone by dawn or they would find her.

She thought back to being with her parents, where she felt safe each night beside her sister's warm body, and she worried for Kath. What if she had run away and died up on the fell? She hadn't come for Ella and if she were safe, surely she would have.

Everything was over, everything was finished. She felt herself fall into sleep. She was so grateful for its sweet release she wished never to wake up.

Ella left her hideout before the sun rose. She was so afraid that the policemen would find her again and this time she might go to prison. Perhaps that's where Kath was. Ella was sure that if her sister was here she would somehow have been in touch by now. Maybe she had tried to go south again. The only thing to do was to leave before anybody found her.

First though she got into the house by lifting a

window. She knew that Kath had left food because they could not carry it all. Some could be eaten without a fire to cook it. Before the light came, she ravished the cupboard, eating to her fill. She drank enough water to sustain her.

She found some small coins in the cupboard in the room where she and Kath had slept. She was grateful for this and gathered them into her pockets. Their weight gave her comfort.

There were clothes that had belonged to her mother that they had not been able to take the first time and she put on as many of these as she could. She stuffed stale bread and cheese into her pockets and set out to leave. It was early – too early, she hoped, for anyone to have realised she was gone or set out after her.

The weather had softened, which was a nice surprise, and the bus could get through the wet roads. A mile out of the village she hailed it and got on. It was so much warmer that she shivered with pleasure.

She asked for a ticket to Darlington, which was the bus's final destination, the driver said. She had been there before and while it took most of her money, she thought it was important to get as far away as quickly as she could, and she knew that it was a big town. It was easy to get lost in such a place and although the idea frightened her, it did not scare her as much as staying in the orphanage had.

Other people got on and off in various small places. She envied them knowing where they were going to and from. She sat quietly where she was, looking out of the window and watching them with their children and baskets, listening to their soft voices as they gossiped. She was glad of the ride; she hadn't been on a bus before and found it a quick way to travel. And unlike the car, she liked the rhythm of it – or at least the company.

When she got off the bus, finally, reluctantly, there was a market on in the main part of the town, striped covers over the stalls. She felt quite excited. Often travellers gathered there.

You couldn't have called the place pretty, but it was interesting with a big wide main street, a huge indoor market and long wide steps that led from the road towards the shops. She didn't know what to do or where to go. Travellers usually stayed out of the town, but where? And if they weren't around, what would she do? She ate the last of her bread and cheese but she was still hungry. She was also thirsty but there was a drinking fountain at the back of the covered market. It even had a tin cup to drink from, so she slaked her thirst. There were also public toilets at the market – these too she was grateful for.

When she grew tired of roaming around and not sure what else to do because she couldn't see any travellers, she came back to where she had set out.

She bought a huge pork pie just before the market closed. She got it half price and nibbled pieces of it, watching the men closing up the market, how they dismantled the stalls and took down the covers and the boards.

The tilley lamps which had been hung against the encroaching darkness were extinguished, snow began to fall and Ella started to panic. Whatever would she do now and how would she manage the night? It was hard enough sleeping without Kath but this would be even worse because she had no shelter of any kind.

When everything was closed and the town quietened, she huddled in a shop doorway. She dared not stay for long in case a policeman found her; thinking movement might keep her warm, she walked up the hill from the town. There she found the railway station.

Lights were still on here and people were getting on and off a train. The waiting room had a fire and comfortable-looking seats. She longed to go inside but was afraid. Eventually sheer desperation gave her courage. Inside it was so warm it made her want to cry – she had never felt such relief before.

She stood in the corner, unwilling to go toward the fire in case somebody came in. Gradually the fire died down and she heard footsteps. She threw herself under a long bench. She could only just get under it and she lay there, her heart thudding so loudly she felt sure it could be heard by the man with the boots who came inside. But all he did was put a guard against the fire that was almost out before he left and closed the door, turning the key in the lock.

Her first instinct was panic at being locked in but she soon realised she could always escape in the morning, and she was safe here. Nobody would expect anyone to stay here for the night, so she crept out from under the bench and lay down by the fire. There was even a little mat to keep the cold floor from her.

It took her a long time to fall asleep. She lay there, staring up into the almost-darkness, eyes open and throat full of terror. She had thought the last two nights were bad but this one was the worst yet.

It was almost morning when she awoke to the sound of footsteps again. She rolled away and under the bench, becoming gradually aware that she needed the toilet and something to drink. This time the stationmaster cleaned and swept the fire and then he lay and lit it. Ella was trying to hold her breath, her bladder, her cough as the thirst in her mouth became dry torture and the pressure to urinate grew. But he went on and on, fussing about while she clinched her eyes shut.

Finally, when she thought he would never leave, she heard his retreating steps. She waited half a beat before she got up and ran. He heard her, saw her, and shouted after her as she ran away down the hill from the station. To her humiliation, the urine was beginning to pour down her legs.

She ran all the way back into the town and found the drinking fountain. The urine stank and smarted but she splashed water as best she could on to her legs. It was cold but dried without a smell; she was grateful for that. She then wandered into the covered market, where holders were setting up stalls.

One woman looked at her.

'What do you want?' she said. 'Out you get. We've seen your like before, pinching stuff. Go back to where you belong.'

Ella ran again and this time into a fine department store. It was warm inside and she could smell coffee. She wandered through the different areas and came to the food section and there she saw the most wonderful array of bread and biscuits and cakes, all under glass so that they could not be stolen. Somebody had planned very carefully.

Beyond it was a café. She knew little of such places but here people were eating bacon and eggs.

'Can I help you, Miss?' was the not-quite-friendly question from a large man who seemed to have followed her from the area before this one. She had noticed him but not that he was following her until now. She just shook her head and walked out. He watched her as she went.

She stood outside and asked a passing woman if she could spare some change. The woman didn't even look at her and other people hurried past or glared at her; she was too afraid to ask again.

That day the snow went on and on. By afternoon she was feeling dizzy from lack of food and the terror of her situation. People walked past her. She couldn't understand how they could do this, how they didn't notice her. In the end she was reduced to asking them if they could spare a farthing, she had become so desperate.

One small child put out his tongue and as she reached the end of High Row, she heard a slight scuffle and then a large stone hit her on the head. Somebody laughed. She put up questing fingers and found warm blood.

The shops closed, the pubs opened and she

hovered in the light until she noticed men looking at her. She melted away into the darkness.

Down a side street, with nowhere else to go, she became so exhausted she sat down in the shadows and watched the snow fall. Some time later, a man's voice startled her from her doze. He grabbed at her, first at her breasts and then groping for her whole body. She managed to scream but all he did was hoist her nearer. She fought, kicked and bit. He slapped her hard across the face and over the ear to stop her but she only screamed more. He cursed again and again, his hands inside the little clothing she wore, and then she heard another voice, two more voices and they were cursing, too, so that she was even more afraid. Then somehow she was on the ground and he didn't have hold of her any more.

And then other arms lifted her. She screamed and fought. She didn't know how long it was before a familiar voice said in astonishment, against the light of the full moon, 'Ella?'

She opened her eyes and in the shadows she saw her deliverer. Will Hern, the rich lad who had wanted to marry Kath.

'Will. Oh, Will,' she said.

Seven

As soon as Kath adopted the room she had liked as her own, the brothers made sure the fire was lit and it was warm. They didn't seem to mind that she had taken their mother's room. She was aware how good this was, the fire and the way that they were so open minded with her. She did have a worry that their mother had died there but what the hell, people had to die somewhere, and at least they had something in common.

Their father had died long ago, found in the field by Jake, he told her. He went to see why his father was so late coming home and she shivered and shuddered and thought of how she had been rescued. She told him how her own father had died and it made her feel better.

She began to feel strong again and one morning soon after her arrival, she ventured into the kitchen and found Jake trying to make a meal. She had been reticent to take over, and up to this point had only made bread, but he seemed to need help – at least if the last few days' offerings were any indication.

'What is it?' she said.

'It's stew and dumplings and that's rice pudding.'

She tasted it. The rice pudding was gritty and half-cooked, the meat was tough and the dumplings were rock hard. Carrots wilted in the pan.

'I think I boiled them too long,' Jake said helpfully.

The carrots were cooked to buggery, as her father would have said. People, especially those who couldn't cook, were apt to be dismissive of food, but in this case her father would have been right.

'Can I help?' she offered. He looked gratefully at her and moved out of the kitchen as though he had a great deal else to do, which she was sure he had.

She put the rice pudding back in the oven with a little more sugar and milk mixed with cream and the stew back in the oven. She found suet and flour and made more dumplings. These she would put in twenty minutes before she called Jake and Pat for dinner. She couldn't do much about the carrots, other than take them off the stove and drain them. When dinner was ready, she put butter, salt and white pepper on them and mashed them with a fork.

When Jake came in, and Pat joined them downstairs, both men seemed overjoyed that the meal was edible. When it was over Jake said, 'We thought that we would say you were our cousin to keep folk from talking. Our mother's family way back came from Northumberland, that'll make it respectable.'

'On the coast?' she said gratefully. It was a place she knew and missed.

'Aye. And you would be called Armstrong. Do you think that will serve?'

Washing up afterwards, she was surprised to see

79

Jake lingering, somewhat awkwardly. He blurted, 'We're so grateful that you came to us. We have nobody to help and neither of us is any use in the kitchen as you might have noticed. That was the first decent dinner we've had since Mam was taken ill.'

He went off outside. Kath washed up and took a walk around the farm, taking with her a wicker basket she found in the pantry. A long wide yard led to barns and byres and a big, wooden chicken coop built like a small house. Somebody clearly had a sense of humour and talent with wood. She opened the door and went inside. It felt warm and cosy and she easily found several eggs. She liked gathering them to take back to the house. She wondered if their mother had done just that and she was, in a way, walking in her footsteps.

She went down the cobbled hill to the side of the farmhouse and beyond it were fields which fell to the river. In these they kept cows, some for beef and some for milking. The horses were out and came to the gate and she fed them apples she had brought especially for that purpose. They were working horses with strong backs and legs, big feet, generous manes and sweet brown eyes.

The river was shallow at that point and slow-flowing with lots of big flat stones. She could almost have stepped across without getting her feet wet and would have done so in summer. It was nearly as good as being at the coast, the low winter sun glinting on the water, various animals scurrying away in the distance. She had the feeling they were rabbits but she couldn't tell because the woods across the water were dense and dark even with their bare branches.

She walked back up to the house and realised that to her right, below the house, was a garden. She couldn't get into it from outside, even though she walked all the way round – it was surrounded by high hedges. When she reached the house again, she walked into the room the brothers called the parlour and saw the glass doors that led outside. She was entranced. You could see it from the big front kitchen but not like this.

She unlocked the doors, stepped beyond them and there the garden stood in all its splendour. She could have laughed. It was perfect for a woman.

Myriad sheltered paths led to hidden nooks and intricate flowerbeds such as she had never seen, oblong and crisscrossed with hedges so that the whole garden was lozenge-shaped with different herbs in the middle, those that saw themselves through the winter, like rosemary, bay and thyme. She had the feeling that Jake and Pat's mother had grown a great many other things in this garden. At the end of it there was a summerhouse, wooden and square.

The door was closed but not locked. She opened it and went inside. It smelled lovely and she soon discovered the drying herbs that were tied together and hung on a clothesline that stretched from corner to corner across the room. The scent of lavender was heady. There was also sage and lemon balm and thyme. The men had been grieving for their mother and not thought of such trivialities but she gloried in this harvest. She sat down in a wicker chair and breathed in the scent of the drying herbs.

When she got back to the house she found Pat watching the fire. He did that a great deal of the time. He was almost asleep, she thought. She told him how much she admired the summerhouse. He looked sheepish.

'I did that – before the war.'

'You built it?'

'Aye, I was going to be a cabinet-maker.'

'It's so beautiful. Do you make things now?'

He shook his head and spread out his hands and she saw how they shook. He tucked them back under his crossed arms.

'You did some fine work,' she said. 'You're very clever.'

Pat's face crimsoned but she thought that he looked pleased.

In the dead of night she heard noises beyond her door, somebody crying. She lay still and listened. The brothers slept in the same room even though there were four or five bedrooms. One of them was upset. She could hear the soothing sound of Jake's voice, the same tone that she heard when she came round in the snow and he and Nell had saved her. It went on and on in a lovely sweet way so that Pat quietened and as she listened, she found herself being lulled to sleep.

Eight

Jake had not forgotten the day Pat came home. He saw a shabby man slip in at the gate and wondered what he wanted. Even when Pat came up to him he didn't recognise his brother. When he did, the shock was so awful that he just stood and stared. His brother looked back with a kind of fixed twilight in his eyes that Jake had seen before only in rabbits caught in lamplight.

Pat hovered by the gate like he didn't know where he was or how to move forward, and Jake had gone to him and urged him into the house. He was aware that their mother had been waiting four long years for one of her sons to come home.

Their mother had stared at him before urging him to sit down and eat, but Pat didn't want to. Finally, they gave up and escorted him upstairs – he didn't seem to remember the layout of the house – and she went back down to the kitchen by herself and closed the door.

That evening, Jake had slept as soon as he lay down – he worked hard and was tired – but somewhere in the depths of darkness he heard screaming. He had stumbled into his brother's room. The curtains were open and moonlight poured in through the window. Jake could make out Pat lying on the floor in the corner, as tightly curled up as he could be.

They were so far apart in age that Jake didn't

quite know what to do, so in the end he did what he thought was right and got down on the floor with Pat and lay still for a long time. He could hear his own heart beating.

Then Pat said, 'You've changed so much. You're nearly grown up.'

Jake smiled and looked into what little he could see of his brother's face in the dark shadows.

The next morning Jake thought that Pat would come downstairs and go with him to see how the farm was faring. Jake was looking forward to that because there was so much work to do. Pat did not move and when Jake went into his bedroom he was sleeping so deeply that he didn't like to wake him.

Jake thought then that Pat was probably so tired from the last four years that it would take some weeks before he could help, so he allowed time and his mother did the same. Even so, she always seemed to be calling up the stairs to see if Pat was coming down for breakfast, dinner or tea and he never did.

Jake told himself that he couldn't afford a doctor but after several weeks and with his mother in despair, he ventured to the surgery in Stanhope and saw Dr McIver. The doctor looked old. His wife had died several years ago, he had lost his only son in the war, and his daughter had married and gone off to Canada, leaving him with his practice.

He said that he would come and see Pat. Jake hesitated. Visits were expensive but there was no way Pat could go to the surgery so he agreed. His mother was not pleased.

'I don't know what you were thinking,' she said, furiously stirring a pot on the stove as though their existence depended on it.

Jake didn't explain himself but he didn't have to; his mother knew they had a problem even if she didn't say so.

The day that Dr McIver came to the farm their mother received him gracefully, though she smiled acidly and said he had no need to be there. Pat just needed time, she said, he had been away for so long. Dr McIver smiled too and said that she was right and the adjustment was hard.

Jake went upstairs and tried to persuade Pat to come down. It was mid-afternoon and the sunshine was bright in his room. Pat did not seem to notice whether the curtains were pulled or not. He slept almost endlessly and didn't appear to know the time, the day, the month, the season or the year.

The doctor went upstairs. It felt as if he was there for a long time but it couldn't have been more than a few minutes. On the way back, Dr McIver hesitated on the stairs as though he didn't know what to say.

'He's not right,' their mother said. 'He's insane, isn't he? I knew he was.'

'He isn't well,' Dr McIver said. 'But neither is any man who has been through four years of war. He will get better, I have no doubt, but how long it will take I cannot say.'

'And who is to do the work?' Jake's mother said.

The doctor looked apologetic. Mrs Sutherland didn't say that they couldn't manage, she was too proud for that, but as Jake watched the doctor get into his car, he become newly aware that he would not be able to rely on his brother for help around the farm and he despaired.

When he got back into the kitchen, his mother was very brisk, saying that she hoped the doctor's bill was not too large because he had done nothing. It had been a waste of money, as she knew it would be.

Jake went outside. His neighbours had helped him with his hay, so now he must go and do the same with theirs.

It was late when he got back. The cows were complaining because they had not been milked. The hens were waiting for corn. He did both and then he found his mother asleep next to the dead fire, the tea grown cold upon the table.

Nine

Pat learned to recognise his bedroom and when he was in it would not constantly project himself back to the noises, smells and sounds of war. His mind had begun to accustom itself to the idea that many of his visions were not real, though he still did not think that he was safe.

Pat's bedroom, where he had once slept with Tom, his closest brother in age, had been his first recovered memory. Tom had been the first of his brothers to die in France, but sometimes Pat felt his comforting presence in their space. Pat had more difficulty conjuring up Ez – he had not mattered as much to him when they were children, being four years younger.

As for Jake, all Pat knew was that the boy had become a man before his time. Jake, the baby, was running the farm with no help other than that of his grieving mother, and – while she had been thankful to see Pat home – she was always shouting up the stairs for him to get up and help out with the work.

Occasionally she would come upstairs and into the bedroom, demanding him to get up and help and when he could not, she would cry, begging him to leave his place of sanctuary. When he wouldn't budge, she would slam the bedroom door so hard that both the frame and Pat shuddered. In the ensuing quiet, he would pull the bedcovers over his head and enjoy the sweet sleep of the afternoon.

At first he cared for nothing and could not distinguish night from day, morning from afternoon. His dreams were so awful that he was left exhausted, drained.

Jake would be there then, the noise having brought him into the room during Pat's nightmares. Often Pat found himself curled up under the bed. He could sleep more easily there, where he felt sheltered. Jake would give him pillows and blankets and stay with him, holding him tight.

If he was in bed, Jake would be there too, close by in Tom's bed, talking to him, soothing him. His murmurations would put Pat to sleep and his dreams were better, of their boyhood on the farm. It seemed to him that they had had all their allotted happiness then.

When they were children, their father read stories to them as they lay in their beds. They had their jobs to do and these they did willingly because their father showered them with praise and encouragement. Harvest time was fun, with the broad-backed horses. He could remember sitting on them when he was so young that his legs didn't stretch as far as their backs' widths and his father had to lift him down, laughing. His mother would bring tea and pies and cakes to the fields and she was happy then, too, proud of her sons.

He had loved the lambing in the spring and the long, warm summer days when everything grew so tall. He could remember picking blackberries in the autumn when the mists were heavy and white above the fields and a low sun stretched golden to claim the green fields. There were mushrooms as big as his hands from the fields behind the house and there was the sweet, thick smell of the elderberry wine his mother made for drinking at Christmas.

Often now Pat awoke during the night after Jake had gone back to his own room, and had to wait the darkness out. It was better when Jake was awake, too, but Jake worked so hard and for so long that he slept heavily.

Pat felt guilty that Jake had to do everything that their mother could not manage. She did the washing, cleaning and cooking. She made butter and cheese and assisted with the milking. Pat wanted to help, but for a long time he could not come out of his bedroom. When he did manage to leave it, he was then afraid of the stairs, half-convinced that a sniper would lurch out and gun him down from the gloom somewhere beneath them.

He had hated that the stairs were open into the enormity of the front kitchen. He found that room impossible to bear. He could not even contemplate coming down those stairs, they were so endless. As he watched, the number of steps multiplied and the floor beneath shifted and disappeared into the greyness of the late afternoon.

Sometimes if he attempted to step onto the first stair he would find himself on the floor, having blacked out. He was ashamed of this and he knew that his mother was also ashamed and then he burned inside, not wanting to be anywhere any more.

There came a day when she would no longer come into Pat's bedroom. Jake gave him clean clothes, hot water, soap and towels for his body and hair. Jake would change the bed, empty the chamber pot, open the window on warm afternoons.

Pat thought that his mother wished he had died. She could have been proud of him as she was proud of her other two sons who were dead. He had sometimes heard her voice below telling the occasional visitor how much she missed them.

He eventually learned to recognise the seasons and loved the softer air of the long summer days. June and July were best because no matter what time of day or night he awoke, there was light covering the house in pink and blue, the sun not yet set when the night should have had its hold or dawn about to break, setting the horizon aglow.

He hated the winter. He dreaded the cold weather, the nearly-unending darkness. The nights crept in at him like ghosts, icy fingers and black mud. Jake would pull the thick, dark red curtains across the windows. Even through his closed door, he could hear his family's raised voices from below.

'Haven't you got enough to do without running after him, lazy bugger that he is?' his mother would say.

It was true. Jake had too much work on the farm to be caring for his brother as well. Pat could never hear his response – Jake's voice was always low and almost indistinguishable. Pat thought Jake had the sweetest, softest voice that he had ever come across. It was never raised in anger, as though he excused the whole world. Jake would bring him food, but Pat couldn't always eat it. Fear drove his hunger away and only water quenched his thirst and saved his parched lips from cracking.

He grew used to seeing nobody but Jake and he was so content in his room he thought he may stay there forever. He had no explanation for the day he decided to venture beyond it.

He had feared the darkness of the hall, the proximity of the other rooms, the great gaping wilderness of the stairs, but in the late mornings when he was awake he often wondered what went on outside his door. One day he felt compelled to open it.

It was summer, the safest time. He clasped the doorknob with his thin white fingers, turned it and gradually pulled it towards him. Sunlight fell into the passage because the other bedroom doors were open. This had not occurred to him. It was so white, and through the open windows he could smell the sweet scent of the cream roses that his mother so loved lifting in the breeze, and the flimsy net curtains danced before his gaze as he slowly passed by the rooms.

He did not know how long he stayed in the hall before going back into his bedroom, happier than he had felt in months.

The next day it rained but even so he was not dismayed. He liked the soft beat of the drops upon the glass, and how later the sun would turn each drop into a diamond and they would race one another to the bottom of the window.

He went out onto the landing and heard the rain beating on the windows in the other rooms. The sun was blacked out. He went to bed with the sound of the rain sweet in his ears.

Still he could not venture down the stairs. That was his mother's territory, and he sensed that she would not welcome him there. Even in the passage upstairs he could hear her voice, harsh in complaint. It was especially fierce at lambing time or in the winter when the snow was deep and animals got trapped and she and Jake were gone most of the day.

Suddenly in the spring he did not hear his mother's voice anymore. Jake was rarely at home during lambing time and there were no more fires. He didn't sleep in his room every night and often forgot to feed Pat. When Pat enquired of him about the change in their mother, Jake said she was just tired, but Pat understood it was more than that.

It was high summer when he finally decided to take the stairs. It was a abrupt decision and he didn't think twice. He took them one step at a time, breathing carefully. Nobody shot at him, he couldn't think now why he had thought they might have done. He made his way into the front kitchen. The room was full of sunshine and the light from the garden spilled in and lit the walls and floor.

Pat had forgotten what a beautiful room it was, with its big fireplace and cosy chairs. The room was covered in dust motes, which danced in the silence.

Slowly he made his way into the darkness of the passage and from there he could see the back kitchen. His mother – he could not remember when he had seen her last – was sitting over the stove, asleep. She had grown thin and looked much older than she had when he had come home. Her body was drooping, the smudges below her eyes were huge, and her hair was wisped and white, showing pink bald patches on her head. As though she sensed his presence, she opened her eyes. Pat stopped in the doorway. He wanted to run back, to take cover before he was mown down and then he watched her eyes gentle on him and their expression grow soft.

'Why, Patrick,' she said, 'you've come back to us.'

Ten

It snowed. Kath had never seen snow like it. Her father had always taken them into low-lying towns when he thought it would snow heavily. She had not understood the advantages of being able to get away. Here there was little to do but go on as usual and the intense cold made everything harder. She had not appreciated how difficult Jake's life was until she saw him in the middle of the night, prodding deep snow with a long pole for any sign of life, lifting sheep from their white suffocation and finding sometimes that they could pull themselves out.

Jake didn't rest and Kath felt she couldn't let him go out by himself. He never asked for help but she could sense his gratitude and relief at having it. Between their nocturnal shepherding and daytime farm labour, they had barely an hour of sleep each night.

She became dizzy for lack of rest and wanted to cry from her frozen toes to her empty belly. The bright frost on the windows blinded her and she could see her breath in every space in the house. Pat kept the kitchen fire on and Kath taught him how to boil vegetables, fry bacon and eggs, and make a simple bread. This was mostly what they existed on when they could not get into Stanhope for supplies. The milking had to be done but she had no time to make cheese or butter and much of the milk went to waste.

She was grateful to shut her eyes, for however short a time, before she had to go outside and see to the animals and climb wearily through the deep snow which clung to the stone walls, heaping six feet high in places so that Jake sometimes had to pull her out before she fell in and disappeared. He would haul her out, impatiently. She wanted to shout at him at these times but she was too tired. Every day they went on lifting the poor sheep from the snow. They didn't lose a single one that winter.

Eleven

Gossip reached the hall via Mrs Witham, the cook. Mrs Banks told Caro with some satisfaction that there was a scandal going on at the Sutherland's farm.

'A young woman is living there,' Mrs Banks said, looking askance at her daughter above afternoon tea, frowning and adding, 'Caroline, have a sandwich.'

Caro knew that she ate too much cake and that it was bad for her figure. Her mother had told her so a thousand times. But she hated sandwiches, especially the fish paste ones which her mother insisted on and never touched.

Caro had also heard about the newcomer.

'I understand she's a cousin from Northumberland who has no family left since her mother died and they took her in.'

'And wouldn't they just say that,' her mother crowed. 'Apparently she looks like a foreigner, very dark skinned.'

'Some Northumbrians are,' Caro protested. 'In the borders, a lot of people vary in their colouring from Viking to Picts.'

Mrs Banks would not have some easy explanation when she could hopefully have a disgustingly complex one which would take up weeks of her time.

'According to the doctor's housekeeper, Jacob Sutherland found her in the snow and took her home. Hardly the way for a relative to arrive. If he deigned to visit the church once in a while, no doubt we could get a good look at her. In the meanwhile is she sleeping in her own bed?'

'Mother!'

'It's possible. Nobody here would marry him – he's penniless and everybody knows it. I don't understand why you don't evict him. You've said yourself he owes you at least six months' rent.'

Caro didn't realise she had been so open with her mother. Usually she took care with such matters.

'His family has been here for hundreds of years,' Caro said. 'How could I?'

'You'll have to eventually or it will give people something else to talk about, favouritism to a young man you barely know. Soon nobody will be paying their rent if they think they can get away with it.'

'That's ridiculous,' Caro said, 'I know him as well as I know everybody else in the dale and his mother worked here. People understand he's fallen on hard times.'

'If he can afford a servant, he can afford to pay his rent,' her mother said.

Caro hadn't seen Jake since his mother's funeral. Half the village, hearing that she was putting on a spread, turned up at the funeral so that the tiny church in the village of Northgate, just above Stanhope, was packed. The new vicar looked pleased that so many people cared about the woman.

Caro's face warmed when she remembered it. And though she would not have her mother suspect more than she already did, she was worried about this girl who had turned up at the farm. If she had been pulled from a snowdrift and carried home by Jake, it was too good a story for people not to pass on. And there was nothing respectable about a woman living with two young men in a farmhouse half a mile from the village no matter what she was doing there.

Twelve

One morning toward the end of March, Jake came in for his midday dinner, but instead of sitting down and eating heartily as he usually did, he took one bite, chewed, swallowed and then put down his knife and fork.

'I think I should go and have a look for your sister.'

Kath felt her heart leap with relief. She had been waiting for him to say something but the weather had been so bad for so long that she knew it was impractical for him to attempt getting out of the dale. They had had two bright days and were coping with everything that had to be done.

'Shall I come with you?' she said.

'I think I should go on my own. We don't want anybody to know that you're nearby.' He smiled across the table at his brother. 'Pat will look after you,' he said and Pat smiled too.

In all the years that Jake had lived in the area he had been to Castle Bank Colliery only a very few times. His parents would never go there – small colliery towns were as far away from their life as anyone could imagine. The two long steep banks that cut the dale off from the fells was a barrier to them both. Children from the colliery who were lucky enough to go to the grammar school came into the dale but there weren't many of them.

Jake hadn't been in a motorcar in ages but he knew how to drive – he had learned because he thought that someday it might be useful. Then he went into Stanhope, wearing the only decent suit he could find in the house – he didn't know which brother it had belonged to and didn't care. From the garage that housed the buses, he managed to get the loan of a car from Mr Filey who owned the buses and a small taxi service.

Jake didn't really like driving. You missed everything when you weren't outside, taking your time. He far preferred travelling by foot with Nell at his side. He loved walking up the steep banks

97

of the dale with her – he never tired of the view, it always felt new. He was proud of where he lived, loved the farm beyond measure.

He was careful to go out of his way on this trip so that nobody would know where he had come from. Perhaps he was being paranoid, but if they found out that Kath was with him, he would not be able to forgive himself.

It was therefore almost midday when he presented himself at the orphanage that Kath had described to him.

The sign before him read 'St Mary's Orphanage'. Although the building was not old there was something about it that he did not like. Orphanages. Abandoned children, poor and left here by dying or troubled adults.

He strode to the door and rang the bell. After a short time a small, fat woman answered him. Jake asked for the person in charge and was ushered into a shadowy office. There a fierce-looking woman asked him to sit down.

'I have heard that my cousin's daughters were here. My mother hasn't seen them in years but she heard that they had bad fortune and their parents died. She wanted to help.' He named the girls.

'Oh, I'm sorry,' she said, 'but they aren't here anymore. The elder girl was never caught, the younger ran away the same night. We did everything we could to try to help them. Gypsies.'

'Their mother was no gypsy.'

'She ran off with one, just the same. The shame of it – her parents died, one after the other because of what she did. Died of broken hearts.'

Jake cast his gaze up to the ceiling.

'The elder girl assaulted a policeman and is wanted by the law – perhaps you have heard that, too. We had no alternative but to take in the younger girl and try to give her a decent life, though apparently she wanted none of it.'

'So, I come here to help these girls and neither of them can be accounted for?'

'It was their own doing,' the woman defended. 'They ran away in such weather. We have had a great deal of snow and ice since then and the roads are a very inhospitable place. We were just doing our best, trying to save them.'

Jake sighed. 'My mother is distraught. They were the only members of family she had left. Have you any idea as to where they could have gone?'

'The elder girl who was running away went off along the fell in the direction of Consett. The younger left here in darkness. That is all I can tell you.'

Jake was so frustrated he felt like he could have choked her. She didn't care; she shouldn't be in charge of children. Jake went outside and saw the children playing in the cold yard. The girls were skipping and the boys were playing football; they seemed happy enough. Perhaps it was the best they could hope for. Kath would not like what he had learned. He wished it could be more.

He motored to Consett. The outskirts of the town were the foulest place that he had ever seen. Everything was covered in a thick, red dust. He went past huge cooling towers where water poured down to road level and then disappeared.

The town itself was row upon row of company

houses but the centre was wide and a bustling theatre gave the whole place an energy that he liked.

Jake went into every shop he came to and asked for Ella. He met nothing but blank stares. Perhaps they thought he was the child's abuser, trying to get her back when she had run from him. He could be her brother or uncle, hauling her back to whatever kind of hell she had known. As a result, he could not work out whether they spoke honestly or not. Who could blame them?

By the time the shops closed, he was exhausted. He had spent much longer days at the farm and had not felt like this. It was defeat. He did not want to go back and tell Kath that he had found nothing.

He could not stay away or she would worry, so he drove back as slowly as he could. He wished things were different and felt stupid. It was completely dark when he reached the farm; he left the car up at the side of the road near the big barn. The lights were on and he was torn between the happiness of homecoming and the sorrow of having no good news to share.

Kath was dismayed at what Jake had to say. He sighed with regret and asked her about the milking and the hens. She waved her hands at him.

'I did everything.'

'Thanks, Kath.'

'I could hardly not when you spent all day searching for my sister. I'm so grateful to you for trying.'

'You mustn't give up. We'll think of something else.'

'Why don't you go and change and I'll make you something to eat?'

He went off. She could hear how slow his steps were. He had wanted to be successful for her, she knew. Would they ever find Ella? Whatever else could they do?

By the time he had come back down again, telling her that Pat was asleep, the broth had heated on the stove and big chunks of bread with butter and cheese were laid out on the table.

'Pat ate already,' she said because she knew he would ask. He always did.

'I don't know how else we can look for her,' Kath said. 'If we ask around here, people will wonder who I am and discover things I don't want them to know. And neither of us knows the area beyond. Unless we find travelling people, I don't know how to proceed.'

'Your friends are bound to find out what has happened; I'm sure they will be able to help.'

'You're right. I just have to believe that she's alive and that somewhere somebody has helped her,' Kath said.

Thirteen

Will Hern had been in Darlington for a week. Since it was a time of big celebration, Christmas and New Year, he hadn't seen much of the place beyond the inside of pubs. There were so many old friends to greet. The travellers always got together at this time of year, sometimes at Thirsk or Northallerton. Word would get round and they would all come together somewhere to keep warm and safe, especially if the weather was bad.

In the north the weather was bad until April so they tended to stay away from the coast and the high ground and keep their heads down as best they could until spring came.

He never worried too much – his family had always made a good living from buying and selling horses, and his father had been in scrap metal for years and was as shrewd as anyone Will had met.

At New Year he and his friend Baz were in town celebrating. They took their beer outside because the pub was packed and smoky. As they leaned against the wall, they heard high-pitched screaming just further down Tubwell Row.

Will had been properly brought up. His mother would never have forgiven him if he let some poor girl be manhandled or worse by an awful slobbering bloke in Darlington, so he and Baz got the old bugger off the lass and hoyed him at the wall and as soon as he could get up, he ran off.

In the meanwhile, in the darkness, Will became aware that he had seen this girl before. It was Kath Watson's young sister, Ella. Baz recognised her, too. She was in a helluva state and although they didn't want to take her into a pub, they didn't really have a lot of choice. In the light she looked even worse. He found a table right at the back and sat her down. He left Baz to look after her and went to the bar and ordered beer and a big beef sandwich for her. He also got two more pints for Baz and himself.

She was almost blue with the cold and her clothes were half ripped off her back so he gave her his coat. Baz took his cue and handed her his thick woolen muffler. She smiled her thanks and wound it about her neck with fingers so pale and thin that they looked as if they might break.

She took the beer and the sandwich gratefully and sank half the beer and then her teeth into the bread. He knew better than to try to talk; the place was too busy and loud. He just let her get on with it, meeting Baz's astonished gaze over her head.

When she had finished, he got her some coffee to warm her through and a piece of cake from under a glass dome on the bar. It was still snowing when they left and she could hardly stand between them. They carried her back to the camp just outside the town. His father was still out but his mother took the shaking girl inside near the stove.

She began to cry. Will, having four sisters, was used to tears, but he still hung back; this required the touch of a mother. After a few minutes, he and Baz left her there and went back to the town for more beer.

He had many questions. He wanted to know why she was there alone and what had happened to her family, what had happened to Kath. But it would wait until the morning. His mother would tell him then.

Fourteen

Ella couldn't stop crying. Her relief at having found her own people and the delayed grief of losing her parents and then Kath overwhelmed her all at once. Mrs Hern had more sense than to interrogate her now. She gave Ella dry clothes, wrapped her in a blanket, gave her a pillow and put her to bed. Not long after that her husband came home. Ella was asleep by then.

'Poor little mite,' he said. 'Something must have gone very badly wrong for a lass like this to be on her own. Thank God Will found her. What would she be doing in Darlington?'

'She wasn't well enough to say. We should be grateful she's with us now. She was always such a bonny little lass. She's almost grown,' his wife said.

In the morning Ella looked much better. With some gentle prodding, her story unfolded. The room was grave. Will's reaction was predictable.

'Kath should've married me when I wanted her,' he said.

His parents were in agreement. Will would have been there to look after her parents and the girls and things would never have gotten so bad. Ella's father, Tom, was known for his bad behaviour. No wonder his wife had died, Mrs Hern thought. The poor soul, she had never been strong and she had always wanted to get off the road and settle down.

She had chosen the wrong man for that – Tom Watson had been more restless than anybody they knew. He didn't care how bad the conditions, he moved when he liked and would take his family with him, thinking nothing of their welfare. Well, it had done for them this time. He and his wife were dead and his elder daughter was missing and likely dead in the snow. At least Ella was saved. Mrs Hern was grateful for that. She didn't mind another daughter – she already had four, what was one more?

Will was their only son and she was grateful that in the middle of four girls she had given her husband the boy he so badly wanted. He was just as clever as his father and had an eye for horses, better than anybody they had ever known.

Will was tall, dark and elegant. It was as though he had picked up the best of both parents' qualities. Who but Will would have given up drinking time to look after a lone young girl? He and Baz were such good lads, his mother thought with pride. They brought Ella to safety, knowing that his parents would take her in – would take in anyone they thought was in trouble – but one of their own, a fellow traveller, was especially of value, so very precious.

Mrs Hern was saddened by the death of Rose Watson, though she knew she had been unhappy. She did not believe that Tom Watson had deliberately killed himself. He had been far too selfish. Because he could not cope with the death of a woman he had never treated well, he had abandoned his daughters to face everything by themselves. He had run away and come to grief because of it. It served him right. But what about Kath?

'Kath will be all right,' her husband said with confidence when they were alone later. 'She's got good instincts, that girl.'

'She must be worried sick about Ella.'

'It will be okay; we'll find her.'

Not if she's died in a snowstorm, Mrs Hern thought, and shook her head. She had not forgotten how much Will had wanted to marry Kath when she was old enough to wed him. She assumed he no longer thought of it but it was the first thing he had mentioned this morning, and he was still unbetrothed when most of the other lads were settling down. Baz was marrying their eldest daughter, Linda. She wondered if Kath Watson had put a spell on her lad so that he couldn't care for any other girl. He never looked at them and he drank too much ... but then so did most of the lads. They weren't all married yet, but there would soon come a day when there would be no girls left for Will. What would he do then? Men were best married; it kept them out of trouble. Mrs Hern wanted to see Will wed.

Fifteen

Kath was determined to learn how to make butter. In the Sutherlands' bountiful years, their mother had made butter and cheese and took it to Stanhope on market day to sell it. It would be a good source of income for the farm if Kath could manage it. She persuaded Jake to take her down to the cellar and after a great deal of grumbling and prevaricating, he showed her how the churn worked. It was difficult, especially for a girl so slight.

Sometimes the butter would churn easily but more often than not her hands and wrists ached from endlessly turning the handle with no result. Inevitably, just when she thought it was never going to turn, it did, and the butter separated from the milk. This moment of triumph made it worthwhile.

The cheese was quite different – she had to set it up so that it dripped slowly through muslin. It would not keep, and had to be eaten right away. There were other ways of making cheese, but Kath's time was limited so the curd style was enough for now. It tasted wonderful – at least, so the brothers said.

Milking was a knack. That was what Jake called it. The cows were patient but the touch had to be gentle or they would be uncomfortable and move about, which made the task more difficult. But

Kath had small hands and was deft; the first time she sat at on the stool, it took only five minutes before she understood the technique – a slow stripping with a slight angle and a pull – and the milk flowed into the pail.

After making three meals a day, cleaning, washing, feeding the hens and doing the dairying, Kath would fall into bed early and sleep dreamlessly. She was glad of that. She spent so many of her waking hours worrying about Ella it was a relief to sleep.

Jake asked her to go to the village church with him. Northgate village was half a mile away up the dale and away from Stanhope, which was the nearest town, a couple of miles away in the other direction. Kath was amazed and horrified. He looked frustrated.

'It's just that if you come to church with me, I can introduce you as my cousin. If you don't, people will have other ideas.'

Kath understood then. She didn't have the courage to tell him that she couldn't read, so she wouldn't understand what was going on.

'I haven't been to a church service before. How will I know what to do?'

'You'll be all right,' he said, 'just follow my lead.'

The next Sunday was fine and dry so she had no excuse not to go, but she left the farm reluctantly. They walked into the village since it wasn't far. Neither of them spoke.

The church was up a side street, next to a waterfall. The hills soared above it and the dale swept below to a view of the river. It was small and friendly-looking. When they went inside, the organ music soothed Kath and made her feel less intimidated.

The other people in the church gave her small sideways glances, but none looked at her as if she did not belong. Jake dropped to his knees so she did too, then they both got back up again and slid on to the wooden pew. She was worried about what would happen next. Would there be reading aloud? What if she was called upon? A distinct hush fell in the sanctuary and two women, one around thirty and one elderly, perhaps her mother, made their way to the front while everybody watched quietly. Kath found this very strange.

She liked the look of the vicar. She had always thought vicars were forbidding old men with whiskers, but he was young and handsome and smiled openly. He waited for the old lady to kneel down and pray and rise again before he went on with the service.

The hymn singing was difficult. Kath shared Jake's hymnbook but since she couldn't make any sense of the words she could do nothing but hum. He didn't seem to notice.

There was also a psalm, Jake said. She liked the sound of it, like poetry, and the music waffling about happily. Somebody read from the Bible and there was another hymn and then the vicar spoke. Jake whispered that it was the sermon. Kath listened carefully; it was such a nice thing, this inspiring talk to get them through the week.

Coming out of the church into a bright morning, Jake introduced her as his cousin to people. The vicar came to them, shook her hand and said how pleased he was that she had come to the service, as though she were doing him a favour. She was astonished. She had never thought that churches were like this, or vicars, either. Despite all the tedious getting up and sitting down, she liked the whole idea of it, local people coming together, sharing a positive message. She felt full of joy.

The young woman she had seen enter late with the older one came across to them and greeted Jake amiably and smiled at her.

'How are you finding the dale so far?'

'It's lovely, thank you.'

'I'm so happy to hear it. Will you be staying with us long?'

Kath was unsure what to say.

Jake jumped in. 'Since we're the only family Kath has left, she'll be staying with us for the foreseeable future while she recovers from her parents' loss.'

The woman nodded and said that she quite understood.

After they left Jake explained that the young woman was Miss Banks. Her dad had been Colonel Banks. They owned all the farms in the valley and lived at the hall and she had run the business since her dad had died. Kath was impressed. She turned to take one last look and found Miss Banks watching her across the lawn.

Sixteen

Caro Banks stared at Jake's supposed cousin and felt sorry for him. If he had found her and taken her home with him, what was he meant to do with her now? How naïve of him to think he could get away with such a thing – and worse still, lie to the people in the village. Had he not tried to find her somewhere she might be respectably taken in?

Everybody had stared. The girl seemed oblivious to it. She was not used to churches, Caro could see. She regarded everything with awe and barely lifted her gaze to meet anyone's eyes.

She was also undoubtedly the most beautiful girl that any of them had ever seen.

Mouths had dropped open. Men stopped and did double-takes and women looked at her and then at one another, eyebrows raised. And yet she was so clearly unaware of her good looks, it was hard to say a word against her.

She wore a coat which had probably been Jake's mother's that hung off her and was tightly belted. A big saggy hat hid most of her face – whether from shyness or modesty Caro didn't know – so there were but traces of her hair visible, only a few tendrils that had fallen around her face. What about this girl was so arresting? The boots on her feet were well-worn and ill-fitting and her ankles could not be seen. She was completely covered up.

Caro thought she had the kind of air that men

dreamt of after a night in the pub. It was something to do with the way that she moved, like a wild animal contained: graceful, lovely and unforgettable, hardly caught or tamed. She was like a cat, watchful yet showing nothing, quick-eyed even though she seemed to look nowhere but down.

Her eyes were dark from what Caro could see, and her skin tanned in that way which young women often had from working the land since small children. The visible strands of her hair were tawny brown.

Caro couldn't decide what to think. She only knew that she hated Kath from the very moment she met her because she lived in Jake Sutherland's house and saw him every day. Caro knew she was possibly being unfair, given how poor the girl obviously was, but she couldn't help it.

Going outside afterwards, Kath clung to Jake's arm. There was nothing possessive or even affectionate about it, Caro could see – it was a gesture of helplessness because she was new there and did not know anybody. Jake's face was innocent; as always, he accepted his lot and asked nobody for anything.

They stood a while with the vicar. Robert Black smiled on Kath as he did on everyone but when she smiled back it was as though the sun had broken through the clouds.

Caro remembered then that Jake Sutherland owed her a great deal of money. Perhaps it was time to remind him of this and maybe, just maybe, he might be persuaded to settle it with a different form of payment.

Seventeen

Will's parents were kind to Ella. They made enquiries amongst the travellers to see whether anybody had news of Kath. Travellers, as their very name indicated, got around a great deal and their friends were all over the northeast and northwest. They went as far north as Scotland and as far south as Liverpool. Mrs Hern reassured Ella daily that they would find Kath and the sisters would be reunited.

After the first few weeks, Mrs Hern's reassurances became less convincing. Mr Hern reminded Ella that bad news travels faster than good and that if anything had happened to Kath they would have known about it by now. Ella took small comfort in that, but she kept hoping.

Will's four sisters accepted her as one of their own. They cooed over her and styled her hair and made her feel grown up. The family was unfailingly generous – Mrs Hern was always taking her into nearby towns and buying gorgeous shawls and jewellery at the markets for her.

She bought Ella neat little boots and pink slippers for dancing just as she did with her own daughters, and told her how beautiful she was. Ella had never seen herself as attractive before. All Will's sisters were luscious and dark like Kath but Ella was blonde and fair-skinned and blue eyed, and much smaller than they were – 'dainty', Wills mother called her. She had always felt like a sore thumb in the company of such exotic beauties. Under Mrs Hern's praise, Ella blossomed and learned to be proud of how she looked.

Will treated her like he treated his other sisters. He played silly card games with her and although she could remember how he had wanted Kath, he never mentioned her, except in reassurance to Ella that she would be found. She figured he no longer desired her and would go on to marry some other lass. She and his sisters liked to guess whom he would choose, which lucky girl would join this wonderful family.

They were richer than everybody else, the Herns. Will had his own varda and he owned several horses. He often borrowed his father's motorcar and the sisters vied to go with him when he took it out. Unbeknownst to their parents, he would take them into town and buy them ribbons and bangles and chocolate.

The eldest sister, Linda, was engaged to Baz. When they got to Harrogate, Baz bought rubies for her neck and wrists and – most importantly – for her finger. A grand wedding celebration followed and Linda and Baz spent the night together. The party afterward lasted for days, everyone dancing around the campfire, singing and clapping.

Ella loved it. She just wished that Kath could have been there. Then it would have been perfect.

'What's the matter?' Will said, catching her in a sorrowful moment.

'Nothing. I just want Kath.'

'We will find her. Don't worry,' he said. 'And

some day some grand lad will want to marry you.'

'Nobody ever could.'

'What, looking like you do?'

'I'm not as pretty as Kath.'

'All the girls here look like Kath,' Will said, 'but you're different, you look like a fairy queen.'

She knew it was silly but she remembered what he had said. It made her feel warm inside. She was different.

That spring Ella found that something had gone wrong with her body and ran to Mrs Hern, crying.

'I'm bleeding down below, between my legs,' she whimpered. 'Am I dying?'

Mrs Hern smiled on her. 'You're growing up, that's all. This is a sign that you can bear children. That makes you a woman.'

Her hiccups subsided. 'I don't feel like a woman.'

Mrs Hern sat her down in private in the wagon and told her that the bleeding would happen monthly. It was nothing to worry about, it was just the eggs in her body breaking.

'That makes me sound like a hen,' Ella said.

'I'll give you some rags to take up the blood so that it doesn't get in your way. You must wash them out between cycles. If it hurts, let me know. I can give you a remedy for that – ginger and a lie-down to start. When you marry, your husband will fertilize the eggs and then you will have a child. But don't worry, you're not quite there yet – you've got plenty of time, Ella, your whole life ahead of you. You don't have to rush into any decisions. I daresay you could have any lad you wanted. Make them wait. Make them suffer.'

Ella laughed at this.

'Just remember how beautiful you are. You are our daughter and we'll look after you, from the respect we held for your parents and because we love you.'

Shortly after this the second eldest girl, Ruthie, was married.

Ella was next in line; the two younger girls were thirteen and eleven. Ella thought back to what her life had been like before but she knew that there was no point in wishing things backwards. Life had to be lived forwards and if you didn't go with it, she had learned, it had a horrible way of dragging you along.

It seemed to her that the lads knew that she had grown up. They hovered around the wagon and Mrs Hern kept shooing them away, like a mother hen who didn't want her chicks bothered. She had lost two of her daughters within a month, she confided to Ella, and that was quite enough for now. But if any lad pleased Ella, she had only to let Mrs Hern know. In the meantime, the search for Kath was always on.

Ella slept well but her dreams were troubled. She was tormented by Kath and her parents and how she couldn't find them. She didn't tell anybody; she didn't want them to know how miserable she felt.

Eighteen

One early morning when Kath saw Pat standing in the doorway of the house she called to him. He hesitated.

'Pat, will you feed the hens for me? I've got so much to do and they must be hungry by now. We also need some eggs for breakfast.' She didn't really mean it – the most he had contributed to the household was his help in the kitchen – but she was in too much of a rush to care.

Kath continued her work, hanging out the first of the washing at the side of the house where the wind blew. She had been up since four and was rather pleased with her progress so far that day.

She went inside to make breakfast and was setting the table when she glanced up and saw a divine look on Pat's face. She thought she had never seen anything like it. In his hands he held four eggs, two in each palm.

'Look, Kath, look what I found,' he said, and she stopped what she was doing and stared in wonder.

'Oh Pat,' she said, 'they're lovely.'

'They're so brown and warm,' he said. 'And I fed the hens.'

'Wonderful,' she gushed and Pat beamed. Jake came in.

'I'm starving, where's breakfast?' he said. Jake was always starving, she rarely heard him utter any other sentence before a meal.

'Look at what Pat's brought us!' she exclaimed.

Jake instantly understood. He was equally en-thusiastic. Kath sat the two men down and served them while Pat told Jake about feeding the hens and how they all were and how he had found the eggs. He thought one of them might be laying away from the coop and he was going to have a look round the yard after breakfast to see if he could find the eggs.

As soon as he cleared his plate, Pat set off. Jake lingered. Kath ignored him, clearing away the dishes as he continued to sit.

'How did you do that?' Jake asked.

'What?'

Jake got up and grabbed her round the waist from behind, leaned in and kissed her cheek. She squealed.

'Get out of here, you reek of pigs!' she said and shoved him away with a sharp elbow but he laughed again before going back outside.

Pat continued to feed the hens every day and one day soon after when Kath was in the cellar she called up to him. He stood hesitantly at the top of the steps with an expression as though she were beckoning him into hell before he trod nervously down to her.

'This is too heavy for me. Can you do it?'

'Mam used to manage it.'

'Well, I can't. Here you are.' It was buttermilk. No matter how small the jug she always found it too heavy, and she normally hauled it one step at a time, cursing all the way. It was important though – they fed it to the piglets or the calves or the lambs, whoever needed it most.

'And come back when you've done that, there's a load more.'

Pat grumbled but he did it. When the butter-milk was all up to ground level and distributed, she heard nothing else from him. She was sure he had gone off to bed, and gave a small smile.

On the first market day after she had mastered making butter, she took her basket with butter and eggs and some dried herbs from the summer-house and got on the bus for Stanhope. Every-body stared at her, but she smiled and looked out of the window and enjoyed the ride.

She passed what looked like a castle on one side and streets of stone houses which went down a bank to the river. A hill on the other side rose up to the top of the dale and houses were dotted a long way up, amidst small square fields and farmhouses.

Jake had explained to her that she didn't need a market stall, she would be allowed to sell from her basket among the other stallholders. She was nervous, but the minute she reached the market-place she felt better; everyone was cheery and the stalls were bustling.

She set up, slightly apart from other people so she wouldn't get in their way. One fat, red-faced woman came straight over, jovial and smiling.

'Aren't you the cousin who's living with the Sutherland lads?'

'Yes,' Kath said. 'How did you know?'

'You can't keep much quiet around here, my

love, and anyway that Jake he called in and asked me to keep an eye on you. They're such nice boys. A shame about Patrick, and their mother not long gone to her maker. They'll be the better for having a woman about the place. You'll sell your wares with no bother. There's plenty that would take more. And these days there's women with money, you know, who have their own jobs and their own purses.'

'What kind of jobs do they have?' Kath asked, curious.

'They manage shops, they sell dresses and hats. There's even a lass in the newspaper office! Things have changed a lot since the war. Men wanted us back in the kitchen but some women wouldn't do it and if they make money, their blokes are hardly going to complain. My daughter started on Darlington market with fruit and veg and now she has her own green-grocer shops, three of them! These ladies with money want stuff for their faces and their bathwater and even those who have nothing more than a pitcher of water want to smell nice. Those herbs will go fast.'

Kath considered this as she turned to her customers, who were already lining up and waiting patiently for her attention.

As Kath was packing up that afternoon, a man stopped in front of her.

'You wouldn't like to buy some beehives?' he offered hopefully.

Kath was selling the last of her butter and why he came to her she was not quite sure. Maybe she looked approachable because she was younger than the others.

'I live in the south,' he said sheepishly. 'I'm not a farmer. I couldn't settle enough for it. My father has just died; he wouldn't come and live in London with us.'

'What do you do down there?'

He looked almost ashamed.

'I'm a banker,' he said. 'My dad was so proud of me. He was good with figures, you know. When he was doing the accounts on the farm he never had to add anything up. He could just glance down it and see the total. I got that from him, but I left. The farming life wasn't for me.'

'That was what you should have done, surely.'

He looked gratefully at her.

'Was it?'

'I think he would have wanted the best for you. Parents always do.'

'He was devoted to his bees. I don't want to leave them there because the people that are buying the farm aren't keen, but I feel I would neglect them in London. Would you be interested, or would you know somebody who might be? I want to leave them in safe hands.'

'How much are they?'

'Let me put it this way,' he said. 'I have nowhere to keep them and no way to transport them but if I could come up here once a year and have some honey for me and my family, you could have them.'

Kath was quite excited. She knew nothing about bees but why shouldn't she learn?

When she got home that evening, Kath told the

two brothers what the market woman had told her, and all about her new beehives. They didn't seem nearly as excited as she was. Men, Kath thought, didn't understand.

'Lasses want what for their baths?' Pat asked.

'Did you say bees?' Jake interjected.

'They like to smell nice,' she explained. All those herbs and such that your mother dried, I think we could make money from them. And as for the bees, we put the hives where there are lots of flowers, and the bees will gather pollen and make honey! When the time comes, you merely take some of it off them.'

'Aye, and that would be the hard bit,' Jake smirked.

They arranged to visit the farm and pick up the hives in the next few days before the place was sold. They were going to take the horse and cart but Jake, who often paced the yard when he had an idea brewing, came in late that day and said to her, 'Why don't we ask Mr Filey if we can borrow a car and trailer for getting the bees?'

'Because it costs.'

Jake looked at her with an expression she had come to recognise: it was the one he used when he thought that he knew better.

'It would cost more if the bees got out, stung the horse and it fell, broke its legs and we lost everything,' he said.

'Oh, for goodness' sake. Go and ask him then, but at least beat him down on the price.'

'I was going to offer him honey, butter, eggs, cheese and maybe summat for his missus and her bath,' Jake grinned.

They took the car and a trailer, leaving Nell shut
in the house since she would have broken out of
the barn and followed. She howled but Jake wasn't
going to have her upsetting the bees or getting
stung.

The farm was on the heights and had the most
wonderful view of the dale, but as usual there was
a cutting wind at the top. The financier, Mr
Ronald, was there, looking relieved. He helped
them carry the hives onto the trailer and secure
them with ropes.

'There's a lot of paraphernalia in the barn,' he
said, leading the way. Kath and Jake followed
him.

She didn't recognise any of it but she soon
understood.

'These two hats with veils are to prevent the
bees from getting to your face,' Mr Ronald explained. 'The long white gloves allow you to
handle the honey. Tuck your trousers into your
socks and boots and make sure not an inch of
skin is bare.' Taking the bundles, Kath nodded.

There was a smoker, too. He showed her how it
worked – it was to distract the bees while she took
the honey from them. Kath wasn't convinced that
blowing smoke at the bees would do anything
other than annoy them and resolved not to use it
if she could manage without. There was also a
spinner to slot the wooden frames into that held
the honey. When the handle was turned, honey
oozed out with the motion. It had a tap at the
bottom so that you could put the honey into jars.

'My father made lovely honey,' Mr Ronald's voice wobbled.

'I can only hope ours is half as good. I can't thank you enough for this,' Kath said. The extra income from the bees would certainly help them a great deal. Mr Ronald promised to come up in a few months to collect his honey and she offered him a farmhouse tea for when he did so.

When she and Jake got everything safely home, they carried the hives carefully into the garden and positioned them at the bottom. Jake stood back.

'Do you think they're all right there?' Kath asked him.

He frowned in thought.

'I think we should try and tilt them forward slightly so that if it rains the water will run straight through and out the entrance. Also, maybe we shouldn't have them under trees because they drip. If we turn the hives slightly this way, they'll get the morning light.' They moved them around to suit and went back to the house, very pleased with their work.

'I thought I might go ahead with making soap, and perhaps shampoo with rosemary or lavender,' Kath told Pat and Jake that evening. 'I'll need a supply of small bottles, coloured if possible, and corks to go in them, and labels. Then all we need is a name for our products...'

The two brothers looked startled, but pleased. And a moment later she found out why.

'Come down into the cellar,' Jake said and when they descended the steep stone steps, he took the lamp and led her further beyond where she made the butter and the cheese. She uttered a cry of delight. All around were hundreds of bottles coloured green, red and blue, and they were so pretty, all sizes and shapes – the family must have saved every one they had ever used. They would be perfect for what Kath was trying to do.

Kath bought large oblong white labels from the post office in the village and then decided to ask Pat the best way to brand their bath products.

Kath sat down at the kitchen table opposite him as they drank tea. She thought he might try to go back upstairs to bed after his morning feeding the hens but she bribed him with freshly baked sponge cake. He asked her what she was doing. She told him about her struggle coming up with ideas for the labels and after a while he took the pencil from her and started a simple sketch.

She had wondered whether he might be artistic. There was no point in asking Jake – he had no idea about creative things – but she had thought there might be a connection between woodwork and drawing.

Kath's expectations weren't high but after a few seconds, Pat showed her a perfectly formed little sketch of their house. She praised him so much that Pat did a whole load more and was still busy when Jake came in for his dinner.

They chose the name together: Kath's Country Honey, Kath's Country Cosmetics, and so on. Pat made years of progress that day – he was acting almost his age as he worked. He was so thrilled at his success, he was eager to help and do more.

Kath wanted to suggest that he should start woodworking again and make things to sell, but she thought it might be too much so she held her peace. His work on the labels was more than enough. She sent him out again and again to show Jake what they had done when Jake was around the buildings. It paid off: when she went out to milk her cows in the early evening, she found that Pat had already milked one and was proudly on to the second.

'Jake says I'm better than him,' Pat said.

'You have much lighter hands,' Jake said. 'You're a natural.'

It was true. By the end of the week, Pat could milk two cows to Jake's one.

Nineteen

Kath's business was a success. She soon found that most of her time was going to the bath products; the household and dairy work was suffering. One day as they sat down to eat, she suggested that they needed more help.

'Why?' Jake said.

'Because I am out selling often now and I cannot do everything.'

'We can't afford it.'

'There are a lot of people about who would do

126

it for meals and warmth and a few pennies. I'll pay out of the butter money if we can make room.'

Nobody said anything. Neither of the brothers looked at her. Kath happily took their silence for assent.

The next day she went to the village post office. She hadn't been in there often and the silence that greeted her reminded her of the old days when she had been a traveller, though now she looked very different from the girl she had been. Some folk, like the lovely fat lady who was at the market in Stanhope, were nice to her, some people were indifferent, and some were just downright unfriendly. She was learning not to care.

In the mirror in her bedroom she saw a new person: no bangles, no bracelets, no big gold earrings. No velvet, no satin, no lace. She felt frumpy and sometimes she yearned for the prettiness of her old things. Even so, she knew that with these people it did her no disservice to look so dull.

'I need help in the house,' she told the postmistress, Mrs Paterson. 'I thought you might let it be known.'

Mrs Paterson looked hard at her.

'My sister's girl is looking for work. She's been widowed young, poor lass. I can go and get her,' and Mrs Paterson disappeared into the back, ignoring the queue. Moments later, she returned with a small, skinny young woman, pale-cheeked with big grey circles under her eyes.

Kath was astonished to see this girl almost in rags, the soles of her shoes flapping free from her feet, with her sleeves torn and her head covered with a cloth that could not be called a headscarf. Her face was sunken, her cheekbones high and her eyes only just alight.

She followed Kath out of the shop.

'My auntie says you're looking for help in the house and on the farm. I have a small bairn,' the girl muttered.

She looked so defensive as she said the last bit that Kath told her, 'You can bring him with you. I will give you a week's trial.'

The girl's eyes finally lost a little of their darkness.

'He's no trouble, honest, but he's just two and my auntie took us in only because we had nowhere to go. I would be grateful and will work very hard.'

'If it doesn't work, then you can't stay, you must understand.'

The young woman nodded vigorously.

'I don't even know your name,' Kath said.

'Mercy.' She paused. 'I know, isn't it awful? My mother had God.'

'Well, you have to have something,' Kath giggled. The other girl joined in as though she had not laughed in many days; it was a release. The tension broke.

'Mercy *Potts*,' she said and they giggled again.

On Monday morning, Mercy walked the half-mile from the village with her son in her arms. When she opened the gate, came down the cobbled yard and into the house, Kath was suddenly glad she had taken a chance on the girl.

Ethan, the little boy, was bonny. He had bright

128

blue eyes and, when put down, ran about the kitchen, cooing with delight. He was very thin. Kath sat them both down that first morning and gave them platefuls of eggs on toast with lashings of butter and saw how fast they ate. She gave them mugs of tea, the little boy's thick with milk, and with his mother's help, he drank it down quickly.

Kath showed Mercy where everything was kept and what she expected her to do that morning. Then, at dinnertime, Kath shouted up the yard for the men. She was not sure how they would greet the new help. Pat had been cleaning out the hen house and came in first. When he spied the child, he hovered in the doorway, unsure. Ethan stared straight back at him in the interested way that small children do.

Finally, he managed to ask, 'Who's this then?' in such a friendly tone that the little boy laughed at him and with him. Pat came to the child and Ethan smiled in delight and held out both arms to be lifted.

'No, no, Mr Sutherland is busy,' Mercy said and that was when Pat looked across the table at the girl and smiled and she smiled back.

To Kath's amazement, Pat lifted Ethan high in the air, threw him up to the ceiling and caught him safely as he came down. The little boy screamed in delight. Kath realised that these lads had had a good father who had taught them to play.

Jake came in shortly afterwards, bemused at the scene. Ethan sat next to Pat and stuffed in his food, mouthful after mouthful. They watched transfixed as he reached for what was on Pat's plate and then Jake's. Since it was Monday, Kath had made minced beef and dumplings with carrots and potatoes. Ethan devoured everything within reach. He didn't slow down when the apple crumble and custard were served.

When the meal was over, Jake went back to work, Pat disappeared into the yard and the women washed up. Ethan lay down on the settee and was soon fast asleep.

'Thank you so much. We haven't eaten this well in ages,' Mercy said. 'My family here can't afford to keep us. The older members of the family are ill and the doctor's bills take almost everything.'

Kath didn't mention that Mercy's aunt was well-known to be tight-fisted, though she would have thought to see Mercy and the boy so skinny and ill-clad she might have taken pity on them.

At the end of the afternoon, Pat came in rather embarrassed and presented Ethan with a small wooden train he had carved. The little boy was so thrilled that Pat's face glowed. Mercy told him how clever he was, and Kath thought she could have boiled a kettle on Pat's face, it was so warm. All evening, the shine in Pat's eyes did not go away.

Kath asked how long it took to make and he shrugged and said not long.

She said casually, 'I could sell them on the market if you had a mind to make any more.'

Pat looked surprised but pleased.

'We have lots of dry, old wood in the cellar, I could try,' he offered and later on he sat by the fire and set to work.

Mercy repaid Kath's faith in her that first day, and on the days that followed. Kath was glad she had hired her. She scrubbed floors and washed plates and cups like the Queen was visiting. She cleaned windows with newspaper and vinegar so vigorously that they could see out of them, which was new for everyone. Kath's window cleaning had been terrible, leaving great big streaks. Mercy was so good that even a low sun could not fault her.

At the end of each day during that first week, Mercy went back to the village. Kath was worried because it got dark early, and although the country was fairly safe, she wasn't happy about Mercy and the little boy walking in the cold darkness alone.

It played on Kath's mind that they had a spare room in the house – two in fact, and a box room – since the brothers slept in one and she in another. Still, she waited for several days to propose the idea. She wanted to make sure she wasn't just being sentimental. But when Mercy continued to prove her worth, Kath's instincts were confirmed. After she and Jake got back from church one Sunday, she tackled the two brothers. She thought Mercy and her little boy should move in.

'She's a poverty-stricken widow,' she pointed out, 'and we need the help. She and Ethan are skin and bone, I don't think their family wants them there, and after what she's been through, I think staying here would be good for her. And we could certainly use the extra hours come lambing season.'

Jake said he thought it was a good idea. Pat

131

didn't say much so she took that as agreement.

The following day, Kath offered Mercy their proposal. Mercy sat down on the kitchen sofa and cried, which was not the response Kath had intended. She showed Mercy the room she had done out for her, with clean sheets and pillowcases on the bed and a rag rug beside it that Jake and Pat's mother had made. A little bedraggled bunch of daffodils sat in a vase on the dresser.

'It looks out over the garden,' Mercy said, as though it was a mansion.

Kath hadn't thought about it. She liked her view of the road, but then, she grew up a traveller. She could see how another woman might prefer a garden view and consider it a luxury. Kath had put a pink and white counterpane on the double bed which she got at the Stanhope market from another stallholder who made quilts for a living. She had swapped it for cheese and butter.

Sunshine was pouring in through the window and though the furniture was old, it had been well looked after and was ornate and handsome. A lovely black half-moon fireplace was laid, ready for the fire to be lit.

Jake came in for tea; Pat had been with him in the top fields for the first time in years.

The week after Mercy and Ethan moved in, Kath heard a knock on the back door and opened it to find the vicar standing there.

'Good morning! I do hope you don't mind my dropping in, Miss Armstrong. I deliberately didn't call on washing day.'

Kath was a regular church-goer by now and knew the vicar well enough to suspect he had come here with some intention.

'Oh, yes,' Kath said, rubbing floured hands on her apron. 'How kind of you to come and see us.'

The vicar was handsome; she had to admit that. He sounded educated and southern, with a gorgeous accent that was lyrical to her ears. She enjoyed hearing him speak on Sundays. His face was open and his eyes were intelligent and twinkling blue.

'You're baking,' he exclaimed in delight. 'I can smell it! Scones. Did I time it well? May I have one?'

'I've just taken them out of the oven, your timing couldn't be better. I just need to put more in.'

'I won't stay more than ten minutes, I promise you.'

She took him into the back kitchen. He looked odd there, she thought. But then Ethan dashed in and the vicar knelt and spoke softly and the boy went to him.

'What a grand little lad! I've seen you in church before with your Mam,' the vicar said warmly.

And that was when Kath understood the purpose of Robert Black's visit. She was so grateful she could have kissed him: his presence there made them respectable. Once he had met Mercy and her little boy living there, nobody would talk of the two young women living at the farm with two young men. His approval was all that was necessary. Kath called Mercy through.

She came in, shy and blushing. Kath brushed

aside the flour, sat them down at the table, and laid out scones, butter, plum jam and tea.

'Jane and myself have three boys,' the vicar said. 'You must bring Ethan to ours on Sunday and they can play. Jane makes very good cakes, and we have tea and coffee as well as sherry for those of us who like that. We also serve beer to bring the men in. Jane is very keen to meet the young women in the area, and you don't often come across to the vicarage after the service, Miss Armstrong and Mrs Potts. Please come, we need to meet our parishioners. We are from Devon and don't know this area at all.'

'Devon must be beautiful.'

'We miss it but Jane is determined that I will be a bishop so this is a better place for us. I have to do as I'm told!' he chuckled.

'A bishop?' Mercy said, forgetting to be shy. 'The Bishop of Durham lives in a palace.'

'The vicarage here is enormous,' he leaned forward over the table and confided, eyes twinkling. 'We're lucky this area has coal mines and forests otherwise we'd struggle to keep ourselves warm.'

He stayed for a brief half-hour and when he had gone, the two women went back to work, giggling about how handsome and kind he was. Kath was aware of the benefit of making friends with the vicar, so the following Sunday the four of them stayed on after the service to visit the vicarage. Robert Black beamed on them, greeting them at the door, shaking hands all round and calling Ethan by name.

The vicarage was as big as he had said, a large

Victorian home with enormous rooms and a sweeping staircase. Nearly everybody who had been at the church was there, the vicar by then being well-known for his generosity. He opened his home on Sunday afternoons to everybody in the village, of any faith; he didn't want the afternoon to be about church.

It was like a party. Kath thought him very clever, uniting people who were divided by different ideas and allowing those who lived on remote farms to socialize and have tea and cake before they set off on their return journeys. Kath felt that Mr Black would make a wonderful bishop – he was tactful and kind and made everybody feel welcome.

Jane, the vicar's wife, gave them tea and cake. Well-dressed and pretty with the same kind of accent as her husband, it was rumoured that she was socially above him in Devon but she had taken him for love. Her parents had expected her to marry a lord but she had shunned him when she fell for the learned vicar.

Kath was sceptical about this but she liked the idea. She too understood the pressure to marry well. Jane looked supremely happy with her husband and children. She was pleasant to everyone: telling the ladies of the parish how wonderful they were, including everyone in the conversation, smiling and encouraging more tea and cake. She was so glad that Mercy had brought Ethan across to the vicarage – she had been hoping Mercy would bring him for some time; they were always welcome.

Jane told them she was so pleased that Mrs

Potts had found work at the farm with the Sutherland brothers and Miss Armstrong – they were such good, industrious and God-fearing people. Kath felt she was nothing of the sort but it still made her feel warm inside. Jane took Ethan outside to play with her sons, urging them to look after him because he was young. Mercy watched anxiously for a few moments but when the biggest boy took Ethan by the hand and led him off, she smiled and turned from the garden to drink her tea.

The respectability that Jane granted them encouraged the other ladies of the parish to come over with their teacups. They chatted and gossiped with Kath and Mercy in a way they hadn't done before. Kath was pleased.

Twenty

The beehives were moved just beyond the garden, not far above the river, into a more sheltered space, well away from the cattle and the sheep. Kath and Mercy had begun taking their tea into the garden so they could watch them collecting pollen from the flowering thyme, pink and white, the dusty purple lavender, the rosemary that flowered twice on a good year, and the pink sage which seemed to have flowered for months. The white phlox at the top of the garden bloomed tall, with great balloons of flowers that seemed to flow one into another. The bumblebees buzzed in great clusters as though they could not get enough of the nectar.

Kath adored the garden. She had always liked flowers but had never had the idea that she might sit amongst her own; one rarely cultivated a garden as a traveller. Best of all was the summerhouse, with its lush green heat and dried herbs perfuming the air. She loved going in there to collect the bundles for her soaps.

The days were so warm and calm that Jake grumbled. Farmers, Kath realised, always complained about the weather no matter what it was. This was drought, as far as Jake was concerned.

'It's rained heavily twice this week,' she reminded him one day in August.

'It wasn't the right kind of rain,' he said.

'What on earth do you mean?'

'The ground is baked so hard from the summer that the rain comes straight back off it and doesn't do any good.'

One day when Jake was in the lower fields, Kath heard him shout her name in a note that could not be ignored. She ran to the bottom of the garden and down the narrow cobbled pathway that led to the river.

She soon spotted Jake and Nell in the field with the beehives and immediately saw what happened. One of the stirks had found its way into the field and knocked over one of the hives. It was now running away, lowing as the bees pursued it, and Jake was doing his best to right the hive. Nell was yelping as the bees stung her.

'Get Nell to the river.'

She called to the dog and Nell, who would normally not have left her idol, ran with her to the bank. Seconds later, Jake righted the heavy beehive and raced after them.

Kath's hair came loose from its bun as she ran and bees were flying into her long tresses. She tried to swat the bees but they just got more entangled. When she and Nell reached the river, they dove straight into the middle; Jake splashed in on their heels.

The bees retreated when they surfaced. Because of the dry season, the water was only waist-deep; they all stood there, Nell paddling, soaking wet. She could see that Jake was anxious about the young bull, but it was now across the next field, eating with the other animals, so it couldn't be that bad.

'How the hell did he get in there?' Kath asked.

'It leapt over the wall,' he said, 'like a bloody horse. I've never seen owt like it.' They both began to laugh as they sloshed back to the bank.

They waded across to the other side of the river so they could avoid the field with the agitated bees and walked around the pasture until they got beyond the farmhouse.

Mercy and Ethan were inside and looked up in shock when they all entered. Kath told her what happened as she knelt down and investigated Nell's stings – luckily her fur was so thick that she had taken no real harm. Jake appeared to be stung everywhere but they weren't swelling so he only had to apply bicarbonate of soda to relieve the itch and put up with the discomfort. Mercy brushed and combed Kath's hair and gingerly pulled the crushed bees out of it. Kath was stung on her hands and arms as well.

'They say bee stings stop you from getting arthritis,' Mercy contributed helpfully.

In the end it was worth it: a few weeks later they took the honey from the bees and spun out the liquid. They poured it into clean jars with little round labels containing Pat's house sketch. Kath was able to sell as much as she could spin and jar.

Twenty-One

It was late summer when Miss Banks came to the farm. Jake had been worrying each day, hoping that she would not appear. Their finances were getting better with their market sales, and Mercy wouldn't take payment over room and board, but they were still in debt and he knew he wouldn't be able to pay his overdue rent. He had been half-telling himself that Miss Banks might have found a husband in whatever high places she spent her free time and would look kindly on the brothers who had so little, though he knew he would've heard if that had happened.

Therefore it was no surprise but certainly a disappointment when the motorcar stopped outside the farm gates and Miss Banks slid out. She opened the double gates and walked down the cobbled farmyard, stepping delicately around the cowpats and into the little square yard which led to the back door.

Jake had been in the cowshed and to his shame, hid there. He heard knocking on the door, heard Kath say to Miss Banks that she must come in; the brothers were about somewhere and she would find them. He heard the door close and knew she would be sitting Miss Banks down and giving her tea and cake. If he did not come inside soon, she would be obliged to scour the yard and the rest of the farm for him.

He must go inside and face Miss Banks. He was trembling. This was the reality he had been putting off for so long, that they would have to leave this place, that he had finally caused them to lose the farm. He was shaking so much that he didn't see how he could go inside.

He wiped his boots meticulously at the door before taking them off altogether. He made himself go into the gloom of the parlour, plunging like a bad swimmer into a waterfall, into a room they never sat in because it was off to the side of the house and even though it overlooked the best of the garden, it was cold, just another fire to light. There Miss Banks sat with coffee cake and tea looking very happy, and so she would, he thought, Kath's coffee cake was to die for.

'Jake,' Kath said, and she sounded relieved and confused all at once. The tension was awful. Kath would know that this was nothing simple or unimportant, she knew what was going to happen. Miss Banks would only come to the farm in person if she had to evict them. 'Will you have some tea and–'

'No, no, thanks. I'm grand.'

Even a sip of tea would have choked him. He managed to sit down but his hands trembled, those hands that had drawn many a lamb from its mother, that were gentle enough to milk a cow swiftly and delicately. He did not have farmers' square stubby fingers; his mother had been fond of saying he should have been a musician. It was a joke between them. He could barely hold a tune and when she had tried to teach him the piano, he could not get his fingers to obey him, just as they were not doing now.

He couldn't say anything. He couldn't even look at her. Kath discreetly excused herself and left them. He wished he could shout at her to come back.

Miss Banks didn't look at him – she went on sitting there with teacup and saucer in her hands, both hands, so maybe she wasn't happy either and her smiles had been nothing more than a polite veneer.

He subsided into his chair, wishing that Nell would come inside. He felt such a coward. What would he do with the dog, the cats, the horses, the sheep, the cows and the hens? Whatever would he do when they had nowhere to go?

She was smiling at him again now. Was it a smile of triumph? He was not sure.

He asked her whether she was well and she returned the same to him and he lied, telling her that everything was fine.

'The thing is,' she said, finally getting to it, saying the words that he had dreaded for so long, 'you owe me a great deal of money.'

'I know,' he said quietly.

'You keep avoiding me.'

'Yes. I don't know what to say. If I could pay you, I would. I want to. My family has never been behind in the rent, however long we've lived here. We must have paid this house's worth a hundred times by now.'

She didn't like that, he could see.

'You've had the living of it. Your family would never have owned anything if it hadn't been for mine.' That stung. It may very well be true, Jake thought, but it seemed cruel for her to say it. She must have realised it, too, because she quickly added, 'I didn't mean that, Jake, I'm sorry. I know it isn't true. I don't want you to have to go. Do you see any way to pay me what you owe?'

'I could sell the cattle, but then we'd have nothing.'

He could no longer read her face since she was sitting in shadow. Was that the reason they had never really used this room? The light left the garden before it reached inside, as though it were unwelcome, as though it knew that nobody had time to sit there, and the darkness reigned.

In all the years he could remember, they had sat there maybe half a dozen times, and only on special occasions. The chimney wasn't great. If the wind was blowing in the wrong direction, smoke came back down and into the room. They laughed about it but it was never important enough to be fixed.

His family had been there for so many hundreds of years that he had no idea if they ever lived anywhere else. Should these things matter? He had a feeling that they shouldn't but they did.

He thought he would die if he had to leave this place. He would do anything to stay there – if he didn't he would spend the rest of his life paying for his failure, blaming himself.

'I've got a – a business proposition to put to you.'

Jake didn't understand but his heart lifted, even though he was wary and tried to tell it not to.

Miss Banks was not looking at him and her face was so red you could have fried potatoes on her cheeks.

'You must be aware that a good many men have asked me to marry them, for my money and my estate. It was never for me – I'm not beautiful and I'm bad tempered.' She smiled a little at this and Jake could feel the pain through that smile.

'I need to marry somebody honest, who won't cheat me,' she said, 'who does his best and knows farming and this valley better than most. I don't pretend that it would be anything more than a – a business arrangement, though I would like to have children before I get too old. We could live here and I could let the hall – maybe somebody would move in and put up with my mother.'

She smiled again and it was so forced, so tight that Jake thought her face might crack. Worst of all, she was actually looking at him and her eyes were full of tears. 'I'm sorry if this sounds stupid so I'm going to go now. Just think about it, if you will,' and she shot out of the door like she was being chased.

Kath knew there was something wrong by the way that Miss Banks left the house without a word of thanks or goodbye. She got into her car and peeled away from the farm so quickly that Kath was left staring.

Moments later Jake went too, striding so quickly across the yard that Kath didn't like to follow. By the time she had collected herself sufficiently to enquire what was wrong, he had gone. He wasn't in the outbuildings. She walked around the outside of the house, but Nell was gone too. She wouldn't let Jake take a dozen paces without her.

Kath went back to her work but when it was almost dark and getting late and he still had not come back for a meal, she was worried. What if something had happened to him? She knew if he were hurt that Nell would have run back to the farm and alerted them, but it didn't help to lessen her growing anxiety.

She didn't say anything to the others and they assumed that he had gone off to do something important without telling anybody. Pat milked the cows and Kath helped him, then she locked up the hens. Just before it was dark, she went around to do all the things that he normally did, making sure that everything was secure.

She gazed down to the low fields, standing on top of the stone where the milk churns were. She could see almost to the river from there, it sloped so very gently, and as she strained her eyes what she saw was not him but the dog, the white patches on Nell's coat bright against the deep shadows of the sky.

And then she saw Jake's outline. He was walking up the field toward the house very slowly. She hadn't seen him do anything so slowly before. She almost went back in so that he wouldn't think she

144

was spying on him but thought better of it – he needed somebody watching out for him, too. He had had to endure for so long with no help when Pat had been ill. She climbed down into the field and walked slowly towards him. She stopped and he stopped when they were just feet away from one another.

'What is it, Jake, what's happened?' she said.

'Nothing.'

'What did Miss Banks say?'

He stood there for so long that she thought he wasn't going to reply and then he said, matter of factly, 'She asked me to marry her.'

At first Kath thought he was joking, but then she saw his expression.

'What on earth for?' She didn't mean to say it, but she was shocked.

He laughed. It was a cool sound, nothing like his usual bright laughter.

'Well–' Kath fumbled. 'You know what I mean. You're a nice lad but you're not exactly a catch.'

'Thanks. I did know.' He sighed and they set off walking, even more slowly than before. 'She said she wants to marry somebody decent and honest.'

'You are that,' Kath allowed. 'I don't suppose a decent, honest man would ever ask her. She's powerful and rich, she must attract all the wrong sorts. I'm sure she's too clever by half for most. Whatever would you talk about over breakfast?'

'Oh, that bit would be easy. We could talk about farming.'

'God, Jake, you're such a romantic.'

This time they both laughed.

'How desperate is the poor woman?'

'She would let the hall if we got married.'

'Does that mean her mother would move in with us?'

Jake said nothing to that and it was only then that she understood what the farm meant to all of them.

'I can't marry her and it's not because she isn't lovely – she's one of the best people I've ever met and really good to her tenants – but she's above me in many ways and I wouldn't know how to go on.'

'Oh Jake,' she said, 'I'm sorry – for her and for you and for all of us. Whatever will we do and Miss Banks do if she can't find a good man to wed? We will lose the farm and she will lose what she thought the future might be.'

'She didn't really think this through,' Jake said. 'I think she just didn't want to put us out.'

It was the following morning when Jake walked up the road to the hall. He took Nell with him but commanded her to sit when he reached the front door. It was opened by a girl from the village, much younger than he was. He couldn't remember her name. She kept him waiting what seemed like an age before coming back.

'Mrs Banks says you're to go round the back.'

Jake wasn't having that and stepped past her into the hall.

'It isn't Mrs Banks I've come to see. I said I wanted to see Miss Banks. Now go and tell her.'

The hall was a gloomy place with dark stained-glass windows covered in shields and lions. The

146

girl – Daisy Wears, that was her name, he remembered – scuttled away into the shadows at the back of the house and came back soon afterwards, ushering him into a room that was equally somber. Small windows looked out over the side of the house. It was Miss Banks' study by the look of it, all books and papers.

Here she stood, scarlet-faced and miserable. She waited only until the maid shut the door and then looked apologetically at him.

'I'm so terribly sorry, Jake.'

He was astonished. She rarely addressed him by his first name and had never looked at him with shame.

'You must think I'm deluded.'

'Of course I don't,' he said with a frankness he hadn't imagined he would manage. 'You want a home and family. Isn't that what everybody wants?'

'I know,' she sighed, gratefully, 'but you–'

'The problem is that you're better than everybody and all the men you could marry are – are ... well, in London, or somewhere like that. I think you'd grow tired of me pretty quickly. I've no education and no ambition and I talk about sheep all the time.'

She recovered her countenance enough to acknowledge this attempt at humour and he could see the relief on her face and he thought, *no, she doesn't want to marry me any more than I want to marry her* and a weight was lifted.

'I just wanted to see my mother's face when I told her,' she said and then they laughed. He was relieved at the ease of it, but dread was not far behind. The farm was his whole life. What would he do without it?

'Well, in that case... I have prospective tenants for the farm,' Miss Banks said, 'and they are ready to move in. I'm going to have to ask you to leave as soon as can be arranged. They would be happy to buy anything you want to leave, such as furniture, equipment, or the stock. It should provide enough to pay at least a little of the rent you owe.'

Jake was soon outside again. It was only when he saw Nell sitting with her head cocked to one side, listening for him, that he could have sat down and bawled his eyes out.

Jake went for a long walk to grow accustomed to the idea that they would have to leave the farm. When he returned, everybody was gathered in the kitchen for dinner. He broke the news.

He couldn't look at Pat. How would Pat leave this place when months ago he could barely leave his bed?

'Miss Banks is putting us out of our home?' Pat said, staring so that Jake was obliged to meet his eyes.

'We owe her almost a year's rent. The sale of the stock will hopefully provide what we owe her, but if not, I'll have to work and pay the rest off as I go.'

There was sheer panic in Pat's eyes and then he got up from the table and went upstairs as Jake had known he would. Even from the kitchen Jake could hear the closing of his bedroom door. God knew how long it would be before he emerged again.

'When do we have to leave?' Kath asked, later when she and Jake were outside in the yard and could talk, where they often did when they wanted privacy.

'As soon as we can find somewhere to go. There are people waiting to move in,' Jake said.

Kath was aghast. She knew the cows by name, she knew each hen, she loved the buildings, the summerhouse, the fields. She was happy here – but for her sister, she could have stayed forever with Mercy and Ethan and these two shy men.

Jake paced as though he might somehow walk off the burden of losing his ancestors' place.

'I'm not leaving Nell,' he said. 'She would miss me.'

Kath sighed.

'Unfortunately,' she said, 'I think we may have more than one dog to worry about.'

He stared at her. 'What do you mean?'

'Oh, Jake,' she said, 'Nell is having pups.'

'She can't be,' he said.

Kath raised her eyes to the heavens.

'Biology, you know, like sheep and pigs and cows.'

Jake stared at Nell.

'I hope it was another sheepdog,' he said, looking severely at Nell who seemed to understand and was avoiding his gaze.

'Oh God,' he said, as they went back inside, 'Mrs Hanson in the village has a fine white poodle called Ephraim. Nell likes him.'

'Called *what?*' Kath said in horror as they went inside.

That evening they sat over the table and talked. Kath didn't say it out loud, but thought it was even worse that they would lose the farm now, when Pat was getting better. She looked at them over the table and they were sitting like a family, Ethan almost asleep in Pat's arms. Pat looked so much happier since Mercy and Ethan had arrived.

'I'm not family,' Mercy was saying. 'You took me in when nobody else would so don't worry about us.'

Pat's eyes registered dismay and Jake, seeing it, leaned over the table and said, 'We're in this together. Miss Banks says that the people who will be taking over the farm might take the stock. We should be able to pay what we owe; even if we have to start out with nothing, at least it's a clean slate.'

Twenty-Two

Kath and Jake discussed where they would move between themselves. They tried to include Mercy, but she felt at fault for the move and kept deferring to their opinions. Pat would simply leave the room.

Kath favoured Northumberland but it was too far, and the part that she liked best was the coast. She also didn't think they would get Pat so far away. There were big farms, and no doubt they needed help, but she couldn't see the five of them in a tiny cottage – it would look bad and also be difficult.

150

'There are a lot of farms in Teesdale owned by Lord Barnard,' Jake said. 'If we could find some kind of living there, Pat might manage that far. I could work as a shepherd if I found somewhere.'

'We won't all fit into a shepherd's cottage,' Kath said.

'I thought maybe you and Mercy and Ethan might find a little house in Barney itself and you could sell things.'

'We wouldn't have the beehives or the garden or the animals that produce milk and eggs. What are we supposed to sell?'

Jake looked at her.

'I have hired a car for Thursday and I thought you and I could go over there and see what might be done.'

Kath and Jake motored over the tops to Barnard Castle where they had a market. It was a lovely country town that she had passed through more than once.

The town itself was substantial, lots of big stone houses in terraces and market stalls all along the main street. Kath knew some of the stallholders from the Stanhope market and greeted them.

There were teashops with windows full of fancy cakes. Jake insisted on taking her into one of these. She loved the little round tables with the white cloths. They sat down near the window so she could watch the passers-by. She could barely decide which cake to get, the selection was so lovely. Finally Jake ordered carrot and she settled on chocolate and they shared while they drank their coffee.

They had an appointment with Lord Barnard's agent. His office was in the middle of the main street, part of a large stone building. Inside, the building was high and wide and made Kath feel out of place, but she knew that Jake needed the support so she went with him.

They had to wait for almost fifteen minutes before a woman ushered them into the office. The agent was a middle-aged man with maps on the walls and photographs of the white-washed farms that were Lord Barnard's signature for his property. Some of them looked pretty and only served to remind Kath that they were going to lose their own farm soon.

Jake was obliged to explain why they were losing their property and the man looked sympathetic. Jake explained that he had always kept sheep and he was hoping that he might find work on someone else's farm.

'I also have a brother and a maid,' he said. 'Mrs Potts makes cheese and butter and helps in the house.'

When Jake stopped speaking, the agent sat back in his chair.

'I'm sorry, we have no openings right now, and without money, no properties are available, either. But your skillsets are strong; if I find a vacancy that suits, I'll write you and let you know.'

Jake gave him the address of the local post office.

Jake was silent afterwards and Kath couldn't think of anything helpful to cheer him up. He said they should go somewhere nice to eat and when she pointed out they couldn't afford it, he said that he didn't damned well care. They had a midday meal sitting in the garden at the back of one of the big hotels.

She was always happy eating outside. He had beer and she had cider and the sun shone down. They shared a ham, eggs and chips. The ham was freshly fried, the egg yolks were dark and golden, and the chips were shiny with salt and vinegar, thick and brown outside and fluffy white within.

They were just about to leave when somebody called her name. Kath froze and then turned. It was Will Hern. He looked so handsome, so young and rich that she stared. His hair was black and shiny, his eyes dark and mysterious; he looked pleased to see her.

'Will!' she exclaimed, and he laughed and gathered her into his arms and swung her round and she laughed, too.

'Why, Kath,' he said, 'after all this time. How good to find you! How are you, what are you doing here?'

'You look wonderful,' she said, as he let go of her and she stood back, surveying him with pleasure. She was so glad to see him – he was part of her past and she had lost so much.

'Not as wonderful as you! We heard about your parents. I worried so much and we searched everywhere for you, but we had no clues to help us.'

'Have you seen Ella? Do you know where she is?' Kath asked eagerly.

He opened his mouth and closed it, seemed confused for a few moments. Then he looked between her and Jake before saying softly, 'We

153

searched and searched for both of you. I couldn't imagine how awful it must have been when your parents died and you were all alone.'

'They took Ella from me and put her in the orphanage. They wouldn't let me near and I – I ran because the police stopped us from leaving and then they – they came after us. I had to fight them to get away. Mr Sutherland here has helped me but we were afraid that if we made Ella's absence known, the police would come for me. Ella ran away from the orphanage where they left her.'

Will looked back at Jake.

'This is – this is Mr Sutherland, my employer,' she explained. 'He and his sheepdog found me half-dead and took me home.'

Will looked harder at the other man; she felt she had to close the gap.

'I keep house and help on the farm,' she said.

'We searched in three counties, trying to find out what had happened. Come back with me, my parents are here and lots of people you know.' He cleared his throat, then added, 'We'll, um – we'll help you find Ella.'

During this she was aware of Jake standing there like a statue, saying nothing. She couldn't say to Will that although she wanted to go, she couldn't.

She had never had split loyalties before and while she knew she had long since paid her debt to Jake – though to be fair, he would never have considered her in his debt to begin with – she couldn't just leave him. There was a part of her that dearly wanted to go to the travellers but she

154

had only to think of Pat and Mercy and Ethan to know she wouldn't, couldn't.

'I'm sure Mr Sutherland here wouldn't mind if you had your own people around you again. We'll find Ella for you, I feel sure.'

Kath wavered. She did desperately want to find her sister, but Will's confidence did not seem right to her – if he and all their friends had failed to find her so far, then why was he so sure now?

'I cannot leave.'

'Why not?'

She couldn't tell him, he wouldn't understand. She was torn in two, standing there. She felt such pain, she was dizzy with it.

'I can't at the moment,' she tried to explain. 'I feel closer to Ella in Weardale, it's not that far from Castle Bank Colliery where the orphanage was.'

Will's face changed then. His expression became harder, and his eyes scanned the farm boy disparagingly. Kath saw his expensive black clothes, his red neckerchief, his traveller's swagger – just like her father had been, all colour and glamour and excitement.

She could picture the campfire then, smell the smoke, hear the chatter and see the gold on the necks and wrists of the women and the rubies or sapphires in the ears of the men. She should go with him but she couldn't move.

'So you don't care about the people you come from?'

'Of course I do.'

'But you don't want to come back to us.'

'Not like this.'

He stood for a minute or so gazing at her and then he scanned Jake up and down. He looked Jake in the eyes.

'I wanted Kath to marry me. If I thought it was you–'

'Don't be ridiculous!' Kath said.

She waited until he looked at her and then she demanded, 'Do you want me to marry you because I have no other choice?'

'Is that how you think of me?'

'I want to make my own decisions. It has nothing to do with any other man or anybody else. And all I want now is to find my sister. Are you listening to me?'

He was looking at the ground.

'Well? Are you?'

Finally Will looked up and his eyes seemed to burn into her.

'You turned me down when you knew how I felt about you, as casually as though I would always come back. What makes you think I would?'

'I don't think that.'

'So you don't want me, but you want me to help you.'

'She's my sister, Will. What if something has happened to her?'

'You don't care about anybody but yourself,' Will said. 'You've kept me dangling all this time when you were promised to me years ago.'

'I was nothing of the sort!' Kath declared, glaring at him.

His gaze disconcerted her.

'Your father told me I could have you. You are bound to me.'

Kath didn't know what to say. Surely he wasn't going to make that claim. But she wanted her sister back and he might be the only person who could really help. He had so many contacts. She made a sudden decision.

'If you find her for me, I'll marry you,' she told him.

Will's whole face darkened. Kath wanted to unsay the words but it seemed the only way that she could save Ella. She would have given anything for her sister's safety. Ella was all she had left of the family she had loved so much. Her throat went thick and her voice failed her when she tried to speak again.

'Don't worry,' Will told her, 'I'll find her. You will come to Appleby next year and she will be there, I swear it.' And he turned and walked away.

Jake was silent as they walked back to the car. Kath turned to him as they reached it. She could feel the anger coming off him.

'What is the matter with you?' she reeled on him.

He looked hard at her.

'Have you lost your mind? What the hell were you doing, saying you would marry him when you never wanted him?'

'He'll find my sister for me. Now I know he'll do it–'

'And he's not a good enough friend to do that for you anyway?'

Kath looked beyond him.

'Not for me.'

'Why not?'

'It was very shameful for him when I wouldn't marry him. He's very well-off – in our circles he's a catch, a very big catch. He was really angry and upset at my rejection.'

'How long ago was this?'

'I was nearly sixteen.'

Jake stared at her. She couldn't look at him.

'My father had promised me to him. My mother fought to help me because I didn't want him. It was a really bad time. But I'm older now and things have changed so much. My parents are dead, I've got nothing. I didn't know that things could get so bad – often I think I should have just married him then. He would have provided a home for Ella and me, and she wouldn't have been lost like this. I have to get her back, no matter what it takes. After that he will take care of us.'

'I never thought I'd hear you say such a thing when you are perfectly capable of taking care of yourself.'

'But not of her or we wouldn't be apart now.'

'The whole thing is ridiculous.'

'Well, you couldn't find her,' Kath said.

Twenty-Three

Kath observed Nell looking for somewhere to have her puppies. She tried to get into the corner in Pat's room, dragging the bedclothes with her, and when they were retrieved back to the bed, she wandered the house whimpering. In the end

Jake made a bed for her in the front kitchen and put the fire on; she settled down there to have her pups.

Jake sat with her when the evening grew dark, yet nothing happened. She didn't appear to be in pain but it was obvious that she would have the pups soon. He lay down on the settee with a cushion and a blanket and fell sleep next to her.

Kath didn't know what woke her. She knew that Jake was downstairs and that he knew more than she did about such things – he had helped many a piglet, calf and lamb into the world – but still she woke up. It was dark. He had left a lamp burning below. She lit her own and ventured to the top of the stairs. All was peaceful – Jake lying asleep on the settee and Nell on a mound of blankets, cosy on the floor.

Nell whimpered sharply and in that second Jake rolled off the settee and toward her in one movement. Kath had never seen anyone move so fast. She didn't think Nell was in distress, but it showed how much Jake loved her.

He began to talk softly to the dog and to feel for her puppies while he stroked her. Kath came down the stairs. He saw the light and nodded and she came the rest of the way. She put down the lamp on the big table in the middle of the room and slid down on to the floor.

'Will it be long?'

He shook his head.

'Is she in pain?'

'Of course she's in pain. She's giving birth.'

'Sounds awful.'

'It is awful. It's also the most glorious thing on

159

God's earth.'

She saw him differently after that.

'That's because you won't ever have to do it.'

Jake grinned.

'Aye, well, mebbe but then you can't get closer to another being than giving birth.'

'I didn't think of it like that.'

'She's not hurting too bad,' he allowed, 'it'll be all right, don't worry.'

Nell did a lot of whimpering and Kath wished for a moment she had stayed in bed, but Jake soothed the dog and stroked and encouraged her in a low sweet voice. When the two puppies were finally born, Kath was glad that she had stayed. She cooed over the pups quite as stupidly as other women did over babies.

'Oh Jake, they look just like Ephraim.'

'Hell, yes,' Jake said. 'Thank God there weren't half a dozen.'

'But they're sweet, all white and fluffy.'

Nell, evidently very pleased with herself, began to bang her tail on the rug.

'I've a good mind to dump them on their bloody sire's doorstep,' Jake said. 'They'll just be more mouths to feed and they'll hardly be any use. Poodles, for God's sake.'

Jake put them down beside Nell and she licked them happily.

'You are a very bad sheepdog,' Jake said gravely. 'Look at them. I could round up more sheep myself than these two ever will.'

That made Kath giggle.

'I can just see myself at the mart with them,' he said.

She pictured it and laughed. He built up the fire, ostensibly for the puppies' sake, but Kath was happy to sit there with the new family. She thought of the loss of her father's dogs, saw again so clearly the image of her father as he rode out of the yard, the dogs after him, and felt satisfaction in Nell's pups that she had never felt before.

Twenty-Four

Will had never been so angry. He had never felt anything that came close to the way that he felt when he saw Kath in Barnard Castle with the stupid woolly-backed farmer. Everything went out of his head.

When he first saw her, his instinct was run to her and tell her that he had Ella safe with him. But then he noticed Jake, saw the situation as it was and remembered when he had asked for her and she would not marry him.

Her father had been angry with her at the time and would have forced her, but Will was too proud to take a woman that didn't want him. It had not occurred to him that she would not be grateful to be his – he was the best of his kind and he knew it. He had always known that she was to be his; it had been planned by their fathers since they had been children. Once she reached womanhood, Will had known that it was time to take her for his bride.

He could not believe it when she did not agree. Her father had taken her away and knocked her from one side of the wagon to the other and they could hear her screams. Will went to him then and told him not to bother – he would not take her now even if she crawled to him, bare and sobbing and offering gold.

She and her mother had both suffered. Will knew that her mother had tried to protect her and for this, she too was bruised and beaten. After that, Kath no longer lifted her head high, no longer spoke or sang, and Will kept out of the way. He had meant to keep it that way but today he saw how beautiful she was and was filled with new desire for her.

After Kath had turned him down, rather to Will's satisfaction, nobody would have her. Her father had declared that she wasn't fit for marriage, that he was ashamed of her, that from then on she would not be allowed out. She was sure to be an embarrassing encumbrance on her parents for all their lives, staying inside the wagon because they were too ashamed to let her outdoors.

This lasted for some months but then Will suspected her father forgave her because she began socialising again. She was so beautiful the lads clustered around her once more, but she wouldn't have any of them, either. Now she was with that stupid dales bloke, poor, ignorant bastard that he was.

Will could not believe how much more beautiful she was now than she had been the last time he saw her. She was full of fire now that her father was not there to dampen her down. She was sleeping with that woolly-backed farmer, it was obvious, and they were not even married.

The shame of it, and yet she had the nerve to tell him that she would have him when he found her sister.

Will laughed as he made his way back to his varda. His groin might ache for her but he knew how to remedy that. He would have her and then take a different wife. He would triumph and she would see it and know that he had his revenge on her for going with a shabby shepherd boy who could not even afford to buy her a decent dress. He was going to see his day with Kath, indeed he was. She would be sorry to her dying day that she had not accepted his offer.

The first person he saw when he went back to the camp was Ella. She looked so pretty; sitting outside his mother's wagon, sewing. His mother was teaching Ella all the things that her mother had neglected to teach her, which was, his mother had confided, just about everything. Kath had done nearly everything for their family and perhaps that's why Ella knew so little, but even so, Ella was as unlike Kath as it was possible to be and Will could not help being pleased about it.

She looked up, smiling as she saw him, and he wondered whether she saw him as a brother since she was being raised with his sisters. He thought he saw envy in her eyes when she found out he had gone into town.

'Why don't I take you out tomorrow?' he suggested.

'With the others?' She meant his two sisters who were younger and she did not sound or look as if she wanted them there.

163

'What about just you and me?'

Her eyes shone.

'That would be lovely but I must ask your mother. It wouldn't be any good leaving her to do so much.'

Mrs Hern, having lost two daughters to marriage, was apt to complain about the workload, and Ella was all too aware of how much his family had done for her to overlook his mother's needs, even for a treat like going into town. Mrs Hern came out of the wagon then.

'And where have you been?' she demanded. 'Your father's been looking for you this past hour. He wants you to go and look at a horse for him.'

She beckoned him into the caravan and said softly, 'Your father's seen a pony he thinks would be just right for Ella. A grey. Your dad says she's a beauty.'

'Great. I'll find him and go check it out.'

His mother looked satisfied.

'Can I take Ella into town tomorrow? I think she'd like a look around.'

Mrs Hern frowned. Good as he was, Will was not often inclined to take his sisters out.

'So long as you look after her.'

'What do you mean?'

His mother sighed.

'How typical of you. Don't you see how beautiful she's becoming? There's many a lad who would misbehave to impress her. And half of them you know,' his mother added severely. 'She's grown up a lot since she lost her family, and I won't have what happiness she can find with us ruined because some fool thinks she's pretty.'

'God's honour,' Will said and his mother clipped his ear lightly for taking the Lord's name in vain.

That afternoon Will went with his father to a farm not far away. The pony was perfect.

'She'll love it,' Will said.

'Well, I thought we might go to the seaside in time, and Ella would need a horse to ride on the beach like your sisters do.'

His father loved the sea – the spray, the wind, the wild surf.

When they got back home, Will and Mr Hern brought Ella out to see the pony. She looked at it in astonishment.

'It's for me?'

'Try it,' Will said, and he lifted her up by her tiny waist and put her on it. All the travellers' wives and daughters could ride from a young age, but Will thought Ella looked better on a horse than any lass he had ever seen. Her dress lifted to just below her knees as her legs closed upon the horse's body and Will was shocked to find himself imagining what it would be like to touch them.

'But it isn't my birthday,' she protested as tears filled her eyes.

'Every lass should have her own pony,' Will's father said gruffly, pleased, and he stomped away into the wagon.

That afternoon Will took her riding on the country lanes he knew so well. The sun shone as brightly as their conversation, and he found himself so happy that he almost forgot about Kath and her woolly-back in Barney.

The next morning was another fine day and as promised, he took Ella into town. Will had often walked around towns with his sisters but he had never enjoyed it like this. Ella was pleased with everything; she wanted to see the ruins of the castle and go for a walk down by the River Tees and explore everywhere. This was new to Will – shops and pubs were his forte – but she was so thrilled by the sights that he couldn't help but enjoy himself, too.

They eventually wandered back into town. He was already told by his mother that he was not to take Ella anywhere near a drinking establishment so he opted for another first: a shop which sold ice cream. With the joy of children, they ordered enormous ice creams with chocolate topping. Ella ate hers greedily and then half of his, laughing.

She loved the various stalls that were set up for the day on the cobbles of the wide street beyond the northern road. There was a lot of foodstuff being sold – Will wasn't interested in that – but then they came to a jewellery stall. Ella tried to hide the gleam in her eyes but Will could see her coveting a lapis lazuli necklace and bracelet and he couldn't resist buying them for her. She argued that he shouldn't but he insisted it was nothing. She kissed him on the cheek and Will felt himself blushing for the first time in years.

Back at the camp, the two younger sisters were unimpressed.

'You never buy anything as nice as that for us,'

the youngest said.

'If you helped more, you might get more treats,' their mother said. 'Anyroad, you've got so much stuff you're already spoiled.'

'Can I borrow it then, Ella?'

'Of course you can,' Ella said.

Other girls wandered across to see Ella's new jewellery and one of two of them looked enviously at her and frowned at Will.

They had a wedding that week so that night there was a big fire with feasting and dancing, and Mrs Hern was even more bothered when all the lads crowded around her adopted daughter.

She kept saying to Will, 'Don't you let her have any of that drink, mind. And watch the lads – I don't want any clever so-and-so putting his hands on her.'

Will laughed but his mother noticed that though he didn't dance with her, he watched her most of the evening. When it was late and Mr and Mrs Hern were sitting about the fire on their own – everybody else rather the worse for drink, food and dancing – she said to him, 'Do you think our Wills got something on his mind?'

'Like what?'

'Like Ella.'

Her husband looked sharply at her in the moonlight.

'Has he? I didn't notice.'

'Well, you wouldn't, would you? He hasn't looked at a lass since Kath wouldn't have him. I was starting to worry.'

'About what?'

'Everything. He's the only lad we've got and if

he doesn't take a wife where are the grandchildren to carry on the line? Mind you, we've had enough weddings around here lately.'

'If Will and Ella wed, she'd be around quite a bit. Wouldn't mind that, I reckon, what with the rest leaving us.'

'Mebbe but you know what young folk are like. I wouldn't have wanted to be around your mother too long.'

'You wouldn't be alone in that,' Mr Hern said. 'Ella's a good and bonny lass. I like her better than I ever liked Kath – that girl was too clever for her own good. I still don't know why she wouldn't have Will. You'd have thought she'd have given anything to get away from her father.'

'He knocked her and Rose about something shocking,' his wife remembered.

'I did try to stop him.'

'I know you did your best. It's difficult, interfering.'

In the days that followed, Will spent all his time with Ella and she began to look at him with shining eyes. His mother wasn't sure he noticed but she drew her husband aside again.

'Have a word with Will before it goes any further. If he means nothing by the lass, it's not fair on her when they practically live together now.'

That evening Will's father took him to the pub. They were in Northallerton, one of their old haunts, and one of his father's favourite towns. The pubs were full of farmers but they knew Will's father of old and greeted him with a wave.

Mr Hern was generous with everybody; if he grazed his horses in another man's field, he always asked for permission and paid for it. And because he peddled a good many items at cheaper rates than the shops, the farmers liked seeing him. It was often the only way they could afford jewellery and trinkets for their wives. They also knew he was the best source if they needed to buy or sell a horse – he was fair and knew everything there was to know. And he dealt in cash.

That evening Will's father took him for what he called a 'quiet drink'. Since the day was rainy, they sat over the fire with their pints of beer.

'Your mother asked me to talk to you.'

Will raised his eyes to heaven.

'She's a little bit concerned about Ella.'

'She worries more about Ella than she does all the rest of us put together.'

'I know, but with good cause. I just wish you could find her sister. She doesn't say much but I know she frets.'

'I have tried.'

'I know. So have I. Kath seems to have disappeared into nowhere and I know your mother is worried that she may be dead.'

'I think it would take more than that to get rid of Kath.'

'You sound as if you care.'

Will didn't answer that. He downed half of his pint and watched the fire.

'If something has happened to her,' his father said, 'it's all the more reason for us not to hurt Ella.'

Will finally understood.

'Who's hurting her?'

'You may be.'

'Me? I've done more than anybody to make her welcome. I spend a lot of time with her.'

'We know. That's just it. She is very young and she cares for you.'

'I should hope so.'

'Perhaps too much?'

Will stared into his father's face.

'What?' he said.

'There are a great many lads who would wed her given the opportunity. Now your mother and me, we are not inclined to give her over to anybody unless he's the right man, but if you are not the right man, then you need to be very careful and give her some space as she gets older.'

'I offered for Kath when she was not much older.'

'I think Kath was more worldly than Ella.'

'She was worldly enough to know she didn't want me.'

'That still stings?'

'I think I could love her sister just as much, if not more.'

His father's eyes warmed.

'That was what I wanted to hear. I knew you wouldn't play any lass false nor give her hope when there was none. Your mother will be pleased as long as you are certain.'

'Quite certain,' Will said.

Twenty-Five

Kath dreaded the whole idea of moving. She wanted to take everything with her when they left. She grieved over the horses and the hens, the summerhouse, the farm itself, the very fields. She couldn't imagine how hard it would be for Jake and Pat.

Kath and Jake sat around the back kitchen table and discussed what to do. Mercy had taken Ethan to bed and Pat was upstairs. He was spending more and more time in his bedroom as the day to leave drew nearer.

'I wish we could go far away so I never have to be reminded of what I lost, but it's going to take everything I have just to get Pat out of here. For his sake, we can't go too far,' Jake said. 'There's a little house right on the end of the village up past Crawleyside. The rent is hardly anything and it stands on its own.'

'How many rooms?'

'Three: two up and one down.'

'A garden?'

'A back yard before the land hits the moor. It's tight on the road at the front.'

'What about your furniture?'

'It'll be sold with the rest; the extra money will help to pay the rent and give us a little bit until we sort ourselves out.' Jake stopped but Kath knew he was going to say more. 'It's not much of

171

a place but at least it's a roof until we can manage something better.'

'It's a start then,' Kath said.

Jake got a note from Miss Banks stating that Mr and Mrs White and their two sons would be taking over the tenancy of the farm. If he was in agreement, she would bring them the following Thursday and together she and Jake might show them around.

The two White sons were a good five or so years younger than she was, Caro thought, and they obviously did not want to move from Teesdale. They were perfectly polite – they didn't say or do anything in particular – but she could sense their distaste. When their father blustered and said how wonderful everything was, she saw them exchange glances.

'We need a place to give our lads a chance,' their father said and their mother nodded and smiled.

As Jake led the parents through the fields, Caro took up the rear with the two young men.

'Why so unhappy?'

They seemed surprised at her soft question. The elder boy turned away without answering but the younger one, Sam, said, 'I wanted to stay on at school, but I was made to leave when I turned fifteen. I've spent the last ten years working.'

His father, catching his words, turned and scowled.

'Farmers don't need school,' he said. 'You can read, write and add up, can't you?' He turned back to Jake and asked him another question about the farm.

Mel, the older brother, stayed silent, his face like thunder. Caro hung back slightly, and to her surprise, so did Sam. He smiled at her.

'What would you like to do, instead of all this?' she asked Sam and he considered. She saw his gaze on far-off things and could tell he was no farmer.

'I would like a library, to sit by the fire and read in the evenings.'

'We have a library at the hall. You can come there and read as many books as you like.'

He shook his head and looked down.

'That's kind of you, Miss Banks, but my father would never let me. Do you really own all the farms?'

'A good many of them.'

'Was that what you wanted to do?'

Nobody had ever asked Caro this question. For this young man to do so now seemed strangely kind.

'I had no choice. My father had no son and I was brought up to inherit it all. I did have a London season, though.' She was surprised at how freely she found herself talking; she was rarely this candid. Was it Sam himself, or just that he was young and guileless, whereas most men were intimidated by her position?

'What's a London season?'

She told him. The others had gone so much further on that she could speak freely. She found the comedy in the telling of it and he laughed. She hadn't made a man laugh before. She couldn't believe how open and friendly he was.

'It sounds awful,' he said.

'It was. I didn't take. That was what they called it. I was a colonel's daughter and had no station.'

'You were supposed to find somebody to marry?'

'Yes, I can't think why. It's a stupid idea really, don't you think? Of course it's all about people marrying for land and money.'

'Hell,' Sam said.

'I did have several offers – one was from an elderly peer who had four children and no money, and the other from an inveterate gambler who thought I was desperate and would take him on because he was tall and handsome. The rest were either dull or greedy.'

Sam laughed again and she joined in. She hadn't allowed herself to find amusement in her failure in London but now she saw what a ridiculous thing it was. She had only gone to please her mother – and, naturally, disappointed her instead by coming home single – when all she wanted was to be home with her father and the land that she loved.

Later they moved inside and Mrs White confided to Kath, 'The lads were getting into bad company and Walter was worried about them. We've always been very respectable. That's the main reason we wanted to move. We want them to go into farming, to have a farm each. There's much more chance of that here – Miss Banks has said that she might offer them land if things work out.'

Kath wanted to hate the White family but couldn't. They were so down-to-earth: friendly, earnest, keen, ready to take the farm and love it. Her instinct had been to run away when they arrived, but instead she waited in the kitchen for

Jake and Miss Banks to finish taking the family around the property. Mercy had enlisted Pat's help in taking Ethan down the fields for a walk to see the river; it was the only way they could get him out of his room.

When they all returned to the house, she smiled and asked Mrs White if she would like to look round while Jake showed her husband the garden. She laid out tea and coffee cake in the parlour for Miss Banks and their sons.

Mrs White looked relieved. She was clearly worried about whether she'd be welcome. She followed Kath from room to room, saying how beautiful it was. When they were done, they joined everyone in the parlour. Mr White was raving about the farm and the good condition of the stock.

Jake and Mr White talked about the sheep and he commented, 'That's a fine dog you have. I'll be glad of her help.'

Kath waited for Jake to say that he was taking Nell with him but he didn't, he just looked at Mr White thoughtfully. The talk went on, the afternoon wore itself towards four, and Miss Banks suggested it was time for them all to take their leave. Jake escorted the Whites out, smiling at them all the way to the gate.

Kath went back into the house, expecting him inside any moment. After she had waited for about twenty minutes, she went into the yard. He wasn't there. She looked across the road and wondered whether he had gone up to the top. She checked the hen house and when she still couldn't find him, she returned to the house. He was kneeling in the back kitchen and he had his face buried in the dog's neck.

He heard Kath's footsteps and drew back.

'She can't come with us,' he said. 'She's a farm dog, she would hate it. Mr White said he'll take the pups, too.'

Kath and Jake went to see the house in Mr Filey's car and she could see why he had insisted on driving rather than walking. It was much too far on foot unless you had nothing to do. They took Crawleyside Bank, the long narrow winding road that led up from the middle of Stanhope, on to the moors. The car chugged as Jake tried for the tight gears on the rise. The road wound to the left and then back.

Houses nestled at either side of the road. The ones on the left had wonderful views as the hill became steeper and steeper. Kath thought it wouldn't be so bad if the cottage was one of these because though the majority of them were terraced, some of the better houses stood alone. But Jake drove the car further, taking a turn off to the right. Here were two streets of terraced houses which looked across at one another. They nestled together, not facing the oncoming winds. It wasn't what she would have wanted – they didn't even have views – but she could make do. Still he didn't stop.

He drove right to the top and there was a tiny house just to the left. Beyond it were decent-sized farms. On the tops it was barren. There was nothing but sheep. He stopped the car.

The house had no outbuildings, only a tiny

176

yard with a bricked wall around it. No garden, no land at the front, only the road and moorland, short and sparse. The wind was cutting against her face. He led the way inside. He had been right – there was one room with a boiler for hot water, as well as a kitchen, dining room and sitting room with a tiny pantry on the end.

Upstairs were two small bedrooms. In the yard there was an outside lavatory and a coalhouse and in the middle a drain where the yard sloped. Land wound its way up and down across the fields to the tops and on to Blanchland and Hexham on one side, Castleside and Consett on the other.

As Kath stood there she wanted to laugh at herself. At one time she would have considered this place huge and forbidding, but having lived in the spacious farmhouse, she had experienced luxury and now felt this might be the meanest house that she had ever come across.

To make things worse, the house had been built sideways – no doubt to try to hold off the worst of the weather – so that, other than in the sitting room, the views were lost for the most part.

'At least we won't need much furniture,' she said.

'And we'll need a car,' Jake said.

They drove to a small secondhand shop in the marketplace in Wolsingham and bought two double beds, a small bed for Ethan, two shabby wardrobes, a table, four chairs and a couch for the sitting room.

The view from the sitting room was the finest

thing about the place, one of the best Kath had ever seen. The view from the kitchen was not bad either – it looked out across the road, at buildings far away, and sheep and hens and other creatures that stirred there up on the tops, pheasants, partridges, grouse, moorhens, curlews, lapwings.

They were taking with them bedlinen, some of the curtains, pans, cutlery and crockery, a rocking chair Pat had made when he was a lad, their clothes, a few books, various tools for Pat's trade, some herbs and spices, as many vegetables as they could store, flour, sugar and the last of their cream, butter and milk.

They moved out the day before the Whites moved in, towing a trailer with their belongings. Jake made four trips and when he went back for his brother on the last trip, Mercy asked if she could go with him and take the little boy.

Jake was worried about this. He would far rather have gone by himself. But he couldn't think of a way to say no, and Ethan was jumping up and down in excitement at the idea of getting back in the car and of seeing Pat so quickly again.

Jake took the long winding bank carefully but it was not far. At the bottom he turned right out of Stanhope and made his way up the slight incline, past Greenfoot and then following the curves and narrow bends of the road with fields on either side. It was not long before they reached the farm for the last time.

Jake didn't want to go into the house but he knew he had no choice. Mercy opened the white gates and Ethan ran down the yard and through the open door straight into the house, calling

Pat's name.

When Jake reached the front kitchen, it was as empty as he had ever seen it. Ethan would have run up the stairs but Mercy caught hold of him, promising that he could go in a moment, after Uncle Jake.

Jake made his way softly up the stairs. He half-expected Pat to be hiding under the bed as he had done for so many years, so he was surprised to find his brother standing by the window. Pat turned as Jake made his way into the room and closed the door.

'I'm sorry you had to come back for me,' he said.

'It's no trouble,' Jake said. He could see Pat's eyes gleaming and not meeting his gaze.

'You always say things like that.'

'It's true,' Jake said, coming to him. 'It's hard to leave, I know.'

'We were born here and our father and grand-father.'

Jake said nothing. Just then the door burst open and Ethan ran into the room and straight to Pat, who picked him up in his arms.

'It doesn't matter where you're born – it's what you do while you're here, isn't it?' he said.

Jake stared after him as Pat strode from the room with Ethan in his arms. Jake had such a feeling of joy and wonder that he didn't mind locking up the house for the last time and driving away.

Twenty-Six

It was not so bad while there was something to do, but once the house was set up, Kath was aghast that there were no hens to feed, no cows to milk, no sheep or pigs to be concerned about. She missed every animal. What did people without farms do with their time?

There were no eggs to go to market, no butter to churn, no cheese to curdle. She did have the last of the honey, however, so she and Mercy learned how to make beeswax candles. She wouldn't be able to make the soaps when her herbs ran out, but they had to make money somehow.

She suggested to Mercy that with the money they had made in the past few months they might buy material. They could make up curtains – or even dresses, if anybody would buy them – and take a market stall just as she had before.

'I used to make all kinds of things for my sister and me. Let's go to the market in Wolsingham tomorrow and see what we can get.'

'My granny was a seamstress and taught me enough to help,' Mercy said, delighted at the new idea.

That first few nights were strange, but Kath discovered she liked to stand outside. The best thing about the location of the house was that there were no lights around it, nothing to interrupt the clear sky. The stars seemed brighter up here, so many of them, whichever way you turned.

She thought of Ella and promised herself anew that she would go to Appleby. She believed Ella would be there – Will always kept his word and he would do everything he could to discover where her sister was. She may have lost the farm and everything that went with it, but when she was reunited with her sister the world would turn again.

Pat liked the tiny house; he liked that you could hear where everybody was and what they were talking about. He liked that the big room downstairs had both the women in it nearly all the time. They scrubbed the little house until it shone even in the dark rain, which fell for days when they moved as though in sympathy. Jake shovelled coal into the coalhouse until it was full. He also got loads of wood for Pat. Pat didn't know what arrangement he had with Mr Filey, but the car and its trailer appeared regularly outside their house now.

He was happy making dolls and engines for children. Kath and Mercy dressed the dolls and they sold well. Pat also made cars and wooden trucks with blocks for younger children and painted them in primary colours.

He liked being where Mercy was, either at the house or at the markets. People would stop and watch him work, which he did rather shyly at first and then with increasing self-confidence as they admired his skills.

Somehow their attentions and questions made

it even more worthwhile. He became proud of his craftsmanship.

Mercy would sing when they were at home while she was doing the washing or chores – not hymns, but old songs about ships. She came from Middlesbrough and her father had been some kind of docker. Pat had the general impression that her father had left his wife and children, though she didn't talk much about her family and not at all about her husband.

When it was sunny, Mercy would persuade him out of the house and they would take Ethan between them for walks across the bleak landscape. Pat liked it up there, nothing but the odd barn and the views as you went away from Crawleyside, the ups and downs of the hills and the huge sky beyond.

Ethan would take a hand on either side and then play a game where he ran and they lifted and swung him. It made him laugh. Mercy was teaching him his letters and though the books they brought with them were far too hard for the little boy to attempt, Pat would read to him – not just at bedtime, but often when the days were short and the nights drew in.

Ethan loved being read to; he would stay still against Pat's side and listen intently. Pat thought he was happier now than he could remember having been since before he went to war. He would also make up stories for Ethan and sometimes catch the others listening. None of them read much – he wasn't sure that Kath could read at all – but he would find her hovering by his elbow when he told his tales. He loved the late nights as they sat by the fire and the little boy, who had become so dear to him, fell asleep in his arms.

Jake was restless just as he had always been. Pat worried about him. It was strange – for years he had thought about nobody, now he was concerned for all of them. He liked the closeness of the little house; it took away his remaining fear. Who could have nightmares when they were all together?

The two women had one room and he and Jake had the other, but sometimes Ethan would come into their bed and snuggle between them. It was on one of these nights that it occurred to Pat that he would like to have a child. He lay as the little boy slept and imagined himself married and being a father.

He began to look at Mercy differently – not as a widow whose husband had fallen in the Tees, drunk one dark night – but as a young, single woman. He found her small figure attractive and began to think what it would be like to touch her. It was a kind of sweet torture to be around her so much.

He liked it best when she washed her hair and sat before the fire, untangling it with her fingers. It was the prettiest shade of brown, almost red reflected in the flames and it was long when it was free. Not that it ever was free – once she combed it, she put it into plaits that she twisted up and knotted out of the way at the back of her head. Her neck was so vulnerable-looking that Pat found himself wanting to kiss her there.

Twenty-Seven

Jake couldn't tell whether it was Nell and the pups and the animals or the land or the house itself that he missed so much. He dreamt every night that he was being put out of the only home that his family had known for so many generations that nobody knew when they had lived elsewhere.

He blamed the war, he blamed the weather, he blamed his family, but most of all he blamed himself. This house was even smaller than he had thought it would be. He had not known how much he would hate the lack of rooms or privacy, or how he could not keep from getting up as soon as the dawn broke.

He would lie there amazed that there was nothing to do. His life had stopped and he missed Nell so much that he hurt. The day after they moved, he took the car and its trailer back to Mr Filey and paid him what he owed. Mr Filey had looked carefully at him.

'Why don't you hang on to it?' Mr Filey said.

Jake couldn't look at him.

'I can't pay for it,' he said.

'It doesn't matter.'

Jake stared at him. Mr Filey was not known for being particularly generous. Why would he be so now?

'But I don't know that I ever will. I've got

184

enough money to buy coal and wood and food and that's all.'

Mr Filey hesitated as though embarrassed to be having this conversation, and then he looked Jake straight in the eye.

'Your father was very good to us when we first started up. He would let us go for months owing him money for milk and cheese and butter and meat, and your mother used to send us food, cakes and stews. You hang on to the car. Treat it like your own.' Mr Filey smiled and wandered back in among the buses, leaving Jake dumbfounded. He had known nothing about his parents helping Mr Filey; it uplifted him to hear how good they had been.

When he got back to the house on the tops, Kath turned around from where she was cooking at the stove.

'I thought you'd be ages yet. Did you catch the bus?'

'Mr Filey asked me to hang on to the car.'

'Why?'

'He said my parents were kind to him when he and his wife had nothing. While I've got it, we should stock up with more wood and coal and other heavy things like flour and sugar.'

'You could also take Mercy and me to the market at Wolsingham, and maybe even Crook, so that we can sell our goods for as many days as possible. We have materials for making clothes and I think Pat might start making furniture – just small to begin with – like little cupboards and maybe jewellery boxes. We've put up notices in the post offices' windows so that people know we're doing mending and dressmaking and will be selling on the markets. If all goes well, maybe in time we might have a shop.'

'It's a good idea,' Jake said. 'Where is everybody?'

'They went out for a walk.'

'A what?'

'You know.'

'I can't say I do.'

She looked patiently at him, her cheeks tinged with pink.

'For heaven's sake,' she said, 'use your imagination. A lass and a lad, like other people.'

Jake stared at her.

'Never,' he said.

'And don't let on.'

At that moment Ethan burst through the door, his face rosy from the cold wind, Mercy and Pat following together. Ethan spent a long time over the meal telling Jake what he had seen on their walk.

'Two sheeps.'

'Sheep,' Mercy said.

'No, two,' he insisted.

'And what else?' Pat said.

Ethan frowned.

'It was a sparrow hawk, up high, wasn't it?' Pat said.

Jake looked across the table at Kath but she was avoiding his gaze. More change. Would he never catch up?

Twenty-Eight

Ella felt safe among Will's family; she loved the smoke of the wood fire when they camped at night, the shared meals, the stories and laughter. It made her think of her mother and father and Kath, the days when she had been a child and they had been all together and happy.

Will's family were rich. The caravans were sumptuous. They all shared the children between them and she liked how Will treated his friends' little ones. He let them pretend to drive. When they stopped, he let them crawl all over him and play on the ground and when they were tired, he took them in his arms until they fell asleep.

Their mothers did not put them to bed; it was warm by the fire and the men, women, children and dogs were all there. Some Spanish gypsies had joined them, a man who played the guitar and a woman who danced.

Ella could not remember having been so happy since before her parents had died. She was at home here among her own people. The women provided good food and Spanish wine flowed.

'Don't you let Ella drink too much of that,' Wills mother directed him as she went around seeing to everyone's needs.

The wine made Ella feel heady and happy. She liked the music and the woman dancing. Another woman sang and though Ella didn't understand

187

the words, she knew the sentiments. It was all about love. Everything had gone wrong in her life, now it seemed as if everything would come right.

Will stopped her from drinking any more wine after a glass and a half and she fell asleep against him. She could feel him picking her up and carrying her; she was only half aware of what was happening as he put her down on a bed in the wagon where his mother was putting the younger girls to sleep. He kissed her cheek and left her there and his mother soothed her brow and told her that they were just outside if she was afraid or needed anything.

How could she have been afraid? She closed her eyes and settled down with the children. She could hear the music and voices from outside and to the lull of those she fell asleep.

The next time that they stopped she thought that Will would go to see the horses with his father but he was soon back and took her into the town. He wanted to buy her sapphires to match her beauty, he said. Ella could not help being flattered, but was also aware of the other girls they travelled with; none of them had spoken to her in days.

It was Northallerton and there at a tiny jeweller's down a little side street, he showed her some lovely blue stones. He wasn't happy until they were in her ears and around her neck and he bought her a blue stone for her finger. Will knew the jeweller well; he said his father had bought jewellery for his mother there for as long as he could remember and that the old man would give him a good deal. Ella was entranced by the sight of such beautiful things.

When they got outside, he took her to a little café, nicer than their usual. People stared but nobody said anything. One or two old ladies blushed and smiled and looked at one another under their hats. Will won the women round with his charm and good manners. He bought Ella coffee and chocolate cake and there in the corner, far away from other people, he leaned in close.

'If you marry me, I will love you all my life. Please say yes.'

Ella was shocked.

'I – I'm not sure.'

'Ella, look. I know that your first concern is your sister and that you feel you can't go forward until you find her, but I swear that I will find her for you. I will bring her to Appleby next year. I promise you that, so stop worrying about her and let me sort it out. We always said we would find her and we will. So please; you must say yes. You're my chosen bride.'

After that, Ella didn't hesitate. She knew that she loved him and it was not just because he was a fine and handsome lad. She admired him and she loved to see him riding his horse, laughing with his friends, and being obedient to his parents. But most of all, she desired him. It was so indecent that she blushed to think of it. She was eager for his body. She was not a child any longer. She had met the man that she wanted to spend her life with. She had never been as sure of anything as she was of this.

They made their way across country and the days were fine. The children danced by the wagons and were lifted up when they grew tired. The bigger ones would ride the horses and the little ones would sleep by the fire with the dogs.

Every morning Ella would awake and his mother, who always seemed to get up before anyone else, would get the fire going and make tea. She would come in and present Ella with a mug, thick and sweet with condensed milk.

'You just sit there and give yourself a little time,' she would say and Ella did for the first few days, but then she found that she was getting up earlier and earlier, careful not to disturb the girls who almost always stayed up late. She wanted to help Will's mother with the fire and the tea and the breakfast. Mrs Hern was obviously delighted with her, smiling and saying what a good help she was. This was bliss to Ella – she loved Will's parents more than she had loved her own: they were kinder than her father and more involved than her mother. They were wonderful to her. She was grateful to them and to Will. If her sister could have been there, her life would have overflowed with joy.

The next decent-sized town that they came to was Thirsk. Here, Will's mother said, the men would buy and sell horses but she left the children with friends and took Ella into the town. Ella had been there before and remembered how pretty it was, a typical Yorkshire country town with an old market square and lots of shops.

His mother insisted on buying her dresses such as Ella had never seen, in gorgeous hues of blue.

She bought her delicate shoes as soft as slippers and even underwear – silk delicate wisps the likes of which Ella could only gasp at – and silver ornaments for her hair.

When they got back, Will looked admiringly at Ella. She felt beautiful.

That evening his mother gave Ella a lovely white silk shawl for her shoulders as the night around her was cool. Yet Will didn't touch her and she wished that he would. She saw other girls casting envious eyes at her but most of her attention was taken by Will; he was so sweet to see. She was proud that he would be hers. As the music played and he still did not look at her, she kept stealing glances at him. His features were perfect, his body was long and lean, and she wanted to be in his arms and for his lips to be on hers.

When Ella and Will named the night that they wanted to be married, his mother and her friends cleaned his wagon so that it almost squeaked. He carried her to it and it was only then that she was shy. She didn't know how to look at him and felt awkward in her body. But the moment that he kissed her, she thrilled and became impatient to feel his body against hers. She wanted to tear off his clothes to reach him. He was too gentle for her mood and she was only happy when they were naked together; her body had never felt more alive.

It did hurt when he took her for the first time but her body was on fire and so desperate for him by then that she welcomed him. Urged on by her youth, clinging so tightly to him, she felt electric, aware of every nerve in her body. Their bodies were slippery with sweat and when she tasted his skin it was salt and sugar. She liked the way he pulled her to him and paced his body's rhythm with hers so that they moved as one person. She finally knew what it was like to really love a man this way.

When it was over, he seemed worried that he had hurt her.

'Are you all right, Ella?' he whispered.

'Oh my God,' she said. And she laughed. She felt powerful. She felt as though she would never be unhappy again.

'I love you, Will, you're my whole life now,' she said.

He kissed her a hundred times and told her that he loved her. They fell asleep intertwined and it was unlike any sleep she had ever had. This was even better than sleeping next to Kath in their wagon by the sea, the summer before their mother had died and everything had gone wrong. Nothing could go wrong now. She had found a family and the love of her life and he had everything she could have wanted in a husband: skills, money, and most important, she could tell that he adored her. She fell asleep and slept deeper than she had in months.

Twenty-Nine

Jake had talked to some of the farmers and they had agreed he could shoot pigeons and rabbits over their land as long as he shared some of his bounty. He spent a lot of time outside after that, hunting. He still went to the mart even though he had no animals to buy or sell and there he encountered Mr White, who seemed very pleased to see him, though Jake couldn't understand why. They went to the pub and Mr White bought him a pint, steak pie, peas, chips and gravy and they talked about the farm.

Jake had told himself that he would get by without it but the truth was that he had found it more difficult than anything he had had to do before. But his spirits rose when he got to see Nell. He was afraid he'd be shunned by her but she bounded over immediately and put her warm head into his lap so that he was able to caress her face and ears.

Afterwards, Mr White encouraged him to come back to the farm with him. He obliged and once there, Mrs White sat him down and gave him tea and cake and asked after Kath. When she heard that they were looking for a shop, she said she thought she knew of one and could help.

They went back outside. Mr White paused halfway up the cobbled yard to the gate and said what he had been wanting to say since they had met that morning.

'I don't know if you've got enough to do,' he said, 'but my lads haven't taken too well to being here – it's so new to them – and I wondered if you would be good enough to come back and help us for a while until they work it out. I know it's a lot to ask, this having been your home, but I don't think I can manage without somebody who knows the land and the animals. You could stay with us if it suits you. Mrs White would give you three good meals a day and we'll provide a warm bed at night and I would pay you well.'

He didn't look at Jake, as though he couldn't bear the idea that Jake would say no, but Jake's heart was singing. He could come back and it meant more to him than anything in the world. They talked about pay and he was satisfied. He got into the car, left Mr White at the gate and waved goodbye. Jake didn't feel the same pain on his departure this time.

Kath liked going to the markets but still she longed for somewhere more permanent that was just theirs. She found it difficult to sew by the fire when there was so little space. That evening, as she was engaged in making a rabbit pie and congratulating herself on the thinness of the crust, Jake came to the stove.

'I think I've found you a shop.'

She put the pie into the oven, closed the door and looked carefully at him.

'Really? Whereabouts?'

'Near the Pack Horse. It's around the corner, on the narrow road that leads down to the river. It's on the left, before you get to the vicarage, and it has a big back garden and bay windows.' Jake's eyes were lit with excitement. 'It's not big enough for all of us to live in but it has three little rooms and then one of those galleries, you know, upstairs. One of the rooms is a kitchen and I thought maybe in the summer you and Mercy could bake cakes and sell teas outside. I could plant herbs for your body products and Pat could make tables and chairs. There are some trees for shade so if you made tablecloths and such, it might work.'

Kath thought that the best thing about Jake was his enthusiasm and his foresight.

'That's such a lovely idea!' she exclaimed.

'I know,' he said, grinning suddenly. 'And I've found you a proper sewing machine. That's how this place came up: Mrs White has a cousin who lives in Stanhope and they wanted to sell the sewing machine and they knew of the shop. It's cheap to rent because it isn't on the front street and it's been empty for a long time. The back garden opens on to the front street, though, and there's a gate into it, so if you put a notice outside with the gate open or some pots of flowers, people would soon find out that it was there.'

'When did you see the Whites?'

'I ran into Mr White at the mart today and he invited me over. He wants me to help him on the farm.'

'I thought he had two sons.'

'They're useless,' Pat chimed in. 'I heard folk the other day talking about it. They're always at the Cross Keys in Eastgate or Stanhope at other pubs. They sleep until mid-afternoon and go out

195

in the evenings.'

'But he took the farm so that they would have a future,' Kath said.

'Mrs White says that I can stay there,' Jake added.

'You won't be here at all?' Kath asked.

Jake shook his head.

'It'll just be for a little while, until his lads grow up a bit and learn how to run it,' he said. 'I'll come back part of every day so that I can help with the shop and everything.'

She understood his desire to be there. It wouldn't be the same as when his family ran it, but he was grateful for any presence he could have and the money would be useful.

Jake tried not to delude himself that his work on the farm meant more than it did. Jake wanted this to be his homecoming so badly. But when he got there, all he had to do was open the gates and go down the yard to remember that this was only work. Mrs White had opened the door and the pups ran out at him, bouncing about and greeting him like they had never met anyone so wonderful.

Mr White came outside, smiling and saying how fantastic the pups were; Jake knew they were nothing of the sort but he nodded and agreed and then Nell came out too. She was no longer his dog, he thought, throat thickening, but she was still affectionate and wagged her tail for him. He thought she would soon get used to him being back at the farm.

Jake was happy to tell Mrs White that he was

taking Mercy and Kath to look at the shop premises she had suggested. She reminded him of his mother, especially in the smell of her cooking. He could smell breakfast, and just like his mother, she sat him down to bacon and eggs before he did anything because she understood they needed food to sustain them for their work.

One of her sons stumbled in.

'I need breakfast, Ma.' He slumped down at the table, clearly the worse for drink. Jake wondered at such people.

The elder son was about his age and had both his parents, he thought in envy. The brothers had hope and work and a future and they wanted none of it. The other son did not appear.

Mrs White conducted Jake upstairs to show him where he'd be sleeping. To his relief, it was not the bedroom that he had slept in with Pat, but a smaller room off to the side. The fire was laid ready to be lit and she said to him that as long as he stayed with them, Jake would have a hot brick in his bed and a fire in his room and plenty of food and drink.

Jake was glad of it. In a way, it was the easiest lambing that he had ever known. All he had to do was make sure that the sheep birthed their lambs safely. Mr White, being a sensible man, did as Jake had suggested and brought many of the pregnant ewes down from the tops in case it snowed too deeply and they could not be dug out.

It was cold but it didn't snow much, and Mr White had enough sense to ensure that one big barn was available for the ewes before they lambed, and another one ready for after. They still had to be diligent, but the bigger hazards were gone. Full of good food and with a warm bed and room all to himself, Jake slept better than he had in years.

He also got to work with his beloved sheepdog, and in that time, she was almost his again. He tried not to be too familiar – she was Mr White's dog now – but he took comfort that she had not forgotten him. That winter in the starlight with Nell at his side, he remembered what farming was about and how much it meant to him.

Kath was impatient to get to the shop so when she discovered that Jake had arranged for them to see it the first day he had time – and it was almost immediately – she was pleased.

The car juddered over the cobbles in the market-place and he parked it right outside. It was as he had said, down a cobbled road that led eventually to the river. It was quite steep at this side but once she stepped into the building she could see that it led beyond the back door and out to a large garden. The shop itself was so full of light that it made you feel better just to be there. Two smaller rooms led off to the right and to the left, from the first big room you walked into, and beyond the room on the right was a wooden staircase which led up to another room which overlooked the central downstairs one.

It was perfect for what they wanted, she thought and Mercy, though she said little, thought the same; Kath could see it from the look on the other woman's face. Each of the rooms facing the hill had big windows and the small square panes bounced light off the walls and back down the narrow lane.

At the other side were windows and a wide back door and when Jake opened it and led them outside into the garden, she saw that he had been right, it was the perfect place for teas. It had several trees which would serve as shelter and the lawn was level for tables and chairs.

There was a gate, as he had said, which led out to the front street and it could be opened so that people could enter in that way for tea and the garden. Though it was currently wild and neglected, the garden could be made a pretty place. The beds could be dug and turned; the ground would hold flowers and herbs, though she knew she may not be able to afford the plants yet.

Jake had followed her.

'Mrs White says we can go into the garden at the farm and gather what you want. My mother and grandmother planted so much, it's all choking each other now. I could dig up whatever you liked and replant it here and both gardens would benefit.'

Jake was rarely at home. He stayed at the farm, only coming for them in the car and taking them back and forth to the shop. It was hard trying to manage everything at once and often when they got back to the little house on the tops they were so tired that it took everything they had to light the fires and make a meal and see to Pat and Ethan and the household jobs.

The winter seemed a very long one, stretching weeks into an overdue spring. There was snow

199

and ice and it was dark and cold and there was always too much to do. Kath encouraged Pat to make tables and chairs for the garden at the shop but he found it difficult to envisage something which seemed to him so far ahead and he could not concentrate for long.

It was difficult to be cheerful. Jake was missed. She thought he was too happy at the farm to come home. It must be almost like it had been but without the problems and now he had money in his pocket. She missed having him there to bring in the coal and wood – though Pat did what he could – and when Jake was at his busiest with the lambing, he arranged with one of Mr Filey's drivers to take them to and from the shop. She rarely saw him then, and was surprised at how much it mattered.

Thirty

Shortly after lambing season was over and Jake returned to stay with the family, his brother came to him. Pat had been very quiet lately and Jake had thought that it was just Pat missing him, but even after he came back to sleep in the same room, Pat was silent. There was a reason for this, he discovered.

'I want to get married.'

Jake stared at his brother.

'I know it sounds daft but I like Mercy and her little boy and – and more than that. I love them.'

Pat moved about awkwardly. They were standing outside the house. It was pitch black out there and freezing and Jake had already suspected what Pat was going to say. Strangely, he was jealous. He had never thought he would be able to marry and now here was Pat, who had been so ill, looking so young and shining with love more every time Jake saw him. Jake was pleased for him and sorry for himself. He knew that was pathetic but he couldn't help wonder if he would ever turn over in bed and feel another warm body beside him, the sweet breath of a woman.

Then he realised something: he didn't have the responsibility of the farm anymore. He wasn't a man with no prospects and a bankrupt property. If he could continue finding work, he would not be poor and he could lift up his head in the society he had here. He could do anything he wanted, and once Pat was married, he was free. It was such a dizzy feeling that he was astonished.

'You don't have to get permission, Pat,' he said, smiling at his brother in the darkness. He hoped Pat would hear the smile since he couldn't see it.

'It isn't that, it's just, you know. Me, the war, the panic, the way I can't manage anything.'

'You're managing a lot,' Jake said. 'Does she know how you feel?'

'How can I tell her?'

'How the hell am I supposed to know?' Jake asked, laughing.

'Do you think she might even like me?'

'Why don't you ask her?'

'I don't know how to. And I'm worried she'll think I'm too damaged.'

201

'You're a lot better. You've been a different person these last few months.'

'I don't think the war is ever going to go away for me, Jake.'

'But it's lessened. You aren't having those awful nightmares. Or are you and you haven't said anything?'

'They aren't as bad as they were. I can come out of them now without screaming and wanting to hide. Sometimes I even know that they're just dreams and that I will wake out of that hellhole and be back in my own bed. Other times I lie and shake. But mostly if I leave the curtains open and I know I'm back here where I'm safe, I can manage the dark nights. I didn't know it would be possible, all those awful days and nights on the war front when I would close my eyes and pray to be back in my bedroom, and now here I am, and beyond. I've even found some peace. I think the little boy has done it. He's so vital, isn't he?'

'He's a lovely little lad.'

'I wish he was mine.'

Mercy burned her fingers trying to get the dish into the oven with the liquid Yorkshire pudding in it. It was tricky but she didn't usually burn herself. She started to swear and then remembered Ethan was in the room, playing on the floor with a truck that Pat had fashioned for him from a piece of wood.

Ethan eventually climbed up onto the old settee at the back of the room where the pale spring sunlight created a shadow under the windowsill and went to sleep. He sometimes still did that after a

big meal. He would be up later but it was no problem; he was happy to sit with them in the evenings
and listen to the talk. Pat would take the little boy
on his knee and read to him or conjure up stories
of distant lands they would visit one day.

'You like Pat?' Kath said now to Mercy, seeing
her looking at the truck.

Mercy's face showed slight panic and her cheeks
turned crimson before she spoke.

'I thought it didn't show,' Mercy smiled tremu-
lously. 'I didn't know men like him existed.'

She looked like a star in the sky, Kath thought
and laughed and then Mercy joined in and they
embraced.

Mercy was putting Ethan to bed, later than usual.
He had slept too long earlier and didn't want to
go down now so Pat came up the stairs and into
the room and Ethan got out of bed and ran to
him. Pat was their hero, and her son needed a
hero. Doesn't everybody?

Pat smiled, the smile that told her that she
needn't stay – he would tell Ethan stories about
the animals and the dale and the things he remembered from childhood. He would talk to him
in that slow, sweet dales tone which could have
put angels singing in heaven to silence.

Mercy thought she had never heard a voice
better than his. In her dreams, he spoke to her in
bed and they held each other close. It was all she
had ever wanted, and being with him was banish-
ing the memories of Mack hitting her in the
kitchen and ripping into her body in the bedroom.

She didn't know she would be able to move

beyond her fear, but she had for Pat. She thought he was the sweetest man that she had ever known and she wanted him so badly that when they all went to bed she couldn't rest knowing he was in the same house, in the next room.

Later that night, Mercy couldn't rest so she went downstairs. She got halfway there when she saw that Pat was sitting over the fire, still dressed. She couldn't go back because he heard her and saw her. She wished that she had stayed in her room. He beckoned her down.

'I couldn't sleep either.'

He looked at her in her long, white nightgown with the wrap over her shoulders – it was something that Kath had made for her, dramatic, unusual, with black, pink and green embroidery. Kath had said it was for the summer – it was too lightweight for the winter chill – but Mercy loved it so much that she wore it anyway. Pat thought she was the most beautiful thing that he had ever seen.

'Are you cold?' he said.

'I'm fine,' she replied.

'Then let's go outside.'

He went out and she followed him and for God's sake it was the most beautiful night of the year, even though it was freezing. Each star was a diamond. She wished it had rained. She wished it had been dull and windy as so many nights were, but the heavens had no pity. A full white moon and thousands of glittering stars, like nobody had ever suffered, like nobody had ever grieved, like nobody had ever died.

In other circumstances it could have been awkward, but she knew what was coming and couldn't believe it. She couldn't say anything or move. He turned around and she saw how tall and lean and sweet-bodied he was.

He was a man any woman would have been proud to call husband but he had never courted a woman in all these years. He had nobody to call his own except his brother, and no place on earth where he could survive but this. He had not been happy since losing everything in France.

She could not bear that having ventured this far, tried this hard, he should not have the life he was attempting now. Ethan was not even his child and yet she knew that Pat cared for him. She had always worried that if she died, her child would go into an orphanage or a workhouse where nobody would care for him, where he might be abused or mishandled, and she could not bear it. Pat would never let that happen and that mattered to her more than anything.

Pat had come alive as she had never seen him. He was animated, keen, and his eyes were so soft on her that she couldn't help smiling.

'I hardly dare–' he said. 'I've never met anybody like you. Would you – would you–'

She said she would and he took her into his arms and kissed her. She felt her body yielding and it was the first time for many years that either of them had known joy. He wasn't going to let go of her and she hoped that he never would.

Those kisses did away with the memories of Mack, and she felt confident here, and womanly, and she wanted to be in his arms like she had never wanted anything in her life.

His breath entranced her as it slowed. They had gone back inside, to the warmth of the fire, and lay now on the rug. His body was so smooth. If the war had cost his mind, at least it had not done damage to his limbs. She liked how sweet and firm he was, how he was all hers and she knew he was. She didn't think any woman had had him before this, but even if he had found a love in France, it was not important now. Your first love didn't have to be your last.

Her body was yielding as it had not done before, and she liked the way that he was with her – as though she was a precious jewel – and he spoke so softly. It was nothing dirty like Mack had talked, it was sweet words, about her, how long he had wanted her, how much he had loved her. His mouth was low on her body now but she waited and waited so that when they were finally together she had to suppress the sweet cries. When she couldn't and the happy tears ran down her face, he made her laugh.

'Hey, don't wake the household,' he said. 'You might get a better offer.' But amidst the tears which soaked her face, she knew that she never would.

Mercy said that she didn't want a new dress for her wedding but Kath insisted and designed it herself.

It was not white – that would have been silly, Mercy knew – but it was still new and she was pleased. She had not had a new dress at her first wedding. She tried not to think of it now. She had

had to drag Mack from the pub because she was pregnant with his son. She knew even then that he did not care for her but she had no choice; she had been stupid and had let him have her body and there were consequences which could not be denied.

It only happened once and she hadn't wanted to do it, but he had insisted and she could not get away. She could not even tell herself that he had forced her. She had loved him, wanted him; afterwards he had left her alone in a dark room all night. She could not call on her parents then, they would not take her back – especially her father, even though he drank nightly and had more than one child to a woman he was not married to.

She pushed the memories away. She had moved forward now and could forget the past. She was entitled to a man who loved her, just this once.

The dress was pale gold – that was the only word she could think of to describe it – and she was sure that it was the most beautiful dress in the entire history of the world.

It was long and swept down from her waist like silk folds. It very respectably covered all of her so that she could go to church, and it had sleeves that fell just below her elbows. When the light fell on it, it changed colour; it was sand and ivory and pearlescent and so beautiful that it made her cry and clasp Kath to her.

'Oh Kath,' she said, moving back, hands on her cheeks as she gazed into the mirror. Kath had insisted on taking it with them from the farmhouse and it sat on the floor in their room, enormous. 'I never thought I could look this way.'

'You're beautiful. Every woman deserves one perfect dress.'

Mercy turned around and hugged her.

'It's lovely,' she said, 'thank you.'

Kath, having talked to Jake, had done up the front bedroom for the newly married couple.

'I'll sleep on the settee,' he said and since she couldn't think of a better plan, she had to let it go. She wished they had more space.

Thirty-One

When Caro Banks first heard there was to be a wedding in the Sutherland family, her heart clutched at her insides and she felt sick. She thought that she had come to terms with the idea that marrying Jake had been a stupid idea – it make her feel ridiculous just to imagine it – but she could see now that she did care for him, more than any other man she had met.

Her mother heard the gossip from the cook, who couldn't make a decent meal but had been with them for so long that Caro put up with the dreadful food. The cook was really her mother's only friend, though she would have been horrified to think so. She came in one early evening to find her mother gleeful with news, her face almost pink.

'Who would have thought it? A Sutherland wedding!' her mother said.

Caro had long since thought that Jake would marry Kath. Why wouldn't he? She was so beautiful she brought a whole new meaning to the word; it would be strange if he didn't notice her, want her. She was in fact the only woman he could marry, in his circumstances.

Caro was so sick with envy that she was amazed to hear her mother go on, 'And she's a widow, for goodness' sake.'

'A widow?'

'The maidservant from Middlesbrough. She came here without a rag to her back and now look at her, parading her shame for all to see. Young widows are used to – well,' her mother blushed, 'a *man* and now she's captured him. And when everybody thought those four young people living together was respectable! I blame the vicar.'

Caro couldn't understand why Jake would want Mercy Potts, skinny and white-faced and obviously through hell, when he had a young lass like Kath Armstrong, as bonny as sunshine, living in his house.

'It's shameful, that's what it is. Apart from anything else, he's much older than she is, not that men care. Indecent, I call it. Being married once should be sufficient for any woman,' and she shuddered.

Caro stared, blinked.

'Older?' she repeated.

'Patrick Sutherland has never been the same man since the war drove him to madness, but he should know better.'

Caro hated herself for being pleased that it was not Jake getting married.

'Never mind that,' her mother said, 'I've had a letter from your cousin – this is my cousin's son actually, so he is only your half-cousin. I haven't seen them in such a long time and they are going to come and stay. He's called Frederick Melville, such a good family, just as good as mine. They have breeding and they're a very handsome crowd and they know all the right people. They number dukes and earls among their acquaintance. My cousin Bel has asked if they could call in on their way to London so I have invited them to stay for a few days. She is bringing Frederick with her and it would be lovely for us to become reacquainted.'

'That sounds lovely, Mother, but you know how busy I am.'

'Caroline, you really ought to try to do other things.'

'I don't have time to do other things.'

'Then you must make time. I have missed my family all these years because your father never had time for meeting up with anyone and I suffered for it. We have no society here of any kind and I am determined that just for once we will.'

Caro only argued when there was a purpose to it and there was no point in asking her mother why her family had decided to come now. She thought she could vaguely remember them from her father's funeral but she had been in such a bad way and there were so many people in the house, she couldn't be sure. All she remembered was that nothing had been good enough and that they had brought their own servants with them. It would have made her father laugh. They not only filled the house but they required so many

210

meals, and so much hot water and bedlinen, that Tandy, who had looked after such things, told Caro that if they stayed any longer she was giving in her notice, despite it all being for the Colonel's funeral.

Since then, there had been correspondence but thankfully no more visits. At one point her mother had declared that she would like to go to Melrose, where her family came from, but Caro had told her she must go alone since there was too much to do. At the time it was true – she was having to get used to her father not being there and between her grief, her mother, and the running of the estate, she could not face any more.

Mr Murchison, her agent, had been a guiding light in those days. Now he was old and near re-tirement, but she wasn't inclined to replace him; she was afraid to trust any one else. He had been there for so long and knew everything. He was her accountant, her general adviser, and he came from Stanhope and knew everybody. Now he was starting to mix people up and he remembered the dead better than the living.

Her mother could never go anywhere alone and had complained loudly and bitterly that since the Colonel had died, her life was truly over and she would never see her family again. She had wept copiously, but Caro was unmoved.

'When are they coming?' she asked nervously.

'Next week. Wednesday,' her mother said. 'I do wish we had somebody we could invite to dinner so that they wouldn't feel as though they were in the back of beyond.'

Caro did not point out that it was the back end

of beyond in so many ways and that was one of the things she liked best about it.

Tandy had long since married and left their employ, so Caro had an audience with Pris, who now looked after the house. She would have been called the housekeeper, and Caro paid her as such, but the cook would have objected at the title and gone through her mother and caused more problems. Caro asked Pris to order extra linen. She wasn't sure how many of them were coming so all the beds should be aired and made up.

Pris stiffened.

'The beds are always aired and ready, Miss Caroline,' she said.

'Oh, I know. Don't take any notice of me. I don't want them to come.'

Pris smiled at this – she and Caro were the same age and shared a similar humour. Caro hoped Pris would not go off and marry but unfortunately she was courting and it could only be a matter of time. The housekeeping role would soon be free again, which would make yet another problem for Caro to deal with.

'How is Mr Grey?' she asked. Pris' intended was the local butcher.

Pris smiled.

'He's coming on a treat,' she said, 'any day now.'

'Oh God,' Caro said with mock horror, 'how can you think of leaving me like this?'

'The amount you pay me, it's a scandal to leave,' Pris laughed and went off to sort out the beds. She would then prepare the sitting rooms and dust and clean until the hall shined. The cook was due a holiday in Whitley Bay that week – Caro had already told Mrs Witham that she was working too hard and needed a week off – and she had booked her a nice hotel as a surprise. Mrs Witham protested that she did not see how they would manage without her, but duly went off to her sea view and her holiday. Pris brought in her sister, who cooked 'all right' she said, and Caro knew that however badly her sister cooked, it could not be worse than Mrs Witham's burned potatoes, scrawny meat and yellow mushy vegetables.

Caro was out when they arrived. Mr Murchison needed her in the office that day. She was getting worried about him. He wasn't well but she didn't know who else could do what he did. She didn't really want people from the dale to know all about her business, but she was likely to need assistance when he retired. There were decisions to be made about various pieces of land, repairs to the farms, and the problems some of the farmers and their families had. She was so busy she forgot that her mother's cousins were to be there mid-afternoon. When she got home, it was almost eight o'clock.

When she walked in, it was like a party. And so it should have been – she had spent a great deal of time making sure it would be just as her mother wanted. Everywhere sparkled and there were vases of flowers in every room and she had asked Herbert Attlee to come and play the piano. The moment she stepped through the door, she was greeted by music and the hum of conversation.

Her mother did not turn to acknowledge her. She was late so her mother would not do. Caro attended politely to the room's occupants and then went upstairs to change. When she came down again, her mother deigned to speak to her.

'We have had dinner put back for you.' She smiled falsely.

'I hope not too far,' she said.

The house was full of her mother's relatives. She didn't remember any of them.

The meal was perfect in spite of the delay she caused, and she was beyond pleased at the work of Pris' sister; she would pay her handsomely for it. She thanked Mr Attlee for his piano playing and made sure he was taken back to St John's Chapel where he owned a small house.

'It was a pleasure, Miss Banks,' he said, with old-fashioned courtesy, and she knew that Mr Murchison had paid Mr Attlee outrageously. As she saw him out, she found a man by her side.

'Is everything all right?' he said.

'Fine,' she said as she always did, and then she turned to him. She was startled to find a tall, handsome young man smiling at her side.

'You don't remember me, do you?' he said, disarmingly. 'I'm your half-cousin, Frederick. You can call me Fred. But don't let my mother hear you – rather like your mother, she is, let me say, difficult.'

Caro could react to this. She smiled and they went back to the party. She picked up a glass of champagne – that she had paid for – and while she didn't know much about it, it seemed dry and easy on her palate. Fred seemed to down the stuff like water and Caro could not help mentally calculating how much it was costing her. She blamed her father for this – he was doubtless looking down and shaking his head at the expenditure over people he didn't care for.

They seemed very nice, Fred and his parents and his sister and her husband, and they were only staying for two nights, for which she was grateful.

'Are you going on to London?' she asked Fred.

'We are. We have another cousin who is being married later in the month and we have to be there. But your mother has rather cut herself off from us – so my own mother says–' he cast up his eyes dramatically at the ceiling and Caro, two glasses of champagne in, laughed '–so we thought we would call in here on our way. And I'm so glad we did, because I've made your acquaintance at last.'

They strolled into the gardens, and because every window was lit, it looked lovely. Caro was rather proud of these, the neat hedges, the verdant lawns, and beyond them and down the slope was the river which she loved beyond anything. When she felt overwhelmed by problems, she threw wide her windows at night and listened to the River Wear and she thought about how it had gone on for hundreds of years. She loved how it ran, like the tide up and down a beach. Its beautiful monotony was her saviour.

'It's very wild,' he said.

'I'm used to it. It's home, I love it.'

'I'm sure. Didn't you have a house in London?'

'My father gave it up.'

'I think your mother has felt the lack all these years.'

'She hasn't lacked for much.'

'Oh, I think she has. I don't think your father

ever liked our family. He had no aristocratic relatives and because your mother did, they were always at variance.'

That was one word for it, Caro thought.

'So,' he said, 'will you come to London and visit us? We will be there for several weeks.'

'I have a great deal to do.'

'I'm sure you have people to help. Why don't you come? You could bring your mother and we could leave our mothers together and go with friends to the opera and the ballet and all kinds of parties. I know so many people.'

It was very tempting. She loved music. She had enjoyed such things in London, but she had a niggling feeling that this was about something more. Why would her cousins come now? She felt that they went to London very often and had never called before.

'That's very kind, Frederick–'

'Fred,' he corrected, moving so close that she felt obliged to move back.

'–but I am very busy here.'

'Oh Caro, do come,' he wheedled ever closer.

'I'll consider it,' she replied politely, before bidding him a swift goodnight and fleeing upstairs. She locked her door though she knew that was ridiculous. He was unlikely to besiege her but the very thought of his oily presence put her off and she only wished they would be gone the following day.

She got up early and went out for fresh air. She took her car up Greenfoot towards Rookhope and followed the winding road. She stopped and got out of her car and she could hear the pheasants making their plaintive sound in the fields and she could see one of them slowly gaining ground as he went on his way. Partridges were almost invisible amidst the long grass, their mother making her way as though through a maze, the half-grown chicks following her. The lambs were lost where the meadows were high and the black and white cattle were knee deep in grass. It was a good year, plenty of rain and sunshine.

She went back to the house replenished and her visitors were not yet awake. They were apparently late risers. They all came down for breakfast mid-morning, her mother with them and as happy as Caro had ever seen her. Caro had been up for four hours.

'Do you hunt?' Fred asked her as he downed bacon, eggs, tomatoes, mushrooms, coffee and several slices of toast, butter and plum jam.

'No,' she said, her appetite lost. At this rate, if her mother's family stayed long she would be thin as a rail.

'You must have good horses in the stables; perhaps I could borrow one and go for a hack now and then.'

Caro stared at him.

'I thought tonight was your last night.'

He laughed.

'Oh, no. Your mother invited us to stay for a couple of weeks at least.'

'I only keep one horse and she's much too small for you,' Caro managed.

'You must know where I could borrow horses.'

'I'm afraid I don't. And I only allow tenants to hunt over my land.'

He pulled a face.

'Oh, dear,' he said. Well, since it isn't hunting season, I suppose I could amuse myself with a decent horse. You could come riding with me. Surely one of your farmers can spare one.'

'You must excuse me. I have a great deal of work to do today,' she said and got up from the table.

'Then what shall I do?' he said and that was the last thing she heard. She was furious. Had her mother really invited them to stay that long? Had she not thought of the cost, of the effort, of the organization?

Mr Murchison was coughing so badly that day that Caro sent him home, and for the first time he agreed to go. He lived in a pretty house high up on the hill behind the church in Stanhope and she worried that he might not make the incline. She would have insisted on going with him except that he was so proud that he wouldn't let her.

She understood a great deal of what he did for her, but she had not underestimated his skills. What she really needed to do was employ another accountant, but he would not hear of it. Even then it would be but a small part of the work involved in running the dale. That day she had an appointment with a stone waller as several of the farms needed walls repairing. If it was a small job the farmers did it themselves, but a harsh frost the winter before had caused real damage. She showed him around and gave him instructions.

That afternoon she was at home, giving out wages to the people who worked directly on the

218

estate, and then she returned to Stanhope to meet with her solicitor, who was going to a farm sale with her to negotiate for a tiny farm up at Daddry Shield. The owner had died and she had a young couple who had just got married who would do well as tenants, she thought.

She did not get home for dinner and it was nine when she finally parked her motor. She noticed another car in the yard beside the one which the Melvilles had come in. Laughter and noise came from the house and Pris saw her come in by the back door and caught her there.

'My sister has come back to cook but she has a family and can't stay long and – that man has drunk everything in the cellar–' she said in despair.

Caro wanted to say that he could not have done anything of the kind but Pris was obviously in distress. Patting her on the arm, she promised to deal with it. She went through to her sitting room. It was full of young men.

'Cousin,' Fred greeted her, staggering up from one of the oldest antique chairs. Somebody had spilt what looked like whisky on it. The other young men greeted her enthusiastically. They too were on their way to London and knowing Fred was visiting his family had just called in for the night, he told her. They had dragged a small table from its niche by the window and were playing cards. Caro had nothing against games like that except that they were very drunk, shouting and swearing.

She went into the other little sitting room and there her mother and Mrs Melville and two other women – there just for the night as well apparently – were drinking tea.

'I hope you don't expect dinner now,' her mother said, 'everything was long since cleared away.'

'I hope you enjoyed it,' she said.

One of them laughed.

'Oh my dear,' she said, 'you must come to London. You cannot possibly stay in this place for any longer. How you haven't died of boredom before now I cannot think.'

'Caroline, that woman who is taking Mrs Witham's place has no manners,' her mother interjected. 'She tried to stop cousin Fred from drinking whisky.' She turned to the other women. 'They are all Methodists here, you see.'

'Good Lord, how awful.'

Caro went to bed and tried to sleep but her bedroom was over the sitting room and the shrieking and shouting grew louder and louder. They were young, she knew they didn't mean any harm. They were not wrecking her house or hurting anything beyond a chair or two, but she lay there all night, waiting for them to go to bed.

When she came down in the morning they were asleep on chairs, on the floor. Bottles were strewn everywhere, glasses were smashed, and a photograph of her grandfather had been stood on and was almost unrecognizable.

Pris was crying in the kitchen. Caro tried to console her but she was too upset herself to do much good. She went into her study and began to work. There was no point in saying much now. The smell of bacon frying began to make its way through the house, and in the dining room the young men were talking and laughing and eating and making just as much noise as they had the night before. She entered the room just in time to see one of them shout at Pris, 'Hey, you, girl, is there any more tea? I asked you ten minutes ago.'

'Please don't speak to Miss Walters like that,' she said.

The young man leered at her.

'And who might you be?' he said.

'I am Caroline Banks and I paid for the wine you drank last night and for the breakfasts you have consumed this morning. When you have finished eating, I would be grateful if you would leave.'

She went back to the study but her hands were shaking. Fred came to her. He put his handsome face around the door. His blue eyes were full of light, his blond hair the colour of corn.

'Sorry old thing, we didn't mean anything, you know. Battersby has shocking manners and he didn't understand a word of what that girl from the kitchen said.'

'I would like your friends to leave when they have finished breakfast.'

'Of course, of course, except that they had come to see me and visit and–'

'No. I want them to leave and I want you and your mother and the other two women, whoever they are – all of you – out of my house by noon.'

He stared at her.

'But we have nowhere to go.'

'I thought you were on your way to London.'

'This is hardly direct,' he said.

'I thought you had a house in London.'

'Good Lord, no, we stay with relatives. It gets us away from our appalling old place in the country. It's just as bad as here, you know, up at Wooler. I try to spend as little time there as possible. Your mother's invitation was a godsend and you are so sweetly situated here. You seem to own everything.'

'If I had to have you and your family here for more than a week, I would be bankrupt,' Caro said.

He smiled sweetly in acknowledge of the jest.

'Apologies,' he said. 'I will tell my friends to leave after breakfast. Then perhaps you and I could go and look at a horse for me to borrow. It's lovely country here, so wild, I would like to ride across some of it.'

He turned to leave.

'Fred. I mean it. I want you out by the middle of the day.'

'We've let our house for six months and our relatives won't expect us in London yet. We need somewhere to stay.'

'It won't be here.'

'But what are we to do?'

'I neither know nor care. Pack. No, better still, I will get that "girl from the kitchen" – as you so charmingly call her – to put your clothes together,' and she swept past him.

Pris looked sharply at her as though she was intruding.

'They're leaving,' she said. 'When Betsy comes, tell her the beds are to be stripped and their clothes packed and put by the outside door. When it's done, tell me and I will put them out if I have to lock the doors to do it.'

Pris nodded eagerly.

'She's already here. She came in early. She thought she might be needed.'

'She was right,' Caro said.

Her mother was still upstairs and she looked happy, drinking tea as ever. Caro told her that the Melvilles were leaving and she should prepare her farewells.

'But they can't. I haven't seen them in years and I was so looking forward to showing them around. I was going to ask Mr Filey for a car so that we could go shopping in Durham and see the cathedral. You can't ask them to leave. Whatever will I do?'

'If you like,' Caro said, 'you can go with them.'

Her mother burst into tears and as Caro left the room, she regretted saying this but not for long.

Fred was sitting on her desk looking penitent.

'I've ushered the lads out, but Caro, we really can't leave. My mother thought yours would be glad of the company and I would like you to show me the area.'

'Frederick, this is not a hotel.'

'I should think not. Ghastly places,' Fred said. 'Look, Caro, I would really like to spend some time with you, get to know you.' He smiled a little. He had perfect teeth, his skin was softly browned from the early summer sun. He leaned forward and took her hands in his slender fingers and then he leaned over and kissed one. 'We could have such fun.'

She yanked her hands back, resisting the temptation to wipe them on her dress. 'Mr Eves and his son, John, are working in the yard. If you don't leave by the time I have asked you to, I shall get them to pitch you out.'

Fred laughed.

'Oh dear me,' he mocked, 'and do you think a couple of country yokels can take on a man like me?'

'I don't know where your talents lie, but Mr Eves used to wrestle – you know, that stupid thing we do in the country – and John is six foot four and has solved a number of problems for me.'

'I see.' Fred got off her desk, glancing at the mounds of paperwork. 'What a dull little life you do lead. What a fat, plain, pedestrian old maid you are.' The last thing he said to her as he walked out was, 'I thought considering how rich you are that I could bear to marry you, but nothing would induce me now, even poor as I am.'

Caro stayed in her study with the door closed until she heard the sounds of people moving about, of doors being slammed, and finally the outside door closing. Only then did she open her study door and listen with her eyes closed to the sound of the motor in her yard. She wanted to heave a sigh of relief but she remembered again Frederick's parting words and rogue tears threatened.

She would have to go and see her mother soon and she did not suppose that she would not have a great deal to say on the subject. She must not cry; it was over now, it didn't matter.

Thirty-Two

The sun shone on Pat and Mercy's wedding day. The ceremony was to be at eleven o'clock. Jake had not slept the night before wondering whether his brother would be able to go through with it.

'Are you sure about this?' Jake said as Pat stood in front of the spotted mirror in what had been their room and was now to be for the married pair, gazing at his reflection. His suit was years old and he was so thin that it hung on him, but he looked back at Jake with a smile.

'It's what I want.'

'You will be able to come straight back here afterwards you know, none of that running away to be together.'

Pat smiled again.

'Stop going on about it. You've said the same thing to me about twelve times. I'm going to do it. I care about her and her little lad. I want them to be mine and I can cope, I know I can. I'm making toys and helping out with everything. This will be fine.'

'I'll be there and Kath too, we'll be right with you.'

There was to be no do afterwards. Jake and Kath had agreed that the groom would never stand it. They would be pleased to get him the three miles down the road to church and then back. Jake knew his brother had said he could do it, but this was different, this was a huge commitment and he worried.

Mercy seemed reluctant to leave the house. Kath wasn't surprised.

'Have you changed your mind?' she asked, as she heard the car stop outside the house to take them to church.

'No.'

'Don't worry about Pat.' Kath was concerned enough for them both. She had the awful feeling that the groom might never get there.

Jake had driven a few yards down the bank when his brother yelled at him to stop. He brought the car to a screaming halt and had only just skidded to the roadside when Pat got out and stood there, trembling.

Jake went to him.

'Are you going to be sick?'

'No, of course not.' Pat gazed up at the top of the hills and took deep breaths.

'Do you want to walk the rest of the way?'

Pat looked at him like he was stupid.

'It's too far.'

Jake had wondered whether they should have rehearsed this, but he couldn't say that, he couldn't lend weight to it.

Pat stood there for so long that Jake half expected Mr Filey's car to come down the road with the bride in it. But he and Kath had worked it out and there would be a fifteen-minute distance between the two in case something like this should happen.

'I just feel as if I'm putting on you and I've been

putting on you for twelve years.'

'That's absolutely daft,' Jake said.

'No, it isn't. I just want to say to you – and I know brothers don't say stuff like this – but I love you, Jake. Where would I ever have been without you?'

'Oh, don't,' Jake pulled a face and squirmed.

'We would never have lost the house if I'd been–'

'Don't do that to yourself. It wasn't either of us, it was that bloody war. It took almost everything we had. But now you've got a new chance with a lovely woman and the little lad. Come on, man, let's get back in the car or she'll be there first.'

Pat nodded and got back in. He was quiet and looked out of the window as Jake negotiated the road, worrying every second. He took it slowly as though it might help but even so they reached the village in a very short time.

Several people were standing outside. Jake had known that they would be. He got out, greeted them and encouraged them into the church. He didn't think that Pat could go through them to get to the door. It was set back from the road and up several steps which would be challenge enough. The church – which had been a chapel of rest for hundreds of years before becoming a place of worship in the mid-eighteen hundreds – was where his parents had been married and countless others, before and after them.

Pat got out of the car and without looking anywhere but straight ahead, he walked towards the door. Jake didn't let him go inside. If Pat had to wait at the front of the church for any length of time, Jake didn't think he would manage.

'Let's just stay here.'

'Isn't the groom meant to go inside so that he doesn't see the bride?'

'I don't think it matters,' Jake said. 'After all, you saw her this morning.'

'She had her nightie on.'

'Well then,' Jake said comfortingly.

They waited. Jake didn't think it could be long but he was restless. He made himself not walk up and down or look impatient and turn to the road. He made himself stand still and look at nothing in particular. After five long minutes, he wondered where the hell they were and what was keeping them.

He could feel the tension coming off Pat. He wanted to suggest that they take a walk around the graveyard but it was not a good idea. Their parents and grandparents were in it and their brothers were not, so either way it couldn't be good.

He had not thought that so many people would gather. Since there was to be no wedding breakfast, he had expected and invited nobody. But he could hear the hum from within and was pleased so many people cared enough to celebrate with them.

The moments went by and Jake had half convinced himself that the bride would not turn up when he heard the sound of Mr Filey's motor. He turned around at that point, made sure that it was so, and then marched his brother into the church. They looked neither to the right nor to the left, though he could see that the church was packed, all the way down to the front where the vicar stood, beaming.

He came forward and greeted them by name, enclosing Pat's hand in both his own. The bride arrived at the door with Kath and Ethan and Mr Black signalled to the organist to strike up. Jake went to the back of the church and accompanied Mercy up the aisle. He could see the encouraging smiles of the people around him.

He got Mercy to the altar. He could feel her trembling as they walked. The music faded. Pat and Mercy did not look at one another. The vicar smiled again, both at them and at the congregation, and the service began. Jake gave the bride away and retreated to his seat beside Kath and Ethan on the front pew. Kath was beaming and Ethan was looking confused. He moved towards Jake and Jake took the boy on to his knee.

He waited for the service to go on. It would not be long. He and Rob had agreed that it must be as short as possible. Pat gave his utterances softly but they could be heard. Mercy was more tentative and just before they got to the bit where the vicar would have pronounced them man and wife, Mercy gazed at him for a second and then turned and ran from the church.

Kath got to her feet and stood for a few seconds, thinking that this could not be happening, that she was dreaming, it was a nightmare. Ethan wriggled in Jake's arms, broke free and ran after her, shouting, 'Mammy, Mammy!'

Kath tried to pretend that she was invisible as she followed. She did not pick up pace until she got outside; the sun had appropriately left the sky

229

and rain was falling in great big sheets that blinded her.

She hurried to the graveyard. She was wearing no coat and was drenched within seconds. The little boy ran screaming to his mother, down by the gate, just outside as though it was sanctuary.

Kath walked slowly towards them and Mercy turned to her.

'I'm sorry,' she said, 'I couldn't do it.'

'We can go back inside.'

Mercy shook her head.

'Why not?' Kath said.

Mercy didn't answer. Kath gazed at her while Mercy's eyes turned to glittering sapphires and salt water began its journey down her cheeks, to shelter in the neck of her dress as though it could hide.

'We must go back,' Kath said.

'I can't.'

'What about Pat? It took everything he had to get here.'

Mercy shook her head.

'I thought I could go through with it.' She set off down the road to where the car was waiting, Ethan screaming at her as she continued to ignore him. Kath ran after her.

'You cannot go, not like this.'

'I will leave. I just need my things.'

'What about Pat?'

The driver got out. Mercy, ignoring him, took Ethan by the hand and began to walk back across to the road which would take them toward Stanhope. She turned left before they reached the middle of the village up toward the house. It was a long climb and she was wearing a dress and already soaked. Kath didn't know whether to follow her or go back into the church. She saw Jake standing in the doorway, looking in vain for his brother's bride.

He came to her.

'Is she coming back in?'

'She's on her way up to the house.'

'What the hell happened?'

She couldn't answer that.

Jake hesitated and she could see that he would have followed but he couldn't leave his brother.

'I'll go,' she said.

Kath gave the driver instructions and they set off. They caught up with Mercy and he stopped the car. Kath got out.

'You're too upset to go further like this and Ethan is in a bad way.'

The child was incoherent with fear; he didn't understand what was happening. His face was soaked in tears and spittle ran down his chin and on to his clothes. His limbs did not seem like his and flailed. Mercy picked him up and walked on.

'Please come back,' Kath begged her. 'You're just frightened. You can't leave Pat like this. It took everything he had to get to the church. Come back and marry him. He's the nicest man in the world. Please, Mercy.'

Mercy stopped. She cradled Ethan in her arms and after a few moments he began to quieten.

'It can be all right,' Kath said, 'I know it can. The car's just there, look, it would only take a couple of minutes. Everybody's waiting.'

Mercy gazed at her from a face that suddenly

looked old. 'I can't marry him,' she said. 'I'm already married.'

Kath took Mercy and Ethan back to the house and then she got into the car and it drove her to the church. There she walked as slowly as she could – considering that she wanted to run inside and drag Pat away from the front without anybody noticing – but the church was full. As she walked down the aisle by herself, heads turned and whispers started, and when she got to the front Jake and Pat were on their feet.

'Where is she?' Jake asked softly.

Kath could see Pat with his arms wrapped around himself. He had seen disaster too often not to recognize it now. He was only just standing, his whole body sagged.

'She's gone back up to the house. This isn't going to happen today.'

Robert Black came across.

'Are we going on?'

'No,' Kath said while Jake stood indecisively.

'Then why don't you take Pat home and I will tell the congregation.'

Mercy ran into the house, lifting up the dress that would impede her progress. She went through the house and up the stairs and into the room which was hers and Kath's. She took a bag from the top of the wardrobe and began throwing into it the little that belonged to her. Ethan was sobbing. Kath caught up with her soon afterwards and stood in the doorway watching her.

'You can't go.'

'I can't stay here.'

'Please, just wait.'

'What for? For Pat to come back here and wonder why he ever asked me? Look at what I've done.'

'You can't leave like this.'

'I can.'

'You don't have any money.'

'Kath, you pay me.'

'You've given most of it back to me for the shop and we're doing that together,' Kath said.

'I suppose you think that they want me here after what I've done.'

She continued to throw things into the bag and when there was nothing else to pack, she took off the dress and put on another. Pulling on her coat and boots, she lugged the bag down the stairs, Ethan sobbing beside her.

As she and Kath reached the bottom Jake came in, his brother by his side. Pat was like something broken, his head as low as it could get and his arms crossed protectively across his front. Mercy let the tears fall again. Pat couldn't move by himself, he needed his brother to hold him up and when they reached the settee Pat slid on to it, like he could go no further.

Mercy's eyes were fixed on the wreck of the man she had tried to marry. Jake advanced, his eyes on fire and fixed on Mercy's face as though he wanted to kill her.

'What were you doing?' he said, his voice soft and menacing.

'Leave it, please,' Kath said.

'What were you thinking of?' he said.

'Jake, don't,' Kath said.

'How could you do this to him? All these years he couldn't go anywhere and today he did it for you. Twelve years it took him to come this far and now look.'

Mercy let the bag slide because she couldn't hold it any longer. The child had cried so much by then that he slumped to the floor too; his mother wasn't taking any notice.

'I'm sorry,' she said, 'I wanted a decent man for myself. My husband left us with nothing. I thought I could stop thinking about him, stop believing that we had been married. I love Pat. I thought I could go through with it. I wanted a place here so very much.'

Nobody said anything.

'You were going to marry my brother while you were still married, after all the help we've given you? How could you betray him like that after the life he's led? His new life was only just beginning.'

'My husband hurt us,' she said. 'Every night he hurt me but when he started to hurt Ethan, I couldn't stand it. I had nobody to help me so I ran. But we are still married. I have no right to Pat, I have no right to anybody.' She picked up the bag once again and lugged it across the floor. Kath went to her and twisted it out of her hands and she glared at Jake.

'Just go,' Jake said, 'and leave us alone so that he has time to get over you.'

'You are not sending her from here with a small child when she has nowhere to go,' Kath said.

Jake turned his hot gaze on her and in that

moment she could have thrown something at him.

'Don't tell me what to do, Kath,' he said.

In a way she was pleased he was arguing with her. The air seemed full of noise and she liked that. She needed violence of some kind and this would do for now. Mercy was hurt and Pat too and there was no justice in it, no pity.

Jake didn't move and he didn't say anything else. He was waiting for her to respond.

'Why not?' she spat back. 'This house isn't yours alone. We work hard and pay bills and you are no more entitled to be here than anybody else so don't say she has to go. We have as much right as you.' She could hear her voice clear in the air. In a way he was giving her room and she was giving him space, like one of those boxing tournaments her father would go to where the contestants moved around and around, watching one another but not attacking. It was as though they needed to lock their gazes before they moved forward or back and she was glad of her own loud voice and not afraid of his and she could not be sorry that they had brought themselves here to this arena when the day had been so hard. It was a release.

'Don't fight over me, please,' Mercy begged.

'You are too keen on what's yours and what isn't,' Kath said, straight into his face.

'She has humiliated my brother!' Jake was shouting now.

'You have no right to tell us what to do.'

There was a long silence. Mercy picked up the bag and as she moved toward the door, Ethan following and in tears, Pat got to his feet. He moved in front of her and stood against the door. He didn't look at her, he looked at the floor and then he said clearly, 'She's not going anywhere without me and I'm not leaving.'

Jake turned around, Kath stared. For a long time, it seemed to her, nobody said anything, nobody moved, but then Pat looked into Mercy's face and he took the bag from her hands and set it aside. He picked up the little boy and then he looked at Jake and there was anger in his eyes.

Kath had never seen Pat this way. Jake saw it too and as Pat urged the woman and the boy back inside, Jake pushed past, hauled open the front door and slammed it after him.

Pat led Mercy and the little boy upstairs but not into his room, into the other room that Mercy and Kath shared, then he closed the door. Kath heard the sneck fall. Then he went across the tiny hall and into his bedroom and he slammed the door shut and after that there was silence.

She ran outside but Jake was gone and the day had turned so dark that she couldn't see. It was so cold that she could barely breathe. It was as though the summer had gone. She went back inside.

When it was very late, Kath told herself to go to bed but she couldn't. She didn't think Jake would come to any harm out there but she was worried. He didn't come back. She finally fell asleep on the couch when the dawn began to break somewhat unevenly upon the unforgiving sharpness of the wind. She woke when she heard him come in.

He went past her without a word.

'Jake,' she said imploringly.

He ignored her.

'Jake, please.'

He went upstairs, opened and closed the bed-room door. Kath followed him. Mercy and Ethan lay still in the bed, though Kath could tell he was asleep and she was not. The fire was cold in the grate. Mercy opened her eyes against the dark-ness. The curtains were open and Kath could see the glint of tears in Mercy's eyes. They didn't even fall, as though she knew she did not deserve the luxury of tears.

'I'm so sorry, Kath,' she said. 'I will go.'

Kath peeled off her clothes and got into bed.

'No, you won't,' she said firmly. 'You make a lot of money around here. You've earned your place. This is just as much your house as anybody else's.'

'Jake didn't mean it, Kath, he was just upset about his brother.'

'We were all upset,' Kath said.

She didn't think she would sleep but she was so exhausted that seconds later she could feel herself falling off the cliff into sweet oblivion.

When Kath awoke a couple of hours later, Mercy was in a deep sleep. She suspected that she had been awake most of the night. Ethan, however, was lying in the gloom awake but not moving. For a small child, she knew that was not good.

She whispered to him to get up. He did so reluctantly and she led him downstairs. He sat on the sofa while she laid and lit the fire. Once it was burning, he came to her and she put her arms around him and whispered into his ear.

'Don't worry,' she said, 'you're not going any-where.'

It would have been the worst thing she could say to a travelling child, but this one needed a place to stay, to live and rely on, and he knew that his security was in doubt. He put his arms around her neck and she gathered him to her, as much for her own feelings as for his.

She heard Jake come down the stairs. His gait was unmistakable. She could feel him glaring across the room at her. That was progress, she thought; she had imagined he would go clashing out of the house like he had last night.

'I'm making some tea shortly,' she offered.

It wasn't true. She couldn't put the kettle on yet, it would take ages to boil. But he sat down sideways at the table and spoke to Ethan.

'Do you know what I'm going to do today?'

Ethan let go of Kath.

'Church?' he said, voice quivering.

'No, I think we had enough of that yesterday,' Jake said and Kath couldn't help smiling at his soft tone. 'I'm going to see Nell and the pups. The pups are really big now. Would you like to come to the farm with me?'

Ethan nodded enthusiastically.

'And I'm taking Uncle Pat. He is going to build Mr White a big, new hen house.'

This was news to Kath.

'Can I come too?' she said.

'No. You yelled at me,' Jake said. 'You have to stay here and peel potatoes.'

If Kath had had anything to hand other than the poker she would have thrown it at him, but she felt better now and smiled to herself.

Ethan ran back upstairs to tell his mother about the pups and the hen house. Kath tried to stop him because she wanted Mercy to sleep, but she didn't want him shouting in protest so she let him go. When the child had gone, she brought herself to look at Jake.

'How is he?'

'He didn't have any nightmares. On the other hand, you don't when your life is complete shite. It takes care of the problem.'

Kath sighed and went to find water for the kettle. She was surprised when he came after her and spoke softly right behind her.

'Kath, I'm sorry.'

She turned around but he didn't meet her eyes.

'You were worried about Pat,' she said.

'I shouldn't have yelled at you.'

'Maybe we each needed somebody to yell at.'

That was when he looked at her and it was almost as if he had touched her face with his fingers. He turned away with a half-smile.

The following evening when all was quiet, Mercy, unable to sleep, trod softly down the stairs only to find a lamp still burning and Pat there alone. He opened the door and stood just outside. It was a lovely night, warm with a soft wind and she could feel the air come in. She turned to sneak back upstairs but he heard her and looked back into the house.

He was smiling at her. She tried to smile back but she felt as if all the joy in her life was over and she shook her head.

'I had better go back upstairs. I remember what happened the last time we met like this.'

'Don't go,' Pat said.

'I don't think talking about any of it will help.'

But she didn't go and she went outside with him and it was so much like before that when he turned and took her into his arms, she nearly sank into them. She came to her senses and pushed back.

'No, don't touch me,' she said.

'I love you. You're the only woman I've ever loved. I don't see why we can't be together.'

'Yes, you do. We can't and that's all there is to it.'

'We can still hold one another.'

'No.' She took another step away.

'I don't mean you any harm.'

'That's what Mack said to me and then we ended up having to get married because I was expecting and I don't want that to happen again.'

'We can go away.'

'I don't want to go away. I've found good things here, not just you, but everybody – Kath and Jake and the people who live around us and the business. I have a life here now.'

'So you'd rather have that than a life with me.'

'I'm sorry for what I did. I thought I could have both but it would have been no better than the first time. I couldn't do it again, lying and thinking things would get better. The only way things get better is if you fight like hell and work every hour that God sends.'

Pat tried to take hold of her again, pleading with her in a soft low voice, but she pulled back even harder this time until he let her go. She was almost crying, she wanted him so much, but she knew how wrong she had been twice now. This was worst of all; she had hurt him so badly. If she had held back in the first place, things would never have come to this. She hated herself for what she had done to the most decent man she had ever known. She almost gave in to his embrace but she knew that she couldn't.

'If we ended up with a bairn in a place like this when we weren't married, it would be the end of respectability for us.'

'I said, we can go away.'

'You, from here? How far could you go?'

'I could go anywhere for you.'

'It still wouldn't make it right and I'm not doing it. How would either of us face Jake again, after all he's done, looking after you all these years.'

'I *know*.'

She could hear the frustration, the pain in his voice.

'I love you,' he said, but his voice broke in the middle of it and he began to sob. He put his hands over his mouth so that nobody would hear him.

'This is my home now,' Mercy said. 'I've been happier here than ever in my life. I'm sure that people here think badly of me for leaving you at the altar. I can't change that, but it was the right thing to do and maybe in time I'll be forgiven for it. I want to bring up my son here. I'm sorry for what I did to you, I wanted you so very much because I love you. I feel more than a hundred

241

times the love for you that I ever felt for Mack, but it can't be because of mistakes I've made. I'm so sorry.'

She ran into the house and up the stairs and found Kath waiting for her on the landing. Kath took Mercy into her arms and there Mercy cried soundlessly so that she should not wake Ethan.

Jake had heard all of this. He had sensitive hearing from a lifetime of listening to animals and his damned bedroom window was always open. He tried putting a pillow over his head but it did no good. Mercy finally clattered upstairs and soon afterwards his brother came too, his feet weary on the stair treads.

Jake feigned sleep. His brother lay down and began to cry very, very quietly.

That Monday Mercy proved difficult to rouse.

'I don't want to go to the shop. There's plenty to do here,' she muttered at Kath.

'There's nothing.'

'I could do a lot more cleaning, washing, ironing and baking.'

'We do that anyway. It's a three-roomed house, how long does it take?'

Mercy stared at her for a few seconds and then turned away. 'I don't want to go,' she said. 'I don't know how to face people after what I did. They'll think I'm horrible.'

'I don't think they will,' Kath said, but she didn't care. She wasn't going to have Mercy hide upstairs. 'Besides, you've already gone through more than a woman should have to. The only way to get people to stop talking is by not giving them anything to talk about. Your absence would just create speculation and fodder.'

Pat and Mercy didn't speak that day. It was a good thing there was only one room downstairs, Kath thought – if there had been more than one, they would have avoided each other entirely. As it was, they didn't look at one another. Pat went off to Mr White's barn and made his new hen hut, even though the wind howled through the buildings because the weather was so wet and blustery.

Thirty-Three

Mr White's sons went on getting drunk every night. How unjust, Jake thought. Mr White should have had good sons like his own father. But then again, his own father had died brokenhearted with two sons dead, one with a lost mind, and the fourth not able to hold the farm together, so who was the worse off? Mr White's sons knew nothing of conflict – they were like children – but were they the worse for that?

Did it take war to make sons into men? It should not have done so – he hadn't gone, after all – but Mr and Mrs White had lean and lined faces full of disappointment.

Jake could not help trying to take that look from them. He yearned to be a decent son and revelled in Mr White's praise, and ate up not only Mrs White's cakes and dinners, but how she looked at

243

him with pleasure.

In a way, his job was dependent on the sons getting drunk and not helping, though he felt guilty about thinking this way. He was only being kept on here because Mr White needed the help.

He sensed that the two lads didn't know what to do and felt a bit lost; maybe they had been up-rooted from somewhere they cared about, maybe one of them had left a lass he loved. Somewhere things had gone wrong and they were going downhill. He wished he could blame the farm for their troubles, but the truth was that until the war, his family had lived here in relative peace for centuries.

He was glad not to be dismissed, however. He knew every blade of grass and all the animals and he had even recovered Nell. The pups, who were big now, would follow him round, thinking they were sheepdogs. He was training them to round up the sheep and to come to a whistle. It was quite funny on a windy day to watch their fleecy coats blowing around.

The local farmers might scoff, but these two were turning into first-rate sheepdogs – though they did still hang round the kitchen door hoping that Mrs White would feed them extras.

Jake would return home late and tell his family about their progress. Pat didn't talk much any more, Mercy was stiff-bodied and Kath had little to say. Only Ethan was normal and his normality had nothing to do with Jake.

Jake didn't have Pat's affinity for small children, he thought, and his irritation wasn't helped by how small the house was. So unless it was pouring with rain, he would go outside when he came back from the farm.

One such evening, when the silence on the tops was peaceful, he heard the door and turned to see that Kath had followed him out with a cup of tea in either hand. He began to wonder what it would be like here when she left, when she married her gypsy boy. How on earth would he manage with Pat and Mercy not getting on and himself the odd one out?

'I didn't think you'd be at the farm quite as much as this any more,' she said.

'Mr White's sons are clowns,' he said, accepting the proferred teacup with a nod of thanks.

'Did they kick you in the playground?'

Jake smiled a little and shook his head.

'It hasn't been a barrel of laughs here, either,' Kath said. 'I've been thinking that maybe we should go to Middlesbrough and see if we can find Mercy's husband.'

It was getting dark outside now but Jake still turned and looked reproachfully at her.

'I'm not going on another one of your excursions,' he said. 'I've still got Appleby to face and your – travelling man.'

'Do you think he will have found Ella? What if he hasn't?'

'I'm more bothered about what happens if he has and he wants you to jump over a broomstick, or whatever it is heathens like you do.'

She thumped his arm. Luckily Jake saw it coming and moved his tea to the other hand so that he wouldn't waste any.

'He'll know I didn't mean it.'

'He didn't look the kind who forgave things,' Jake said.

'I never stop thinking about her.'

'I'm sure he's a man of his word. If he says he'll bring her to you, then he won't fail you.'

Kath let drop the proposed trip to Middles-brough, but Jake – even knowing that it was a fruitless venture – could not help dwelling on the matter and wondering about Mercy's husband. And her aunt at the post office – whom Jake had never liked after she proved what a mean woman she was by not helping Mercy and Ethan at the beginning – had somehow discovered that Mercy's husband was still alive.

The village gossip was that he had appeared on the wedding day – or some such rubbish, Jake thought – and since Mercy had thought him dead for so many years, she was shocked and could not bear to tell Pat and had had to rush from the church as a consequence. It was a lovely scandal for the village and had provided weeks of talk for the women. Jake had been happy for them not to know the truth, which was, in its way, much worse.

It did not occur to them that a woman would run from her husband, no matter how she was treated. Once one was married in church, they stayed married. They believed that Mercy had not left the village to join her husband because he had gone off and she didn't know where he was.

Soon after, Jake learned from another farmer at the mart that Melvin, the older White lad, was getting married since he got a serving maid at one of the local farms into trouble. The only good thing about it, as far as Jake could see, was that Melvin would be moving to Stanley, the pit village up on the hilltop not far from Consett where the lass came from. They would live in her parents' front room until the baby was born and Melvin would become one of their family.

The Whites were embarrassed and heart-broken. Mr White said nothing and Mrs White made so much cake that she ended up giving it to Jake to take home with him. The younger lad, Sam, was quiet and sober. Perhaps he thought he would end up the same, or maybe because his brother was leaving, he knew that their brotherly outings were at an end and he was lonely.

After the hasty wedding in the pit village, things began to settle back down. Sam stayed home by himself and mooched about the farm. One morning he came to Jake when Jake was milking his favourite cow, Emily.

'Could you show me how to do that?'

'Aye,' Jake said in surprise. He had assumed the two lads knew such things and just didn't want to do them, but once he sat Sam down and saw his technique, he realised otherwise. He gave him brief instructions and the lad picked it up straight away, looked pleased with himself. Jake left him to it.

Jake didn't know much about the Whites' back-ground other than they had come from some-where in Teesdale and Mr White had been head stockman at one of Lord Barnard's biggest farms, but he guessed that the two lads had never done any farm work and it was only their father's expectations that had got them to here. Maybe they had been mothered too much, Jake thought, with a twinge of envy. Whatever the cause, the lad had no idea what to do. He asked Sam to collect the eggs and he hesitated as Jake opened the cree.

'I've always been frightened of them. They flap such a lot,' he admitted.

Jake had never heard of such a thing but he went inside. It wasn't too dark and the hens were used to him. He put his hand under one of them and he brought out a perfect oval brown egg. Sam gazed at it.

'That's Phyllis' work for today,' Jake said.

'Hens have names?' Sam said, almost smiling.

'That's Mary,' he said, pointing to another one, 'she's a good one, she won't hurt you.'

Carefully Sam reached into the warmth and he too drew out an egg. He gazed at it like it was a magic trick.

'Miracle, isn't it?' Jake said.

Sam smiled properly this time and Jake found a container in the barn. Mrs White had a wicker basket for such matters but this old pot would do. They gathered up the eggs that some of the hens laid away and Sam was so absorbed in the hunt that they spent longer than Jake's patience would typically allow looking inside and outside all the farm buildings. He sent Sam into the kitchen with the eggs and heard Mrs White's surprised tones turn to pleasure. She was no fool, Jake thought.

That day he kept Sam busy. The lad was soon tired and would have gone to the pub to escape in the early evening, but Jake made him work until the light went and Sam fell gratefully into the farmhouse and went to bed without his supper. Mrs White called Jake into the kitchen, and there to his enormous embarrassment, she got hold of him and kissed him on both cheeks, big warm smacks.

'Oh Jake,' she said, 'your mam would have been so proud of you.'

The following day Sam was up as early as he would have been after going to bed so soon the night before, and Jake called him out of the house and set him to milking. He gave him various other jobs and kept him working for a good two hours before they went in to eat. Sam ate the biggest breakfast that Jake had ever seen and he was eager now to do more. Mr White snorted critically at his enthusiasm.

'You were never good for owt but book work.' Turning to Jake, 'He was in Lord Barnard's office, not a fit job for farm lads.'

'He's got good hands,' Jake said. 'He milked two cows this morning.'

'We had people to do that where we were,' Mr White said and Jake saw for the first time that he imagined this labour was not only beneath himself but beneath his sons. He had come here with the idea of employing somebody like Jake and thought that miraculously, somehow, his sons would turn into gentlemen and have to do nothing. No wonder they had not taken to any of this.

Jake continued to teach Sam. He became so keen that he risked boring even Jake because he talked about it nonstop. He had grown attached to the hens and knew them all by name and had taken to picking them up and cuddling them and stroking their heads. Jake had to admit that though he found it bizarre, their egg production was better than ever.

On mart day, Jake was going with Nell and the pups – not for any particular reason, he had nothing to buy or sell – he just liked to go. It was an old habit and at this point no more than a sociable day off. He asked Sam if he wanted to go and he nodded with excitement. Jake drove them in Mr White's truck with Nell and the pups in the back. Once at St John's Chapel, Jake parked the truck and took Sam into one of the pubs where the farmers gathered, the King's Head, on the main street.

If Jake had had to live in a village, he would have preferred this one above all others. It was no prettier than the rest – all the villages in the dale were lovely – but he liked the community of the mart.

Some of the old men who lived alone and had little company would stay there all day in the pub with one pint, sitting over the fire if it was cold, playing dominoes with a friend or two, or shove halfpenny, watching the smoke from fire and pipes mingle and drift.

It was a three-storey building with views of the fields from its doors and it was friendly. There were three rooms downstairs and on mart days the farmers would spill into the big hall and on fine afternoons even outside. The couple who owned the place were welcoming and kind and the fires were replenished often. The brasses were well-polished, the floors shining.

The bar on the left had a big fireplace and it was this room that Jake took Sam into. It had a polished wooden bar down the right-hand side. There was another room with a piano and small tables and chairs, but the younger members of the farming community gathered here.

'Two pints, no more,' he said to Sam, and then introduced him to several lads of about his own age and went to the bar. Jake then stayed quiet for the most part and was satisfied to see that Sam's beer went untouched as he listened to the lads talk. Some of them were farmers' sons who did not necessarily want to become farmers themselves and he thought it might do Sam good to know he wasn't alone and could try for something else. His enthusiasm at the farm could be just novelty; he was discovering that he could be good at a great number of things, and that in the end he might have some choice.

Even though he had dealt with Pat, Jake had no idea how to show a younger lad what to do. But his experience with Pat at the farm had taught him a lot and he thought it was good for Sam to be among lads his own age who thought of more than beer.

It was for most of them their only sociable day of the month and the talk was the kind that Jake loved best. He took Sam into the other rooms and introduced him to older farmers and other men of the area who had various trades. They were all kind to Sam. No doubt they had heard of his exploits but they were experienced enough to hold nothing against him and kind enough to include him as one of them.

Some knew his father and had known of him when he worked in Teesdale. Jake bought Sam and himself pies, peas and chips.

People scratched Nell's head and laughed at the pups and several of them asked Jake how the pups were getting on and were promised a look at them when they went back to the truck. It was a source of continual joking in the dale that the pups were sheepdogs in trade and poodles in style.

At the end of the day, Jake took Sam back to the farm with him and there Sam milked his cows and they fed the animals and when it was dark they went around with a tilley lamp securing everything. They finally stood leaning against a gate as night came down.

'This isn't what you wanted, is it?' Jake ventured.

'I don't know. I was brought up on a big place where there were lots of farmhands to do everything. It was like there was nowhere for us to be and nothing to do. Then my dad saw that we couldn't have anything there – at least not any future that he wanted – so now we're here. I worked in the estate office back home and I liked it. I was quite sharp at it, but that wasn't good enough. I was nothing but a clerk to him. I miss Mel.'

'Why don't you go over and see him?'

This had not occurred to Sam.

'It isn't that far,' Jake said.

'My dad wouldn't like it.'

'They will when the bairn's born, folk always do. Besides, he's your brother, you should go. I don't think your dad would mind if you asked him in the right way. Why don't I show you how to drive the car I have, and then you can ask your dad if you can go over there? We could talk to Mr Filey about getting you a motor.'

Sam said nothing more that night, but when they had some free time, Jake took him into the field to learn. The weather was dry and there was no fear of the vehicle getting stuck and within a few minutes Sam could drive up and down the pasture.

'Not too close to the water,' Jake said, half joking. 'I don't know what your swimming's like but I can't.'

'I'll be careful. This is easy!' Sam was thrilled. He understood straight away everything Jake was teaching him.

Jake was astonished at how quickly Sam learned and told him he was brilliant. He hadn't thought anybody could learn to drive a car that swiftly. Sam clearly had a lot of abilities that his father did not appreciate.

It occurred to Jake that Mr Filey might take on Sam as a driver. He didn't like to say anything to Mr White, but by the end of the week Sam was actually better than he was, so he talked to Mr Filey and then to Mr White.

'Mr Filey has offered Sam a job.'

Mr White glared at him.

'You've gone behind my back, taught my lad to drive and then got him a job doing something other than farming?'

'But you don't want him on the farm. You got me here instead. He had nothing to do.'

Mr White's face was the same colour as his name.

'You're very free with what you say for some-body your age,' he said.

'Sometimes when you're close to a problem you don't see it like other people do. You said you got this farm for your lads but I don't think you want them farming.'

Mr White hesitated as though he was going to pull Jake's head off, but then he calmed down.

'I'm disappointed,' he confessed. 'I thought they would both run big places like I did, but the agent couldn't help and I thought keeping them on at school would give them other ideas, make them bookish. I wanted them to be gentlemen. Taking over this farm was a bad idea from the start. It was Mrs White, she pushed it. She didn't want them drinking and going with lasses in Barney and now look, we're no better off.'

'Yes, you are. You've got a grandchild on the way, maybe he'll like farming. And Sam is very good at a number of things. You only have to show him a thing once and he can do it. Miss Thompson, the retired schoolteacher who used to teach at the grammar school, takes classes in the evenings, science and such. Her dad was a famous astronomer. You could encourage him to do stuff like that. You never know what he might be capable of.'

Mr White looked sad and somewhat perplexed. They were sitting in the little office opposite the back kitchen.

'I think Sam is a really bright lad. You can't make people want to do things,' Jake said.

'You did it.'

'It came naturally.' He didn't add that he had

had no choice but he was lucky in that he loved farming.

'When I get older, we'll have to leave if he doesn't take over.'

'Sam might have had enough of driving long before then. Or Mel might not like mining. A lot of men would prefer this. If you're honest with yourself, you have to admit you do like it here,' Jake said.

'You help us enjoy it,' Mr White said. 'You make it easy.'

Jake didn't know what to say to that but he couldn't help feeling pleased.

Best of all was Sam's expression when he came into the barn a couple of days later, clearly embarrassed.

'Thanks for taking on my Dad. Mr Filey's given me a full-time job. I get to drive people around the dale and he's going to teach me how to drive the buses. And best of all, I get to learn all about car engines. And I went to see Miss Thompson – she has this telescope at the top of the house and she's teaching me all about stars.'

Thirty-Four

Ella found that being Will's wife meant she wanted to be with Kath even more. She wanted to tell her what had happened and to make sure Kath didn't mind because she had the feeling that if Will asked

255

Kath to marry him now she would have said yes. They had been through a great deal and if Kath had been married to Will when their parents died, they would never have lost one another.

It was not a scenario she liked to bring to mind. She could not imagine why her sister had not wanted him and she could not imagine what it would have been like if she had burned for Will and he had been her brother-in-law. It would have brought endless misery. But now having married him, she missed Kath even more.

Would Kath be angry that Ella had married the man who had loved her, and would she resent all that Ella had? A womanly part of Ella loved to think she had married better than anybody else. She could not but be pleased that other women envied her. Some wouldn't talk to her any more so she had nobody to enthuse with or admire the pretty things that he bought her. She liked having the most successful, most handsome husband, so tall and lean and well-dressed with his glossy hair. She admired his gait and his bearing, she loved his songs and his ability with horses and how he was all hers.

She liked how proud his parents and sisters were of him. But she did want to tell her sister. She wanted Kath to be pleased over her marriage and maybe sometimes she selfishly wanted Kath to envy her.

She kept on mentioning Kath's name to Will. One morning when she was in a bad mood because she was helping his mother to wash the dirty clothes and it had rained when they were hung outside to dry, she brought her up again.

'I told you that I would find her for you,' Will said, with a touch of exasperation.

'But you haven't done it.'

'It's not that easy.'

'Your father could do it, he knows everybody.'

'We have talked to people and set other people on her trail but she could be anywhere by now.'

'She wouldn't. She would never leave this area without me; I know she wouldn't.'

She meant the northeast and northwest; they were in Cumbria just away from the coast.

'It's a very big place here, from the border down to the end of Cumbria and Yorkshire. It'll take some time, Ella.'

'You think she's dead, don't you?' Ella said, gazing miserably at him and he thought this was the real problem. 'You just don't want to tell me that you can't find her. That day I left her – I shall never forget it and I don't want it to be the end of my sister and me and if she is dead, then I need to know. We could go back to that village where I last saw her–'

'Ella, that's miles and miles away. It would take weeks to get there and it would be pointless. She can't be there if she's wanted by the police. She wouldn't go back, she would know you hadn't stayed there.'

'Maybe she's dead then,' Ella said. 'Maybe she died in the snow and I'll have lost everybody,' and she burst into tears and ran away, sobbing.

Will swore under his breath and then his mother came out of her wagon. She never missed a trick.

'What have you done to that lass now?' she

said, as though he was guilty of upsetting his wife daily.

'She wants me to find her sister.'

'She wants you to try.'

'I have.'

'No, you haven't. I don't think you want to find her.'

'Why would I want that?'

'Because she wouldn't have you and because she probably wouldn't have wanted her sister to marry you.'

'That doesn't make sense.'

'That's because you're a man. Get yourself after her. Go on.'

So Will had to pretend to go searching for her, though he could have located her in hours. He brought news, first that she was alive and had lived on a farm, and now that she had moved. His spies knew all about her, they knew that she was living with that woolly-backed farmer as his wife.

Thirty-Five

Jake was still thinking about going to Middlesbrough. He didn't understand why his mind had changed and cursed Kath silently for having put the thought into his head, but he kept turning the idea over and over. He found it hard to bear, Mercy and Pat going about with dark faces.

Ethan had become a horrible little boy, kicking at everything and crying a lot. Jake was not surprised; children must know when the adults around them are seriously unhappy. Mercy worked hard and was always at the shop and he threw tantrums to get her attention. He had worked out that if he lay on the floor and kicked and screamed she would stop what she was doing and pick him up and talk softly to him.

Pat was still whittling away at wood, making toys for the shop, and there came the odd commission for furniture. Having completed the bigger hen house at the farm, he continued to work there. Mr White seemed happy to have him around, there was plenty of space, and he brought with him a strange calm. And Mrs White always liked having young men at her table, like they were her sons. Pat felt at home just as Jake did. Also Jake was around a good deal and kept popping into the barn where Pat was working so between that and the shop he was fully engaged.

Stanhope was the wrong place for Pat's skills, Jake thought.

He could have done with a bigger town like Bishop Auckland where there was more call for such items. Here people had no money or made their own or made do. They would rather have old or secondhand furniture which was much cheaper.

The evenings at the little house grew longer and longer when there was nothing to do, but the farm beckoned. The work on the farm went on late when evenings were light and he preferred to be there anyway. Mrs White would feed them at six and he would go on working until it was dark, Pat by a big lamp in the barn when dusk fell.

Jake was not sure whether he created the work or whether it was just there. He would have given a great deal to live back at the farm and deny the difficult parts of his home life which had nothing to do with him.

Pat, however, was beginning to lose his grip on reality. He was fine at work but he spent longer and longer staring into the fire at night, not acknowledging anyone's presence. He rarely spoke to Mercy, nor she to him. Kath got Jake outside one evening. It was late and dark by then and the others had gone to bed.

'I don't know what to do about Pat,' she said. 'I think maybe we should go to Middlesbrough and see what we can find out about Mercy's husband. I'm not sure it will make any difference but I can't think of anything else and at least it would be something to do.'

Jake was grateful to her for thinking about his brother when he knew that she worried enough about her sister. He too had been thinking that there must be some way that the situation could be bettered, but he didn't know what it was.

The trouble was when Jake went to bed he couldn't sleep. Pat didn't sleep either. He hadn't slept properly in weeks, Jake acknowledged to himself now. He wasn't having nightmares but he lay there in the darkness and worried. Finally in the darkest hour of the night, Jake turned toward him.

'Do you think we should go to Middlesbrough?' he asked.

Pat didn't answer at first.

'What for?' he said finally and there was such tension in the reply that Jake almost shut up.

'Well, I just thought it might help if we knew–'

'Knew what?'

'I don't know. Maybe somebody threw Mercy's man into the Tees and–'

'Don't be stupid, Jake. We don't even know where she comes from. Middlesbrough's a big place.'

'Couldn't we find out?'

'Why don't you just leave it? This is because we aren't speaking, isn't it? Damn well leave it, will you?'

Pat turned over. Jake knew that he wasn't asleep by the rigid way that he lay there. Jake always thought there was a solution to every problem and he couldn't shake this one. He lay there wishing the dawn would come sooner than it did and then wishing it wouldn't because he was tired now. He felt trapped, like he would live in this awful little house forever as surely as he had lost the farm.

He decided not to mention the idea to Pat any more. It wouldn't do to get him riled up; it was a ridiculous idea. But the trouble was that the more he tried to put it from his mind, the more he thought about it.

One Sunday when Mercy and Ethan were still at church and Pat was out taking a walk, Jake decided to talk to Kath about it.

He came inside and closed the door. She turned half in protest and then saw his face and put down the coal bucket. She had been heaving coal at the back of the fireplace, ready to pull forward as the flames faltered.

She didn't say anything.

'I was just thinking, you know, Kath, about Middlesbrough.'

'I thought you didn't want to do it.'

'I mentioned it to Pat but it's too far a reach for his head, if you know what I mean.'

She nodded and he saw how open she was to the idea. That was what he loved best about her, that she was always ready to go on. Was that the traveller in her?

'One of us should go to the post office and try to find out where they lived,' Jake said.

'You mean me.'

'It would look funny me going in there and asking questions when I never did.'

Kath was rather pleased; she thought that he had dismissed her idea without thinking about it. She was glad too that he had mentioned it to Pat. Even though he thought no good had come of that, he had sown the idea in Pat's mind and maybe Pat, who thought that Jake could do anything, would be glad if there was a positive result. If there wasn't, he would at least acknowledge that they had tried.

In a way, though Pat's love for Mercy had turned out to be yet another difficult thing he had to bear, it also made him into an adult again. He had taken the idea that he couldn't have her and borne it, and still he was kind to her. She responded with her own kindness but it was a fragile thing and Kath wasn't sure how long it would last under the pressure.

She knew they weren't more than friendly with each other; that was one advantage of the tiny house. There could be no sneaking across landings, meetings behind bushes in gardens. There was nowhere for Mercy and Pat to be alone and they did not attempt to contrive it. They silently acknowledged, she knew, that it could not end well.

Kath and Mercy were always busy in Stanhope now that their shop was open for business. Pat had finished the tables and chairs for outside and Jake had dug up a lot of plants from the farm garden. He had been given stone troughs by Mr White which he had planted so that they were pretty with marguerites and all kinds of flowers. Pots and containers all over the garden were filled with blues and pinks and whites and lilacs.

Mercy and Kath bought lengths of blue and white material and made tablecloths. They bought tiny vases and Jake took herbs from the farm garden at Mrs White's insistence. She even came and helped and said how much she admired what they were doing.

She loved the shop and the little café and she made coffee and walnut, chocolate and ribbon cakes. Jake thought her involvement in the café offset her disappointment about her sons though things were going better there. One was now happy driving a bus and taxis and the other came over often with his wife at weekends. She was pleased enough with this and could turn to other things.

One good thing had come of Pat and Mercy's

not-quite-wedding: a lot of people from the dale had seen Mercy's dress and told their friends and neighbours about it. It had since provided a stream of customers through the doors of the shop, wanting dresses for brides and bridesmaids and outfits for other occasions.

One woman asked Kath if she thought she could fashion her a professional costume – she was a businesswoman in Durham and liked the work she had seen them do and wanted them to make a suit for her. The woman had a carpet factory in Durham and loved the colours of the dales. Kath protested that she had never made such a thing.

'You know, like they made Harris tweed for the autumn. I know that sounds pretentious but I love the heather and the green of the fields and the yellow flowers. I want you to find the right material and put together a suit so that when I do business in the town, I look serious about it.'

Kath said she would do it and then worried. She scoured the various markets for the material until she found exactly what she wanted. After she made it, the woman was so pleased that she ordered two lighter suits for summer and two more for winter. Business then flowed in from other women who worked outside the home and wanted to look sharp.

Kath worried about the trip to Middlesbrough and how to obtain sufficient information from Mercy's aunt so that they had somewhere to start from. How on earth would she broach the subject? She couldn't just walk in and ask for Mercy's address. Maybe she hadn't even lived in Middlesbrough, maybe it was Stockton or Normanby. The ironworks covered a great deal of ground, as did the huge docks and lots of other industries. There were too many places to cover. There was nothing for it: she had to talk to Mrs Paterson.

She let Jake drive her to the edge of the village and she went into the post office to buy stationery to write to her mythical relatives in Northumberland. She needed a pen, too, and by the time the postmistress had found these things for her they were in accord. Mrs Paterson was smiling and asking politely about Mercy, even though it was common knowledge that she had called Mercy a scheming, deceitful woman after Pat and Mercy failed to marry.

'I hear you're doing very well in your little shop,' she said.

Kath hated her for calling it 'little' but she smiled sweetly.

'We are selling afternoon teas. You must come. Mrs White is making the cakes.'

Mrs White by this time had become known for her mouthwatering confections which she contributed to church fundraisers and local festivities. A number of people in the queue nodded their heads, though most were enjoying the gossip which related to Mercy. Kath, aware of the silence which had fallen, was quite enjoying herself.

'Mercy has written to relatives and they are promising to come and visit. They have a motor now, you see.'

The postmistress stared.

'A motor? The last I heard, her family hadn't a

penny to their name. Her father and my father worked at the ironworks, and her husband too, until he drank so much that they wouldn't keep him on.'

Kath leaned closer and so did the whole queue.

'I think it is her husband's family. I don't know much about them.'

'They are dreadful people and I don't suppose for a second that they are doing anything other than telling huge lies. Don't take any notice, Miss Armstrong, they've never gone further than Cannon Street in the heart of Middlesbrough. She's well out of it, lucky lass, for all she's done wrong.'

'Cannon Street?'

'Somewhere just off there. It's a great long road. Sometimes I miss the town. We used to go to the Café Royal on Linthorpe Road before the war. I never thought I'd end up in a place like this, running a post office and keeping Jackie Paterson's family, and him dead all this time. I weren't short of menfriends; I could have done much better than this, looking back. Eh, I remember the first electric tram–'

Kath was eager to get Mrs Paterson back to the subject as she continued to bring nostalgic views of Middlesbrough to people who rarely ventured further south than Bishop Auckland.

'My mother came from Acklam...'

'Cannon Street,' Kath put in. 'It rings a bell with me.'

'Mercy should never have gone down there. Hilda's Place. Folk knew he couldn't be good coming from there. St Hilda's was the worst place in the town, a terrible yard,' and Mrs Pater-

266

son shuddered.

Kath went off with paper, envelopes and a pen she didn't need. She was pleased with her sleuthing: their search had been narrowed down to one street, though it was in a big town with the industry around it. She went back to the car where Jake was waiting and told him.

'It's not enough, I know,' she said, 'but if I could get Mercy to talk about it, I could find out more or less where it is we need to go.'

'No, she would be sure to work it out,' he said. 'We need to just go and try and find it. We'll say Mr White has asked me to go to a farm sale for him and you are going to look at some market or other. We'll think of something.'

Middlesbrough was a town that Kath had been to before but only on the outskirts. She remembered Darlington and Stockton but Middlesbrough had always been too big a centre, not the place for traders of horses and the like. It was industrial, the ironworks, the steelworks, the docks and all the mess and business of a big town, and it scared her.

She couldn't possibly have gone there without Jake. He didn't seem bothered about how overwhelming it all was. The centre was very big with lots of grand buildings, shops and trams, the streets full of fairly prosperous people. But there were many poor streets where the workers from the iron- and steelworks lived, near the river and beside the railway and the docks. It was dirty and had about it an air of people overworked and badly paid, skinny, scantily-clad children, narrow back streets and dark alleys.

There were street names but they weren't always to be seen and she didn't want to ask anyone – it was such a big place that it seemed pointless. However, after a long time of going up and down various streets, they came across a post office, and Jake, very sensibly stopped the car and said he thought they might know. She got directions to Cannon Street but when they arrived, they soon saw a new problem: it was a great long road, and so many streets led off it at both sides that they were soon lost again looking for St Hilda's.

The streets became poorer and darker and the rainy day didn't help. The railway was at one side and the river beyond it followed by big gasworks towers. The streets were narrow and dismal and then just as suddenly as they had turned all the corners, they found it. Hilda's Place. She stared, appalled.

The street was so narrow that Jake hesitated and stopped the car and she saw what Mrs Paterson had meant when she said that it was a yard. It had no way out at one end and on a day such as this one, it made her want to turn and run for home. It was dark and smelled of rotting sewage and old vegetables and there was sludgy water on the ground. A child stood in the open doorway of a house and was so ragged that he was near naked, his face so dirty that she could barely see him.

The doors and windows were rotted and almost falling out and the stonework was dislodged as though it had been hastily contrived and not meant to last; it had gone a long way beyond its intended lifetime.

She got out and approached an old man, smiled and asked him if he knew of a man called Potts.

'Mack Potts? Aye, he's always around somewhere.'

'Any particular house you know of?'

The old man smiled and shook his head and walked away.

'What are we going to do?' she said, getting back in the car.

'If we knock at doors, people will wonder what we're doing.'

'We could say he's been left some money.'

She frowned at him.

'You'd better do that.'

So he did. She sat and tried to look unobtrusive, but cars in such an area were rare and everybody stared as they walked by. She thought that Jake was a very long time. When he got back in the car she waited and when he didn't say anything, she got impatient.

'Don't they know where he is?'

'Oh aye, since there's money involved, they all know where he is but they will need money to find him.'

That made her laugh.

'We should've known.'

'There's an empty house at the end and that's where he used to live.'

'How did you find that out?'

'An old lady. She just pointed and shook her head and said his wife, wherever she was, was better off without him and she hoped he would never find her.'

It was getting late and the sun was fading. People had gone home for tea and there was no way that Jake and Kath could get home and come back the next day. He looked at her.

'We need to stay here.'

'I'm not staying here, Jake, it's awful.'

'We can find a nicer part of town, but we can't go all the way back home. Tomorrow we need to go to that house and find out everything we can, and I saw a pub at the other end of the street that we can ask around. We'll see what we can find out.'

Kath sighed.

'We need to find somewhere respectable.'

'Kath, somewhere respectable will never take us. We should just aim for not dangerous.'

She glared at him.

'Even if we have a room each?'

'That's a lot of money.'

'I'm not spending the night with you,' she protested.

'I don't believe I asked you to. And since you are more or less promised to that gypsy, you have nothing to worry about. When I take up with a lass, it won't be somebody else's.'

Kath was stung by this and it didn't matter that he was quite right.

'Give me that ring then,' she said briskly.

He handed over the little ring he wore on his smallest finger when he was not at work.

'It's my dad's signet ring.'

'I'm not going to pinch it, I'm just going to put it on and turn it round so it looks like a wedding band.'

They drove east and then south away from the town and its industry, and came to a little place beside the sea. It was a tiny village with a pub between two hills, nestled in the valley high above the water mark but closer to the waves than any other building. They parked the car and got out. The sun was just disappearing and the sea was flat.

It was a lovely evening. Kath could hear the waves; they always made her think of Northumberland and Ella and her parents. Nobody questioned them but then, only well-to-do people had motors and it was a good-looking one at that. Jake had cleaned it for the occasion and she had never seen it so shiny; she had always thought of it as a workhorse until now. No wonder it looked so out of place around here.

They sat outside and drank beer and watched the tide and went for a walk before it got dark. She liked that. She wasn't afraid to spend the night in the same room; she knew he would go to sleep and not notice her. He was used to sharing with Pat.

They went inside and ate an indifferent stew, then went upstairs to the room. To her delight, it faced the sea. She wasn't tired and sat watching as the moon rose high above the water.

'Look at it, Jake,' she said and when he didn't respond she glanced back; it looked like he had fallen asleep on the bed.

She went back and lay down.

'Jake,' she said.

'Go to sleep, Kath,' he said and turned over away from her in case she talked any more.

271

She had never thought about sleeping alongside a man; it was very odd. He didn't snore, which she was thankful for – sometimes both he and Pat did and she could hear it through the walls – and he didn't move much. Maybe he was so tired that he lay down and that was it.

She didn't fall sleep. She could hear the waves crashing on the shore and she liked it so much she wanted to see it again. She got up and went back to the window.

'Are you all right?' he said softly.

She jumped.

'I thought you were asleep.'

'You moved.'

'Does it matter?'

'No, it's just that to farmers movement means sheep are having lambs or there's a storm or–'

'I'm not having lambs,' she said and was rewarded with a slight chuckle. 'I'm just looking at the moon. It's a long time since I was by the sea and I miss it.'

'When you make your fortune, you can buy a house here.'

'What would you do if you made a fortune?'

'Buy the farm.'

'Is that because you want to or because you think you should?'

He didn't answer for a few seconds.

'I'm not sure. It was always the same thing.'

'Maybe you're meant to do something your family hasn't done.'

'I was thinking about it,' he said.

'What do you mean?'

He turned over and propped himself up on his elbow and looked at her. For once it was serious, she could tell.

'If things work out and Mercy and Pat end up together and you get back with your travelling man, I could go to Canada or Australia or somewhere. There'd be nothing to stop me.'

Kath was astonished. She hadn't known he was thinking anything of the kind. Every time he spoke about Will or she thought about him, it made her feel nervous, on edge, as though her stomach was about to give up.

'You would leave without Pat?'

'He wouldn't need me if he had Mercy and Ethan.'

This had not occurred to her. Nobody spoke for a long time after that, and he lay down and turned over away from her again. She was becoming sleepy and wanted to get into bed but she was still a bit nervous. She knew that she was being ridiculous and he would never touch her so she pulled off most of her clothes and slid inside the covers. Jake appeared to be asleep just where he was. She wasn't sure but it didn't matter. She felt safe here and fell asleep listening to the sound of the waves breaking softly upon the sand.

When she awoke it was full morning and he had gone. She got up and looked out of the window. The tide was well in. He was standing, looking out to sea. He wasn't used to the seashore, she knew, and he looked as though he liked it. She pulled on her clothes and ran down the stairs and outside.

He turned around when she reached him.

'Do you wish you had a horse so that you could race the waves?'

'That's exactly what I wish,' she replied.

'Your Will knows a lot about horses. He'll most likely buy you one,' Jake said.

Her heart pounded and to stop it she changed the subject.

'My father's horse was called Diamond and he was the most beautiful animal on earth.'

Jake looked gravely at her.

'Are you telling me he was more beautiful than Nell?'

She laughed.

'He couldn't have been,' she said and they walked back up the beach to breakfast.

The houses in the streets nearest to St Hilda's Place were a sorry lot and the one on the end beside the wall where apparently Mercy had lived was the darkest and smallest of all. It was also empty. When they got to the door, it was not locked and she could see why. The glass from the windows lay in great shards on the dirty floors. The furniture was nothing more than a table and chairs, so frail that no one had bothered to loot them. The fireplace was full of soot and the smell was cloying.

Downstairs were two small rooms and upstairs the same, but there was nothing to suggest that Mercy and Ethan and her husband had ever lived there. Kath believed – though it could have been because she knew Mercy – that there was an overwhelming sense of misery in the place.

'I don't like it,' she said to Jake.

The wind howled around the far end of the street and she was glad to go outside. She thought she might never forget the smell of poverty, the squalor, the cold, bare empty rooms, the gritty floors and how small and mean it was and how it stank so that you could barely breathe without choking.

They had left the car at the far end of the road, so having driven around the area, they went into a pub, The Vulcan on Denmark Street. The landlord jerked his chin at the window.

'Is that your motor?'

'Borrowed,' Jake said and the landlord shook his head in admiration. That put them on an even footing, Kath thought. Jake certainly had foresight.

'Canny,' the landlord allowed.

'Aye,' Jake said. He leaned over the bar and said gently, 'Do you know a man called Mack Potts? We were told he used to drink around here and his family wants to find him.'

'He used to come in here a lot a while back,' the landlord said as Jake asked him for beer and ordered Kath a gin and tonic, whatever that was. She watched fascinated as the drink came all fizzy and clear and in a round glass with a stalk sticking out of it.

'You never know who's coming or going,' the landlord said. 'We have all sorts here, you know, and it's hard keeping track of them. We have more temples, mosques and churches than any place you can think of.' He drew himself up tall as he said this. He was proud of his hometown and its inhabitants and why not, Kath thought, how

275

fascinating to meet so many people from so many different places.

'I think he went to Saltburn the last time I saw him,' the landlord said. 'He had relatives there, well, he said he had. If his money hadn't been good, I would have barred him. He was always making trouble and the lass he married,' the landlord shook his head, 'she was a lovely lass but eh, she should never have married him. This is the trouble when you're young, you think the world belongs to you.'

'Saltburn, you say?'

'Aye, it could be Emerald Street, or Ruby Street, or summat daft like that.'

Jake thanked him and carried the drinks over to a table by the window.

'Where is Saltburn?' Kath said.

'It must be near the sea,' he said and smiled just a little as he tasted his beer.

Kath thought the gin and tonic very strange. To her it tasted as perfume might; it was horrible. It reminded her of the Spanish gypsies and their red wine and though she had tasted little of that, she thought it tasted better than this fizzy stuff.

'Why did you get me this?'

'It was the only thing I could think of besides beer and I needed to spend money with him since he was so helpful.'

After they finished their drinks – Kath coughing dramatically at every torturous sip – she stood up. 'Come on, let's go.' She set off and left him to follow and when he didn't, she waited outside. 'What were you doing?' she said when he finally reached her.

'Getting directions.'

Saltburn was some miles down the coast but it was a lovely town, right on the sea, and the Victorian buildings were big and brash and well put together, with hotels everywhere. It was a proper holiday place, she thought, where people stayed in the summer. Her father had always shied away from these. He did not think that travellers would be welcome.

There were several streets which led away from the front and one of these was Sapphire Street. Jake parked the car and they began to ask door to door whether anybody knew of Mack Potts. Halfway down the street, they got lucky. The woman sighed at her open door. She was big and fat and obviously poor by her dress and the lines on her face.

'Aye, he was here at one time,' she said, 'but I don't know where he is now.'

'Are you related to him?'

'Oh aye,' she said, 'I'm his wife.'

Kath tried not to stare. Mercy's husband had been married to another woman? It couldn't be true, this woman must be forty and he had to be younger than that.

'He buggered off and left me. Three bairns we had, half-grown now. I've got another feller now but it was hard.'

'You were married to him?'

'St Patrick's Church, Cannon Street. I'm Pearl Potts. Aye, it sounds daft and it were daft; the worst thing I ever did was wedding that bugger,' she said and she slammed the door.

Kath and Jake walked slowly back to the car.

'Do you think she was telling the truth?' Kath said.

'Would she have any reason to lie?'

'But I can remember Mercy saying they were married at this really nice church, close to where they lived.'

'And it was called?'

'I can't remember now or maybe she didn't say.'

They motored back to Middlesbrough, to Cannon Street, and there they found St Patrick's. It was huge – or looked huge to her because she had not been inside many churches and the one she now attended was very small. This was brick built and seemed to tower over the whole area.

They knocked on the door of the house beside it, where presumably the priest lived. A tall slender woman answered the door, smiling. She let them in and took them through into a study where the priest sat at a large desk covered in papers.

Kath was losing her awe of religious men thanks to knowing Robert Black quite well by this time, and she no longer saw them as scary and beyond her ken. This man was quite elderly but he smiled kindly at them and beckoned them to sit. His housekeeper brought them tea and biscuits while they explained that they were looking for the marriage records of Mack Potts.

'I married them,' he said, 'I remember very well. She was called Miss Pearl Michaels then, as far as I can remember. How are they?'

This was difficult and both Kath and Jake hesitated. Eventually Jake said, 'We believe he might

278

have married again. We're trying to find out so that there is no mistake.'

'Married again?' the priest frowned. 'Did Mrs Potts die?'

'No. She's living by the coast with three children, but he isn't there.'

The priest went on frowning and then he said, 'I think you had better tell me the rest.' Jake did and the old man listened without speaking until the tale was done.

'I think your friend has been led up the garden path, so to speak. Mr Potts, as a Catholic, couldn't marry again while he had a wife living, and it must be ten years since I married them. Perhaps a ceremony took place but no respectable cleric would do such a thing. None of the churches here would countenance it if they knew. But this is a big town and there are several churches, and we have different religions here owing to the fact that this is a port town, so it's possible he could have found one that would perform the ceremony. But it would have been illegal and fraudulent. This poor second woman has no marriage.'

It was late afternoon when they finally got back. Mercy was cooking. She looked up in relief.

'Wherever have you been? We were so worried when you didn't come back last night. How busy are farm sales, even that far away?'

Pat came in too, Ethan with him, and Kath and Jake sat down and told them exactly where they had been and what they were doing. She thought that Mercy would be pleased, overjoyed, grateful, and when none of these expressions appeared on her face Kath sat back, the tea cold in her cup since she had not stopped talking since it was poured.

'You went there without saying anything to me?' Mercy's face was dark and straight.

'We didn't know what we would find.'

'So now I know that I was never married, that's supposed to make me feel better?'

'We thought–'

Mercy got up and began clearing the dishes and then she put them back down and went outside.

Kath put down her cup and saucer and followed Mercy. It was pouring rain. How very typical, she thought. Mercy was crying, her back turned and her shoulders hunched.

'I'm sorry,' Kath said, 'I just wanted to help.'

'You can't imagine how this makes me feel. He never cared about me, he only pretended to marry me because I was pregnant with his bairn while he already had a wife and three children. I was the biggest fool in the whole world.'

'But you didn't know. She doesn't even live there and it's such a big place.'

'Nobody told me, not his drunken bloody father or his friends. My God, they must have had such a laugh at me. Nobody cared enough to try to stop me, but then I was expecting so what else could he do but deceive me. Being on your own in a place like that with a bairn is the worst thing that can happen to a woman.'

Mercy stopped crying and blew her nose.

'He must have been nothing but a bairn when he married her. I wonder how many other children he has.'

Thirty-Six

Ella began throwing up in the mornings. By then she and Will had the wagon to themselves and he had to admit, she kept it spotless. They travelled with his parents mostly but sometimes with younger people. There was another set of young couples and he liked that, he liked that it wasn't his old drinking cronies. They had laughed at him for taking on a wife, though they were in line to do the same.

'Not that she isn't a bonny piece,' one of them said, 'but now you're paying for two dinners to get one of them cooked when your Ma did it for nowt.'

Will wasn't always happy with the arrangement, sometimes he wanted to go off drinking with his friends, but the trouble was that when he suggested it, Ella merely nodded and told him what a good idea it was – she didn't intend to be the sort of wife who would let a man neglect his mates. He went with them, got drunk, and instead of shouting at him when he came back at three in the morning, she was sympathetic and took care of him. Going out with his friends no longer had any zest to it; he just felt guilty at his poor behaviour.

He was concerned, however, when she became ill and pale, and he went to his mother. They had been away from his parents for a couple of weeks

281

and he thought that Ella, caring about his parents so much, might have minded. But Ella didn't seem bothered who was around. She sang and cleaned the caravan – she loved it so much – and he liked how everything shone and how appreciative she was. Her cooking skills improved every day.

She never expected presents when he went away so it gave him particular pleasure to buy them for her. She was so delighted with whatever he gave her, and beamed her smiles on him and kissed him and told him that he was the most wonderful husband on earth. He never left her overnight except when his mother and her friends were there to keep her company.

He often worried about her – she seemed blissfully unaware of danger – and he found himself wanting to look after her, to make certain she was not distressed in any way. His wife was so damned near perfect and she adored him so much that it disconcerted him. Her eyes shone when she looked at him, she admired everything he said and everything he did. Nightly in his arms she told him how much she loved him, that he was the only man she had ever loved. She would love him forever and ever. He had not thought he could make anybody so very happy. He was beyond thrilled with his match.

He wanted to get his mother by herself to ask her about the changes he noticed in Ella's health. It was a difficult task with the girls around but his two sisters, who were the nearest in age to him and married, swept them out of the way and he found himself with her outside the caravan.

She was busy of course, as she always was, this time washing clothes. It was a complicated business because the fire had to be kept high and the clothes steeped in boiling water, dunked with soap, then rinsed and squeezed and put on lines, and all the time she was saying how glad she was that the sun had come out and it was not as cold as it had been recently. Could he ever remember a colder spring and early summer?

'Do you think Ella's all right, Ma?'

His mother looked up from where she was pushing clothes into the hot water with a long stick. Her face was red with exertion and slick with sweat.

'What do you mean?' she said.

'She isn't well.'

'She was a bit pale last night but she didn't say anything.'

'She's been sick.'

'Sick?' His mother looked at him.

'Really sick.'

'Every day?'

'For the last few days, every morning, and she's not herself. She's ... difficult.'

He didn't like to say that since his wife was never difficult, but she had shouted at him three times that week. It had never happened before and he had actually been cowed.

His mother bent over her knees for a few seconds, shaking with laughter.

'Oh Will,' she said affectionately, 'all these babies I've had, and you've never noticed.'

Will stared at her.

'But she can't be.'

283

'Why not?'

'Well, she – she just can't, not yet. We're barely married.'

The whole idea made him want to run away. He stood for a long time and could have howled like a child. He couldn't be a parent, he couldn't be a father, that would make him like his own father, old and responsible and, oh my God, she could have lots of children and then he would never get away. He stood, taking this thought and tossing it around in his mind. He had not thought about leaving her before. There was no reason for it. He felt trapped.

'Maybe it isn't that,' his mother soothed, 'it could be just a stomach upset, I'll go and talk to her.' When she had finished the washing, wrung it all out and got her two elder daughters to hang it on the line, she went off to Ella and Will's caravan. There she asked her daughter-in-law about her illness.

'I feel fine,' Ella said. 'It's just that as soon as I wake up I want to be sick.'

'I think you're having a baby.'

Ella stared at her. They were sitting outside the caravan and despite the pale weather, the sun beat down.

'It's nothing to worry about. You're young and strong, it'll be fine.'

'Does Will know? What does he think?' Ella's eyes were full of tears and Will's mother couldn't tell her the truth, that he was horrified and appalled, as most young men were, as his father had been at first. Will's mother put an arm around her.

'Don't you worry,' she said. 'We'll look after you and I'll be there when the baby comes, along with all of our friends. Between us, we know everything there is to know about babies. This sickness will pass and I will make mint tea for you which will help, and give you ginger to chew, and you will do very little work until you feel less tired, and you will soon. I'll send the girls over to help and in the meantime, you must rest. The first time I was pregnant I was so tired. Sleep now and your energy will come back.'

Word got round that Ella was pregnant. Will's single friends laughed and clapped him on the back and told him how clever he was. Will liked being the object of their admiration but he didn't want to get drunk with them when they invited him out.

'You can go out and celebrate, you know,' she told him. 'I don't mind.'

'I don't like to leave you.'

'Your mother and all the other women are here. I am well looked after and I have nothing to do. And I'm tired, I just want to go to bed,' she said and kissed him.

He went but the beer would not go down. He left his friends celebrating in the pub and stood outside. He shouldn't have been out, it was a horrible night, the rain was throwing itself sideways into the River Ouse. He was just beyond it. He walked over and could see that the river was swirling and turning itself inside out and he thought how easy it would be just to walk into it; since he couldn't swim he would go down after a few panicking breaths.

He stood there amid the noise of the full river and something turned in him. He had done this to show Kath that he despised her. He had used her sister and his actions had borne such fruit that he was glad. He could not wait to see her face when she saw that he had not only married Ella, but made her big with his child by Appleby fair.

He laughed in glee at the idea. What good fortune. Kath had tried to better him and he had hated her for it. Why should he put up with the likes of her? He had offered her marriage and she had turned him down. It smarted more and more as he considered it. When she saw Ella with his child, she would regret every second of what she had done.

She did not know that destiny and the past were coiled together as surely as men and women in marriage. She had defied these things and therefore she was entitled to nothing, and he was about to give her more than nothing to show her that she could not treat him in such a way. He would give her a shock such as she would never recover from.

He went out drinking night after night that week. Ella did not complain but his father came to him, and he wished they had not been in the same camp.

'Are you all right, Will? Ella is looked after and it's unlikely that any harm can come to her, but you know unpredictable things can happen and it's good to be ready. That's why we're here, within distance of a doctor.'

Will muttered that he did know.

'Then why ... this?'

They had moved on from York and he was glad, he had hated so much of it, sometimes he thought he would choke for loss of freedom. They were camped outside Harrogate. Why did they bother with it at all? It was a dreadful place, full of self-satisfied people. The travellers' women did not go into town. The men went to pubs on the river and were welcomed there by the landlords because they had a great deal of money, but that was the only thing going for it. He had been there every night, drinking brandy and remembering why he had done what he had done and being glad of it.

Sober now before his father, he could not meet the older man's eyes.

'I didn't see that I would be a father so soon.'

'I was a father of two at your age. It will be all right. She is the loveliest girl that I have ever seen.'

Will wanted to shout and say that she was not as lovely as Kath. Kath had been the loveliest girl in the entire world and he had wanted her so badly that he could not get beyond it. Every time he thought of her, he sought revenge, and he was about to exact the kind of revenge that would send angels screaming back to heaven.

He was glad of it and terrified at who he had become.

When he came in, Ella would awaken and speak his name so sweetly that he could sleep and forget and justify it all, counting down the seconds to when he would be able to show Kath what she had done. It was all her fault, it was all her doing.

Thirty-Seven

Pat thought a great deal about what had happened in Middlesbrough and though little was said since Mercy had become so upset, he went on thinking about it. He didn't understand why nobody spoke about the fact that there was now no reason why he and Mercy should not be married.

She had changed since the news, since she saw that she had never been married. He thought she had been upset about the fact that she had deceived him over their wedding. She had been ashamed, and even though he would have given anything to have gone away with her, she would not agree to it. He was glad in some ways; he was worried that if he moved away, the old Pat would come back and he would end up in hell again and this time for good. So he had accepted her decision though it hurt him dearly.

But now he could not understand why they should not marry. She was so obviously hurt by what Mack Potts had done that she grew silent and Ethan with her. She would not even go for walks. Pat still read and took the little boy to bed but she had stopped thanking him, stopped including him in her conversation. He doubted she even noticed he was there any longer.

He wanted to get over her, but he still wished that he had somebody of his own, and perhaps a child. Surely that was natural, it was another step forward. Men of his age had children who were almost grown up. Now he seemed to have no one. He didn't think he had ever been as lonely.

That night Ethan screamed and cried and Pat went in to comfort him as he often did. Mercy came bounding up the stairs a moment later.

'What did you do to him?' she accused, reaching for the boy. Ethan went sobbing into her arms and Pat was so astonished that he couldn't say anything. He went back downstairs and after that he did not offer to take the little boy to bed anymore.

Several days later they were working at the shop and he was trying to make a particularly difficult chair and felt as though he wanted to throw it through the window. Kath went out on some errand and left him there with Mercy.

'I didn't do anything,' he said.

She glanced around. She was busy and had a mouth full of pins.

'What?'

'The other night. You said about Ethan, "what did you do to him?" I didn't do anything.'

She concentrated hard on the material she was pinning.

'I know. I'm sorry, I was just tired. You're so good with him. Bairns are hard work.'

'I suppose. Does it mean I can't read him a story any more when he goes to bed?'

'Of course not.'

That evening as usual he picked Ethan and the storybook up, but Ethan screamed and fought and kicked him. Pat put him down and he ran to his mother. She took him to bed and when she came back down, she found Pat alone by the fire.

'It's nothing to do with you, bairns take on like that all the time.'

'It doesn't feel like that. It's like he knows things aren't right.'

'What do you mean?'

Pat looked at her.

'Do you really not know?'

'Know what?'

'We could be married now,' he said.

She stared at him and then she looked down at her worn red hands and she said, 'We've been through all that.'

'Not since Jake and Kath found out that you hadn't been married. It changes everything. We could get married, find a nice little house here, bring up Ethan and maybe even have more children. Don't you want more children? Don't you want to marry me?'

She didn't answer. She stood there for what felt like an age to him and then she said awkwardly, 'After what he did to me you think I want to marry again?'

'I'm not like him!'

'I know.' She still didn't look at him. 'But for the first time in my life, I can see my way forward. I don't need to marry, I'm not afraid or expecting a child or poor, and I have Kath and my own skills to thank for that. I don't think I'd be willing to give that up for anybody.'

'But you were.'

'Things were different then.'

Pat couldn't understand and worse than that,

he wanted to cry. He left the shop without a word and began to walk by the river. He could see now that he had no place here. What would he do?

He didn't come back. When Jake came in with some material for her, he enquired after his brother and she managed to say, red-faced, 'We had a – a row.'

'A row?'

She looked blankly at him.

'He wants us to be married. I can't do that.'

Kath arrived in time to hear this and to see Jake glare at Mercy.

'My God, Mercy, I ache for the day when you know your own mind!'

He crashed out of the shop.

Kath looked at Mercy and she explained.

'Weren't you expecting Pat to say something?' Kath said.

'I kept pretending to myself that he wouldn't and then I tried to persuade myself that I did want to marry him but I don't, I can't. I don't ever want to be put into that situation again, where I can't control where I go and what I do and how I bring up my child and how I spend my money. I know it sounds unfair and that Pat is a lovely man, but I think I only wanted him because I thought I needed somebody to see out for me and my boy. But I don't and that's all there is to it.'

Pat wasn't far. Jake was so relieved. He no longer had Nell to help him when Pat went off like that, though he hadn't done it in ages – and to be fair,

291

hadn't really accomplished it now – but then the house was too far away for him to make it on foot and that was something to be grateful for. He glanced around when he heard Jake, who sat down beside him on the grass on the riverbank.

'She thought I was going to hurt Ethan, like those awful men who like children too much.'

'No, she didn't. You wouldn't hurt anybody.'

'I killed men in the war.'

'Weren't they trying to kill you? That's different.'

'I feel as if I've gone into another war now,' Pat said.

'There are other women.'

His brother looked at Jake with almost amused affection and he said, looking more like himself than he had in years, 'Oh Jake, don't talk soft. I've got work to do.' And then he went off to the shop, leaving his brother bewildered in his wake.

It was time to go to Appleby but Kath hesitated. She didn't want to leave Pat and Mercy here on their own. She also wanted Jake to go with her and yet there was no reason why he should. Pat was silent so much of the time now that they were both worried about him and Mercy crept about as though she had done him harm.

'I don't think you should come with me to Appleby,' she said, several days before they were due to set off. 'I don't think you should leave Pat and I don't think Ella will even be there, so I could just go for one day and come back.'

'And how are you going to get there?'

'There'll be a train.'

He laughed in scorn.

'It would take forever.'

'All right, but I still don't think you should leave Pat here.'

'I've looked after him for years, he'll be fine for a few days on his own. I don't want you going there alone.'

'Then I won't go. Ella won't be there. Why would she be? Sometimes I think she died up on the fell and she's lying there, dead and forgotten.' Kath got up from the table and began to throw dirty dishes into the sink to hide the tears she was holding back from Jake.

'I'll take you,' he said, coming to her and turning her to him.

'What if something happens when we aren't here? What if it's too much for Pat and he does something awful, like kills himself?' She didn't realise she was going to cry and when it came it was a veritable storm.

'You are being terribly morbid tonight. None of that's going to happen and I'm not letting you go by yourself,' he said, holding her to him. She liked being there, it was so warm and safe.

'I'll stay here,' she offered.

He released her so that he could look into her face.

'No, you won't. Pat's a lot stronger, and he needs to be given time to be himself. You need to find Ella. We haven't managed it and neither has anybody else. We're going.'

'But—'

'Nobody can cover everything, no matter how they try. This is for Ella.' As he let go of her, Kath felt a wrench. She wanted to be close to him again; he smelled of the country, of hay and stars, and she longed to put her hands into his hair.

'This has to be the last time,' she said. 'If nothing happens and I have no news of her, I must accept that I'm not going to, even though I don't want to – I want to go on hoping forever. Having lost my parents, I don't want to lose Ella, too.'

For a week before they went she couldn't sleep and she couldn't think of anything else. She told herself over and over that she was being ridiculous, that she could always change her mind and stay at home.

Pat was still getting up and working in the mornings but on difficult days he retreated upstairs by noon. Mercy was sombre and silent. It made Kath want to stay and mediate but she knew that she had to try to find Ella once more. These people mattered to her so very much but her sister mattered most of all.

Every night she planned to talk to Jake in the morning and cancel the trip and each morning she changed her mind and didn't say a word. She began to panic as the days counted down. Now that the time was fast approaching, she was dreading it. And yet the day that they set out was the loveliest day of the year.

She enjoyed the drive, she had nothing to do but watch from the window at summer taking over the dale. It was only when they finally reached Appleby that she felt nauseous. It was the day before the big horse sale. The streets were thronged with men standing outside the pubs, jostling one another into the road.

Kath and Jake walked around the river and it

was just like it had been. She could almost have believed that her parents and Ella were somewhere nearby but her heart ached.

She couldn't see Will or his father, but she could see now that a lot of these people didn't recognise or remember her. Time was passing and she had another life. It was all long gone.

They left the car and went into a hotel nearby where Jake asked for two rooms. She hadn't even been thinking about it, she was wholly focused on the idea of how she would face Will and whether her sister would be there. She was all excitement and anguish. She was certain he had found her sister, sure that she would see her again, but would he keep her to her stupid promise? Of course he wouldn't. Therefore she said nothing to Jake. They had a quiet dinner and said very little to one another. She went upstairs and felt that she had never been more alone than this.

Half a dozen times she nearly went and knocked on his door and each time she stopped herself. It didn't seem fair somehow, though she couldn't work it out. It hadn't been like this in Middlesbrough, but somehow in Middlesbrough he had seemed like somebody different. No, she thought, he seemed like somebody different now. In Middlesbrough he was himself. Here he wasn't.

On top of that it was such a lovely evening, far too nice to be stuck in a hotel room alone. She opened the window and could hear the sound of a Spanish guitar. She remembered being younger and walking about the streets here, her mother buying pretty bangles for her, blue and pink, and a lilac-coloured shawl. She remembered Ella being little and skipping along the pavements and their father throwing her up into the air and catching her when she came down, laughing and hugging her to him.

She panicked. She wanted to go and bang on Jake's door again but she couldn't. It wasn't right, she had to remind herself that he wasn't hers, he might even have gone out and found a girl and had a few pints of beer. It sounded so unlike him that she quashed the thought. Then she decided that he had not done such things previously because he had not had the opportunity, and now perhaps he had, and why shouldn't he take advantage of it?

What kind of girl would he like? He had no experience, she hoped he wouldn't get drunk and go with a girl who was dirty. She lay listening for sound but since his room was across the hall she couldn't hear anything. She convinced herself that he had gone out. Anybody would on such a beautiful night.

Travellers would be lighting their fires and there would be dancing, singing and feasting. She missed it more than she ever had and suddenly she couldn't stay in her room any longer and flung herself down the stairs, out of the door and into the street.

It would not get dark, being early summer. The skies at that time of year were light; perhaps that was why this horse fair had come about. It was about getting together and having a good time after the trials of the winter, and now there was all the daylight anybody could reach for.

She didn't know what to do. It was mid evening

and the men were drunk, laughing and shouting. She shouldn't be out there. It was the time when fights started and the police arrived. She hoped Jake wasn't in it. She went back to the quiet and the hotel owner, a woman with a kind face, said, 'Are you all right, my dear?'

'I just wondered whether Mr Sutherland had gone out?'

'A couple of hours ago. It's such a lovely evening.'

Kath went upstairs, lay down on the bed and tried to sleep. After a long while she thought she heard the door open and close over the landing. She wanted to get up and go to him but she couldn't. She didn't think it was fair. He was nothing to do with her, she couldn't ask him about his comings and goings. What if he had a girl with him?

She waited, listening, but there was no sound. In the end she couldn't stop herself from going across the landing and knocking softly on the door.

'Jake?'

'Kath?' He opened it quickly, his face full of concern. 'Are you all right?'

She peered inside, really concerned now. What had he done?

'Come in,' he offered.

She had the better room – his was on the back and though the night was warm and the window was open, it didn't have the same appeal. The noise here was not as at the front where she felt as if she was missing a party, though considering her mood, it might have been easier had she had the back room.

'Did you go out?' she said.

'Just for a walk and I met this lad, I'd seen him before at St John's show every year and I knew he bred sheepdogs so we had a couple of pints.'

Kath looked gravely at him.

'You told him about Nell and Ephraim and the pups.'

'He was amazed when I told him what good sheepdogs poodles are.'

Kath sat down on the bed and laughed. She hadn't laughed for days and it felt so sweet.

'What?' he said, frowning. 'You were all right, weren't you? I would have asked you to go with me but you looked so tired. If I'd known you wanted to come–'

'To talk about poodles?' She smiled at him. His face was so reassuring.

'You're worried about tomorrow, aren't you?' he said, sitting down on the bed beside her. 'It'll be all right, you know. I think he's a man of his word. You will see your sister and it will make you happy.'

'It won't make me want to marry him,' she said. 'I never did want to marry him.'

'He won't expect it. How could he? It was just a way of getting you here.'

Kath was trembling.

'You won't go anywhere without me?' she said. 'I'm so scared. What if he hasn't found her?'

'If he hasn't, then we will.'

'But we couldn't. What if she's dead?'

'You would have known by now.'

She looked into his face.

'You're so kind.'

'No, I'm not. I just think you would've felt it.'

The following morning they went into town to watch the boys parading the horses up and down the main street. She spied Will's father, talking to several other men, but he didn't see her. Then she saw Will, nearer, standing by the river. They made their way over to him. He stopped talking when he heard her say his name. He turned towards her and her insides went cool.

He had changed. He was a swaggering man now and it was a different thing than a swaggering lad, and not nearly as attractive. Will was clearly the most important man in town, expensively dressed, so at home there that he merely smiled in acknowledgement at the farm boy he despised. Jake nodded and said nothing.

Will greeted her with politeness and that was all. She was relieved that any feeling he might have had for her appeared to be gone. She would not have to marry him.

She asked him about Ella and he said that he had had news of her.

'You found her! Is she far away? Is she all right? Where can I find her?'

'She's just as good as ever – in fact, you might say better.'

'How did you find her?'

He told her about Darlington and said that some friends of his father had been looking after her and they were bringing her to Appleby.

'They've been very kind to her and have promised that Ella will be here tonight.'

She smiled into his face and kissed him on the cheek and said how grateful she was to him.

'And you could meet my wife.'

Kath stood back and suddenly the day was even brighter with sunshine than it had been.

'You married?' She beamed on him and it was as though a huge weight lifted off her heart. 'Oh, I'm so glad for you. How wonderful.'

'I'm very happy with my choice. We'll be going back for supper mid evening. You must both come.'

She accepted the invitation, thanked him and they moved on. She wanted to sing and dance but she didn't want to do such a thing in front of Jake. She felt as if a bubble was bursting inside her. Ella was there, and Will was good and kind and he had done what he had said he would without her stupid promise.

She was thrilled when she realised that she had brought a suitable dress to wear to the camp. She had made it herself. It was full length but low over her breasts and off her shoulders. She had never thought herself as beguiling but if she did, it would be in this dress.

At the hotel she tried it on behind a room divider while Jake hung over the balcony in her room and regarded the main street with more concentration than she thought appropriate.

'Is something happening out there?' she enquired, finally stepping out.

He turned around and then stopped and stared. She was pleased at first at how he regarded her and then uncomfortable when he did not speak.

He made a kind of gesture with his hands.

'That's – that's amazing.'

'Do you think I should wear something else?' She didn't have anything else and she thought she would have killed him if he had said that he thought it was not a good idea.

'No, no,' he said hastily, 'it's perfect.'

They set out for Fair Hill. Jake insisted on taking the car.

'It's a lovely evening, why shouldn't we walk?' she said.

'I would just rather not.'

'You walk almost everywhere.'

'By the time we get away, from what you've told me of these evenings, it's going to be very late. Will you want to walk back then?'

Kath shrugged. She didn't really care, she was so excited. It would be like the old days, with people singing and lots of music and wine and good food; she might even get up and dance. She thought of the fire on a summer evening, the grass dry, the air still and some woman's or man's sweet voice lifting in song on what slight breeze there might be.

There were two ways in to the camp once you turned off the main road and she wasn't sure where Will's caravan was. She knew instinctively that he had his own wagon, so she directed Jake to take the left fork; if his caravan wasn't there it would be easy to go the other way.

She couldn't see his parents' caravan, which always stood out because it was so much shinier than everybody else's and had a gleaming motor beside it. Nothing like that was here but she could guess which one must be Will's; it was a smaller but just as flashy model. She could see the couples outside their wagons and was surprised. She had thought most of the men would still be in town rather than here with their little ones and their wives and she was impressed. Things had changed.

There were no older people about and although that was unusual, she liked that the younger people were with their children. She could almost imagine that her parents were somewhere about, maybe in the other part of the camp with Will's parents, laughing and talking, drinking and dancing.

It was very quiet. No movement, no music, no kind of gathering.

The car moved toward the caravans and she could see Will. Jake drove as near as he could and then he turned the car around so that it was facing the road out. Will saw them and waved and came across.

'There you are,' he said, hugging her.

'It's lovely to be here,' she said.

She thought there would have been a party going by now but nobody was sitting around the fire outside Will's caravan that she could see. She had the awful feeling that she and Jake were somehow intruding and had come at the wrong time. She drew back.

'Are you about to eat?' she said. 'We should have waited.'

She thought they had been invited to eat and drink and celebrate the evening but she was starting to feel uneasy. She had never heard of tightness among travellers – they were always open handed, even if they had little. And poorness was clearly not the case here: these people were prosperous, the women well-dressed and the caravans shiny and new. But there was nothing generous about it.

She looked around and there were suddenly lots of men but no women. How strange, she thought, and the children also disappeared. She caught a glimpse of one or two as their young mothers lifted them up and took them away. It was almost deserted. She had a strange feeling of apprehension.

'Your parents aren't here?' she said.

'They're over the other side of the hill.'

'I was hoping to see them.'

'I did tell them you were coming.'

'I can see your caravan,' she said, laughing and trying to shrug off her sense of foreboding. 'It's always the best one.'

It was very handsome, just like him, so, smiling, she followed him. She had been right, it was an expensive wagon with a new car beside it. A woman stood over it, checking the food, her back to them, a slight figure. Will's wife, no doubt, wearing a dress of shimmering blue, so expensive that Kath felt momentarily envious. She had waist-length golden hair shiny down her back, just the kind of girl that Kath had thought he would choose; she was glad for him.

Will's wife would have a good stove inside, Kath knew, but she was right to cook and serve their meal outside on such a fair evening. Hopefully soon the musicians would play, the wine would flow and everybody would be singing and happy. Why would you stay inside when every nerve of you wanted to be out? The food smelled very good; no doubt she was making something special in their honour.

Kath wondered whether his wife was anybody she had known. Lots of girls would have been glad to marry him; he was such a catch.

Then the girl straightened and turned around. She was big with child, about six months along, and held her hands across her stomach in protection as pregnant women so often did. Her face was thin and her eyes were troubled and grey rather than the blue they had always been but when she looked at Kath, it was as though they had known one another for a thousand years.

Kath's heart did horrible, unbelievable things and she felt dizzy, her whole life impossible. The girl that Will had married was her beloved sister and she was having his child. Kath cried out, crumpled, and would have fallen had Jake not caught and steadied her around her waist.

'Ella,' was all she could say, gazing across the space between them; it was huge like an ocean.

The girl stared as though she didn't know who Kath was.

'Ella, it's Kath.'

The girl's eyes registered her with joyous disbelief but still she didn't move. Kath looked at the swelling of her sister's stomach and then she whipped around as Will said, 'What do you think of my wife?'

Kath, had she had a weapon about her, would have tried to kill him at that moment. Then she understood and wished as she had never wished anything in her life that it was not so. She saw the excitement in his eyes, how he had anticipated this meeting, planned it, executed it and was now gloating, his eyes like jet, his mouth a thin, smirking line.

'Oh God, Will,' she said, feeling sick and not believing what was happening. Then knowing coldly that it was, 'How could you do this to us? How could you treat my sister this way?'

He was so gleeful that he almost danced and his eyes shone as he went across to his wife and grabbed her close to him.

'You thought I couldn't love anybody but you?' he taunted Kath.

She stared at him. Her heart felt as if it was trying to crawl out of her body, trying to get away from what he had done. It was despicable. He had betrayed their origins, their honour, their customs, their whole way of life. She couldn't speak. She didn't understand.

'Ella's not much more than a child.'

'She's old enough to bear me a son, as you can see.'

Kath went on staring at him. She couldn't move. She wanted to go to her sister but sensed that she could not. Her first instinct was to take her sister out of the situation but when she looked around, she saw that she couldn't. She was surrounded by Wills friends. The women stayed inside their caravans and the whole place was deserted except for the young men. He had planned this, it was clear to her now.

None of the decent men that she had known

305

were there. He had chosen his new friends so carefully. He had tricked her, had meant to hurt her very badly because she had rejected him. He could have hurt her, she would have accepted that, but why did he have to hurt Ella, who had never damaged anyone in her life, and after all they had gone through?

'We fell in love,' he said.

For some stupid reason Kath wanted to believe him, she wanted to think that her sister was happy. But when she looked at the distance between them, as Ella realised what was happening, the tears spilled down her pale face and her expression was one of lost hope. Ella knew, as Kath did, that he had done this for revenge, that he had hurt them both to the fullest extent that he could. Kath could not stop looking at her sister, could not move her gaze. Why had he hurt Ella so much?

His eyes glinted in triumph, and Kath could see the men moving closer. She felt trapped, stupid. How could she have believed him? How could she have let herself and Jake be lured here like this? For the first time ever amongst her own kind she was afraid, and saw that she did not matter, she was not one of them any more. They didn't care about her or her sister. These people had seemed like her family but it was gone. They were not the men she had grown up with, he had chosen those who felt as he did.

She could not see a way out. Her heart raced and she was on the verge of panic. How on earth was she to rescue her sister from this situation? How would any of them get out without more pain, more regret? She had trusted a man who wished her nothing but ill and who had done the cruellest thing he could have to her sister.

Will advanced, his face screwed up with triumph, gleeful, laughing. Ella came forward toward Kath but only as far as her husband would allow because he caught and held her. Ella looked up into his face in confusion as though he was a stranger. She said nothing, just gazed at him in despair.

Ella was so much taller than Kath remembered and now she was looking at him from brimming eyes.

'You married me for revenge?' Ella asked.

He didn't reply.

'Answer me!' Ella screamed, struggling, twisting to be free, her thin arms flailing, her eyes raining. Yet he held her fast.

'What can you do?' he said. 'You're my wife now, you will stay with me, you will do as I command. You're having my son.'

'You did this to me because of my *sister?*' Nobody could have mistaken the catch in her voice.

'Why, what can you do to alter any of it? What can you possibly achieve now? She's here and her stupid shepherd boy had no more sense than to come with her. You are mine and you will stay here with me and be my wife and have my children. You will be satisfied with that and I will be glad that every time I look at you you don't look like her.'

'You bastard!' Kath said.

Will stared and saw the face of the girl he had wanted, had desired beyond anything. He had loved her. She was so beautiful, she was possibly the most beautiful thing that he had ever seen, and he hated her for it, he hated her for denying him. He glared at her.

'There's nothing you can do,' he said. 'You gave everything up for your farm boy. You betrayed me and us and everything that we stand for. You went and lived with him.' He jerked his chin scornfully at Jake. 'How many times has he had you? You gave yourself to an outsider. You're his whore. You don't deserve for any of us to care about you. You have betrayed us.'

Kath saw Ella's face, stunned, and so pale that she thought her sister might faint. She had no idea what to do now, yet how could she leave Ella there?

Will moved towards her, his hands cruel about her sister's swollen form. She wanted to move backward but she couldn't; her heart was pounding horribly as though the night was over, as though everything was done.

He moved in such a menacing way and she was scared though she tried not to let him see it. He came almost to her and then halted and she saw the glee in his eyes. He had bettered her and won and he knew it. He didn't care about Ella or her or anybody else, all he cared about was winning. Her sister had stopped struggling, like a bird resigned to a tiny cage. Her head was down and her whole body was defeated.

Kath felt so sick that she could have passed out but she stood there, defying him, watching him, until she saw that the other men were moving slowly toward her and Jake like an army. She was so afraid that she felt dizzy. Will came nearer.

'Be careful,' he said, 'or would you like to see your farm boy with his bits in his gob?' It was such a disgustingly awful thing to say but she couldn't react – the men stood in a semi-circle to Will's right and left. Soon there would be no way out. She was forgetting how to breathe. She had brought Jake into this and God knew how they would ever get out. Her sister would have to stay and there was nothing to be done but attempt to retreat.

Her sister's small wavering voice sobbed her name and Kath reached for her but Will blocked her. She froze and Ella cried almost uncontrollably. Her body started to sag in sorrow as she held her arms protectively over her unborn child. Kath had to watch her, the sobs and the choked breathing and the tears that spilled.

'Let me go to her.'

'You will never hold her. You will never come close again.'

Kath wanted to bargain with him, to say conciliatory words, but she couldn't think of anything that would help.

Ella seemed to recollect herself. She pulled herself up, drew back and said in a calm way, though her voice trembled and then broke, 'Leave it, Kath, it's done.'

'You want to stay here with him?'

Her sister's gaze wavered just for a second.

'He's my husband, I have no choice. Please go away and take that lad with you or they will treat you both badly.'

'I'm not leaving you here,' Kath said.

'You must.'

Kath wanted to break down and cry but she knew that nothing would come of it and she would not give him the satisfaction. She could not leave Ella there, no matter what it cost, but she knew that they might hurt Jake and she could not ask him to protect them now.

Beside her Jake said softly, 'Come back to the car, easy now. Don't look behind you.'

She understood. There was nothing left to do but attempt to get out of here without further hurt.

He would try to get them both into the motor and away, she knew. It was why he had turned the car around in the first place. How sensible. She was so afraid that they wouldn't be able to get out of there, but Jake's presence was calming and she did as he told her, and was surprised that it was such a short walk away. They would never make it, though – the men were coming towards her in such a way that she was forgetting how to move.

When she got to the car door, she could see from the corner of her eye Jake reaching into the back of the car. She hadn't even noticed that the back door nearer to him was open. He was directly beside it and as she watched, he took from it the shotgun she had seen him hunt with so often. She was astonished.

One second the gun was broken over his arm and the next he had flicked his elbow so that it clicked shut with possibly the most reassuring sound in the world. In seconds the whole situation changed. His eyes were cool and level as she gazed at him, astonished. The men backed up with due respect and she understood as much as they did.

He had killed crows with it when they pecked at the lambs' eyes. She had seen him pick off rabbits as they decimated a garden and pigeons when they scavenged a field of greens. No foxes ever came near his hen house. He was considered a very fine shot in the dale – he could take two birds in the air, travelling in different directions – but she had never seen him like this and it made her shiver.

She had learned respect for firearms. Jake kept two shotguns and a rifle. The shotguns were for moving targets but the rifle was more deadly at a distance. Today it didn't really matter. A bullet from a rifle could kill, but a shotgun cartridge exploding into Will would make a terrible mess.

She knew that for hunting deer Jake put in cartridges that exploded differently since their insides were bigger. It was slower, more lethal and would impact in a narrower way to do more harm, spreading close and damaging a bigger target. A man and a deer were alike in that way, she felt sure, though by the look on Will's face he might never move again. The colour had drained away and she saw fear in his eyes. He did not know and had badly underestimated his enemy. She didn't think that Jake had ever pointed a gun at a man before; he was always preaching how important it was to carry it broken over your arm and never ever aim at anything you were not intending to hit.

She saw and understood the power of firearms for the first time. She was half-ashamed at being happy to see it, yet the relief she felt made up for it. And strangest of all, she did not for a single second fear for her sister. Hope began to make its way through her, tiny yet, but present. She felt sure he had chosen the shotgun because it looked so fearsome. He needed his enemy to be afraid and Will was, she could see. His eyes betrayed it with their unsteady glance once belief had taken over. Even if Jake didn't intend to kill him, he might not be a good shot and at that distance, inaccuracy could cost his life.

Jake didn't move. He just watched in a long and reaching way, as though if anybody flinched he would fire the weapon, and a deep silence came over the men.

Will's eyes wavered and he pretended scorn.

'You aren't going to use that,' he said. 'You might hit my wife.'

Jake smiled, sure of himself.

'I can knock a bird from the sky that you can't even see. From here I could take both your knee-caps with no bother and if you pulled your wife in front of you, as you seem keen on doing, I could take off the top of your head. Your brains, such as they are, would dissipate into a nasty red heap in the air before they even drenched the grass.' Jake's voice was low and cool and convincing. 'And since you are a gypsy,' Jake said the word with relish as though he knew it would anger the men further, 'your word means nothing here. When I explain to the police that you tried to detain a woman you were not legally married to and had so obviously kidnapped, forced and made pregnant while she was underage, I don't think your chances of them taking your side would be big, do you, even if you were still alive? Some of them would think I was doing them a favour if I killed you. Nobody in Appleby wants people like you here.'

Will was sweating. Kath could see the moisture sliding down his cheeks and she was savagely glad. Jake kept his eyes on his opponent but he said to Ella, who had by now almost wriggled from Will's hold that had lessened significantly during his speech, 'Ella, do you want to come with us?'

She hesitated and then nodded.

'Let her go,' he said and as Will hesitated, Jake lifted the shotgun to his shoulder and sighted it neatly at his enemy's head. Will released her.

'Have you anything left in the wagon that you value?' Jake said. She shook her head and the tears slipped down her face like rain.

'Come to your sister, then,' he said, so very softly.

She ran across and Kath gathered her sister into her arms and they backed towards the car. Jake urged them inside and watching carefully, only half turning, he got into the driving seat. He rested the gun barrel on the open passenger window, across Kath's lap. She gripped it carefully.

The car skidded when he put his foot to the accelerator and the dried mud sprayed up behind them, great clods of it, three feet high. He urged the car forward until he had driven it well out of the camp, on to the road and beyond.

Thirty-Eight

Will was awoken by the sound of his wagon door being hauled open and a voice he could not mistake barking at him.

'Where are you, you bugger?' and his father came into the varda, hauled him out of bed, and to Will's horror and astonishment, began to beat him with a horsewhip.

He had never done such a thing before. Will could remember a few clips round the ear when he had been young and threats of further punishment, but his father had never actually beaten him before. He proceeded to do so now with such thoroughness that one would have thought he was an expert at it. His father, who never hurt an animal, who never even argued with his wife, who adored his daughters and was so proud of his children, beat his only son until Will screamed with pain, begging him over and over to stop.

His father didn't stop until the anger had abated, until he stood there, exhausted and breathing hard.

'You are no longer my son. Your mother is disgusted with you and so am I. We don't want to see your face again. Don't go near Ella or Kath and don't you dare come anywhere close to your sisters. You are dead to us, you complete and utter bastard.'

Will knew at that how serious his father was

because he would never call anybody a bastard, especially not his own, most precious child. Mr Hern left him there on the floor.

When his father had gone, all Will could do was lie there in the kind of pain he had never experienced, and cry. Why did his father not understand that he had loved Kath to the exclusion of all else? He had wanted her so much that he didn't see anybody clearly. Although he thought Ella was a perfectly good person, all he had seen when he saw her was revenge and how he could not have what he had most wanted in life. His father was to blame. His father had taught him that he could have anything and everything and now it seemed that he could not.

He lay and wished all kinds of horrible things on his father and mother for leaving him there. He could barely move for the pain. He fell asleep in the middle of his crying and with the memory of what his father had said. He was so tired that the pain came back at him in his dreams. He was hurt, he was dying and nobody would help him. He was falling off a cliff.

When he awoke, his back and sides were a searing hell. He could hardly move. He only got up when he had to because his bladder was full. When it was emptied he went back and lay down again and did not move for a long time. He didn't notice the light or the darkness but he was unrepentant. He knew that Kath would never be happy without him. He knew that Ella would have his child alone and that she would be sorry she had ever crossed him. With luck he had made their lives a complete misery. He was glad.

He relived and relished the bit of their meeting where Kath had looked stricken and her sister had cried and leaned over, six months pregnant as she was. She was his. He had had her first, she would always be his in so many ways, and Kath would never forget that she had refused him. She would always remember this day and what he had done.

He did not think about the rest of it, when he was bested by the farm boy. He stopped the story at his success and went back to how he felt. He cried again and wished he had not had parents and wished he had not had sisters and wished he had not been kind to them or made his parents proud of him. He had done what he had to do to maintain the proud man he was and they should be glad of it.

His mother received his father back into her arms. There were only two girls left now and she was glad of that. They were both asleep and she was grateful they did not see her husband crying over his only son who had betrayed them in the most basic way possible.

The sisters were at the back of their big caravan and didn't hear him but then he was barely coherent. He smothered his cries against her neck. Eventually he spoke.

'What did we do that he should turn out so badly?'

'We did the best that we could.'

'How could he do such a thing to those girls?'

'I don't know.'

'I prided myself and my family on our honour.'

She said nothing; she held him close and she too felt guilty. He was her only son and he had done something that was beyond her comprehension. She could not go to him, she could not forgive him, she could never see him again and the pain was almost unbearable.

Eventually her husband grew heavy. He had gone to sleep. She shifted him slightly so that she had enough space to go to sleep too. She knew that it was the only way to get beyond such grief. Sleep healed. She knew also that word would soon get around and that the two married daughters would be back. She would be pleased to see them, they could bring some comfort to their parents, but the more she thought about Ella the more she wanted to cry. She was such a lovely girl, she had been just like another daughter to them.

Will lay there for several days. He made sure that the door was locked and opened it to no one, even though he heard the sounds of his friends calling his name and banging on the door. He did not want them to see that his father had beaten and cast him out.

After several days when he could move, he got up in the middle of the night, harnessed one horse and left with his wagon. He took with him nothing else, not the car that his father had bought for him, nor his other horses.

He travelled for several days until he reached a place that he did not know and then he left the wagon locked and the horse tethered by the side of the road. He went into the nearest pub and drank himself stupid. When he was about to slide to the floor and couldn't see, he barged back to the wagon and went inside.

The next night when he would have done the same, the landlord spied him.

'You're not coming in here,' he said. 'I can do without customers like you.'

'I have money.'

'I don't care if you're chancellor of the exchequer, you don't come into my pub and behave like that. This is a respectable place.'

'Can I have something to take out?'

The landlord allowed that so Will bought two bottles of whisky and went back to the caravan. He did that the next night and the one after it and the one after that and then he awoke one morning and felt different. He could face the world again. Not his parents, but he had friends in various places and knew where they would gather. He set off and made for just beyond Carlisle. Not many people went that far but he had friends who gathered there; he was glad when he reached the sea and found two familiar caravans, parked with some he didn't know.

His friends greeted him with pleasure, those who thought he had done the right thing, that the two girls deserved what they got. Will didn't talk about what his father had done. He was happy to be there, pleased to be the man he was, proud of himself. And there he stayed, not drinking nearly as much, eating what his friends' wives fed him and glorying in his freedom.

He had been there for a couple of weeks when a band of Spanish gypsies arrived. They were friends of friends and Will took to them immediately. They brought red wine and good food and they would dance and sing. The women were very beautiful, like Kath but not stupid or prudish, and one in particular he began to talk to. He knew some Spanish, his parents had had Spanish friends from his childhood, and they liked that he spoke their language and that he could dance and sing. She was called Rosa, which was so close to Kath's mother's name that he thought it was an omen.

She seemed to belong to no one and when he asked, he learned she was not respectable, she was a whore. He asked her into his caravan when it was late. She tapped him on the chest.

'I need money first.'

'All right then,' Will said and he took a big wad of notes out of his pocket. 'There, that's for the night.'

She looked at the money and then looked at him. She took it and followed him into the caravan.

Thirty-Nine

Ella was silent all the way back to Weardale and Kath was relieved. She didn't know what to say. There were so many things wrong that her mind was in a muddle.

She wished it hadn't been so far. Every minute was hard and when they finally reached Stanhope, the rain was pouring down, obscuring the view from their tiny house up on the tops which was the only good thing about it.

Ella wouldn't think it small, at least Kath didn't imagine so. Her sister stood in front of the house as though she couldn't see it, like she couldn't see anything. Kath urged her inside. Pat, Mercy and Ethan were downstairs waiting but they didn't know how to react; the homecoming was nothing like any of them had imagined.

Kath sat her sister down without introduction. Mercy, sensibly, offered them tea and ginger cake. Kath thought that if she had to swallow anything other than liquid she would choke. Ella accepted the tea, shook her head over the cake and didn't look up or speak. She didn't drink her tea, she just sat there and then a tear trickled down her cheek and she spoke in a trembling voice.

'He didn't want me. He didn't ever really want me. He only did it for spite. How could he do that to me? I'm going to find some herbs that will get rid of his child!'

Carefully Kath took the cup and saucer from her and handed it to Mercy. The incongruity of the situation struck her then. Ella was well-dressed and she wore expensive blue stones on her wrists and around her neck and in her ears, sapphires, and good ones by the darkness of them. Her dress was rich and she was well cared for – the plumpness was not just her baby, she had blossomed into a beautiful young woman.

'He wanted you. All along he wanted you,' she accused Kath.

Kath yearned to say that it wasn't so but she was afraid it was. And she had made it worse by telling him that she would marry him when he found her sister. How stupid could she be? He had bettered her and that was all he cared about. She had been right not to marry him: he was vindictive and petty and he had hurt her sister so much that she wished Jake had killed him. She took back the thought. This was not Jake's problem and yet he had protected them.

Jake stood outside in the late evening. Kath went to him. He always went there when he had hard thinking to do or he had some problem he couldn't solve.

Jake acknowledged her merely with a half-turn, then he went back to looking down at the dale and there was nothing wrong with the view, Kath thought, even if it was dark and your eyes were full of tears.

'I don't know how to thank you. You were so brave,' she said, trying not to choke and not looking at him.

He shrugged.

'It's easy to be brave with a shotgun in your hand. He wasn't so stupid that he didn't know a gun like that could blow his feet away.'

'He was going to use Ella as a shield.'

'From that distance I could have taken his head off easily.'

Kath put a hand over her mouth, racking with dry sobs and her body went on shuddering as though it belonged to somebody else.

'Hey, don't,' Jake said. 'It wouldn't have ever come to that. A threat's always enough.'

'I didn't mean to get you into such a mess. I

should never have taken you there.'

'It's just as well you did, isn't it? You thought he was your friend. You never thought he'd hold you to your promise. You made him feel powerless, men hate that more than anything. You took him on over his own ground. He couldn't bear it. He had to humiliate you.'

'But why?'

'Because he wanted you and you wouldn't have him. Will was part of your life, your childhood, part of the magic of the road and the wagon, why wouldn't you trust him?'

'How did you know he was going to do something?'

'Something about him. But I didn't think he'd do that, go that far. He's a great one for surprises.'

'You thought he was going to try to kill us!' Kath said and couldn't help bursting into tears.

'No, I didn't,' he said, laughing just a little and taking her into his arms. She was surprised and didn't know whether to be pleased or not. 'You're dramatising it.'

'You are the one who took the gun,' she protested, anger winning so that she backed away and searched her pockets for a handkerchief. 'I'm so angry that he hurt Ella. She did nothing to him except love him.'

'It was enough that she was your sister. Go and see how she is. She's safe now and we'll look after her. Don't worry, Kath, it'll be all right.'

'What if he comes here?'

'He won't.'

She smiled at that.

'You always say that everything will be all right, even though you know it isn't true.'

'I don't know anything of the kind,' he said. 'But I do know if he comes anywhere near I'll shoot him between the legs. That'll sort him out.'

Kath could not help noticing that Jake took the shotgun to bed with him. She imagined Will and his friends coming to get them, even though Jake had made safe the windows and doors. For possibly the first time she was glad that they lived in such a small house, it was easily defended. Ethan didn't like how things had changed and went next door to sleep with the men. Kath slept in between Ella and Mercy because Ella was too large to sleep in the middle. Kath determined to buy another bed; a single would fit into the room and they would all sleep more easily.

Kath felt as though Ella was older than her. In a lot of ways she was, being married and having her first child. Will's parents would have been horrified by what had happened, she knew. He would pay dearly for it, which brought her some comfort.

She wished her sister would sleep but they both lay awake in the darkness and it did not resemble their childhood. Kath tried to think about the last wonderful summer they were together but that made her sad too, thinking of her parents.

'I'm so sorry, Ella,' she said eventually. 'I wanted you back so badly. I never thought he would do such a thing to you, honestly I didn't. I'm sorry.'

Ella didn't say anything for so long that Kath thought she wasn't going to.

'I loved him, Kath, I really did,' she whispered. 'He made me so proud to be his wife, when all the girls, older than me, years some of them, they wanted him. And his parents were so kind to me, I had a family again. They treated me like I was their daughter and when I became pregnant they had a party. I didn't know people did such things. They treated me like a queen. What are they thinking now? I miss them.'

It was two weeks later when Kath heard a voice that she thought she recognised at the front door. She opened it very carefully because she wasn't sure whether Jake or Pat was nearby. They tended to make their own arrangements so that one of them was here all the time. She found Jake standing just beyond the door and an older man talking very softly and persuasively but Jake wasn't moving.

It was Will's father. She hadn't seen him in a long time. He didn't look straight at her at first. She took in his rich clothes and how much he looked like Will, but the anxious gaze was completely his. His whole face had dropped with unhappiness.

'Kathleen,' he said, in some relief and why wouldn't he, since Jake had the shotgun pointed at him, 'will you tell this young man that I mean no harm?'

She ventured outside but only just and looked straight at him.

'That depends on what you want and whether he is with you.'

Will's father looked down at the ground and

324

then at her.

'May I see my daughter-in-law? I'm alone and I mean no disrespect.'

Kath had no idea that she was so easily able to be found. No doubt since she had been in Appleby he could trace her from the hotel to here. It made her feel vulnerable. Had they been followed back to Weardale? She thought of how Will might come there with his horrible friends and how Jake was still sleeping with the shotgun.

'Have you told him where we are?'

Will's father looked reproachfully at her while also looking ashamed.

'Absolutely not. We are not speaking. I had a lot of problems finding you, and I am very sorry for what has happened,' Wills father said. 'My wife and I would like to see Ella and our grandchild occasionally. That's all.' Will's father looked at her miserably.

'All right,' she said and Jake moved the gun away, 'but if you upset her, you will be out of that door faster than you ever moved anywhere.'

Will's father nodded and would have gone inside but she stopped him with a raised hand.

'Ella must be told first and if she disagrees then you will not come in.'

He nodded and Kath went back inside.

Ella, who had been tired the previous night and not slept for the baby making her uncomfortable, was sitting by the fire. She looked up as Kath came into the room.

'Will's father is here alone and has asked to see you. Jake is just outside. I think Mr Hern means well. Can he come in?'

Ella hesitated for a few seconds and Kath could see hope in her face. Even now she wanted Will, wanted to see him, to be told that it had all been a mistake, that he still wanted her for his wife. She nodded and Kath went back outside and told Mr Hern to follow her. Once he was in the house, Ella's expression flickered from grief to joy and back again. She wanted to run to her adopted father's arms but she was also afraid, afraid to be hurt again. He raised a hand.

'Oh Ella,' he whispered. 'How can I tell you how sorry I am that my son did such dreadful things to you and to your sister? His mother and I will never forgive him and never see him again for what he did to you and to the honour of our family. He has broken his mother's heart. She sends you her love and cries so often about it that I despair. All I can say to you is that I horse-whipped him and banished him from the family and he no longer exists for us.'

Ella began to cry.

'Do you feel as if you can come back to us?' he offered. 'We would expect nothing of you but we would look after you. My wife loves you like her daughters and she is so pleased that you are having our first grandchild. She's in despair that you have been so injured by our son.'

Ella shook her head but she did get up and go to him and put her arms around him. He held her and his voice broke.

She eventually drew away. 'I want to stay here with my sister and her friends.'

'I understand that and I would like to help you. We would very much like to see the baby when it is born. It means a great deal to us. His mother frets over you. Can I at least tell her that you are safe and that you will have help?'

Ella nodded.

'I won't trouble you any more then,' and he took a huge parcel of paper money from his pocket and put it into her resisting fingers.

Ella stared at him.

'What's this?' she said. 'This is not your fault. You did all the things you should have done for your son and your daughters. I'll be happy for you to see the baby when it's born, you don't have to–'

'Take it. It will make us feel better. The last thing my wife said to me was that if I couldn't make you accept this then I would have to answer to her when I came home. You will need time with your new child and although I'm sure your sister is happy to have you here, it all costs. It's for her, as well, to help her take care of you.'

Ella could see the lines on his face where there had been none and how stricken he was. There were tears in his eyes and he touched her hands with his roughened fingers.

'We will always look after you in every way that you need. You are our daughter and we care for you.'

Kath saw him out. He turned to her once the door was closed. 'I'm so sorry for how he treated you.'

'I feel partly to blame. I promised him I would marry him if he found my sister.'

He shook his head.

'I'm afraid he would've done this even if you

hadn't. You have nothing to be sorry for. You had been through so much. I think you would have promised anything to get your sister back because she was all you had left. I can't believe that he didn't put you and Ella in touch all those months ago after your parents died. Instead he tricked you and dishonoured our family. This is his blame. You survived what would have finished off a lot of people. Be proud of that. If he ever comes anywhere near either of you again, I will kill him.' Mr Hern walked away.

Kath shuddered.

When she went back inside, Ella gave her the money.

'I can't take this. It's a huge amount,' Kath said staring at it.

'You cannot have wanted me here—'

'I have always wanted you here. And I feel somewhat responsible; if I hadn't rejected him, he wouldn't have done this.'

'You didn't think that he was a monster. How could either of us have known?'

Kath closed her eyes against the memories but her sister was clear eyed and still gazing at her.

'Take the money for now, and maybe you won't resent me as much as you might have. The baby isn't born yet. In a house like this, I should think you could hear a baby scream everywhere.'

As the baby grew bigger, Kath would hear her sister get up quietly in the night and she would follow her downstairs. It was her dream come true, in spite of everything. There had been so many times when she had thought that her sister had died and when Ella smiled at her she knew she felt the same. They sat outside on the stone wall until the late summer came and the nights cooled. Ella's baby was almost due. Kath surprised herself by hoping that Will would come to the farm and try to make things better. She wanted him to say that he had made a terrible mistake and wished only to be forgiven, it had all been a stupid fit of madness. But he didn't.

Forty

Having got Rosa into his caravan, Will was gleeful. She was so like Kath that he could pretend she was the woman he had wanted all this time. He could even cry out Kath's name in ecstasy if he liked; he had paid Rosa and she wouldn't care. He would be in paradise.

He was eager for her yet didn't want it to be rushed; he wanted to pretend he wasn't paying for her. He had paid for women before but not since his marriage. In the moonlight, her body was lush, dark like chocolate and slick with summer sweat.

She peeled off her clothes, lifting her brown arms high above her head, so eager was she for his body or his money. He could not stop himself from thinking about the roll of notes that he had paid for her. He wanted to hit her, he wanted her to know that he did not love her, that he would never love her. Instead he closed his eyes and pretended she was Kath and started to kiss her, to run his hands over her body. His mouth followed the trail his hands made and her body was soon warm and eager, lifted for him.

He thought of how good he was at this, how he could make a woman scream with want and moan with satisfaction, how controlled and clever he was. Her body was open for him and he wanted her very badly. He moved to take her and then he couldn't. The more he tried, the less his body responded, until he was as limp as a wet cabbage. How disgusting.

He didn't understand it. He had had a lot of women, had never not been able to take them, but now his body would not obey him; he could not do it.

He told her to wait and he went outside into the cool air. He took a bottle of whisky with him, since he always had it by him now, and he took great swigs of it. He went back inside and got down on the bed and clutched her to him but it was no good. He didn't want her, he didn't want anything to do with her. His body failed him completely. He could no longer convince himself that she was Kath, and there was no way in which she was his wife.

Ella was silken, kind, soft voiced and funny. She loved everything he did, everything he attempted. It wouldn't have mattered whether they made love or not, but they always had. He remembered how she was in the mornings, pale and flushed, like strawberries in cream, her body lithe and her legs exactly right in length and perfectly formed, and how in ecstasy she would wrap them around him and then still make silly remarks and he

330

would not be stopped. She would cry tears of joy when her body reached its height and she would tell him how much she loved him. How no woman had ever loved a man as she loved him.

She had been so practical, too. He had loved her sense of order. He liked how she was respectful to his parents, how she called them Mother and Father and they laughed at this in joy and their eyes were full of love. To them he could not have married anyone better. She was the daughter-in-law that everybody wanted, the wife that every couple loved.

He thought of her with his sisters and how they had accepted her as one of them and how, on her wedding night, they had dressed her hair and put her in the most exquisite blue gown and put a circlet of yellow flowers around her neck because they knew that blue and yellow became her soft blue gaze and her flawless cream skin.

She had come to him that night with love in her eyes. She was all admiration and stars. She was his as no woman had ever been, virginal, excited, terrified and, best of all, so accepting. She cried out with pain and pleasure when he took her for the first time and after they had slept she got up and danced naked around the caravan, laughing. Night after night she wanted him.

When he cried out with nightmares in his sleep, she soothed him and held him and he knew that she was there. He had never felt as comforted in his life as he did with her by his side. Her capacity for care was limitless.

He did not know now why he had not loved her when she had offered everything she had, everything she was. He had forgotten the demon that lived with him, the resentment and the hate.

He wanted to bundle Rosa out of his caravan, he felt sick with embarrassment. But she knew men, she had seen enough and did not react. She did not run or turn from him. She sat up and even offered him the money that he had given her. Will was ashamed. What was he doing, using a woman he didn't love? He was disgusted with himself.

He told her that he was sorry and she should keep the money, and asked if she'd like to sleep now. She politely lay down with him though he could tell she was merely waiting for him to sleep so she could leave. He feigned sleep for her sake and his.

She picked up her clothes and tiptoed her way out of the caravan and as soon as he was alone, he felt the tears slowly making their hot way down his face. He didn't want to face another day. Maybe he could go away from his friends and never come back.

Forty-One

Caro Banks fell over. It was silly, she thought. One minute she was fine, the next minute she was missing the last stair and ending up on her ample backside on the beautifully tiled cream, brown and fawn floor of the hall. How embarrassing. Her mother stotted out of the drawing room at the sound of the thump.

'What on earth are you doing down there?'

'Don't be ridiculous, Mother, I'm not here on purpose. And I think I've hurt my ankle.'

Her mother rang the doctor and she sat there, feeling like an idiot.

It was an hour before the doctor came; she had scooted against the wall by then and begged a book from her mother. He got her to the nearest couch and said he thought it was just a sprain but she should rest it for a few days and no driving. She sighed and thanked him.

She called the taxi service and half an hour later a car arrived. Driving it was Sam White, looking rather serious.

'Can you manage, Miss Banks?' he asked her in a voice which half persuaded her that she couldn't.

'Of course I can,' she said, hobbling with a stick and furious with herself.

'Maybe you could get your appointments to come to you,' he suggested.

'If you lived with my mother, you would understand why I want to get out of the house,' she said, and he smiled and nodded. She didn't usually say things like that, especially not to people she was employing, but her temper was short and her sense of humour barely intact.

After four hours of appointments, he took her home to collect files to go to the estate office.

Sam gazed around him at the papers that were strewn everywhere, great piles of them.

'I thought Mr Murchison did all this.'

'He did, but he isn't very well now and he's

nearly seventy.'

'Which do you want taking to the office?'

'This pile here and that over there and–'

'Has he stopped working for you then?'

'I'm trying not to let him know that he isn't keeping up as he once was so I keep taking stuff down there and then bringing it back and hoping he doesn't notice. I don't want to hurt his feelings.'

'Don't you think he might want you to say you don't need him?'

'But I do need him.'

'No, you need somebody who can take care of some of it. You can't do it all yourself and it looks like a mess to me.'

'What would you know?' she said, offended at his presumption.

'Enough to help in Lord Barnard's estate office for two years.' Caro stared at him.

'I wish I'd stayed, actually,' he said. 'I wanted to but Ma wanted us all to move for our sake. Much good it's done us. My parents thought we'd be better off here and now look.'

They drove to the office and there Sam looked around him in shock.

Caro said, defensively, 'Mr Murchison hasn't been here all week.'

'Maybe I could help just for today?'

'Please do,' she said and ushered him to a seat.

Mr Murchison arrived later in the day, ashen-faced and apologetic. He scowled to see another face in the office.

'I hope you aren't planning to get rid of me, Miss Banks,' he said quietly to her.

'Of course not. Mr White is just helping because I know you haven't been very well lately and I thought it might be easier for both of us if we had someone to take on the less complicated paper-work. Mr White has other work to do; he's also my driver until my ankle heals. It's just a little help needed and he could do the easier stuff.'

Mr Murchison thought about this.

Caro continued, 'If you could tell Mr White what you would like him to do, we could perhaps employ him for a few hours a week – but only if you think it's a good idea.'

Much to her relief, Mr Murchison nodded. She wished she had seen sooner that what he needed was not to be replaced but to be aided. She had not noticed that they needed someone else until it was almost too late.

'Mr White helped in Lord Barnard's estate office,' Caro said, knowing that that would make the older man feel comfortable.

After that Mr Murchison came in as early as ever but happily didn't have to do too much. For the next few days Sam drove her around and got to know the work she did. He was still driving for Mr Filey when people needed a lift to places in the evenings, but he very much wanted a proper job in Miss Banks' office.

After a few days, Caro asked Mr Murchison if he would like Sam's help regularly. After a short, almost offended, silence, he said that he would be glad of the help. Mr White seemed a very nice, competent young man. That was praise indeed coming from Mr Murchison, so the following day, driving herself for the first time, Caro went early to the office.

She knew Sam would be there; he was always early. He looked concerned.

'How's the ankle?'

'Fine. I don't need your driving any more.'

'Good.'

'But–'

He looked worried.

'I've talked it over with Mr Murchison,' she said, 'and we would like to offer you a full-time position working at the office. You don't need to give me an answer until you've thought about it and talked it over with your parents, but I will pay you fairly. It will be a lot of work because Mr Murchison is doing less and less – as I'm sure you've noticed – so if it turns out to be too much, I can employ somebody else too.'

Sam grinned.

'I was hoping you might. I'm a bit tired of the driving, although it's good money and Mr Filey's been really kind to me. But I would much rather do this.'

Sam told his parents about the offer and his mother looked pleased but his father didn't.

'I'm paying Jake when I could be paying you,' his father said. 'I'll have to keep him on permanently unless one of my sons gets his ideas together. I knew you would get sick of the driving, and now we've got something else to contend with.'

'I'd rather do the office work.'

'And what happens when you get tired of that?'

'Miss Banks is going to pay me well.'

'All your generation ever thinks about is

336

money!' his father said.

'Walter,' his wife reproved him and his father scraped his chair away from the table and stormed out.

'Take no notice of him,' his mother said.

'You think it's a good idea, then?'

'I never wanted you to leave Lord Barnard's office; he told me you were very good at it. It was your father's idea and since he was so unhappy I couldn't say anything. He wanted us all together, but it's never going to happen. Sometimes the Lord is good to us when we aren't expecting it,' his mother said. 'I think Caroline Banks is a very fine woman and a credit to us all and you would do well to work for her.'

The following week Caro asked Sam to take Mr Murchison home a couple of times because he couldn't get his breath on the hill and the cobble-stones made him wobbly.

'I need to get you a car,' she said. 'Sometimes I'm going to want you to go places when I'm occupied elsewhere.'

'Shall I ask Mr Filey?'

'I've still got my father's car at the house. It's kept in good working order and though it's a bit old and big, I think it'll serve. If not, say so and we'll find something else.'

She drove them back to the house and opened up the big doors to a building that Sam hadn't noticed before. Inside was a huge silver car. He gaped. Miss Banks' car was a lovely Renault, but this was the kind of car that men dreamed of driving. He stared at the shining silver monster.

'I can't drive this, Miss Banks,' he said.

337

She peered in at the door in an unexpectedly womanly fashion and it made him smile.

'Is it too big for the bends on the narrow roads?' she asked. 'My father was a terrible driver.'

'It's not that. It's a – it's a Bentley.'

'He was very fond of it. And Mr Filey comes regularly and sorts it out. There's nothing the matter with it.'

'I'm not saying there is, but – what if I bash it up against a bus or something?'

She sighed.

'It would be nice if it was used,' she said, 'and after all, it's only a car.'

Sam wasn't sure whether to be horrified or amused at this response.

'Why don't you have it?' he said. 'And I'll drive yours.'

'I like mine better,' she said, with a fine disregard for the entire motor industry.

Sam had never thought he would drive such a beautiful vehicle and though it was big, it was built so that it worked on every level. One didn't have to drive it, it glided. Sam could see why her father had loved the car so much. It smelled of good leather. The dials and the clocks at the front were superbly marked and every inch of it had been so carefully put together that each man who had worked on it must have been a master. The engine purred sweeter than any kitten. After just a day driving it up on the tops, he would have fought off anybody who tried to take it from him.

'What in God's name is that?' his father said when he arrived home in it.

Sam looked sheepishly at him.

'It's Miss Banks' car.'

'Well, I didn't think it was yours,' his father said.

His mother said to his father when they went to bed, 'What did you say about your sons being gentlemen?'

'Huh,' was all he said. 'Folk will think he's getting above himself.'

Forty-Two

Ella's baby chose to arrive just after harvest time. Kath was astonished at how little she knew about pregnancy; she knew many women who had borne babies but it was a different thing when it was your sister. Ella could hardly walk for the last two weeks, she was so heavy and ungainly.

She couldn't sleep, she needed pillows around her so that she could lie comfortably, and she took up so much room in bed that Kath kept apologising to Mercy, who only shook her head and said that she didn't care. Ella was tired and ached all over and Kath spent time rubbing her back; it was the only thing she could do to help. The summer was long and hot, which was, Kath realised, the very last thing a pregnant woman needed.

The sweat dripped off her sister and she was only glad that they lived at the top of a big hill. If there was any breeze, it came across the purple heather. Ella would sit outside and catch at it and let go of her breath in slow release. Her ankles had swollen, her face was shiny and red, and every time she moved it took all her strength.

The baby decided to be born in the middle of the night. Wasn't that typical, Kath thought. Did babies ever come right after breakfast when it was convenient to people?

The night was quiet and all of them had gone to bed. For once Ethan slept close against his mother and Kath wished she had spent more time finding a new bed to go in the room. She was on the verge of falling off the cliff into sleep when Ella caught her breath.

Kath sat up. At that point Ella cried out and clutched at her stomach. Kath knew nothing about childbirth but Mercy was already awake and bounding out of bed and Kath was grateful. Ethan climbed down and ran into the other room.

'Shall we send for the doctor?' Kath said.

'Not yet,' Mercy said, 'it could be hours. First children are usually slow. I used to help with babies; my gran always went to see them into this world.'

Kath was horrified at this show of calm. Ella was soon in even more pain. Mercy encouraged her and she talked about the length of time between contractions and she was right, soon Ella howled at shorter and shorter intervals. Kath was dismayed to hear her sister scream so loudly. Mercy bundled Kath out of the room and she was glad to go. She went outside and gulped at the air and tried not to shake.

Jake and Pat followed her. They stood about,

not knowing what to do. After a long time, hearing her sister scream and scream, Kath went back in and upstairs.

'I think we should go for the doctor,' she said.

'You won't need to,' Mercy said, coming out of the bedroom in reassurance, 'the baby's coming.'

She was right. The baby's head soon appeared. Kath was mesmerised, appalled. Mercy calmed Ella, told her that another couple of pushes would do it, and it did as her child slithered into the world.

The baby was a boy. Ella cried, the tears running sideways and around to the back of her neck. Kath thought that it was relief at being out of pain, but Ella said, in strangled tones, 'I'm so glad it's a boy. He'll come for me now.'

Kath stared at her. She wanted Will back? After what he had done, the way that he had treated them? Had her sister lost her mind when she had a child? Or was it that each woman needed a father for her offspring? Look at Mercy. Kath wished she could somehow pick up Ella and her boy and dash off and hide them somewhere in the hills. It was a stupid basic instinct and there was nothing she could do. She told herself that a woman giving birth might say anything.

The baby yelled. Kath didn't think she had ever heard anything quite so ear-splitting. Mercy washed and wound the baby in a big soft sheet and then saw to the afterbirth. She cleaned the mother with warm water, soap and soft words.

She handed the baby to Ella, who held him close.

'He looks just like Will. He's so beautiful.'

Ella wept and put him to her breast and he shut up as he nursed. Kath was so thankful.

'What are you going to call him?' she asked, several days later.

Ella stared out of the window. She had been staring out of the window for hours on end all week. The baby screamed relentlessly. They were all making excuses to get out. The house had never seemed so small; the screams could be heard everywhere. None of them was getting much sleep.

Jake and Pat were so glad to go off to the farm where they were both working. She couldn't begrudge them – she and Mercy would have left Ella if they could, but someone had to stay behind so they took it in turns to run the shop. Each were eager to dash off into Stanhope on their day.

'I'll call him William, of course. It is his father's name and his grandfather's.'

'Ella, do you really want Will to come here?'

'I didn't but now I have his child and I'm scared.'

'You don't have to be scared. We'll look after you.'

'I know and I'm very grateful but it isn't the same. How could it be? I've never wanted him so much as I do now and I don't understand why after all he's done.'

'Because you've just had a baby.'

'I thought I didn't want it after what he did.'

'Maybe he was scared, too.'

'No, he just wanted you. He always wanted you,' Ella said in such a dismissive voice that

Kath despaired.

'I think that was just because I turned him down. I was very young.'

'So was I,' Ella said.

'The circumstances were so different though by then.'

'I loved him even when I was a little girl,' Ella said. 'I was so jealous when he chose you. I just knew that he was mine, that he was meant for me, always. I suppose it could have been worse – you could have married him.'

Kath couldn't think of an answer to that but it hurt.

Ella thought that she had died and gone to hell when the day came that Kath and Mercy assumed she was all right on her own and went back to work together. She couldn't complain. Her sister had taken her in, and she was so grateful for that, but the tiny house here was haunted, she was sure of it. It terrified her. The wind screamed around it on the tops because there was nothing to stop it and when the others were away during the day, instead of being glad to have time to herself and the baby, she lay there in her bed terrified or by the fire in the same way.

The only thing she looked forward to was their coming home in the evenings. She kept the kitchen fire going and helped where she could, but mostly she nursed the baby and nodded off. When Kath came home from the shop, she would take him.

'Why don't you go and sleep for a couple of hours?' she would say.

343

Ella could only smile in gratitude, stagger up the stairs and fall thankfully into her bed, not to dream but to be aware that she had enough time during which the baby would not cry and waken her.

It took all of Mercy's courage to say to Kath that she didn't want to keep on with the café the following year. They had been successful at it but Mercy wanted to focus on the dress shop. She had determined that if Kath wanted to go on with the café, she would ask if they might split up and each do what they wanted to do.

She wasn't confident but she couldn't rest. She wanted this so much. One day when they had the shop to themselves and it wasn't busy and Ethan had fallen asleep, she took the opportunity.

'I want to close the café and push our dress-making. I'd also like to move with Ethan into Stanhope. It's time for him to go to school and have playmates. I think that's important since he's an only child.' She was looking straight at Kath so that she would know none of this was lightly said.

'You must know by now that I need to get away from Pat. He hasn't done anything wrong but it will be better for both of us if I move off that hilltop and into the town. I'm not used to being isolated and I think I could find some kind of a life in Stanhope.' She rushed the end. 'If you want to keep the café on that's fine, but I would rather concentrate on the dressmaking. Would that be all right with you?'

Kath was relieved. That was her first feeling. It

344

was so obvious that Mercy and Pat now agreed on nothing. They barely spoke to one another. And the café had become the kind of repetition that she hated but she hadn't known where to go from there. She was tired of making cakes and listening to the women talking in the café and garden of their children and grandchildren.

'Why don't we close the café?' she offered. 'To be honest I've had enough, too. I may explore other options. I don't know what I'll do, just that it'll be something different. You could keep on as a dress shop. People know you're here and it's perfect, right in the middle of the village. You and Ethan could even live here. You could walk him to school and spend Sundays with him and arrange your time to suit yourself. You're a natural. You have such good ideas and know a lot more about things like that than I ever could. If you like, we could start doing the place up now and you start spending the odd night here and then move in as you want to.'

'That's wonderful,' Mercy said. 'I'm a bit nervous about it but if I could do it gradually that would be the best way for Ethan and for me. Can we keep it just between you and me for now?'

Kath smiled. 'Of course. Now let's get to work.'

Forty-Three

Will went further south than he had ever done, far beyond the reach, he hoped, of people who knew him, down to the bottom end of Yorkshire.

He drank and took various women to his bed in the hope that he might be able to have sex with one of them but he had no success. After three weeks of attempting this and getting nowhere, he resigned himself to loneliness and celibacy.

He had even tried not drinking but that was no good either, the seconds were minutes, the minutes were hours and he couldn't stand the idea of days, which stretched out endlessly in front of him. He could not bear any of it and the further away he got from the north, the more he thought of what he had done to Ella. He began to realise the enormity of it and it made him shiver.

He couldn't believe he had done something so awful but he had and there was no way he could pretend it hadn't happened. It was horrible.

The funny part was that for the first time in all those years, he no longer loved Kath. He hadn't for a long time; how foolish not to see it. He could live with the fact that she had never loved him, never wanted him and the whole thing had been an illusion on his part. He even remembered his mother telling him that Kath was not for him. He hated that he had not listened to her.

When he dreamed, it was all of Ella. She was

346

always just out of sight, running away, or worse still, dying because of what he had done. He dreamed that she died having his child and the child died, too. During the day his sensible self told him this was unlikely, but at night the demons scorched his brain and Ella died in childbirth over and over until the nights when he didn't dream this became few.

He began to want her as he had never wanted anything in his life. He wanted to go back to his mother and father and beg their pardon and be accepted but he knew that he couldn't. His father had cast him out and he would never be forgiven.

He no longer drank in pubs. It was easier just to buy it and have it in the caravan. He no longer ate, it was too much trouble. He did remember to feed the horse and he was glad that he had let none of the dogs go with him; he didn't see how he could have managed them. The horse was his only companion; he would sit by as it grazed, stroking it on occasion. He had paid for it to have a field to itself a couple of weeks ago. Thank God for money, it was all he had left.

He made sure that the horse had plenty of water. Buying dozens of bottles of whisky at different places a while ago, he had also bought a sack of carrots and a bag of apples. It was the only way in which his life was normal. Animals didn't care how bad you had been, what you had done. He shed pathetic tears into the animal's glossy mane as he brushed it and talked to it because he had no one else to speak to. Nobody cared any more. His self-respect was long gone and so was his life. The only thing that kept him from doing himself in was the stupid idea that the horse would be left waiting for him to come back.

He could down a bottle of whisky in the morning, one in the afternoon and another in the evening if he stayed awake that long. He fed the horse and watered it. Other than that he slept.

During the day, even with a pale sun filtering in at either side of the curtains, he was reasonably content dozing in and out, and when the evening fell there was another bottle of whisky to stave off the feelings of guilt which clawed at his brain.

Then the day came when he had no more whisky left and he had to go out. It was dark and very cold. He had not left his caravan in several days but he vaguely remembered the way to the nearest pub. He went to the bar and asked for a bottle.

He always carried a lot of cash and it spilled from his pocket when he tried to pay. He picked it back up and staggered out with the bottle that he had paid for. That was the last thing he remembered.

Forty-Four

Ella had not been sure she wanted Will's parents to see the baby but when they arrived and Pat allowed them in, she took one look at them and collapsed in Will's mother's arms. Will's father stood about, looking embarrassed, and when Ella showed them the baby, Mrs Hern cried and he looked even more embarrassed. Ella offered her the baby to hold and then he came and stood next to them, like somebody had offered him a miracle.

'He's so beautiful,' he said.

'He looks like Will,' Ella said.

They both gazed at her.

'He has your eyes though,' Will's mother said and Ella gazed down at the infant and saw that he did indeed have blue eyes. How had she not noticed it before now? Blue eyes, black hair and porcelain skin.

'He looks Irish,' Mr Hern said doubtfully, but it was true, the combination was glorious wherever it had come from.

His mother wept so much that Ella hugged her.

'I am sorry and ashamed of him,' his mother said. 'You will always be our daughter and we will always be proud of you and there for you and your son, our first grandchild. Come to us, won't you, whenever you like. You are very important to us and we love you. We will never let Will anywhere near you but I don't think he will come back now. He has no place with us.'

Ella said nothing but nodded and it was only when they were gone that she broke down and cried; they had called her baby 'our first grandchild.'

'How can I still love Will after all he's done? Have I gone mad? How can I learn not to love him, Kath? I must try.'

'You don't have to stop loving him, you just have to go on taking care of the baby, and in time he will be a blessing. Not that he's much of one at the moment,' Kath added, as the baby began to scream. Ella laughed through her tears.

Forty-Five

Will's father had seen a lot of trouble in his life and therefore the morning when two uniformed policemen made their way into the travellers' camp, he didn't think anything much about it. He was used to dealing with the law and in the main got on well with them. He had greased a great many palms and cultivated men when he needed to; it was likely just some of the lads getting rowdy that he would have to deal with.

It was autumn, his least favourite time of year, the beginning of months of dark days and sharp frosts. He had not minded so much until now that he had no son, he had managed to keep busy and avoid thinking about it. But now his heart was so heavy he was no longer sure how he carried it around.

He came out of the wagon and nodded at them. What was their complaint this time?

'Mr Hern?' enquired the sergeant.

'Aye. What's the problem?'

The sergeant looked around him as though somebody was concealing stolen goods.

'We have found your son, Will. He's in hospital in Doncaster.'

Mr Hern tried to pretend that he didn't

understand them, hadn't heard it. They would be wrong; they so often were.

'We don't have a son any more,' he said sorrowfully.

'He's in a bad way, sir. He's been stabbed.'

Mr Hern didn't remember having been called 'sir' by a policeman before. He wished that he had never had a son. Daughters were so much less trouble. And then he qualified it with 'so far'. He didn't wish any more bad luck to catch up with him.

When the policemen had gone, Mrs Hern came out of the caravan.

'Has somebody stolen something?' she said.

'Not us. Don't worry.'

She went back to her cleaning and he tried to dismiss Will from his mind but it wasn't easy. After a couple of hours his wife saw him and came out again.

'There is something the matter, why are you keeping it from me?' She looked hard at him. 'It's Will, isn't it?'

He hesitated.

'Billy Hern, if you don't tell me what it is, you will not come to my bed until hell freezes. Tell me right now.'

'He's badly hurt. He's in Doncaster infirmary.'

'What is wrong with him?'

Her husband looked down at the ground and didn't say anything.

'My God, Billy, hasn't he paid for what he did? Would you have him die? Get in that car right now. No, first go and tell Baz that he must motor to Weardale and fetch Ella. Thank God the others are here and Linda can look after the girls.'

Kath found a young man she did not recognise at her front door but when she looked more closely, she remembered him. She had always liked him.

'Why, Baz,' she said, and then she saw his face and knew that he would not have come here unless something was very wrong. 'What is it?'

'It's Will. I need to talk to Ella. I wouldn't bother her but it's important.'

'Yes, of course,' Kath said and opened the door wider.

As she saw him inside she realised how things had changed. Jake no longer barred the door with a shotgun. It being evening, both men were at home. They were all inside.

Baz looked from one to another and then found Ella's face.

'Will has been badly hurt and is in hospital, in Doncaster,' he said. 'Mr Hern says that he can understand why you would not come, but they think he may not live.'

Ella, thinner than Kath had ever seen her, got up, baby in her arms.

'How is he hurt?' she asked.

'He's been stabbed.'

'Of course I can come,' she said and then she looked at her sister and at Jake and Jake nodded immediately.

'I'll drive you. Kath?'

Kath nodded too.

All the way there, Kath kept remembering the last time they had seen Will and how vengeful and hateful he had become. She would have been content never to see him again, but she knew that her sister had not given up on him and loved him despite what he had done. Although she didn't understand it, she was respectful of her sister and what she needed in her life. Life came back at you again and again, as though you had to work these things out before you reached heaven. You had to do your penance here on earth.

Will's parents motored to Doncaster. They didn't often travel like that, it was against all their ideas, but Mr Hern had had a car for a long time and now it was justifying its existence. He tried not to think. Will could not die, not when he was in disgrace, not when he had been cast out.

They didn't speak all the way there and it was a long time in the car. It seemed like days and yet it was so much faster than how they usually travelled. Guilt crushed him and fear that his son might die alone clutched at his insides so that he had to keep stopping, getting out and going into the bushes to throw up or let his trousers down or both, which was distressing. His wife sat in the car and said nothing. Yet when they finally reached the hospital, she put her hands to her cheeks and cried. Her sobbing went on and on as though her hands had never had any other purpose than to try to prevent tears from falling.

He talked to her, tried to soothe her, but he didn't want to go into the hospital either. He was so afraid that Will had died and nobody had been there to comfort him. He knew then that no matter what your children did, you still had to be there for them and with them, and it was the hardest lesson that he had ever learned. He was heavy with guilt.

He coaxed her out of the car, put his arm around her shoulders and they walked into the hospital together. There was a smiling person on the desk who took them into the ward where their son lay.

It was a big ward, lots of beds, but it was night and most of the lamps had been extinguished. A nurse got up from a desk and table in the centre of the ward. Mr Hern wondered if indeed his son was really there; perhaps they had made a mistake and he was not and Will was in his wagon where he belonged.

The nurse took them to a bed, and indeed their son lay unconscious. Mr Hern wanted to cry and release the pressure building in his chest. Will was so pale and so thin and so unlike and yet so like himself that it was heartbreaking.

His wife stifled sobs again as he held her close to him. They were given chairs to sit by their son's bed. The nurse said that Will was a little better. How bad had he been, Mr Hern wanted to ask. The police had told him that Will had been robbed but that the horse and caravan had been taken by the police and were being looked after. The Herns sat there in the semi-darkness, that awful time before light became day, and their son lay unconscious, badly injured.

Mr Hern got up and left his wife and went to the window and looked toward the horizon where day would surely come and there he found that he wept. It was not for what he had done, it was not for what Will had done, it was just for all of them and how hard it was to get through life even for the short time that one was here.

His wife came over and took him into her arms and told him that they had done what they could. He knew, though, that it was not enough, no matter what you did, it would never be enough to save your children, to help them lead decent lives. Will would die and they would be left, wanting.

They tried to maintain some kind of composure when Ella came in to see her husband. She went close to the bed and sat down, taking his hand and calling his name so softly.

They went back outside where Kath was holding the baby. She handed him to Mrs Hern who wandered off with him, talking to him all the while.

Ella whispered Will's name until she was hoarse, hoping he would hear her voice and wake up. She didn't think it was him lying there, it was so awful, and then she didn't understand why she had thought that the sound of her voice would bring him back round. How conceited was that, especially since he had never really loved her. Always he had thought to gain her sister. The whole thing was so ridiculous now.

She thought that she could sit there forever, except when it came time to feed her child. She was too upset to produce milk and she had to calm herself. She took him away from everyone, sat herself down and breathed very carefully until her milk began to flow and the baby suckled and was silent. When he was full he fell asleep and she cradled him in her arms. At that point all she wanted was for Will to live to see his son and be glad.

She took the baby inside the ward with her and told Will all about him. She talked to him as though he was conscious and told him how she had named the baby after him, and how much she loved them both, and how she wanted him to come back to her.

She told him over and over that she understood and forgave him and that as long as he was true to her, they could go forward with their child. She tried not to weep at the bedside, it seemed so pathetic to do so. She thought she could spend the next ten years sitting there, waiting for him to wake up, if her presence meant he would not die.

Having Will's parents and Kath and Jake there made Ella feel so warm and cared for that she was overtaken by moments of optimism, believing that any moment Will would wake. Then she noticed the dark looks exchanged between the nurses and the doctor, and her heart beat so hard she thought it might fall out and clunk on the floor, heavy as iron.

Kath helped with the baby, offered to stay with her until she slept, but Ella couldn't sleep. She felt as though she would wait forever for her husband to recover. Although Kath and Mrs Hern were happy to take the baby to give her breaks, she felt as though the boy was a talisman for Will's recovery and rarely wanted to let him go. She told herself how stupid she was to believe such nonsense, to hang on to any hope so that he would not die.

Ella made bargains with God so that Will would come through. She had lived in hope since the baby was born that Will would be so glad she had borne a son that he would come and see them. She had altered that picture in her mind a thousand times by now but she could see it fading away. He might never see his son and she might never know any kind of love that fulfilled her.

She had tried so hard to hate him but it was always short-lived, even when she thought of what he had done to Kath and Jake and herself. He was the father of her child and in some kind of better world he would have been a decent man as his father was. And he could not die now because she would be left, not hating him, holding his son in her arms while she grieved.

Ella sat by Will's bed for four days. It didn't seem like four days. How strange it was that life moved differently when things were bad and didn't slow down. Her baby cried often but when she was able to feed him, she did. She let go of her idea that he would bring Will back and delivered him into Kath's arms when he was awake. The baby howled as though he knew his father was badly hurt and Ella was glad to relinquish him.

Ella focused on her good memories of Will. If he was dying, there was no point in dwelling on the bad. She brought to mind how he had rescued her, how she had fallen in love with him. The images in her mind were so clear that the little she did sleep she dreamt of happiness.

357

Mr Hern had made arrangements for everyone to stay at a small hotel next door to the hospital. Ella tried going once but she was so afraid that Will might die while she was away that she went right back and dozed in a chair by the bed. Although his mother begged her to take some rest, Ella wouldn't leave. She couldn't bear not being in the room where the love of her life might be taking his last breaths.

She thought that her whole life had consisted of this hospital and its inside and its outside, its comings and goings, its nurses and its doctors and its visitors. It was strange how something like that became normal. In some ways she wished never to leave. If she did it would mean that Will was dead and whatever he had done, he did not deserve to die.

On the fifth day she was so tired she thought she could sleep forever. She fed the baby and Kath took him outside. Had any woman ever had a better sister than hers? She owed Kath and Jake so much. Thinking of this, she lay back in the chair by the bed and soon she could feel herself drifting on soft white clouds and then there was nothing.

She awoke suddenly in the darkness. A single light was kept burning in the ward and that was by the nurse's desk. Ella came to and looked at Will in the shadows and there was no change. She had wept and prayed and hoped that there might be and forgiven him a thousand times for what he had done. He had been nothing but a thoughtless selfish young man, too young to see what the consequences of his actions might be and by God, he had been paid out.

He was awake, not awake as people usually were, only just conscious. His eyes were not focused, he did not seem to recognise her or anything about him. His gaze was dull, as though even unconscious he had been through a great deal of pain and it was showing in his eyes.

He went on looking at her for such a long time that she didn't move, she didn't ever want to move. She just wished he would look at her like that forever, like she was a star in the sky, bigger than the others and he would follow it.

Then she saw that he knew she was with him. He closed his eyes and went back to sleep. Ella was torn between wanting to tell his parents and not wanting to leave him in case he should wake up again so she sat and waited.

The second time he woke up, she was waiting and smiled and said his name. He said, as best he could in a faint hoarse voice, 'I'm so sorry, Ella, so very sorry.'

'It's okay,' she said and he closed his eyes and went back to sleep.

His father and mother came to the bed and she told them what happened. Later the doctor and nurse came and they said that he was starting to get better. It would take a long time for him to heal but it was a start.

Kath had her own room. She didn't want to be there. She went outside when it was dark, telling herself that things would get better now, Will had regained consciousness if only briefly. The night was dark and still and she heard familiar footsteps behind her.

'Why are you still out here? Blaming yourself again?' Jake asked, and she turned, almost smiling.

'How did you know?'

'You blame yourself for everything,' he said. 'It's a big load to carry.'

'I thought he would die.'

'Well, it doesn't look as if he's going to now,' Jake said. 'I wish we could leave.'

'We can as soon as he starts to get better.'

'No, I meant I wish we could leave the dale. I've had enough.' She stared at him through the shadows that fell from lit hospital windows.

'I never thought I'd hear you say it.'

'Would you come with me?'

Kath went on staring.

'Me?'

'Well, of course. I couldn't go anywhere without you.'

'Why now?'

'I've lost my job,' he said.

Kath just stared.

Forty-Six

Jake didn't want to tell her when they had more important things to worry about, but he was no longer needed at the farm. He felt like a ship that had slipped its mooring and was on the high seas with nobody on board.

He hadn't seen it coming. He liked being there,

working the fields while Pat did his carpentry in one of the big, empty barns. Jake liked being near his brother, he liked the smell of sawdust and how Pat would sit there hour after hour, unaware of anything, as he went about the labour that came so naturally to him. Jake went back up to the little house on the tops every night, happy that he and his brother, like their father and their grandfather before them, were there at the farm as they should be.

Jake was used to Sam coming and going and was glad that Sam now had a job with Miss Banks in the office. He thought if he had been Sam's father, he would have been pleased at the young man going off to work each morning wearing a suit and driving Miss Banks' car, but Mr White was pleased with neither of his sons. Was that what it was like, having sons? Were you always disappointed? Had his father been disappointed in him?

The trouble with being happy was that it couldn't last, and Jake was too happy by half. He whistled as he went about his jobs on the farm. Mrs White still fed him like a son and he worked very hard, though with the coming autumn there would not be so much to do. He dreaded the earlier evenings around the fire in the tiny house where Ethan was always yelling and the baby was always screaming and there was never any peace. He had thought that would be the hardest thing he might endure that winter, the way that the cottage was so cramped.

So when Mel and his young wife and baby had turned up, he assumed that they were just visiting.

They had come on a Saturday morning and he didn't expect to see Mel at all. He mooched about the farmyard, looking into the buildings like somebody who might buy the place and then came into the farm office where Jake was doing the accounts.

'You here every day?' he had asked.

'Just about.'

'Do you think I could do it?'

Jake had stopped what he was doing.

'Do you want to?'

Mel had looked out of the window across the yard as though something interesting might be happening and Jake looked too, but apart from Mary and Phyllis who were looking for corn which might have been dropped between the cobbles, there was no one.

'I've been down the pit,' Mel said and he pulled a face.

'Doesn't it pay a lot better?'

'I think you have to be born to it. I hate every minute. I want to come back here with Violet and the baby. It's a good place and it'll be mine to farm one day if I can get it right. Sam isn't going to be here, now that he's so important. Violet likes it in the country for the bairn's sake and she'll be glad to be away from her mother.' Mel looked down almost in apology and said, 'My Dad would be so pleased if we came here for good.'

After that, Mel was Jake's shadow. For a week Jake took Mel everywhere with him and did his best to show Mel not just what there was to do but a love of this place and everything it stood for. Mel was so grateful not to be down the pit, and in the fresh air, that he did his best. He was apt enough now that he was older and had responsibilities and saw the alternative. He wanted to do it, just like Sam had. These lads didn't lack intelligence, just years, and nothing put years on a lad like a wife and child, Jake thought.

Jake was pleased for him and in private despair. He felt as though he was losing the farm all over again. At the end of the week, Mr White came out of the house, looking apologetically at him but pleased as well.

'You can see which way the wind's blowing.'

'Aye,' Jake said, 'it'll be nice for Mrs White to have your daughter-in-law and the baby here and there's no reason why Mel shouldn't be a good farmer. After all, he's your son.'

Mr White flashed him a grateful look.

'I'm sorry, Jake,' he said.

'When would you like me to go?'

'When Mel can manage without you, if he ever can.'

Mr White was being polite. Jake favoured him with a smile and went back to work. Another week would do it, he thought, and so it did.

Pat couldn't believe that they would lose their last hold on the farm either but his brother said so and his brother was always right about such things. Jake was calm, but Pat was not deceived. He knew his brother well. Jake was smarting as much as Pat was at losing this place completely. They might never see it again.

Pat was more angry now than he had been in years. He hadn't been happy since Mercy had told him she wanted nothing more to do with him. The house was tiny, Ella's blessed child screamed at all hours, and Ethan was always whining. Up there on the tops it was now bitterly cold and at night he was restless and unhappy. After the work stopped at the farm, he found that he didn't want to be at the café and shop in Stanhope, either. Everywhere was suddenly so very full of people and he needed some peace in order to work.

He wanted to push at the walls, both down in Stanhope and up at the farm, and even though the weather was foul, wet with a sideways wind, he found himself going for long walks in the wind and sleet, and eventually in the snow, which came early for God's sake, in the middle of October. Jake had the same problem though he dealt with it better, Pat thought.

He had the car and went hunting over other farmers' lands and he still sometimes went to the mart just because he knew everybody, though Pat could tell by the slump of his shoulders that it was a world lost to him. Possibly because of the baby or the cramped quarters, Pat wished more and more that he had somewhere else to go.

He didn't know what to do and of late he hadn't liked to talk to Jake about it because he was withdrawn and quiet. One night in October when the snow was particularly bad and Jake had been down to collect the women from Stanhope, he came in with only Kath.

'Mercy decided to sleep at the shop,' Kath said, in slight explanation.

Pat stared at her.

'How could she do that?'

Kath met his eyes but there was deliberation in

her look.

'We decided we needed to fix up the rooms upstairs so we found some furniture and bought a bed in case the weather was harsh. If there'd been another bed, I would have stayed with her but there isn't enough space. I think we should take it on as a good idea. She likes being there and is going to go on with the dress shop. We aren't doing the café next year–'

Pat didn't hear any more but it was obvious that Mercy had bowed out of the arrangement they had at this house. He knew that the café had a kitchen with a sitting room and bedroom upstairs and downstairs there was a bathroom of sorts, so it was perfectly understandable that she could stay. He should have seen it coming but somehow he hadn't. It shouldn't hurt any more and yet it did.

Nobody said anything else but that night like a miracle Ella's baby didn't cry. It obviously made a difference to the others but he lay awake all night, telling himself over and over that he would never have Mercy for his wife, how many times did he have to be told?

After breakfast Jake took Kath into Stanhope in the car. Pat begged a lift. He didn't often go anywhere on his own so they both looked at him in surprise but he didn't explain. When Jake left him in the marketplace, he thanked him for the ride.

'I'll get the bus back,' and went off without another word.

He had got all his courage together and he thought he knew where to go for some help. Miss Banks had an office in Stanhope and he needed advice. He didn't know her well but she knew who he was and he didn't know who else to ask.

He half changed his mind when he got there and saw Mr Murchison and Sam White working in the big general office. Sam was easy with everybody, smiled and didn't look at all surprised to see him. He had a gift for remembering everybody's name and treating everybody as though they were important, Pat thought. You couldn't help liking him. He was a good lad and every time Pat saw him he thought about how much he missed his brothers.

Sam said that Miss Banks was just in the other office and he would go and see if she was available. She was and Pat was ushered through into a much smaller office. Miss Banks greeted him like he was an old friend, and that was when Pat realised he had known her all his life and she had had his mother's funeral tea at the hall.

'Why, Mr Sutherland,' she said, taking his hand and shaking it and smiling as though he was the best thing that had happened to her all week. 'How lovely to see you. Have a chair.'

They sat down and Pat had taken off his hat and was now unable to put it down or stop fiddling with it. He was starting to wish he hadn't come.

'I – I needed somebody to talk to. I hope you don't mind. I just thought you might know what to do.'

'I'll do my best,' she said.

And Pat, who never talked much to anybody, found that in that small office with the door closed and this woman looking kindly at him, he could tell her what he hadn't been able to admit to himself.

'To do my work I need to go somewhere else, and I don't know how,' he said.

'Yes, I've seen it; it's very good. You are so skilled. You could attract a much bigger market, I feel sure.'

'We're really cramped in our house and – I need to get out. I need a new place.'

'Somewhere in Stanhope?'

'No,' Pat said bravely, 'somewhere bigger, beyond this area.'

'What about Durham? I feel certain, knowing the quality of work you do, that you could have a shop there. If it was the right premises, you could work and sell from the same place. You could borrow money from the bank manager here to set you up, and I can tell a great many people how good you are so that you will have commissions right from the start. It should provide enough income until the local people there get to know you.'

'I made the bank manager's children some toys,' Pat said eagerly.

'Would you like me to make some enquiries for you?'

Pat agreed and that evening when they had eaten and were still sitting at the table, drinking tea, he told them all what he had done.

Jake stared at him. Pat looked levelly at his brother.

'I thought about talking to you, but you've already done so much for me. I thought maybe I should ask somebody else about it.'

Mercy was looking down. Ethan had gone to sleep in her lap. Pat almost wished that she had not come back. Ella was holding the baby, who was also quiet for once. Kath looked understanding.

'I need to move on,' Pat said when nobody spoke for what seemed to him a long time. He got up and went outside even though the wind was bitter and low in the heather and he had no coat.

It wasn't long before his brother followed him.

'It's a good idea, Pat,' he said.

'I need a place to do my work, and the shop isn't the answer, not with Mercy there. I can do something else, something more.'

'When Miss Banks thinks she has found you a new place, we'll go and look at it,' Jake said.

That changed everything. Pat's heart lifted.

'You'll come with me?'

'Of course I will,' Jake said.

When the others had gone to bed, Jake and Kath sat over the fire.

'You'll leave the dale? You'll leave me?' she asked softly, remembering how sounds went up through the floorboards.

'I can't let him go on his own, can I? And you can't go because of Ella. You could keep this place on and–'

'I don't want to keep it on!' She said it so loudly that she clapped her hand over her mouth immediately. She wanted to cry. Ever since he had said he would travel if he could, she couldn't imagine being anywhere without him. But now it was turning out so badly. He would end up living

368

in Durham and she would end up here, doing God knew what, with Ella and her wretched squalling infant.

Jake came over and got down and put his arms around her but the storm had broken well and truly and Kath couldn't stop crying She cried for how hard it had all been since her parents died, how she had tried to keep everything going, find Ella, make some kind of a life. And now it seemed like none of it had mattered and she would be left here in this godforsaken place without the man who had been propping her up ever since he found her in the snow.

'I don't want to be here without you,' she said.

Pat, gathering up his tools, was so reluctant to leave the farm that he could barely move.

The farm held everything that Pat had lost: his childhood, the memories of his parents in the kitchen, his brothers talking late in the darkness of their bedrooms, the way that seasons changed against the windows, the icy patterns in winter, how his mother would push wide the curtains in summer, the smell of hay in season, the rushing of the river when it rained hard and the sound of cows mooing as they came up the lane to be milked. It had all gone and yet it was there in his head. He thought it always would be.

He wished he could have been Phyllis, or Mary, or one of the other hens, and stayed.

Forty-Seven

Everybody who worked for Miss Banks was invited to that year's autumn party. Sam didn't want to go. It was nothing to do with him, he thought, he wasn't one of her tenants. But his father persuaded him to go with Mel and his wife as a favour to his family. Violet had brought her sister, Agnes, with her. It annoyed Sam, he didn't want to take a lass to the dance. It wasn't helped by his brother poking him, asking if she wasn't the bonniest thing he had seen in months. It was true, she was very pretty; slim and dark like Violet. She smiled at him coyly.

'Well, and aren't you a surprise. What a dark horse. I didn't know Mel's younger brother was so good looking,' she cooed, looking up at him through her lashes. He thought she was daft.

They were greeted by Miss Banks and Mrs Banks in the big entrance of the hall. It was, he thought, a lovely home. He hadn't been to many houses like this. Lord Barnard had his parties at Raby Castle, not his private residence. Sam had spent a bit of time at the castle, at dances like this, playing cricket on summer Sundays, and watching the lovely white deer in the huge park, which he and all the other tenant farmers and people had access to.

Sam had grown to know this house well since he had become Miss Banks' driver and then worked at the estate office. They were always going back and forth between the two. He listened very carefully to everything Mr Murchison told him and in the evenings he drove Mr Murchison up the hill to his lovely house. Mrs Murchison, who had no children, greeted him with joy every time and gave him ginger cake and tea. They all talked and talked by the fire about the concerns of the estate. Sam was soaking it up.

One night as Sam was leaving, Mrs Murchison pulled him aside.

'Thank goodness for you, Sam. He was doing too much, I was so afraid for him. He's a lot better now.'

'Don't worry, Mrs Murchison, I'm here to help. Miss Banks values Mr Murchison very highly and I can't tell you how much I appreciate learning from him.'

With Sam's assistance, Mr Murchison could do what he liked, and in fact he was doing better than he had for some time. He had a good deal of knowledge which made things much easier, and with help he wouldn't have to retire until he was eighty or even more, Sam thought in delight.

The ballroom, where the dance was being held, had enormous windows overlooking the lawns that sloped down to the river. Tables full of food stretched across the dining room and there was plenty to drink, but beer reminded Sam of how he and his brother had behaved when they first arrived in Weardale and he didn't want it. They had moved on, he thought, as he watched Mel holding his tiny son so proudly. Violet wore a pretty dress the colour of her name.

'They must be very rich,' Agnes said, 'but how fat and old and plain Miss Banks is. I wouldn't want to be like that. Aren't you going to ask me to dance?'

Miss Banks wasn't that old, Sam couldn't help thinking, she could only be in her early thirties, not much older than he was.

Sam obligingly danced twice with her and then walked her back to her sister.

'This is my favourite,' Agnes said, as the music started up.

Sam pretended he hadn't heard her and went outside into the fresh air.

Mel came to him a moment later.

'Don't you like her?'

'Not much.'

'I asked her specially.'

'Well, you shouldn't have on my account, I never asked you. Anyroad, there are lots more lads in there. I daresay she could dance all night and still have new partners, being so bonny.'

'It's your loss,' Mel shrugged and he went back inside.

When Sam went in, he saw that he had been right; Agnes was dancing with a lad from West-gate whose parents had friends and relatives here. Only the young people danced, except for the local doctor and local solicitor who asked Miss Banks to dance. They were much older than she was and she was too polite to look bored, though he knew her well enough to see she was. He could tell she was fed up and wanted to be at home with a decent book, a good fire and a comfortable chair. Her mother was long and skinny with a pinched smile, as though she would rather not be socialising in this manner.

What kind of a life had the poor woman had, Sam wondered, to look so sour? He began to think that maybe Mrs Banks would like living in Durham City, where she would have neighbours and friends to gossip with and plenty of church services to disrupt. Or would she miss being so important here? He didn't think she ever went anywhere, but then she couldn't walk anywhere from the hall and she didn't drive. Maybe she was just lonely and needed new company. He couldn't see how a small house in the bailey in Durham wouldn't be the right place for her. Perhaps she wouldn't be interested, but it was certainly an idea. She had no friends here and that couldn't be any good for her. Perhaps he'd approach the notion with Miss Banks.

He was so intent on his musings that he didn't notice when Agnes left the dance floor and her sister followed her. Shortly afterwards Violet came to him.

'Our Agnes is crying because you won't dance with her. I promised that you would look after her.'

Sam glanced across at Miss Banks and could see her struggling with her boredom. She had been smiling for so long her face might set that way forever, though it verged on a grimace after her two clumsy partners who so obviously hadn't danced in years. Sam looked past Violet.

'Excuse me,' he said.

'Sam–'

He ignored her.

As the music began again, Sam reached his goal. 'Will you dance with me, Miss Banks?' he asked.

Miss Banks looked astonished, as well she might, but at least she no longer looked bored. Her mother stared. He didn't look around him. She was his captive. She could hardly turn him down in front of all these people. She hesitated and then she smiled. Her eyes warmed and they really were rather beautiful, as dark as amber, and she held out her hand.

'That's very kind of you, Mr White, I would very much like to dance.'

Sam had never been more grateful than now for his mam and dad making him go to Lord Barnard's dances where he had learned how to do the quickstep, the veleta, the military two-step and, most importantly, the waltz. And this was a waltz. He took the most powerful woman in the dale into his arms and moved her neatly around the room, all too aware of his hand on her back and the warmth of her perfume and how her body fitted so beautifully against him.

She was light in his arms, she danced so well. Nobody spoke though he felt the room hush, and he wished the music would go on and on. When it ended, she smiled at him, lifting her face to thank him. She was quite a bit shorter than he was and it made him feel powerful, too, and slightly protective.

'Thank God for you,' she said, softly. 'It was kind of you to come and rescue me from those poor men who thought they had to dance with me, and even better of you to ask when there are dozens of poor maidens propping up the walls.'

'Dance with me again.'

'Sam, there are lots of lovely young women without partners, surely you'd rather–'

'Please,' he said, gently, and the music started up again. It was another waltz. Sam, possibly for the first time in his life, found the courage he needed and went on smiling at her. Caro hadn't been so full of joy in a long time. She accepted and they began to move.

'You dance beautifully,' she said, 'where did you learn?'

'Raby Castle.'

She laughed.

'No, it's true,' he said. 'Lord Barnard has lots of dances for his tenant farmers. He said my ma was the best dancer in Teesdale and you needn't think I've come up in the world dancing with you because the last partner I had was Lady Barnard.'

Caro Banks laughed again and to Sam it sounded like music. Caro imagined her mother would go off to bed when everybody had gone, but she obviously had something to say and hovered around.

When the outside door closed on the last guest, her mother went off into the little sitting room where tea was always set before she went to bed. Caro didn't want to go in there, but she felt as though she should and found her mother pouring tea.

'Did you have to make a show of yourself like that?' she said.

Oh dear, Caro thought, the only bit of fun I've had in years and I'm not supposed to have it.

'It was a dance,' she said with a sigh.

'It was two dances with that – that boy.'

Sam White was more of a man than almost anyone else Caro had met in months, she thought, turning away so that her mother might not discern her expression. Her feelings would not be quenched. She had never felt so alive as when Sam took her into his arms. She hadn't even felt that way with Jake Sutherland.

She was already reliving those two wonderful dances. For the first time ever she felt beautiful, she felt admired. She wasn't sure why he had done it, whether it was just bravado or to make his brother smile, but it didn't matter to her. Nobody could undo that hour.

She was being ridiculous, she knew, but it was probably as close as she would ever get to a young man who was fit and strong and such a good dancer. She felt like a starving person who had been given a fabulous meal.

'He was just being polite, Mother,' she said. 'And he does work for me. It's not as though he doesn't come from decent people; he's doing well in the estate office.'

'He's in no position to be polite. This is the dale, people will talk.'

'What did you want me to do, turn him down in front of all those people?'

'He can't be more than twenty-four or five,' her mother said.

Did it matter? She would probably never dance with him again, what did his age have to do with anything? In time he would marry a local girl and have children and never think of fat middle-aged

Caro Banks again, except as his employer.

Well, nobody was going to spoil her memories of tonight. She went off to bed, depriving her mother of what was obviously meant to be a great opportunity to shame her daughter.

She lay in the darkness and remembered the music and how happy she had been in an ordinary, nice lad's arms. It was his kindness she couldn't get beyond. She didn't think she would ever want to.

Forty-Eight

Holding himself very carefully, Will walked out of a building he had come to regard as safe. He was terrified to leave. He had never thought a building would come to mean so much. These people had saved his life and not just that, he had been treated with kindness. To them he was not a traveller, he was an injured man, there to be looked after as best they could, and they had saved his life.

Now he could walk out unaided. He made sure that he thanked everybody he had met; he knew that his father would put money into that hospital. His father had always had huge respect for doctors and nurses who devoted their lives to healing.

Ella had gone back with Kath and Jake when his survival was assured, and his parents returned to the camp. His father said he would send someone to drive Will to where they were staying and when he looked up, Will saw it was Baz.

He hadn't seen Baz in months, had deliberately avoided him. Baz had married Will's sister Linda, and had started his own family, but the breach had been deliberate by Will because Baz would have stopped him from hurting Ella and Kath. Baz, happy in his marriage, was fond of Ella ever since he helped Will rescue her from her attack in the Darlington back street.

Will hesitated.

'Do you need a hand?' Baz said and got out.

Will said nothing but thank you. Baz drove. Will couldn't see, his eyes were full of tears.

After a while when they were out of the town and heading north towards more familiar territory, he ventured, 'How is Linda?'

'She's just had our first child, a little girl. You have a niece now. We've called her Amie since my mother has French ancestry; she is so pleased. It means "friend".'

'That's lovely,' Will said. Then he had to get it out: 'My father is trying to forgive me. Do you think you could, too?'

'It's not me you need to think about,' Baz said. 'You were so consumed by the idea of revenge on two lovely young women that you didn't know friend from idiot. What on earth were you thinking of?'

'All I could see was Kath. I'd never asked for anything I couldn't have until she refused me.'

'God Almighty. She never even encouraged you.'

'I think that was why. She was so beautiful.'

'I never thought she was a patch on how Ella turned out.'

'Kath slept with that bloody woolly-backed farmer.'

'That has nothing to do with you. Anyroad, he bettered you.'

'Aye, with a loaded gun.'

'If it hadn't been for him and his good sense, there could have been murder done and you would have been strung up long before now,' Baz said. 'Then how would your parents have felt and your sisters?'

Will stayed quiet after that but he was unhappy. He was anxious about what it would be like when he saw his parents again with their friends around them. He was coming back in shame for all that he had done.

When they arrived, his parents came out of their caravan. He slowly walked toward them and then his mother took him into her arms, and then his sisters did the same, and their friends gathered around and it was nothing like he had thought it would be. He was so grateful to be accepted back amongst them that he couldn't see for tears.

Forty-Nine

When Sam got back to the farm after the dance he hesitated before going inside. He wished he could be anywhere else but here. From the light coming from inside, he could tell that his father and mother were in the back kitchen and Mel and Violet had taken the baby upstairs. He had no idea where Violet's sister Agnes was, and he didn't wish to know, but in the end he knew he couldn't stand outside all night. To his relief, when he went in his mother was alone in the back kitchen.

'Sam,' she said when he tried to steal past her and up the stairs to his own room. How did she know that he was there? He hadn't made a sound.

'Mother. Did you have a nice evening?'

'I did. Did you? The hall is a beautiful building, don't you think?'

'It is,' he agreed, warily.

'And for Miss Banks to live there alone with her mother, that must be quite hard.'

'Not as hard as some,' he said. 'There are lots of people living in the dale who need help and she helps them and – and – I am trying to help her to help them,' he finished lamely.

It sounded really stupid. He choked and his throat tightened and his mother chuckled. Then, kindly, she said, 'I should think that it is very difficult for Miss Banks to mix with other people. I am proud of you for asking her to dance.'

'All the men who were asking her to dance were married and old and acting like it was a duty.'

His mother laughed softly.

'It's hard for them too,' she said, 'having a woman in charge.'

'Like it isn't for her?'

'Those men mean nothing, but you did mean something, didn't you, when you danced with her? It wasn't just your so obviously polite up-bringing,' she nudged.

Sam's face burned so hotly that he thought it

might melt and there would be nothing left other than his cheekbones. He didn't realise that he was so transparent. But then again, this woman was his mother. Nobody knew him better.

'But she's a lady,' Sam said.

'A lady is just a woman with more money and responsibility,' his mother said softly, 'and she might still want to marry and have children.'

'How would she do that?'

'She needs to find a man she can trust, one who won't betray her, won't better her, won't be beneath her or above her. Somebody to be by her side in everything she does so she can then be there in everything he does. That's what a good marriage is all about,' she told him.

'Where would she ever find somebody like that?' Sam said.

'All I know is that, for whatever reason, you made her evening much better,' his mother said.

Sam looked desperately at her.

'Are you saying I can ask her to marry me? But she's landed gentry and I'm – whatever I am. She would despise me and – I'm not clever enough for her.'

'Nothing of the kind, unless you choose to marry her for what she's got.'

'I don't understand,' he said.

'Some men might think they're bigger for driving a car like that and wearing a suit. If you do, too, then you shouldn't go anywhere near her.'

'I like all that but–'

'What's more, you'll be taking on her mother and everyone in the dale. Everyone will say you're beneath her and marrying for her money, and that she's marrying you because you're young and she wants a man in her bed.'

'Mother–'

'They will, so you had best know that now and prepare yourself. It won't be easy. Her mother could live as long as you do, women like that always hang about, and she is awful.'

'I *have* met her, you know.'

'Not over breakfast,' his mother said.

Sam laughed, but only a little. The image of meeting Caro's mother over the toast and marmalade was sufficient to deter even the most enthusiastic suitor.

'Does she care about you?' his mother asked him then.

This was the question that was keeping him awake at night and destroying his concentration every time he was with her.

'She's always nice to me, but she is to everybody.'

'What if she turns you down?'

'Then I'll leave the dale.'

'Oh, Sam–'

'I would have to,' Sam hesitated. 'I really, really like her. She makes me feel more alive. She makes me feel like I can take on the whole world for her. I want to shine when she's there, I want for her to dance and wear gorgeous dresses and go away to places together and have a good time. But I also want to take care of things here, to help her. I know I'm not as good as she is because this has been her whole life, but I want to be there, trying hard to get it right. How will I ever find the courage to ask her to marry me when she has everything and I have nothing?'

'If you never ask, you'll never know,' his mother said.

Fifty

Miss Banks had done her homework, Jake thought, as he looked around the shop premises in Durham City. It was in the marketplace so that visitors couldn't miss it, and none of the shops here had anything as good as the furniture his brother could make. The property was small but had a workshop at the back, and above it was a kitchen, a bathroom, a bedroom and a small sitting room.

Pat was right, he didn't need anything larger. He had a good number of items to display so that people could order what they wanted or see what he could do, and he could work in the back where there was a long room full of light. Some sensible person had put windows in the roof and at the end. The whole wall was windows, including a door which led into a narrow back garden, which in turn led down to the river. From the garden you could see the buildings opposite and Framwellgate Bridge to the left. It was perfect.

'What do you think?' Pat said.

'You couldn't get anything better.'

Pat looked at him.

'You really like it?'

'More than that.'

Pat laughed. He wasn't sure if he'd ever felt this good, certainly not since Mercy had run away from the altar. He was going forward, he was doing something he could shine at. This was his place and he could do good work here, find somewhere to be himself. He hadn't had that up to now.

'It'll be lovely here, Jake,' he said, 'we'll have such good times.'

But then Jake's silence finished off that dream. Pat had tried not to think that his brother might not want to come with him. He had told himself that they needed a new start, that it would be better for both of them, that they had nothing left in the dale, but he had to stop pretending.

His brother wasn't going to tell him that he didn't want to be in Durham, that he would feel stifled anywhere that wasn't the countryside, anywhere that didn't have fields and trees and a river. Durham was a tiny city, which was part of its appeal to Pat. Cars drove through its narrow streets with the cathedral and the castle and the tiny Georgian houses. Durham was lovely but it wasn't the dale.

Jake enthused about the place, talked about the wonderful times they would have and Pat almost let him get on with it. He thought of all those years when Jake had had to manage without him, when he found his father dead in the field without his brothers, and went alone to his mother's funeral, when he had to sink the farm because he couldn't earn enough money to keep going – all without Pat because Pat couldn't get out of bed. How far they had come since then. Although it made Pat feel sick to do it, he looked Jake in the face and summoned all his courage.

'I don't need you here, Jake, I can do this by myself.'

Jake started to say something three or four times but couldn't manage. Pat thought of all those days lying in his bedroom at the farm in the afternoons, grateful not to be in France, to be still alive, and to have a brother like Jake who had fought so hard for so long.

Now they would win in different ways, and he would free his beloved brother just as Jake had freed him from the terrors that war had left him. The thick mud of those terrors had fallen away from him now like snow on a mild afternoon and the sun shone through the back windows of the shop as Jake hugged him and turned away.

Fifty-One

Sam didn't know what to do. He told himself repeatedly that he could go on working for Miss Banks, and she need never know that he had turned into a right idiot and wanted her for his wife. She would laugh at him if she knew. What pretensions! And where on earth had they even come from? Was he turning into his father, thinking he could marry the lady of the manor? It even made *him* cringe.

His mother had been right. The people in the dale would call him names, they would think he was really up himself and he would have no friends and nowhere to go and he would have to live in that bloody great place and Mrs Banks would never speak to him.

Miss Banks wouldn't want him anyroad, she would think he was just like everybody else and wanted what she had. And he did, in a way, but more in that he wanted to sit in the office and talk about the tenants, and go to meetings with her and help her. The sweetest thing in the world to him was when she would talk to him after the meetings and ask him what he thought. In the beginning he had retreated to, 'Why are you asking me?'

But she wasn't having that and responded sharply, 'I'm asking you because I want your opinion, for God's sake.'

He liked that she didn't hold back, how she cursed and it was a private thing between them. Unless they were by themselves, she never swore or let down her guard. She must feel safe with him ... or maybe didn't think he mattered.

Sam loved the autumn, the fires and the darkness and how you had to stay inside. He thought of the library at the hall and wanted to ask whether Miss Banks ever sat in there with the fire lit but he didn't need to ask. She never did. Her mother held court in the drawing room and there was a part of him that felt sorry for her.

Mrs Banks hated the dale, hated that she didn't have a nice house in London and that she hadn't married a lord. Some women needed to marry up. Maybe everyone needed to think of their spouses that way. Sam at least certainly thought of Mrs Banks' daughter as a lady. Miss Banks was the sort of person who knew what to do with cutlery at dinners.

She had read lots of books and though he was dying to ask her about them, it sounded pathetic so he didn't. He tried to read, just so that he could talk to her about it, but he thought he would sound absolutely up his own backside. She would have looked at him as she did when he made a stupid suggestion, or an idea she had already thought of and dismissed.

He could see them going on for years like this until they were both too old to do owt else. Her mother would die eventually and she would be left there like that stupid woman in Dickens' novel who sat over her ruined wedding feast and he would have a little street house in Stanhope and get a small brown dog to walk by the river on fine days.

He kept making bargains with himself. He would ask her tomorrow if she would marry him. He would ask her if she would have a drink with him at the Black Bull in Stanhope. He would ask her out for afternoon tea. But he never did. He lost himself in his work, pulling longer and longer hours. Even Mr Murchison told him he was doing too much – 'There is another day coming, you know, lad' – and encouraging Sam to go home.

Sam liked to linger at Mr Murchison's after taking him home. After Mrs Murchison had gone to bed, they'd take whisky from the cupboard and tell stories and laugh. Sam could tell that Mr Murchison really liked him and he thought that

Mrs Murchison went to bed on purpose, pretending that she didn't know what they were up to. She must hear their quiet laugher through the thin boards of the ceiling.

Mr Murchison had confided one night, whilst slightly the worse for whisky, that they had had a son and he had died a week after being born. It had grieved them so much when it had happened that they had had no child since. Sam knew it wasn't something he could remedy, but he hoped his presence on cold dark nights gave them even half the pleasure that he felt being there.

Christmas came and all Sam wanted was a kiss from his employer. Miss Banks – he could never think of her as Caro – asked him if he was feeling all right.

'You're not going to down with the flu, are you?' she said. Was he sneezing? No, he was not. Was he blowing his nose? No, he was not. Was he feverish? Yes, probably, but not for reasons he could tell her.

'I'm fine!' he said in exasperation, three days before Christmas.

'Is there something the matter?'

'Nothing. I'm going to have a wonderful Christmas. You've given me the day off, at least unless something goes wrong, and I'm spending it with my mother and father and my brother and his wife and child. It will be lovely. What are you doing for the holiday?'

She frowned.

'Well, I'll be handing out the turkeys to everybody on Christmas Eve.'

Sam knew this. He had long since helped her to

put in the orders for turkeys, brandy, sherry, and whisky. Everything but cakes – the farmers' wives would be insulted, they made their own. They had also made sure that the children would have toys, good toys. Miss Banks had insisted and had chosen them carefully in a huge toyshop in Darlington. He knew, he had driven her there. My God, it was expensive. And old women who lived on their own were getting fancy hampers from Bainbridge's in Newcastle. Nothing ordinary like fruitcake, it was all biscuits made out of lemons and half-bottles of champagne. He had argued about that one. Would they appreciate it?

Caro had fired a stapler at him across the office and said that everybody needed half a bottle of champagne at Christmas. In fact, the world would be a better place when people could have champagne every day. The only reason she sent them half a bottle was not to frighten them. The stapler had missed him. She really was a rotten shot. She could never have kept pigeons off the Brussels sprouts as Jake had taught him to do.

'What is the matter with you, Sam, can't you find any fellow feeling at Christmas?' she asked.

He looked at her and then very slowly he got up, went over to her desk and around to her side of it and, still trying to breathe normally and not quite managing it, he knelt down and held her face tenderly in both hands as he had dreamed of doing on so many nights, and then he closed his eyes and kissed her. It wasn't a knockout blow, it was just a whisper of a thing, but it meant the whole bloody world to him. She gazed at him. Sam looked back at her as well as he could.

'I know I'm above meself doing this,' he said, very softly, 'but I can't pretend. I've been pretending ever since we met. If you don't want me, I suppose I could still work at the office – at least until you found somebody else – but I just wanted to know what it's like being close to you. I've wanted to know that ever since I met you.'

She said nothing. He let her go. He hadn't even realised that he still had his hands lightly on her face; the letting go was like the finish of something and he was already mourning his loss. He would have to go from here and leave everything. She was so much cleverer than he was and would think of the laughter in the dale, of the scorn and the way that people talked. It would make her burn with shame.

Sam got up and stood for such a long time that he thought it must be Christmas Day already, and then she got up too and looked at him and said ever so quietly, 'Can you do it again?'

'What?'

'Can you do it again?' And then he saw what she meant and he felt his lips crease into a smile. He lifted up his hands back to her face as he had dreamt of doing a thousand times and had done only once, and then he kissed her and gathered her close and kissed her again and he thought, *yes*, it was really good, it was just as good as he had ever thought it would be.

'Will you marry me, Miss Banks?' he asked.

'Oh, you are a complete fool! Do you mean it?'

'Yes,' he said, laughing in relief. 'I've decided to be posh. I want to move into the hall with you and your Ma.'

'You'll regret it,' she said.

'Not half as much as your Ma will,' he said and they both laughed.

Fifty-Two

Will was almost happy back at the camp. They were at Barnard Castle and as far as he was concerned that was where everything had started to go wrong. For the first few days he talked to the horse, cuddled the dogs, helped his mother and sisters scrub out his caravan and went to a horse sale with his father. He advised his dad on which to buy, and yearned to embrace him. He had come so close to never being able to hug his dad again that he never wanted to stop now.

He had to stop apologising to his parents because they were looking pained. He helped until his sisters looked askance at him and then he retreated to his wagon. His father put his head around the door.

'Are you coming into town?' he said. It was early evening.

'I don't think–'

'Will, get off your arse and come and have some beer,' his father said and that was when he knew he was forgiven.

He was so happy there in the town drinking beer and talking horses like the old days. Somewhere in the conversation he heard his father calling him 'my son' in the proud way that he always had and

Will could hardly bear it. He had not been the son his father wanted. He had been so awful that he couldn't stand himself. He went outside and into the back where there was a garden. His dad came to him.

'What is it?' his father said.

'I just– I just–' Will choked over tears. *My God,* he thought, *I'm crying. I'm pathetic.*

'It's over,' his father said, 'now we can move on.'

'What about Ella?'

'What about her?' His father moved back as though he had been anticipating this problem.

'I want her. I need her.'

'Do you care about her, as you have never cared for anything or anybody in your whole life?'

'Yes, I do,' Will said.

'Then you must go to her and ask. And if she turns you down, you have to accept it. You did a dreadful thing to those girls and I know it and you know it and these things go wide and deep. Kathleen was never meant to be yours. You have to accept that, too, before you can go to her sister and ask her anything. You cannot do this just because she has your son. You have no rights to him other than those she grants you. Do you understand that? And be very careful, because if you screw this up a second time, your life with your family will be over.'

'I know I'm lucky to be here. I won't do such a thing again. I want Ella for my wife now. I want to try.'

'Then there's no time like the present,' his father said and smiled.

Fifty-Three

Jake didn't believe that his brother could manage without him and stupidly in some ways he didn't want him to. He never had before and Jake wasn't quite ready to let him go.

Jake didn't know what to do without Pat. In some ways, his limitations had helped guide Jake. But now all he knew was he didn't want to leave the dale, he didn't want to live in Durham and he didn't want Pat to leave him. Having wished for things to be better for so long, he didn't know what to do now that they were. He wanted to kick somebody very hard indeed and it might even be himself.

Mercy had not offered to go and see the new shop and Jake was glad. He didn't think his brother could stand any more of her company. Her absence was bad enough and Pat might never get over her. Jake couldn't stop disliking her for it even though he knew he was being unjust.

Kath offered to go but Pat said that Mrs Robbins, whose husband owned the premises, had already taken care of the details. So the day that Pat moved there was only Jake and himself. He said goodbye to no one. Jake helped Pat to take his belongings, his clothes, his books, his tools and the pieces he had made for show. Jake loved the way that his brother put these in the window.

Pat now had a future. He would do well and he was finally away from the dale, which held such bitter memories.

They unloaded the rest of the trailer and put the furniture in place. Kath had helped Pat buy a bed and a chest of drawers, a wardrobe and for the sitting room and kitchen, a small square table, two chairs and a settee. He didn't have much in the way of crockery, but there were several good pubs, Pat told Jake, where he could eat. All he would need at home would be a kettle, a teapot and a cup or two.

Pat carefully arranged his tools in the back workshop, where he would spend most of his time. Jake felt sure he could smell the future in the warmth of woodshavings and envisage the floor ankle deep in them, his brother unaware of the golden carpet around him.

Mrs Robbins came in and made up the bed and laid the fires. She shook Jake by the hand and told him what a talented brother he had. Jake wished their mother could have heard her enthusing.

Mrs Robbins lived next door. She had made a stew for Pat for his first day and brought him bread and milk. She said she would not bother him, but if he needed anything he could knock on their door. She and her husband were both retired now but they would be happy to help.

Jake left his brother to his dinner, saying good-bye to him on the doorstep. They did not embrace, they did not look at one another, but their silence said everything. Jake made a hasty retreat from the city, hoping he never had to do anything as difficult as that again. It had been just as bad as losing the farm.

When he reached the little house on the tops, the first thing that met his ears was a screaming baby. Neither woman was downstairs but within minutes the screams lowered and finally stopped. The silence, he thought, was bliss.

Kath came slowly down the stairs. She had the baby in her arms.

'Take him for me, will you?'

'Do I have to?'

'It's up to you. You can either sort the dinner or hold the baby.'

'What if he wakes up?'

She frowned at him.

'He's screamed for six hours. I don't think he'll wake up for a while, do you?'

He took the sleeping child carefully.

'How does he manage to yell for that long? Is there something the matter with him?'

'Oh don't,' she said. 'Just pray he sleeps for a while.'

They sat down and ate. He didn't enquire about Ella, asleep somewhere, exhausted. Jake lay the child on the couch with pillows around him so that he wouldn't fall off and then they sat at the table together. It was the first time they had done that, just the two of them.

'Do you think Pat will be okay?'

'No, I think he yearns for a woman who won't have him.'

'She might change her mind when he isn't there.'

'Huh,' Jake grunted. 'I just hope that by the tim

she discovers she wants him he's found somebody else.'

'That's awful, Jake,' she protested, and he looked at her and his shoulders slumped.

'Sorry,' he said. 'I miss him. I want him to have an easy life. I want things to go well for him.'

'I know. But I think Mercy also had a bad time before she got here. I know what it's like when–' she stopped.

'When what?'

She hesitated.

'When I wouldn't marry Will, my father knocked me around.'

Jake stared at her.

'Why would he do such a thing?'

'Because Will was such a good catch and I was supposed to do what I was told. My mother supported me, so he hit her, too. Ella was the only one who escaped it and that was because she was too young to get involved. She hid in a corner when he went out and got drunk. Every time he came back, it happened all over again. For weeks none of us could go anywhere because we were so battered and bruised.'

'You didn't tell me.'

'What was the point?'

'Hell. I'm so sorry. And now Will–'

'That's the problem. Now she thinks no man could ever love her or look after her, and I think Mercy's the same. They can't trust anybody.'

'And you?'

She looked straight at him.

'I owe my life to you, in more ways than one.'

He looked bashful.

'It wasn't me. It was Nell. I had already turned away and she whimpered. I thought you were a sheep at first.'

Kath choked and laughed.

'You carried me so far.'

'I didn't have any option and hell, you weighed nothing. Certainly not as much as a sheep. Maybe a lamb.'

'Clown!' she said and they laughed.

The baby made a small noise and they quieted, and Kath looked at Jake and Jake looked at Kath and then the baby went back to sleep.

'What are you going to do now?' he asked her.

'What do you mean?'

'Mercy's taken over the business in Stanhope. Pat's gone to Durham. You must have ideas.'

'I just want to look after my sister. She has nightmares. We don't mean to put upon you. We can pay our way. God knows, Will's father gave her enough money. I think we'll just stay here for now, if that's all right with you. What are your plans?'

'I'm going to leave. I want to go overseas, maybe to Canada. I have the feeling I might farm out there. I got some papers to fill out, but I have just enough money to get me there. I'm young and it would be a fresh start ... you know.'

Nobody said anything and then Jake sighed.

'I want you to come with me, Kath.'

'How can I leave Ella? You wouldn't have left Pat in such circumstances. Besides, we'd have t[o] marry. Is that something you want to do? Y[ou] don't even like children.'

'I might if they were mine.'

'I'd want a wedding before I went, and n[o]

travellers. I'd want a certificate and everything. No running out on me.'

'I don't go running out on people.'

'I know. I have never been more glad to see anybody do something horrible than I was when you pointed that shotgun at Will. It changed my ideas about such things.'

'It shouldn't. Guns are awful.'

'Not in your hands,' she said. 'I want to carry the day always.'

The baby whimpered and she picked him up.

'He's wet, so unless you want to help...'

Jake left her to it and went outside and stood looking into the night. He thought about whether he could actually go from here without her. He could get casual work here, he could shoot and fish and help out other people on their farms, but he had never felt the need to leave as much as he did now. It was all he could think about.

He wanted a place for himself; a farm – a big one if he could manage it – something that was for him, not a place where his family had lived and died. He needed something new, but he didn't know if he could do it without Kath. But if he stayed and Ella was always there with her wretched baby, he knew that they would learn to resent one another, perhaps even in time hate one another, like caged birds.

He stayed outside for so long that he almost decided not to return. He couldn't bear to have to o inside that tiny house again and face whatever e future had so cruelly devised for them. In the l he did, though even as he opened the door he d hear the blessed child screaming again.

Kath and Ella and the baby all slept well into the next day. When Kath woke, Jake was gone. She didn't know where. She kept thinking that one day, any day now, she would wake up and find that he had left altogether. He was running out of patience, not just with the baby, but with the whole situation, especially now that he didn't need to be here.

It wasn't as if she and Ella had to stay here, it was just that she didn't know where to go from here. She didn't deceive herself that her sister was happy. Perhaps they would always live together, as so many women did now since the war upset the balance. The towns were full of single women, leading tiny lives with boring jobs and no hope of ever turning over in the night and finding a warm person there who loved them.

'Jake's very restless,' Ella said to her sister when there was a beautiful silence in the house.

'I know. I think he may leave.'

'Go to Durham, you mean? I thought he would, anyway. I'm sure that Pat will struggle without him.'

'He says he can handle it.'

'Of course he does, but he never has lived without his brother. It seems cruel to ask him to do it now.'

'Nobody asked him.'

'No, but he's trying to move on. I think it's ver[y]
[bra]ve, but I'm not sure he can do it. Perhaps i[f]
[i]t if Jake goes, though how we'll manage wi[th]
a car, I'm not sure.'

That was not quite how Kath would have put it, but she didn't say so.

'What would you like to do?' she said.

'I'd like to be a child again and for our parents to be here,' Ella said with a sad smile. 'Other than that, I really don't know. I don't know that I want to be anywhere any more. Everything seems so insubstantial, everything except Will's wretched, squalling child.'

'Oh, Ella, you love the baby.'

'I could throw him out the window at the moment,' Ella said and they laughed. 'If Jake is only staying on here because of us, maybe you should tell him that he doesn't have to. It isn't fair to him, we aren't his responsibility. At least in Durham he won't have to see the farm he can't go to any more. It must be torture for him being so close to it and having so little to do. In Durham he might find something else, something he does want to do. Maybe all he needs is the opportunity.'

Jake anticipated a summons from his brother any day saying that he couldn't cope any longer and either wanted to return or for Jake to join him. He wanted to get into the car and drive to Durham as fast as he could and rescue his brother from whatever demons still haunted him but he didn't.

Several days after this, he encountered Miss Banks in Stanhope in the main street and she regaled him with an account of Pat's shop and of how well he was doing.

'It was kind of you to go and see,' Jake said, surprised.

'I had a meeting at the County Hotel so I

thought I would just pop in and check how he was and he is – well, I think the word is "blooming"! He has several commissions and I've asked him if he'll make some new furniture for the hall. Some of it is falling to pieces and he is so skilled. Your brother has truly blossomed, Mr Sutherland,' she said, and smiling broadly at him, she went on her way.

It was Ella that suggested to Jake he might leave after he told her about how well Pat was coping.

'Don't stay here just for us. We'll be fine. You must have some idea of what you want to do. We can afford to keep this place on for as long as we need to – Mr Hern has been so very kind. When the baby gets bigger, things will get easier and we'll no doubt figure out where we want to go and what we want to do.'

'Are you, too, wanting to leave?' he said.

'I can't at the moment, but I'm the one who always liked travelling. Kath never did. She was like our mother. But the travelling life is not the sort of thing a woman can do without a man, so Kath and I have to think of what lives we want to lead now. You should feel free to go, though. There's nothing to stop you and you've done so much for us. It's not fair that you can't move forward and do something for yourself.'

Fifty-Four

Will spent a good amount of time worrying about how he would get to Stanhope. He couldn't get a horse to pull a bloody wagon up that endless hill he heard the girls lived on and he didn't want to go in a car; it would look so over the top. All he knew was that he needed to see Ella, he needed to ask her if she would take him back, and night after night he lay there sweating because he knew that she wouldn't. He did not deserve her, he did not deserve another chance. He was beyond the pale, beyond hope, beyond redemption.

He tried to act normal to hide his inner turmoil but one day his father turned to him in exasperation, 'For God's sake, Will, if you're going, go. She can only turn you down, and if she does, you come back here and leave her alone. Better to know than to live like this. But you have to let her be if she doesn't want you. Am I making myself clear?'

Will said that he was.

In the end it was Kath who couldn't stand it. Jake's vague moods and silences got her down. She thought of what it would be like to leave, she thought a hundred times about what it would be to journey to another country with him and afresh. They would find somewhere to belong would never have to start again. She knew

402

nothing about Canada except that it was a new country and people were invited there to go and work. She and Jake were both young and healthy and had skills and ability. All of it sounded like a world of possibility and she desperately wanted to go with him. But she knew that she couldn't leave her sister in that awful little house, especially now that everything seemed over for her.

She had one hope, that Mr and Mrs Hern would come and persuade Ella to travel with them. They cared so much for her and the baby. But nothing happened and as the days passed with all of them idle, it became intolerable. So as soon as she could, she got Jake outside and told him to go.

'Without you?'

'Just because we're miserable doesn't mean you have to be, too. And I can't leave Ella.'

'I keep thinking it will get better – it'll be spring soon and the nights will be lighter and the grass will grow and the air will be soft–'

'The air is never soft here,' she said, meaning to make him smile, but he didn't. 'You have to go. I could be stuck here for years. In time I can get used to it, but you have a chance to get out and you don't belong here any more.'

'That's the most awful part,' he said. 'I can't see a future here for me but I don't want to go anywhere without you. You're my whole life now, Kath.'

She shook her head.

'Go. You can always write to me, and if things change here, I can come to you.'

'What if they don't change? What if you're stuck here for good? I know what men are like when women have children, and as far as normal society goes, your sister is an unmarried mother. Who's going to have her? And you, by association. You could be here forever.' He was struck by a thought. 'Why don't we take her with us?'

'I don't think she would leave.'

'Let's ask her. It would certainly make things much easier.'

'Leave England?'

'Yes,' Kath tried to sound jolly but she didn't feel it. 'You're the traveller.'

'If you want to go, Kath, then go. I didn't think you would ever want to do such a thing. There are plenty of places here if you want to move.' She looked harder at her sister. 'You care about him, don't you?' she accused. 'Oh, Kath, you can't.'

'Why not?'

'Well, because he's – he's not one of us.'

'He's not what?' Kath stared back.

'He doesn't understand our way of life at all. You would hate it. Haven't you been stuck here for so long that you want to go? You obviously do. We could talk to Mr Hern and he could find us a caravan–'

'What, on our own?'

'There are plenty of travelling men.'

'Have you forgotten what our life was like with our father?'

'It was a good life.'

'It was nothing of the sort. He behaved badly towards our mother and we never even had decent shoes on our feet. We were always cold and wet and hungry. And people's caravans smelled,'

404

she added at the end.

'Oh, Kath, they didn't.'

Kath wished she hadn't said that. For a lot of people, it was a good way of life and she knew it. She even thought that if her father had been a good man like Mr Hern, who looked after his family so well, that they would have gloried in such a free life and pitied people who were stuck in horrible dirty towns and boring little villages. Ella's mind was influenced now not by the awful things Will had done, but by the way of life she had become used to with his family.

'We could travel with Mr and Mrs Hern. They love the baby.'

'I can't do that. And what about Will? He's there, presumably.'

'He travels with his friends, not necessarily with his family. I don't know what their relationship with him is now but I doubt that it's anything like the way it was, so I don't think it's a question of that.'

'Maybe it is. Maybe you still want him back, after all he's done to us.'

'Well, you want a farmhand.'

'He's not–'

'Yes, he is, Kath. He'll never be anything else. He has no money, no manners, no education. He's lived in this dreadful insular little valley all his life. The people here have no idea what the rest of the world is like and they don't want to. They crouch here because they're scared of what's on the road.'

'My God, Ella, that's cruel after all he's done for you.'

'That's exactly why,' Ella said, turning away as though she would go upstairs, which was the only alternative since it was pouring with rain. Jake had gone out early and hadn't come back. Kath was beginning to think he had left. She didn't dare venture into his bedroom in case his things were gone.

'What do you mean?'

'Every time I see him, he's standing there with that loaded shotgun about to kill my husband. And then I see Will in hospital dying and I associate it with Jake. I know it's not related, but I can't help it. I don't like him. He's the very opposite of a travelling man, don't you see? I don't know how you can consider marrying him; I couldn't stand it. He's plain and dull and has no conversation.'

'Well, you won't have to worry about him much longer,' Kath said.

'Go with him, don't stay here for me. I'll be fine. I think you'll regret it.'

Jake didn't come back that day and the rain poured down. Kath eventually couldn't help sneaking into his bedroom. It was very tidy. It had been a lot more cluttered when Pat was around, with books and ornaments that had been their mother's. But these had all gone – Jake had given them to his brother, to make him feel more at home in his new place. Jake had nothing left other than a few clothes and these were neatly stacked or hung in the wardrobe. Otherwise there was nothing of him here at all. It was as though he had already gone.

She tried to behave as though everything was

normal. Ella nursed her baby near the fire. Kath didn't want to go on being disagreeable but they made little conversation. The night came down early in the gloom and still he was not back.

In the end Ella took the baby to bed. It was very late indeed when Kath heard the sound of Mr Filey's car. She thought no sound had ever been more welcome and as the engine died, she flung open the door and ran out into the rain, throwing herself at Jake as he got out of the car.

'What the hell?' he said, sounding slightly pleased and amused that she was in his arms.

'I thought you'd left.'

'Of course I haven't left. Are we going to stand here and get soaked?'

They ran back into the house. When the door was closed, she kissed him. Jake held her close and she said between kisses, 'Please don't go and leave me. I was wrong, I don't want you to go without me.'

'I won't.'

'Where have you been until now?'

'Off with some mucky lass in the pub,' he said and then he kissed her again and drew her closer and closer and then off her feet. They got as far as the sofa and for once Kath didn't care that her sister might hear them.

For the first time ever, she slept with Jake in his room.

They overslept. In fact, for the first time that Kath could remember, Jake was still asleep well after eight. She got dressed and made her way downstairs. Her sister had lit the fire and was making tea. She looked woodenly at Kath.

'I thought you were planning to stay up there all day.'

'Is the tea ready?' Kath said and she poured two cups, splashed milk into them and went back upstairs.

Ella was so angry with her sister. She tried to tell herself that Kath could do what she wanted, but Ella had been through so much by now that she was afraid her sister would leave her in this awful little house in the middle of nowhere. What would she do then? She had no car so she would have to walk, and where would she walk to with a small baby and her belongings? She didn't even know where Mr and Mrs Hern were staying. They would eventually come back to see her, but that could be months. How would she survive up here on her own with the howling wind and the rain that came sideways?

Kath couldn't help loving Jake just as Ella couldn't help loving Will. They didn't make a decent man between them, her sense of humour told her. Jake was coarse and Will was stupid. Men!

She went back upstairs, making very little noise. She was still aghast with having had to listen to them making love downstairs and then in the room beside her. It was disgusting to listen to and they obviously didn't care that she was alone while they did it.

She began to put her clothes together. The baby slept on. She was grateful for that. She heard talk from next door and then movement and the floorboards creaked. Her door was opened just a little. She didn't turn around.

'What are you doing?' her sister said in a soft, rather ashamed voice.

'I'm going.'

'Where to?'

'Anywhere away from here. You have no idea how sick I am of this horrible little house. I hate houses.'

'Ella, you can't. You have no idea where the Herns might be. They could be as far south as Scarborough.'

'They never go to Scarborough,' Ella retorted.

'Somewhere else then that would take days to get to.'

'I don't care. And you don't care, you're sleeping with your farmhand. I didn't know things had got that far. Have you thought that you might get with child?'

'Not really.'

'He doesn't like children,' Ella said. 'He never goes near the baby.'

'When it's his, he'll have to.'

'I'm not staying here with you two together like that. Have you any idea how awful it is to somebody alone?'

Kath got out of the room. Jake was dressing.

'She's going away.'

'What?'

'Ella's really upset and she's leaving. She can't go. She can't go out there with a bag and a baby.'

Jake went into the other bedroom. He never went in there and just now he wanted to be in there less than he had possibly wanted to be anywhere.

'Don't go.'

'I'm not staying here with you two like that.'

'Where can you go?'

'I don't care.'

Ella finished packing what was a very small bag. She wasn't taking anything other than a change of underwear, nappies and her money. She picked up the baby and wound him in a shawl.

'Can you move out of the doorway, please?'

'Ella, don't.'

'Move!'

He did, calling behind him as he went back into the bedroom, 'Wait until I get the car keys.'

Ella didn't. She ignored her sister, who was standing there between the bedrooms. The door downstairs was already open to the morning sunlight. She didn't even care that it was a lovely day out there. She drew the baby closer, and stepped outside.

In the end, Will took his father's car. His had long since been sold by Mr Hern. It was fast enough, in fact it was too fast – he got from Barnard Castle over the tops in such a short time that he kept stopping, pretending to himself that he admired the view.

What if she wouldn't have him? What if she wouldn't forgive him? He would have to go back and tell his parents that he was alone for good now. He only vaguely remembered his son; all he could really remember was that when he had woken up, Ella had been the first thing he saw.

He wound his way down the hills toward Stanhope and there he turned right and then in the middle of the village he turned left and it was just as though he had done it a hundred times. His heart misgave him. He was so afraid that she would not have him. Why would she, after all he had done. He had cost them all so dearly, Ella, Kath, even that bugger Jake Sutherland. They had all suffered because of him and because he thought that he could have anything he wanted.

He had learned that one's desires were not necessarily one's needs. He loved Ella and it was a much more substantial thing than he had ever felt for Kath. She was his wife and the mother of his son. She was more important to him than anything had ever been. If he failed now, he would be finished.

He set the car at the hill but more and more slowly. He didn't know how to face Ella or even Kath at this point. When he reached the top, brown hens scattered across the road in front of him and there were sheep on either side. The moor was sparse and short. Up here it was a different world.

He got out of the car and the wind nearly knocked him over, and yet it was bright and cloudless. The top of the world, he thought. As he stood there, gathering his courage, the outside door opened and a lovely fair-haired woman, with a bag in one hand and a baby on her hip, came outside.

'Going anywhere in particular?' Will said.

She looked at him, screamed, dropped her bag and launched herself the short, stony distance between them.

Behind her he could see her sister, so different, so beautiful, with those dark eyes he had spent many nights dreaming of. She was so dishevelled he thought she must have only just got up and her hair was blowing about her lovely face. She too looked at him in a surprised way, and then her face changed and for the first time that Will could remember, she began to smile at him. Behind her, car keys in hand, came the farm lad, just as ill-dressed as ever, looking as though he too had just got up. He didn't look very happy.

And then he saw Will and stopped.

'Nice timing,' he said.

Will kept hold of his wife and looked over her head at him. Nobody spoke for a long few minutes and then Kath, prosaic to the last, Will thought, said, 'We have eggs and bacon if you want to come inside and have some breakfast. I'll put the kettle on.' And off she went, closely followed by the farm boy.

'We don't have to go just yet, do we?' he asked Ella. And then, 'Let me see my son.'

She stepped back and unwound the baby slightly from his cocoon.

'He looks just like you.'

He did, Will thought, except for his beautiful blue eyes. Those were Ella's.

This Large Print Book for the partially sighted, who cannot read normal print, is published under the auspices of

THE ULVERSCROFT FOUNDATION